BAD DAY AT THE
VULTURE CLUB

Also by Vaseem Khan

The Unexpected Inheritance of Inspector Chopra
The Perplexing Theft of the Jewel in the Crown
The Strange Disappearance of a Bollywood Star
Inspector Chopra and the Million Dollar Motor Car
(Quick Read)
Murder at the Grand Raj Palace

BAD DAY AT THE VULTURE CLUB

Vaseem Khan

MULHOLLAND
BOOKS
HODDER

First published in Great Britain in 2019 by Mulholland Books
An imprint of Hodder & Stoughton
An Hachette UK company

2

A CIP catalogue record for this title is available from the British Library

Hardback ISBN 978 1 473 68536 9
Trade Paperback ISBN 978 1 473 68537 6
eBook ISBN 978 1 473 68539 0

Typeset in Sabon MT by Hewer Text UK Ltd, Edinburgh

Printed and bound in Great Britain by Clays Ltd, Elcograf S.p.A.

Hodder & Stoughton policy is to use papers that are natural, renewable
and recyclable products and made from wood grown in sustainable
forests. The logging and manufacturing processes are expected to
conform to the environmental regulations of the country of origin.

Hodder & Stoughton Ltd
Carmelite House
50 Victoria Embankment
London EC4Y 0DZ

www.hodder.co.uk

To UNICEF and all the other social activists and agencies that work tirelessly across the subcontinent to improve the lot of the disenfranchised and the dispossessed. Often they are unheralded and unrewarded, but, ultimately, appreciated and adored by those to whom they have dedicated their efforts.

THE PALACE BY THE SEA

Perched on a rocky outcrop thrusting dramatically into the Arabian Sea halfway up the city's western flank, the Samundra Mahal – the 'palace by the sea' – seemed to Inspector Ashwin Chopra (Retd) to encapsulate everything he had come to associate with the Parsees of Mumbai. There was a sense of lofty idealism about the old place, a magnificent grandeur, somewhat dulled now by a creeping decay. Time's inescapable embrace shimmered around the mansion's marbled façade: in the crumbling plasterwork, the faded paint, the creepers that wound unhindered between the rusted railings of the wrought-iron gate.

Truly, thought Chopra, with a twinge of sadness, all things must wither and die.

He recalled Shelley's poem, *Ozymandias*, which he had encountered in his youth. A similar feeling of poignant loss overcame him, for he had always staked some part of himself to the past, even as the future had taken hold of his country, rampaging her along the tracks of modernity like a runaway train. There was still much to be gained, he felt, by reflecting on the millennia-long journey that had laid the foundations for the glittering new society he saw around him.

In Mumbai, foremost among those who had paved the way for this transformation were the Parsees. Over the span of three centuries their industry and acumen had brought wealth to the great metropolis, and with it the lifeblood of commerce. They had worked for and with the British, then strived just as tirelessly for the Independence movement. In post-colonial India, Parsee philanthropy had shaped social welfare, the arts and, to a large extent, the city's cosmopolitan mindset.

Yet, for all this, the Parsees were at a crossroads.

Once heralded as the grand architects of the city, now fewer than forty thousand remained, an ever dwindling population besieged by the twin onslaughts of intermarriage and their own insularity.

In a very real sense the Parsees of Mumbai were dying.

Which made the murder of Cyrus Zorabian, one of the community's most respected grandees, all the more shocking. For if death could so unceremoniously take a man like Cyrus, then what hope remained for those left behind?

Chopra had parked his sturdy Tata Venture beneath a succession of coconut palms lining the narrow road that snaked past the mansion. He stepped out now and walked to the rear of the van. A puff of hot air escaped as he swung open the door and let out his companion, the one-year-old baby elephant that had been sent to him almost a year earlier by his long-vanished uncle, Bansi. In the letter accompanying the little calf, Bansi had failed to explain his reasons for sending the enigmatic gift to Chopra, suggesting only that: 'this is no ordinary elephant.'

In many ways, his words had proved prophetic.

The elephant's arrival had coincided with Chopra's own retirement from the Mumbai police service, a departure forced upon him by a heart condition known as unstable angina. For a man yet to achieve his fiftieth year, a man who for three decades had known only a singular purpose – the pursuit of justice in khaki – the loss of his post, and with it his allotted place in the grand scheme of things, had been devastating.

He had wasted little time in self-pity, instead steeling himself to rise swiftly from the ashes of his former life.

He had opened a restaurant, and, shortly afterwards, a private detective agency.

The restaurant had been a deliberate attempt to embrace the future, but the agency had materialised by happenstance in the wake of a case that Chopra had continued to pursue after his retirement, ultimately unravelling a major criminal network in the city. The agency's name he owed to his new ward. He had christened the animal Ganesha, after the elephant-headed god that inspired such maverick devotion around the country. During that first investigation he had discovered that his unusual inheritance possessed depths of intelligence and resourcefulness he could not have guessed at. A year later there was still much about his new companion that he had yet to fathom. But there was little doubt in his mind that his uncle had been right: there *was* something extraordinary about the creature. He would never claim that the elephant was, in any way, his *partner* at the detective agency – for that was most assuredly *not* the case – but he had quickly fallen into the habit of taking the little calf along with him on his peregrinations about the city. Ganesha needed the exercise, and, though he would be loath to admit it, Chopra had become so accustomed to his presence that he sometimes forgot just how ludicrous it might seem to others, a grown man wandering around the crowded metropolis with an elephant in tow.

Then again, this was India.

There were stranger sights on the streets of the subcontinent's most fabulous city than a baby elephant.

Ganesha trotted down the ramp into the bright haze of mid-morning.

The temperature was already in the high thirties; heat shimmered from the tarmac and came rolling in off the sea in warm gusts that rustled the leaves of the palms lining the road.

Gulls cawed in the silence, a rare commodity in Mumbai.

The little elephant waggled his ears.

For a brief moment he appeared to contemplate the expanse of blue water glittering before him, sweeping out to a sparkling haze in the far distance, then turned and followed Chopra towards the Samundra Mahal.

They were met inside the gates of the Zorabian mansion by a tall, severe-looking white man who Chopra guessed to be in his early forties. Introducing himself as William Buckley, personal secretary to the murdered man, he led them through a formal garden and into the mansion. Buckley, with his blond crew cut, watery blue eyes, sunken cheeks and spare frame put Chopra in mind of an ascetic of the type India had in abundance.

The interior of the mansion was lavishly appointed. Yet, once again, Chopra had the feeling that these fixtures – Carrara marble, Bohemian chandeliers, teakwood sideboards – were the legacy of past grandeur.

Buckley swept them along a wood-panelled corridor, lined with a succession of baroque, robber-baron family portraits: the Zorabians of Mumbai, staring down upon them through a haze of constipated myopia. Chopra knew that the Zorabian dynasty – beginning with old 'Bawa' Rustom Zorabian – numbered among the original group of Parsee families to settle in Mumbai, having fled their ancestral homeland in Persia to protect their faith from an emergent Islam. Combining native intelligence with an unstinting work ethic, they had quickly found their feet in the teeming metropolis, subsequently prospering under British rule. Venerated for their philanthropy and business acumen, the Zorabians, like many Parsees, had managed the enviable trick of amassing great wealth in a land distinguished by its poverty, yet continuing to enjoy the general goodwill of those around them.

When Independence finally arrived – with a cataclysmic political thunderclap – their close ties to the British had not, to all intents and purposes, earned them lasting opprobrium. Indeed, most Indians had a healthy respect, even an affection – if sometimes grudging – for the lovably eccentric Parsee community, heirs to the legacy of their forebears who had created much of Mumbai's wealth, and built many of the city's visionary institutions.

It was no wonder, then, that Cyrus Zorabian's death had made headlines around the country; particularly so because of the shocking nature of his passing.

At the end of the corridor Buckley paused.

He nodded up at the portrait before him. 'Mr Zorabian,' he said simply.

Chopra examined the painting with a critical eye: Cyrus Zorabian in his pomp, a tall, fleshy man with the glossy cheeks of the ancestrally wealthy, an impressive whisky-drinker's nose, and a head of swept-back, darkly dyed hair. Dressed in an ivory-coloured three-piece suit, he cut a dashing figure on the front lawn of his home. Here, the portrait suggested, stands a man of rare influence and power. A man used to bending fate to his whim.

And yet, ultimately, even the Cyrus Zorabians of this world were forced to kneel before the greatest leveller of them all – death.

They entered an expansive drawing room – fitted out with claw-footed furniture and an ancient Pianola – where the woman Chopra had been summoned to see awaited.

Perizaad Zorabian was younger than he had imagined. Elegant and attractive, with shoulder-length jet-black hair parted dead centre of her high forehead, an aquiline nose, and piercing brown eyes, she put him in mind of a mortician. There was something unsettlingly clinical in her look, and in the precision with which she greeted them.

Her gaze rested only momentarily on Ganesha, who shuffled closer to Chopra, unnerved by the scrutiny. For a second Chopra thought she would comment on the little elephant's presence, but instead she turned to address Buckley. 'Please leave us.'

The Englishman frowned, then seemed to think better of objecting. He dipped his head and exited the room. Chopra thought that he detected an unspoken animosity in the air.

'He worked for my father for almost a decade,' said Perizaad, perhaps sensing his thoughts. 'I think he still believes he should be consulted on all matters relating to him.'

'I am very sorry for your loss,' said Chopra automatically, and then regretted the words. He had never been a man for appearances.

Perizaad ignored the sentiment.

Instead, she rose from her teakwood desk, and began to pace the room. She wore a grey trouser suit, belted high at the waist. A cloud of perfume trailed her as she weaved figures-of-eight over the marble flooring.

'Thank you for coming so quickly. I know that you must be a busy man.' Abruptly, she wheeled on them, frightening Ganesha into shrinking back behind him. 'How much do you know about my father's death?'

'I know that he was murdered three months ago. I know that no suspect has ever been identified for his killing.'

'As you can imagine, this is not a satisfactory state of affairs.'

'You are unhappy with the police investigation?'

'The police!' She slapped out an angry hand, accidentally knocking over a vase perched on the corner of her desk. It fell to the floor, where it shattered into a thousand pieces. Ganesha's trunk vanished behind Chopra's legs. 'They have redefined the meaning of incompetence.'

'If I remember correctly they concluded that your father was the victim of a random attack. He was simply in the wrong place at the wrong time.'

'My father was killed inside Doongerwadi,' said Perizaad. 'Murdered on holy ground. In the entire history of the Parsees in this country no one has ever been murdered in the Towers of Silence, let alone a Parsee of my father's standing. No one would dare.'

'And yet it happened.'

'Yes,' she said, a shadow clouding her eyes. 'It happened. And the killer is still out there, somewhere.'

Chopra considered the matter.

He had understood when Buckley had contacted him that Cyrus Zorabian's murder most likely lay behind his invitation to the Samundra Mahal. The PA's call had brought back to him the fuss in Mumbai when the Parsee industrialist's body had been discovered. The sensational nature of the killing, coupled with the victim's stature, had kept the city's news editors frothing at the mouth for weeks.

Eventually, as it became clear that no leads or suspects

were forthcoming, the story had died a quiet death. In a city such as Mumbai, with twenty million inhabitants, twenty million stories waiting to be told – or twenty million tragedies waiting to unfold, as his friend and pathologist Homi Contractor would often put it – there was no shortage of news.

Thinking of Homi – who himself was a Parsee – reminded Chopra that this was a unique situation. The Parsees, so heavily outnumbered in the seething mass of India's billion-strong horde, were, in many ways, under siege from without as well as from within. Chopra had always found them an agreeable and generous bunch – even Homi, with his surly disposition, concealed a heart of, if not gold, then certainly something approaching it.

Gold alloy, perhaps.

'Tell me,' he said, 'what makes you think there is more to your father's death than the police have concluded?'

'Because of how many unanswered questions remain. My father was a careful man. What was he doing inside Doongerwadi, alone, at that time? And there are other things about the case that the police have simply made no headway with. Either because they were incompetent, or because they simply didn't care to.'

'Yet you think I might do a better job? I *was* a policeman for thirty years.'

She arched her eyebrows at him. 'Do you know much about my father, Chopra?'

'He was wealthy. He was a widower. He was well-liked – generally speaking. Beyond that I know no more than the average Mumbaiker.'

'My father is – was – an institution in this city. Because of our family's history here, and our varied business interests, he knew just about everyone with any influence in Mumbai. Yet he was also, socially speaking, a clumsy man. Apt to say the wrong thing at the wrong time. He used to joke that he'd put so many feet into his mouth over the years that he should have been born a millipede.' She gave a wan smile. 'The truth is that he was hated by many of the people who run this city, including the chief minister. My father clashed with him last year over the rise of right-wing militancy in the state. He felt that the CM was pandering to the demagogues – not doing enough to shut down their hate speech.'

'Is this why you believe the police haven't investigated his murder thoroughly?'

'The commissioner of police serves at the pleasure of the chief minister, does he not?'

Chopra made no comment but privately felt that this was doing the man a disservice. He had met the commissioner on two prior occasions, and although he wasn't quite convinced that he was the right man – or woman – for the role, nevertheless he was a far cry from the sort of kowtowing oaf that had for so long distinguished the post. The truth was that no one could hope to run the police service for a city such as Mumbai without being a political animal. Wooden ears, a hollow heart and a forked tongue. That was how Homi had described the ideal aspirant to the role.

'Have you spoken with him?'

'The commissioner? Yes, of course.'

'What did he say?'

'He told me they had done everything within their power to find my father's killer.'

Chopra gave a wry smile. 'Yet here I am.'

'Yet here you are.'

A silence passed between them as he evaluated the situation.

The agency was busier than ever.

Even with the help of his associate private investigator, Abbas Rangwalla – a former policeman who had served as Chopra's deputy for two decades at the local station in Sahar – there was more work than they could presently handle. He did not need this case. He particularly did not need to tread on the toes of the Brihanmumbai police, who had only recently begun to invite him back to work on investigations they did not have the manpower to handle themselves. If it leaked out that the Zorabian family had employed a private investigator to look into Cyrus's killing, Chopra would swiftly find himself the centre of unwelcome attention, a development he did not relish.

And yet, there was something here that did not sit right with him.

That a man as well-known as Cyrus Zorabian should be murdered in the city was bad enough – but in a city of twenty million the fact of a single murder was a statistical inevitability. What set this case apart was the conviction of Cyrus's daughter that perhaps, just perhaps, those who should have followed through in investigating that death had not applied their shoulders fully to the wheel. That, somehow, they had not given of their best because the victim was a man out of favour with those at the very top of the city's power structure.

On the day that he had retired, Chopra had been accused by the mother of a murdered boy of not caring because they were poor. Her words had stung him deeply. He was a man for whom the notion of justice went deeper than rhetoric. If a principle was to have any value at all it had to be applied equally to rich and poor, powerful and disenfranchised: this simple truth had always been apparent to him. Did Cyrus Zorabian deserve less because he was wealthy, or because his family name commanded great influence?

'Very well,' he said. 'I will take the case.'

Perizaad gave a grimace of acknowledgement. 'Buckley will give you the names of everyone the police interviewed in connection with my father's death.'

'Frankly, I would rather speak directly with the man in charge of the investigation.'

'Man?' said Perizaad archly. 'How do you know it was not a woman?'

Chopra raised a surprised eyebrow. 'I—' he began, but Perizaad took pity on him.

'Buckley will arrange the meeting for you. I will also speak to the commissioner. Willingly or unwillingly he will instruct his people to give you all the cooperation you need. But I warn you: the *man* in question is an imbecile.'

'What is his name?'

'Rao,' said Perizaad. 'ACP Suresh Rao. He is with the CBI.'

Chopra's ears rang like tolling church bells. He suddenly found it hard to breathe, as if the air had been sucked from the room.

Rao.

Of all the names that Perizaad Zorabian might have set forth this was the one Chopra had least expected, and would have least wished to hear. For many years, Suresh Rao had served as his commanding officer when Chopra had run the Sahar police station. Even then the man had been a two-chip thug, the sort of incompetent and congenitally corrupt policeman responsible for the terrible reputation enjoyed by the Indian police service. In the recent past Rao and Chopra had clashed when his investigations had cut across Rao's work at the CBI, the Central Bureau of Investigation. There was little love lost between them; Chopra did not relish the prospect of crossing swords with Rao once more.

'Do you know him?' said Perizaad.

'Yes,' breathed Chopra. 'Unfortunately, I do.'

She squinted suspiciously at him, but declined to enquire further. 'I will expect regular updates. If you need anything, anything at all, simply ask Buckley.'

'I would like to ask you a few questions now, to flesh out some background detail.'

She glanced at her watch, then nodded. Quickly, he went over the basics with her, covering Zorabian family history, a rundown of her father's closest friends, an insight into the business behind their fortune. Perizaad appeared in a hurry, and he sensed that there was more to be dug out here.

When she was done, she swept past him, then turned back at the door. Her eyes alighted on Ganesha's backside. 'I was informed that you seem to be wandering around with a pet elephant. I thought it might be some sort of elaborate joke. Clearly, I was wrong.'

'He is not a pet,' said Chopra stiffly. 'His name is Ganesha.'

'Ganesha,' echoed Perizaad, as if testing out the name.

Hearing his name spoken out loud the little elephant flapped his ears, but declined to turn and face the woman. His bottom trembled gently.

'He appears to be of a somewhat nervous disposition,' said Perizaad dryly.

'He's not normally like this,' mumbled Chopra. 'I'm not sure what's got into him.'

'I hope his guardian has a stronger stomach for the fight.' She turned and left.

Chopra glanced down at his ward. 'Well, thanks for embarrassing us both,' he muttered.

Ganesha gave him a sheepish tap with his trunk, then went back to examining the intricate mosaic between his blunt-toed feet.

Chopra swallowed his irritation. The little elephant had been increasingly distracted of late. He wondered what was going on beneath that knobbly skull, with its little cluster of short hairs.

He was prevented from dwelling on the matter further by Buckley, returned to usher them out of the building.

As he swung briskly along, he handed Chopra the list that Perizaad had mentioned. 'Ms Zorabian has asked me to arrange an appointment for you with ACP Rao. I shall request that he meet with you first thing tomorrow morning at the CBI headquarters in Nariman Point. I trust that will be satisfactory.'

At the gates, Chopra paused. 'Perizaad said that you worked for Cyrus Zorabian for almost a decade.'

'That's correct,' said Buckley, glancing impatiently at his watch, an elaborately expensive platinum affair, Chopra couldn't help but notice.

'In all that time did you become aware of anyone who hated him enough to want to kill him?'

Buckley blinked from behind his spectacles. 'The truth? No. He was not a dislikeable man. Yes, at times he did or said things that upset others, but enough to kill him? It's unthinkable.'

Chopra nodded, then headed back across the road towards his van, Ganesha following closely in his wake.

THE POO2LOO CAMPAIGN

It took an hour to drive from Worli back to Sahar. Chopra's first port of call was the restaurant.

He had named the place after his wife – known to friends and family alike as Poppy – and it served now not only as a base of operations for the detective agency, but also as a home for Ganesha, who lived happily in a little mud wallow in the rear courtyard, beneath an ancient mango tree.

The restaurant was also home to Irfan, the ten-year-old street urchin Chopra and Poppy had all but adopted.

The boy had swaggered into the restaurant the previous year, pulling up his tattered shorts with his deformed left hand, flopping his mop of unkempt dark hair around as he stared Chopra down and convinced him that he would make a first-rate waiter.

Chopra had never regretted his decision.

Irfan – whose recently deceased father had, for years, forced him into a life of petty thievery – had proven to be an enterprising and hard-working addition to the place. He had also become firm friends with Ganesha, the pair of them as thick as thieves, and as adept at getting into trouble. Irfan worked a day shift at the restaurant. The evenings he spent playing with his elephant companion, at least on those occasions he wasn't being smothered by Poppy's lavish attentions.

In the twenty-four years of their marriage, Chopra's only regret was that he and Poppy had been unable to have children. Nevertheless, they had weathered the disappointment together, their shared adversity serving to settle their long-standing affection for one another deeper on its foundations. Yet the arrival of Ganesha and Irfan had changed things irrevocably – Poppy had found an outlet for her long-suppressed mothering instincts, and there was little Chopra could do about it except get out of the way.

Chopra left Irfan to settle Ganesha in and arrange his evening feed, and drove home.

Edging the van into the compound of the complex in which his apartment tower was located he discovered, to his mild shock, Poppy engaged in a heated argument in the courtyard of their building.

Poppy and Chopra lived on the fifteenth floor of Poomalai Apartments, another of Mumbai's ubiquitous tower blocks. As with most people in the city – those who didn't live in the slums, at any rate – these high-rise prisons were home. Poomalai was one of three towers, all corralled inside a walled and gated compound, ostensibly guarded by young Bahadur, though, in Chopra's opinion, a corpse might have proved more vigilant.

A peanut bounced off his shoulder.

He glanced up.

A number of his neighbours were leaning over their balconies looking down on the evening's impromptu entertainment.

He returned his attention to the spectacle before him.

Poppy, hands aggressively attached to hips, stood beside a technicolour poster pasted to the side of the tower. Bahadur, the scrawny security guard, was attempting to make himself invisible behind his wife's slender form. A glue brush was clutched guiltily in his hand.

Standing directly before the pair of them, arms folded across her narrow chest, stood Mrs Subramanium, the president of the complex's managing committee. The old woman, resplendent in her habitual black sari – complemented by an iron-grey hairstyle that had always put Chopra in mind of India's formidable former prime minister, Indira Gandhi – was glaring with ill-concealed anger at the poster.

It was clear that Poppy and Mrs Subramanium were engaged in another of their frequent stand-offs.

He sighed inwardly.

Early on in their tenure at Poomalai, Poppy, realising that Mrs Subramanium ruled the complex with an iron hand, had set herself up to oppose the old martinet's reign of terror. And so had begun a campaign of guerrilla warfare that had left most of the building's hapless residents either trapped beneath the boot-heel of Mrs Subramanium's increasingly draconian edicts, or harried into joining Poppy's well-meaning subversions.

He transferred his attention momentarily to the poster, in an attempt to understand the present impasse.

The poster depicted a series of cartoons of an average-looking Indian man walking along the street, before stepping, with exaggerated disgust, into a pile of excrement. A glaring slogan, in foot-high red letters, stretched across the top of the poster: JOIN THE POO2LOO CAMPAIGN.

Chopra had heard of the campaign – who hadn't?

It had been everywhere these past weeks, with its catchy theme song 'Take the poo to the loo'. Everyone knew that public defecation was a serious problem in India, but until now no one had ever bothered to do anything about it. And then UNICEF had launched its campaign, hot on the heels of which came a wildly successful Bollywood film depicting the travails of an educated young woman marrying into a rural household without an internal lavatory.

UNICEF claimed that millions of people defecated out in the open in India each day, delivering some fifty million kilos of solid human waste on to the nation's streets.

Chopra wasn't surprised by the figures. Sometimes, it felt as if the whole country was slowly being buried under this avalanche of shit.

Clearly, his wife – an inveterate pursuer of social causes – had decided to bring the campaign to their doorstep.

'This poster is an offence to public decency,' Mrs Subramanium was saying.

'The offence,' countered Poppy, narrowing her eyes, 'is the disease caused by human waste.'

'Look around you, Mrs Chopra,' said the old woman. 'There is no waste, human or otherwise, here. I do not allow it.'

This much was true, Chopra thought. The old tyrant ran a tight ship. A man with rampant dysentery would not dare soil a single square inch of the building for fear of incurring her wrath.

'But we must think of society at large,' muttered Poppy, through gritted teeth. 'Out there, people are defecating like there is no tomorrow, defecating all over the place, defecating left, right and centre. We must educate them. It is our duty.'

'Instead of educating them, perhaps we should punish them,' suggested Mrs Subramanium curtly. 'A sound thrashing or a night in jail each time some incontinent loafer decided to leave their calling card on the street. I think *that* might be more effective than your obscene posters.'

Sighing, Chopra waded into the fracas.

It was going to be a long night.

Following his evening meal, he shut himself into the small office he maintained at home. He logged on to the Internet and began to search for information on Cyrus Zorabian to add to the sketchy details he had obtained from Perizaad. A polished calabash pipe stuck out of the side of his mouth. Chopra did not smoke; the pipe was a prop, something that helped him to think. He had been a fan of Sherlock Holmes ever since he had seen Basil Rathbone playing the iconic character in *Sherlock Holmes Faces Death*, and the pipe helped settle him into the great detective's mental shoes. On the TV behind him India were playing cricket abroad;

he turned briefly as his favourite player Sachin Tendulkar dropped a catch.

In Chopra's opinion, it had been a tough one.

The Internet search returned far more than he would have liked – Zorabian was not as uncommon a name as he had supposed.

He bent to his task, clicking through the various references, only stopping to scratch in his notebook whenever anything of significance caught his eye. Midway through, he took out his mobile phone and dialled Homi Contractor. What was the point of having a Parsee for a friend if he couldn't pick his brain? Homi was glad to help, and his information supplemented Chopra's own research.

Two hours later, he sat back and examined his efforts.

Given that they were one of the country's pre-eminent business families, the Zorabians had managed to maintain a relatively low profile. Much of the information Chopra had found centred around Cyrus's legendary ancestor Rustom Zorabian, a larger-than-life character whose deeds had entered the annals of both Parsee and Mumbai folklore. The line of heritage from Rustom to Cyrus was distinguished by a cadre of dependable, if unspectacular, men who had steadily grown the family business into an empire that spanned the country. The sole blip in this progression of excellence had been Cyrus's great-great-grandfather, known to history as the 'Mad Zorabian', who had earned that sobriquet thanks to his numerous well-documented peccadillos, which included dressing in petticoats for formal occasions and playing bagpipes below the Gateway to India as a means of serenading incoming ships.

Cyrus himself was an only child. His father and mother – nondescript characters by all accounts – had both died in his teenage years. He had grown up in the traditions of the Parsee community, attending a staunchly Anglo school, followed by a few years abroad in England pursuing a degree in aeronautics at Cambridge University (the article failed to clarify whether he had actually graduated), and then a return to Mumbai to take the helm of the family business.

In 1981 he married a fellow Parsee.

In short order, they had two children, a boy and a girl. The marriage, by all accounts, was a successful one – there were no rumours of affairs or marital strife, at least none that had made the society pages.

Cyrus's wife had passed from cancer six years previously.

A year later Cyrus *had* made the news when he banned two Parsee priests from performing rites at Mumbai's so-called Towers of Silence. The priests had attracted Cyrus's ire by overseeing a number of cremations in response to the scarcity of vultures at the time. Cremation went against the Parsee practice of excarnation, of permitting birds of carrion to consume their dead in the towers.

Cyrus had made it clear that he would never permit such 'modern' practices at Doongerwadi, the site where the towers were located. The preservation of the community's values, he had publicly stated, was paramount.

To his surprise, Chopra found little information about Cyrus's children, Perizaad and Darius.

Clearly they too valued their privacy.

A knock on the door, followed by Poppy. He smiled at her. 'You know Mrs Subramanium isn't going to let it go.' Poppy had won the first round – the poster would stay, for now – but Chopra knew the old woman was smarting. No doubt they'd hear from her soon.

'I know. It's just . . . We spend so much time telling the world how incredible India is, I think we sometimes forget that for so many people it is anything but. Don't you think it is our duty to help?'

'You know that I do.'

She put an arm around his shoulders. He smiled again, and allowed her to lead him back into the living room.

CRIME BRANCH SHOWDOWN

The next morning he picked Ganesha up from the restaurant, then headed south to Nariman Point and the CBI headquarters. Traffic was already snarling the streets as he drove out towards the Western Express highway, a dual carriageway that speared in a single sinuous line to the southern half of the city, and along the length of which appeared to have been compressed enough trucks, vans, cars, motorbikes, bicycles, rickshaws, taxis, bullock-carts, stray flocks of goats and the occasional suicidal pedestrian to fill the traffic lanes of most good-sized countries.

It took almost an hour to get there.

Having parked the van on a busy side street, he picked his way deftly through the throng of morning commuters rushing to their offices, brandishing briefcases and lunch tiffins, jabbering on mobile phones; a heaving, Brownian motion of humanity flowing along the city's streets. The fact that a small elephant accompanied him elicited almost no interest, aside from the occasional muttered oath as Ganesha prevented a would-be titan of industry from advancing along the road.

For his part the elephant seemed perfectly at home; yet Chopra recalled that when he had first arrived in the city, a despondent and underweight calf, he had been distinctly ill at ease in the boisterous crowds for which Mumbai was infamous.

At the CBI HQ, Chopra discovered a dispirited-looking constable on reception duty who looked as if he'd been hammered into the plastic seat in which he now sat. He barely looked up from his ledger as he barked at a nearby peon to escort them to a cell-like interview room where Chopra found himself waiting an hour for his nine o'clock appointment with Assistant Commissioner of Police Suresh Rao. He had expected as much; such petty gamesmanship was part and parcel of Rao's make-up.

When the man finally deigned to appear, it was with a fellow officer in tow.

He entered the room as Caesar might have entered Rome, glancing imperiously at those in attendance, expecting tribute, or at least plaudits. When neither was forthcoming, his round balding face, with its comical little moustache, compressed itself into a grimace.

'Perizaad Zorabian must be desperate if she has employed *you* to look into her father's death,' he said, by way of greeting.

'I can certainly do no worse than you already have,' replied Chopra.

Rao's eyes fell on Ganesha. He flung out an arm. 'Who let that elephant in here?' he roared. 'Is this the CBI or a petting zoo?'

'He is with me,' responded Chopra, his own temper flaring. 'I believe Ms Zorabian informed the commissioner that she has retained my services. I understand he assured her of your full cooperation.'

Rao's moustache did a little fandango above his lip. 'Cyrus Zorabian was murdered by a random attacker,' he hissed. 'That is all there is to it.'

'We shall see,' said Chopra, struggling to resist the urge to hurl himself across the room at his old nemesis. After all, it was only recently that Rao's machinations had landed him inside one of the state's blackest prisons. Only good fortune, and the assistance of friends and family, had delivered him from his ordeal. The man was incompetent, unscrupulous and thoroughly untrustworthy; a stain on the uniform he wore. That he now worked for one of the country's most powerful police institutions was an irony at one with the malaise that lay behind much of his nation's problems.

The CBI – the Central Bureau of Investigation – was a federal police force, with offices in each state, only called in when a case had political ramifications. There was little doubt that Cyrus Zorabian's murder qualified on that basis alone. As one of the most powerful Parsees in Mumbai his influence had been felt far and wide; his sudden death had left more than a few politicos sitting uneasily. No doubt Perizaad Zorabian had pressed for the CBI's involvement.

Well, she had got her wish, if not the officer Chopra would have assigned to the case.

Rao opened his mouth as if to reply, then seemed to think better of it. He turned and would have swept from the room in a grand gesture, had he not walked straight into his junior colleague, the pair of them tumbling to the floor in a heap.

Rao scrambled to his feet, as did his fellow officer.

'Get out of my way, you imbecile!'

The policeman folded swiftly out of the way, allowing Rao to finally depart the room.

When the door had closed, he sagged, taking a handkerchief from his pocket and wiping his brow.

'My name is Avinash Kelkar,' he said. 'I ran the investigation into Cyrus Zorabian's murder. Under ACP Rao, of course.'

'Let me guess,' said Chopra. 'You did all the work, while he took all the credit.'

Kelkar's silence was answer enough.

He watched as the man squeezed himself into one of the reedy-looking chairs behind the room's solitary desk. The chair creaked ominously. Kelkar was a big man, clearly the beneficiary of a generous diet; Chopra doubted that he would have passed the physical fitness test currently mandated by the Mumbai police service.

Then again, getting around the regs had never been much of a problem in the Brihanmumbai police.

Kelkar pulled off his peaked cap revealing a sponge of dark brown hair sitting on his otherwise shaven skull like a chocolate blancmange. He set down the cap, then pushed a thick manila folder across the desk's scarred surface. 'This is everything we have. Rao was right about one thing: we found nothing to suggest Cyrus's killing was anything other than random.'

'Perizaad is convinced that you did not put your best foot forward. In light of her belief that Cyrus and the chief minister were not on the best of terms.'

A pained look flashed over Kelkar's square, clean-shaven face. 'Yes, she has made that opinion clear. But the fact remains that we did everything we could.'

Chopra picked up the folder and began to leaf through it.

First, he examined the crime scene photographs.

They depicted the body of Cyrus Zorabian lying face down inside a dakhma – more popularly known as a 'Tower of Silence' – located in Doongerwadi. Doongerwadi, a fifty-acre wooded plot in the very heart of Mumbai, was owned by the Zorabian family, its sole purpose to house half a dozen Towers of Silence. It was here that the Parsees sent their dead. According to Zoroastrian belief, corpses had to be left to the ministrations of birds of carrion for disposal; in Mumbai this meant the community of vultures that lived inside Doongerwadi.

Cyrus's body was fully clothed, lying beside a partially decomposed corpse that had been deposited in the dakhma the day before. The back of his head had been caved in by repeated blows from a blunt object; blood could be seen caked on the collar of his jacket and the silk cravat he had been wearing at the time of his death.

Chopra next examined the autopsy report.

There was little to go on.

Cyrus had died as a result of the injuries sustained to his skull, three blows that had fractured the cranium in multiple places, sending blood and fragments of bone into the brain. Death had been all but instantaneous. The pathologist speculated that the killer had first struck Cyrus with his right hand, then, in an attempt to disguise his 'handedness', had struck him twice more with the left hand. He further speculated that the weapon in question had been heavy and blunt, a length of steel pipe, or a billy club, possibly something with a rounded head.

Whatever it was, the attack had been brutal and swift.

Chopra stood back from the thought in order to give it due consideration.

On the face of it the information fitted the pattern of a random assault. A surprise attack, from behind, in an out-of-the way location.

But why was Cyrus attacked in the first place?

'Where, exactly, did the assault occur?'

'Not far from the dakhma where his body was found. A hundred yards, if that. We discovered blood on a walking path inside Doongerwadi. Drag marks and a trail of droplets led from there to the tower.'

Chopra looked at the inventory of items found on the victim's body.

'It says here his wallet was still with him, as was his gold watch.'

Kelkar shrugged. 'We never suggested that the motive for his attack was robbery.'

'So your theory is that a complete stranger bashed his skull in for the heck of it? Then dragged his body a hundred yards and dumped it into a Tower of Silence?' Chopra could not keep the ridicule from his voice.

'There are plenty of lunatics in the city,' countered Kelkar. 'Maybe a stressed-out banker had a bad day at the office. Some fish seller got into a fight with his wife. Or one of those wild-eyed ascetics finally had enough of contemplating the mysteries of his own navel.' The rotund policeman sighed. 'Our best theory is that a homeless man climbed the wall into Doongerwadi looking for a place to get high. Apparently there's been a recent epidemic of that sort of thing. Cyrus crossed his path, probably attempted to eject him from the premises, and got it in the neck. Or the back of the head, to be more accurate. The tower was simply the nearest convenient place to dump the body.'

'Why would a homeless murderer, high to the eyeballs – if we accept your theory – worry about hiding the body?'

'Who knows how a madman thinks?' replied Kelkar stubbornly.

'The time of death was established as late in the evening. What was Cyrus doing in Doongerwadi then?'

The policeman shifted uncomfortably in his seat. 'We think he went for a walk.'

'A walk?'

'Yes. A walk. Apparently he was in the habit of doing so. Liked the solitude inside Doongerwadi. God knows there aren't many places in this city to be alone.'

Chopra conceded the point. 'Do you have a last known movements timeline?'

'You'll find it in there. There's nothing that stands out. He had a succession of meetings during the day, then went to his club in the evening. He left the club some time before he was killed. Wasn't seen again until his body was discovered the next day.'

'Who found the body?'

'The head corpse-bearer. Got the shock of his life seeing the boss laid out in one of his precious towers.'

'The boss?'

'Well, technically, as the owner of Doongerwadi, Cyrus had the power to appoint – or get rid of – the corpse-bearers.'

Chopra salted this away, then leafed through to the forensics report.

It made sparse reading.

Nothing untoward had been discovered on or near the industrialist's body. No stray fibres, no viable shoeprints, no blood other than Cyrus's own. No forensic artefacts of any kind that might give a clue as to his assailant.

'What about enemies?'

'We made enquiries. Business rivals, disgruntled former employees, even rumoured female acquaintances – though, according to his family and friends, he's been single ever since his wife passed on a few years ago. We also spoke to his son – apparently, he's estranged from his father. The truth is no one really hated him enough to bash his brains in. And if they did, they had rock-solid alibis for the time of death. His son, for instance, was at home with his wife. She says he never left the apartment.' He sighed. 'ACP Rao wanted a quick resolution, and that is exactly what we achieved.'

The fact that Kelkar couldn't meet his eyes convinced Chopra that the investigation had been a lot shoddier than the man was painting. With Rao in charge, he would expect no less. Perizaad Zorabian was convinced there was more to her father's death than the official investigation had concluded. Chopra owed it to his client to follow the matter through as far as possible.

He went back over the paperwork as Kelkar waited impatiently, occasionally eyeing Ganesha, who was occupying himself by snuffling his trunk into the room's corners, no doubt investigating the various ripe scents on offer.

'What's this?' said Chopra.

He tapped the piece of paper he was holding, a list of personal effects discovered on the victim. 'It says here you found a piece of paper with some indecipherable text on it.'

'Yes,' said Kelkar.

He took the folder from Chopra, leafed through it, and pulled out a photocopy of a single much-folded sheet of A5 on which was typed:

INDUKNAAUIKBAHNXDDLA

'It's gibberish,' said Kelkar.

'You mean you couldn't work out what it meant,' corrected Chopra.

'No,' admitted Kelkar, deflating somewhat.

'It says here that this sheet was found inside a book of poetry that Cyrus had on him at the time. Clearly, he valued it enough to keep it close.'

'We thought it might be some sort of password. But he wasn't the type to use a computer, or online accounts. He was, however, a closet poet – probably why he was carrying around that book of poetry. Maybe this was one of those nonsense compositions you hear about.'

'Can I see the poetry book?'

Kelkar rang outside.

Minutes later, a junior officer arrived with an evidence bag.

Inside was a pocket book featuring works by the premier Romance poets: Wordsworth, Coleridge, Keats, Byron and Shelley. The fact that the book had been found on Cyrus said something about the murdered man; it was too early for Chopra to say what that something meant.

He picked up the paper inscribed with the enigmatic 'code', then flicked through the book of poetry in which it had been found. There seemed to be no plausible connection.

He held up the sheet. 'I would like to hold on to this. And the book.'

'Technically, they are evidence,' pointed out Kelkar.

'Usually I would not ask,' said Chopra. 'But I feel there is something here that may give me an insight into Cyrus. I need time to study these items further.'

Kelkar looked momentarily unsure, then shrugged. 'Well, the commissioner has ordered us to give you what-ever you need. You'll have to sign for them, of course.'

Chopra did as he was bid, then returned to the list of items found on the victim's body. 'You also found a small key inside Cyrus's wallet. What was it for?'

'We think it's the key to a secure bank locker.'

'You're not sure?'

Kelkar looked embarrassed. 'We haven't been able to find out *which* bank the locker is held at. The registration numbers have been filed off, so we couldn't trace it through the locksmiths' association. We tried checking with all the major banks, but no one recognised the key. But it's hardly important, is it?' He shook his head. 'You're looking at this all wrong, Chopra. These details are meaningless. The man was murdered by a random assailant. There's no more to it than that. No complicated murder scenario; no skeletons in Cyrus's closet. He was simply in the wrong place at the wrong time. The sooner you accept this, the sooner we can all get back to our lives.'

LUNCHTIME AT THE VULTURE CLUB

The Ahura Mazda Parsee Sports and Social Gymkhana had long served as one of Mumbai's oldest bastions of fraternal enterprise. Established more than a century earlier on the bustling Swami Vivekanand Road in the affluent suburb of Bandra West, the club – known informally as the Vulture Club – was the brainchild of a group of Parsee grandees keen to establish a venue where they could meet to discuss matters of both commercial and philanthropic endeavour.

The magnificent sandstone building, recently renovated, was fronted by enormous carved wooden gates copied from an ancient Zoroastrian fire temple and inscribed with lines of Persian text. To either side of the wooden gates stood two fifteen-foot-high pillars, atop which perched a pair of colossal stone vultures, staring, beady-eyed, down into the road. The vultures, pitted and scarred by decades of monsoon bombardment and the corrosive effect of bird droppings, gave off a distinctly minatory air. Most passers-by tended to hurry quickly on, as if the twin birds of carrion were, perhaps, measuring them up for leisurely consumption at some unspecified later date.

Chopra was let into the compound, where he parked the van before releasing Ganesha from the rear.

They were met there by the club's secretary, Zubin Engineer, a decrepit-looking elderly gentleman in a billowing white shirt and black trousers who shuffled along with a cane as he squinted myopically from behind bottle-bottom spectacles.

'Thank you for taking the time to meet me,' said Chopra, as they approached the grand portico fronting the club. He had come here as a first step in retracing the police investigation into Cyrus's death, in particular Cyrus's last known movements.

'I am happy to help in any way I can,' responded Engineer. 'Cyrus was the club's president, and an old friend. We have known each other since we were boys. When Perizaad told me that it was her intention to employ a private investigator, I was delighted. The police, I am afraid, have been most ineffective. Perizaad heard about you from the owner of the Grand Raj Palace Hotel. I believe you recently took on a similar investigation for them – concluding the matter to the satisfaction of all parties.'

Chopra remained silent.

It was not his habit to discuss previous cases with new clients, though Engineer was correct in that there were similarities between that investigation and the current one. The body of American billionaire Hollis Burbank had been found in his suite at the Grand Raj Palace, the city's most iconic hotel. Unhappy with his senior officer's desire to label the death a suicide, an old colleague had invited Chopra to look over the case. Chopra had uncovered a wealth of motives and suspects, and a truly shocking secret from Burbank's past, ultimately unmasking a killer.

He wondered if his path to the truth behind Cyrus Zorabian's death would be similarly circuitous.

Chopra paused before a sprawling display in the lobby, consisting of memorabilia from the club's history. Old sepia prints of ancestral Parsees newly arrived in the metropolis; items of ceremonial clothing handed down by the club's forefathers; a collection of personal bric-a-brac: an old pipe, a snuff box, even a stuffed vulture said to have fed on the club's founder 'Bawa' Rustom Zorabian – Cyrus Zorabian's revered ancestor.

The centre of the display was taken up by a waxwork of the late founder, sitting on a throne-like wooden seat inside a spotlit glass case, dressed to the nines in traditional Parsee skullcap, loose silk trousers and long, white double-breasted coat, clutching the club's ceremonial mace. Chopra found the waxwork disturbingly lifelike; the old Parsee progenitor looked ready to bounce to his feet and begin laying down the law, as he was reputed to have done in his pomp.

'The Parsees of Mumbai owe the Zorabian family a great debt,' Engineer explained. 'Rustom Zorabian was a true pioneer. He led the way for many of our families to establish commercial activities which later flowered into thriving businesses. But he was more than that. He was a keeper of the sacred flame, a staunch supporter of our oldest traditions. He believed fervently that no matter how far from home we found ourselves, we had a duty to preserve the rituals and customs of our forebears. It was Rustom who purchased the land on which the Towers of Silence now sit; it was he who enclosed it behind a wall and brokered an agreement with the British that Doongerwadi would be classified as Parsee holy ground. Because of Rustom Zorabian we continue to be connected to our past.'

'Did Cyrus come to the club often?' asked Chopra.

'Yes, of course. He was the chairman of the club's managing committee, as was his father before him, and his father before that, all the way back to Rustom. Cyrus was never one for details, but he insisted on being involved in the life of the community. He personally oversaw the club's charitable programme.'

'According to the police investigation he visited the club on the evening that he was killed – is that correct?'

'Yes. He was here for a meeting of the managing committee. After that there was a presentation – given by myself – to be followed by a late-night supper. But he never made it to the dinner.'

'He left early?'

'Yes. Apparently he left during my lecture,' said Engineer, sounding somewhat miffed.

'Apparently?' said Chopra. 'Did you not see him leave?'

'I was on stage at the time and the lights had been dimmed – so, no, I didn't see him go. But my colleagues did.'

'What was your presentation about?' asked Chopra, intrigued.

'Oh, it was a slide lecture on the results of a study I have been conducting for the past decade,' said Engineer modestly. ' "A reflection and analysis of the Parsee patronage of Bombay's architectural renaissance in the late nineteenth century as evidence of the complex colonial relationship between Parsee, British and Indian populations of the period – with a discussion on the methodological underpinnings of the study".'

Chopra was unsure how to respond, and even less sure that he had understood what Engineer had said. 'I'd like to speak to your colleagues, if I may. Those who attended the lecture.'

'I anticipated as much. They are waiting for us in the drawing room.'

Engineer led the way to the lifts, which they took up to the second floor. Ganesha bundled in beside them, squeezing Chopra against the mirrored rear wall.

The drawing room, a magnificently chandeliered space, was every bit as lavish as Chopra might have expected. The Parsees, on the whole, did not do things by halves. He recalled Homi explaining that Zoroastrians, unlike the pious of other religions, did not eschew wealth as necessarily evil. In fact, they actively embraced it, as long as it was utilised to the benefit of others. For this reason, Parsees rarely donned sackcloth to head off into the hills in search of the ascetic life.

The polished white Italian marble floors gleamed, and the walls were hung with canvases and tapestries depicting morally invigorating motifs from the long history of the Zoroastrians. A common theme running through many of the paintings was the depiction of the club's founder Rustom Zorabian in a prophetical light: Rustom standing resolutely at the prow of a boat as it churned through choppy seas – presumably on the long and desperate flight to India; Rustom engaged in ardent negotiation with British representatives of the East India Company. A particularly striking canvas depicted a bronzed and muscled Rustom kneeling atop a mountain, a torch of sacred fire held aloft, as he gazed into the heavenly ether communing with Ahura Mazda.

The image, intensely hagiographical, gave Chopra pause.

Clearly Cyrus's ancestor had held a high opinion of himself, as both a leader to his people and a devout Zoroastrian. He wondered if this hubris had been passed down the family line – had Cyrus also viewed himself in this manner?

He quickly reviewed what he knew of the Parsee religion.

The sect had been founded by Zoroaster – known also as Zarathustra – a priest living in ancient Persia who claimed to have received a revelatory vision from the god Ahura Mazda, the Lord of Wisdom. Ahura Mazda urged him to preach against the polytheistic religions of the time, and to embrace the inherent duality of existence, namely the eternal battle between good and evil – with evil being personified in the entity known as Ahriman, the Destructive Spirit. Zoroaster had been one of the earliest to preach belief in a single god, and the concept of paradise. Through good deeds, the righteous could earn immortality. Those who opted for the path of evil were condemned by their own conscience, and must expect to be punished in the afterlife.

He briefly wondered where Cyrus Zorabian might fit in this grand scheme of morality. Perhaps it was too early to say.

Chopra himself had never had much time for piety. He was content to let others believe what they wished, but he held no illusions that the world was a better place because of it. If the current state of things was anything to go by, it seemed evident that the exact opposite was the case. With so many recipients of the 'truth' throughout the ages, it was a wonder that anyone had any idea what was going on.

'This way,' said Engineer, and led them to the rear half of the grand drawing room, where clumps of comfortable-looking red horsehair sofas and bucket seats were arranged on a thick Persian carpet. Scattered among the seats were half a dozen ancient specimens – the members of the Vulture Club's managing committee.

They were even older than Chopra had anticipated.

One of them, a perfectly bald gentleman in white slacks, slept the sleep of the dead, a newspaper propping up his chin, drool escaping from his lower lip; another, wearing a red Parsee fez secured under his chin with an elastic strap and clutching tightly to a mobile catheter stand, eyed Chopra with a rheumy glare, as if he suspected that the detective had designs on the half-filled pouch of murky yellow liquid hanging from the stand. A silver-haired woman in a floral dress gave him a slightly bemused smile, then went back to the crochet hoop in her lap. Ganesha, instantly intrigued, trotted over to her, and attempted to investigate the hoop. The woman took this in her stride, allowing him to run the tip of his trunk over the intricate embroidery.

'Attention, please,' said Zubin Engineer, rapping his cane on the floor. 'This is the man I told you about. His name is Chopra, and he is investigating Cyrus's death.'

'What?' said Catheter Man. 'Speak up, Engineer. Can't hear a word.'

Ganesha, losing interest in the crochet, walked over to the sleeping gentleman and prodded him awake. The man opened his gummy eyes, the newspaper sliding off his chest, then mumbled: 'By Ahura Mazda, Engineer, your nose gets bigger by the day.'

'That's an elephant, Dinshaw, you senile old fool,' said Catheter Man, who was seated opposite him.

'Who are you calling senile, Forhad? I'm every bit as sharp today as I was seventy years ago when I used to thrash you in the weekly chess tourney.'

'Is that why you're wearing a bib?' said Forhad nastily.

'He's a fine specimen,' said Dinshaw, patting Ganesha on the head. 'You don't see many of them around any more. When I was young they were everywhere, hauling timber, charging madly at trucks. Great days, great days.'

'When *you* were young, Dinshaw,' said Forhad, as he pulled his catheter stand away from Ganesha's curious trunk, 'dinosaurs still roamed the earth.'

'I have some questions,' interrupted Chopra.

'What?' said Dinshaw. 'What did he say?'

'He said you're an idiot,' muttered Forhad.

'Really? Why would he say that? I've only just met the man.'

Chopra raised his voice. Five minutes with the methuse-lahs of the Vulture Club and he could feel his blood pressure heading skywards. 'I *said*,' he bellowed, 'that I have some questions. About Cyrus.'

'Well, why didn't you say so?' said Dinshaw. 'And there's no need to shout. We're not deaf.'

'I have been told that Cyrus left the evening lecture early on the night that he died,' Chopra ground out. 'May I ask which of you saw him leave?'

'That would be Dinshaw,' said Engineer. 'Tell the detective what you heard on the night of Cyrus's death. Dinshaw . . . DINSHAW!'

Dinshaw, who had drifted back to sleep, jerked awake. 'What's happening? Is it the end of days?'

'I wish it was the end of *your* days,' muttered Forhad. Then louder: 'The detective wants to know what Cyrus told you when he left the lecture. On the night he died.'

'Oh, that,' said Dinshaw, shifting on the sofa. 'He was sitting behind me in the lecture hall. And then he got a phone call. I could hear him mumbling away, so I turned and asked him to be quiet. Young people these days, no manners.'

Chopra wondered just how ancient Dinshaw was if he considered the sixty-five-year-old Cyrus Zorabian to be 'young'. 'What was the conversation about?'

'I don't know. My hearing isn't what it once was.' Dinshaw grimaced. 'But Cyrus was disturbed by it, that much I recall. He told me he had to leave urgently, and that I should convey his apologies to Engineer after the lecture.'

'What time was this?'

'Around nine thirty, I think. The lecture had just begun. It wasn't due to finish for a couple of hours. Engineer does so love the sound of his own voice. Not to mention the two hundred slides!'

As Zubin Engineer bristled beside him, Chopra considered Dinshaw's testimony.

Nine thirty.

The pathologist had concluded that Cyrus had died between 10 and 11 p.m. Given the evening traffic in the city, this meant that Cyrus had left the Vulture Club – following the unexpected phone call – and driven directly to Doongerwadi to meet his fate in the Towers of Silence.

What had convinced him to leave?

The sound of a bell being rung cut through the conversation.

Chopra turned to see a large man in an apron wheeling a trolley into the room. 'Lunch is served!' he bellowed.

There was a marked stirring of interest, as the gathered committee members enlivened at the prospect of their midday meal.

'What's on the menu today, Izad?' asked the urbane woman with the crochet hoop.

The chef, adjusting his apron over his substantial belly, began to read off a menu card. 'Chicken dhansak, lamb dhansak, mutton dhansak, prawn dhansak.'

There was a loud groan. 'Dhansak? Again? When are you going to cook something else?' said Forhad, glaring at the chef.

Izad's face swelled. 'Something else? What do you mean *something else*? My family has been making dhansak at this club for over a hundred years. Our dhansak is the best dhansak in the country. People would give their right arms for just a taste of my dhansak.'

'Man cannot live on dhansak alone,' muttered Forhad.

'Well then, man can bloody well go hungry,' said the chef, brandishing his serving ladle as if it were an axe.

Ganesha, drawn by the delicious aromas of the iconic Parsee dish – a stew-like mixture of spiced meat, vegetables and cooked lentils – had trotted over to investigate the lunch cart.

'You see,' said the chef, 'even the elephant cannot resist!'

'Perhaps we can finish our conversation outside,' suggested Chopra, leaning into Zubin Engineer.

When they had returned to the lobby, Engineer said, 'I must apologise for my colleagues. They are a little set in their ways.'

'This is a sensitive question,' said Chopra, 'but was Cyrus well liked here?'

Engineer squinted from behind his spectacles. 'What do you mean? He was the club's chairman.'

'Are you saying there was no one here who wished him anything but well?'

Engineer hesitated.

'This is no time to hold back,' Chopra prodded. 'I am not a policeman. You can be assured of my discretion.'

'Well, I suppose there *was* Boman . . .' said Engineer reluctantly.

'Boman?'

'Boman Jeejibhoy. He is – was – a member of the managing committee, until he quit last year following a disagreement with Cyrus. We all thought it would blow over – they've been friends since they were children, after all. But I don't think they had reconciled by the time Cyrus died.'

'What did they fall out about?'

'I don't know. Neither of them would explain it. All we know is they had a bust-up in the lobby, ending with Boman threatening to kill Cyrus.'

'Did you tell the police this?'

'Of course not. It was just an argument. Boman didn't know what he was saying.'

'You never tried to find out what the disagreement was about?'

'Certainly. But they were both as stubborn as each other.'

'I'd like to talk to this Boman,' said Chopra.

'It won't do any good,' sighed Engineer. 'But I will give him a call. Perhaps he has had a change of heart since Cyrus's death.'

THE TOWERS OF SILENCE

Chopra decided to continue in the footsteps of the initial police investigation by next visiting the crime scene. Doongerwadi was a brisk, forty-minute drive from the club. He took the Bandra-Worli Sealink, the new flyover that speared across Mahim Bay, then sped the Tata van along the Khan Abdul Gaffar Khan Road running all the way from the Worli Sea Face to Mahalaxmi. From here it was a quick loop around Haji Ali and Cumballa Hill to the wooded tract of land sitting in the very heart of the city.

By the time they arrived it was two in the afternoon.

The heat had become unbearable. With the air-conditioner in the van temporarily out of action, he and Ganesha had sweated like lobsters in a pot, and were glad to be back out in the open.

They were met at Doongerwadi's eastern gate by Anosh Ginwala, the head corpse-bearer assigned to the Towers of Silence. Ginwala, dressed in black pants, a long white shirt and a red, fez-like hat, was a dour man. His sunken eyes looked out from beneath thick eyebrows, sullenly observing a world he appeared to hold in contempt. His lips twisted into a grimace beneath a thick moustache as he let Chopra into Doongerwadi. 'A few years ago, no non-Parsee would ever have been permitted to set foot on this hallowed ground.'

Chopra knew that this was true.

He had had to call Perizaad Zorabian to arrange the visit. He wished to get a feel for the scene of the crime. He also needed to speak to the man who had found Cyrus's body – Anosh Ginwala.

'I am told that Cyrus was a frequent visitor here,' he began as Ginwala tramped ahead along a rutted path. The path meandered through a thicket of trees, blocking out all but the odd shaft of lancing sunlight. The darkness pressed in around them, thick and textured. He felt Ganesha trot up closer behind him.

'He has been coming here regularly these past months,' confirmed Ginwala. 'Doongerwadi is one of the few places in the city where he knew he would not be bothered.'

Chopra considered this. On the evening of his death Cyrus had been scheduled to sit through a lecture at the Vulture Club. He had left only after receiving a mysterious phone call.

Whatever he had been doing in Doongerwadi, it was a good bet that he had not come here to be alone.

'Does anyone stay here on a permanent basis?'

'A number of us call Doongerwadi home.'

'Us?'

'Khandias – corpse-bearers.'

'Where do you live?'

'We have been given accommodation by the main gates, on the far side of Doongerwadi.'

'It seems a grim place to wish to reside,' mused Chopra.

Ginwala turned to glare at him. 'Do you think we do this because we *wish* to? Have you any idea what it means to be a khandia? We handle the dead, Chopra. Because of this we are considered untouchable – in a community that claims to be casteless. Hah! Once upon a time I used to live in the suburbs. But when I lost my job, this was the only work I could get. And once my neighbours, my friends, discovered what I did, it wasn't long before we found ourselves ostracised. They stopped coming to our home; they refused to eat from our kitchen. Even now, those who wish to tip me for escorting their dearly departed into the netherworld will not touch my hand to give me their money.' Bitterness dripped from Ginwala's tone, forestalling Chopra from asking any more questions.

They proceeded in silence until, some ten minutes later, the path opened out into a clearing.

The Tower of Silence that rose before them was built of ancient sandstone bricks, a roofless, circular structure some three hundred feet in circumference and eighteen feet high. A stone ramp led up to a wooden door built into its outer wall.

A trio of vultures were perched on the tower's rim. One of them shook out its wings and snapped its beak at them.

'When I first came to Doongerwadi,' Ginwala began, 'there were so many birds there was not enough space atop the tower for them all. They would flap and wheel above us in a great cloud, blotting out the sky.'

'What happened to them?'

'A decade ago their numbers were decimated. That was when life began to change for us.'

Chopra had seen many photographs of the legendary Towers of Silence, but now, as he stood for the first time before one, he felt a blast of emotion that unsettled him. He could not have named the reason for his discomfort – he had been around death so often that death alone was not enough to unnerve him.

No. It went deeper than that.

The idea that inside this macabre monument had lain the corpses of innumerable men, women and children, left to the predations of scavengers, seemed somehow perverse to him.

And yet he knew that it was precisely this feeling, born of little more than ignorance and an instinctive xenophobia, that had led to the vilification of the Parsee practice of excarnation, ordained by the prophet Zarathustra so that the elements that the Parsees held dear – earth, fire, water – would not be defiled by burial or cremation.

In recent years, this unease had grown into a clamour. The residents of the high-rise towers that surrounded Doongerwadi had petitioned the state government to have the practice outlawed; the idea of human corpses rotting in the open for lengthy periods of time in close proximity to their homes had become intensely unpalatable.

The Parsee community had, unsurprisingly, responded with a belligerent refusal to buckle under the pressure.

Nevertheless, there were some, Homi included, who believed that change was inevitable. Homi himself had championed the heretical notion that Doongerwadi might be better utilised as a centre of cremation. 'Once you are dead, who really cares, anyway?' he had baldly asserted.

Chopra thought that his friend was being purposefully naïve.

Religion warped the minds of men in ways that continued to astonish him. Set against the blind adherence to that-which-had-been-enshrined, common sense and logic could rarely hope to prevail.

'Do you know what Doongerwadi means?' said Ginwala. ' "The orchard on the hill". But if this is an orchard, the only fruit it bears is the fruit of death.'

He shuffled up the ramp, pushed aside the wooden entry door and vanished inside the tower.

Chopra turned at the door as he realised that Ganesha was no longer behind him. 'It's OK, boy,' he said, sensing the elephant's distress. 'Wait for me here.'

Inside the tower, he found himself looking down upon three concentric tiers of stone, moving downwards towards a central well. A number of decomposing corpses lay on the tiers; some exhibited the signs of having been scavenged. The central well seemed to exude a camphorous breath that hung in the air.

Even though he had been expecting it, the ghastly pano-rama sent a shiver through him.

'Males are left on this outermost circle,' explained Ginwala. 'Females on the middle tier, and children on the innermost. Beyond that is the well – though it is no more than a pit paved with stone. When the bodies on the tiers have sufficiently deteriorated we push them into the well.

The well is connected via channels to underground chambers containing charcoal and sand. The putrefying matter is washed into these chambers by rain, and gradually filters away. At least that was how it used to be.' Ginwala grimaced. 'In the old days, the vultures would reduce the bodies to a heap of bones in half an hour. There was little left to go into the well. Since the vultures vanished, things have changed. Now the bodies lie out on the tiers for far too long. Five years ago, we installed solar concentrators to help focus the sun's rays and aid the process of desiccation. This is only partially effective. Sometimes bodies take weeks to decompose. In the rainy season they become bloated, like sludge. Have you seen a piece of bread when it gets soaked? A body becomes gooey like that. It is not pleasant.'

Chopra shuddered. 'You found Cyrus's body in the central well – is that correct?'

'Yes.'

'He had been thrown inside?'

'I doubt that he got there himself.'

'What were you doing in here?'

'My job,' said Ginwala flatly. 'I had come to deliver another body to the dakhma. I checked to see how the previous incumbent of the central well was coming along – and saw Cyrus in there. I have observed many terrible things inside these towers, but none so terrible as a fresh corpse inside the central well.' The corpse-bearer's brow darkened at the sacrilege.

'How did Cyrus get into Doongerwadi? Presumably it is locked.'

'He had his own set of keys. This is ancestral Zorabian land, after all.'

'Could he have been meeting someone here that night?'

'Who would he meet? The corpse-bearers are generally shunned, and the only other human residents are incapable of meeting anyone.'

'The police believe he was killed by a drug addict. Apparently, they have been climbing the wall.'

Ginwala's expression folded into a frown. 'Yes, it happens. And ever more frequently as the city becomes more crowded. We patrol the grounds regularly, and throw out anyone we find. But we cannot stop them all.'

'So it is a possibility?'

Ginwala shrugged. 'Anything is possible. The plot is fifty acres. There are only a dozen khandia families living here – and we generally don't come into the woods in the evening.'

Chopra sensed that he had gained as much as he was going to from the surly corpse-bearer. 'Thank you for your time,' he said, as they made their way back out of the tower.

He passed back through the wooden door and immediately noticed the vulture squatting on the ground near Ganesha. The vulture was unusually large, almost a metre in height, with the bald head and white neck ruff common to its species and a distinctive white band across its hooked beak. The little elephant was eyeing it with some trepidation, unsettled by its scrutiny.

As Chopra appeared, he padded with relief to the foot of the stone ramp.

'Come on, boy,' said Chopra. 'Let's get out of here.'

Ginwala led them back along the trail to the eastern gate. Here he locked the gate behind them, then, without a word of farewell, turned and vanished back into the gloom.

Chopra, glad to be back out in the sunlight, herded Ganesha into the van, then slipped into his seat and started the engine. He paused, foot poised on the clutch, looking back at the gate into Doongerwadi.

The encounter with Ginwala had left him uneasy.

He could not shake the feeling that the man had left something unsaid; not exactly lied, more omitted details from his stilted and grudging testimony that might prove to be important. The case was swiftly entangling itself, suspects shimmering into view. He needed to lay the groundwork, establish the veracity of the 'facts' presented to him by the initial investigation, then begin checking alibis – such as that of the murdered man's estranged son – and other testimony that felt less than airtight. Ginwala would be high on that list.

Ganesha's trunk tapped him on the shoulder. 'You felt it too, did you?' he said, glancing at the elephant in his rear-view mirror as he slipped the vehicle into gear and stepped on the accelerator.

There was a bump as the front fender struck something below his eyeline, followed by a loud squawk.

Instinctively, he slammed on the brakes.

Cursing, he leapt out of the van.

On the baking tarmac, beside the van's front tyre, was a vulture. He realised that it was the same one that had been eyeing Ganesha inside Doongerwadi.

He knelt down beside the bird.

Its eyes were closed. Up close, the arch scavenger gave off a horrible stench. Clumps of rotting flesh stuck to its beak. The realisation churned his stomach. He wondered just *who* the bird had been snacking on.

He reached out with a finger and jabbed the vulture in the ribcage.

The bird's wings fluttered feebly, jerking him backwards.

He watched as it snapped open its eyes, scrabbled to its feet, then attempted to take off, managing only to flail around in an ungainly circle. He realised that its right wing was broken, sweeping along the floor at an unnatural angle.

He was glad now that Ginwala had vanished with such alacrity. Heaven only knew the fuss the man would have made had he seen Chopra mow down one of the few remaining vultures. He had no idea what the penalty was for running over an endangered holy bird, but he guessed it wasn't pleasant.

A VULTURE OF SUBSTANCE

'*Gyps indicus*. Otherwise known as the Indian vulture.'

Rohit Lala, vet, grinned at Chopra.

'I know what it *is*,' said Chopra through gritted teeth. 'Can you fix it?'

'Her,' said Lala. 'Can I fix *her*.'

Chopra had become well acquainted with Lala – a large, voluble and gregarious man hailing from a rich Marwadi family whose paterfamilias still could not believe that his only son had eschewed the ancestral jewellery business for the suspect pleasures of fiddling around with the private parts of animals – since Ganesha had arrived on his doorstep. He found the man's inveterate good humour generally insufferable, but he was a more than competent practitioner of the arcane craft of animal husbandry.

A regular Doctor DooLala, as the man himself was wont to joke.

'This is a rare animal you've chosen to run over,' continued Lala. 'A decade ago there were more of these around than you could shake a stick at. And then, almost overnight, 99 per cent of the population died off. Can you guess why?'

Chopra shook his head.

Lala pointed his finger at Chopra's chest. 'You, my friend, are the reason why. Humankind. A drug called diclofenac. Administered to livestock in order to promote good health. Unfortunately, the drug is deadly to vultures. When they fed on dead cattle, they ingested enough of it to knock out their kidneys. Pretty much wiped them out.'

'But they have recovered now, yes?' said Chopra, glancing at Ganesha, who was looking on with some concern.

'Barely. And nowhere near the numbers they once were. Captive breeding programmes have reintroduced a few to Doongerwadi, but they remain critically endangered.' Lala grimaced. 'They are a truly remarkable species. We love to hate them, but the truth is that vultures do a great deal for us humans. Do you know that when the vultures died off, the rat and wild dog population in Mumbai exploded? Which, in turn, meant the spread of diseases such as rabies. With the absence of vultures, crows stepped in to pick at the corpses in Doongerwadi. Unfortunately, crows are fussy eaters. They have a habit of flying off with body parts – fingers, eyes, tongues – occasionally dropping them into the surrounding homes.' Lala stretched his lips into a grisly grin. 'Whether we like it or not, we need vultures, if only to clean up after ourselves.'

'Can you fix her?' Chopra repeated.

'She has a broken wing,' explained Lala. 'If left untended it could prove life-threatening – simply because the bird will not be able to feed. But it is a simple matter to set.'

Lala called over his assistant, a rat-faced individual named Stephen De Souza. Together, they transported the bird inside.

With the bird set on a worktop, Stephen gently held the broken wing in its natural position as Lala cut a length of gauze and wrapped it around the bird's body, slipping it over the damaged wing, and under the functional one. In this way, he immobilised the injured limb, but not so tightly that the vulture's breathing was restricted.

'All done,' said Lala, stepping back, as the bird attempted to scratch at the gauze with her beak. 'You need to keep her in a confined area for about two weeks. Indoors. Otherwise she will provide an easy target for a feral dog or a passing leopard.'

'Me?' said Chopra in alarm. 'I thought you were going to keep her here.'

'I wish I could. But I just don't have the space.'

'But where will *I* house a vulture?' Chopra could not keep a trace of horror from his voice.

'You're a smart man. You'll think of something.' Lala turned back to the bird. 'You know, there's something not quite right with her. Even accounting for the fact that you bashed her with your van, she seems to be quite sickly. Look at this plumage; she's been losing feathers. And her tongue – it shouldn't be that colour.'

'Perhaps it is that chemical you mentioned? Diclofenac.'

'No. That was banned years ago.' He continued to stare at the bird, then took out a small torch and shone it in her eyes. When he straightened, moments later, it was with a shake of the head. 'I'll take some blood. Have it tested.

We'll get to the bottom of it.' He looked down with affection at the bird, which clacked her beak and returned his gaze with a beady-eyed stare. 'Parsees believe that these vultures serve as intermediaries between earth and heaven. By consuming the body, they liberate the soul. Look after her, Chopra. She is the future of her species.'

With Stephen's help Chopra bundled the bird safely back into the van.

'By the way,' he said, turning to Lala, 'my little companion here seems to be somewhat distracted these days. Do you think he's ill?'

'Let's have a look,' said Lala. He slipped out his torch and gave Ganesha a quick once-over, which the elephant submitted to without protest. 'Nothing that I can immediately detect,' concluded the vet.

'It is probably nothing,' agreed Chopra.

Lala smiled. 'Don't forget, elephants are highly emotional creatures. In that respect, they are very much like us. Don't you have days when you don't feel quite at your best?'

'I suppose so,' said Chopra.

'And you have yet to get to the bottom of Ganesha's past. Who knows what trauma he may have suffered? Perhaps he is troubled by bad memories.'

Chopra looked down at his young ward, who was busy investigating Lala's shoelaces.

The vet was right, of course.

Over the past year, he had made little headway in uncovering Ganesha's history. The truth was he did not even know where to start. His uncle's letter had given no clue as to where Ganesha had been born, or under what circumstances Bansi had come into contact with him, let alone why he had sent the calf to Chopra.

It was a mystery that needed to be solved; one day, he would do so. For now, all he could do was look after his young ward as best as he was able.

He patted Ganesha on the head. 'Let's head for home. Irfan will be preparing your bowl of evening chocolate.'

At the sound of the word 'chocolate' Ganesha's ears perked up. The little calf was addicted to the stuff, which Irfan would melt into a bucket of creamy milk for him each evening.

Like the humans he lived with, it appeared that chocolate was a sure-fire pick-me-up for an elephant.

A CLIENT AT THE RESTAURANT

Back at the restaurant, Chopra parked the van, then carried the vulture into the rear compound.

He found the chef, Azeem Lucknowwallah, sitting out on the veranda, a thick cheroot stuck out of the side of his mouth, concentrating fiercely on an ancient typewriter perched on a rickety table before him. As Chopra looked on Lucknowwallah lifted a finger and hammered at a couple of keys. He then ripped out the vellum sheet, examined it, swore, curled it into a ball and hurled it into the compound, adding to the drifts of abused paper littering the parched earth.

'What are you doing, Chef?' asked Chopra, temporarily halted by the odd sight.

'I am penning my memoirs,' said Lucknowwallah, as if this was the most obvious thing in the world. The cheroot jacked up and down between his lips. 'But I just cannot seem to get the opening right.'

By now Chopra was used to the chef's eccentricities. Highly combustible and intensely driven, Lucknowwallah had cooked for some of the finest restaurants in the country, only coming out of retirement to work at Poppy's because his own father had been a policeman, killed tragically in the line of duty by a rampaging bullock.

'Your memoirs?' he echoed.

'These days every two-chip burger mechanic is out there hawking his autobiography, so I thought why not Azeem Lucknowwallah? There are people who would literally bite my arm off for my life story.'

'Why are you using a typewriter?' he asked, for want of something else to say. 'Don't you have a computer?'

'You can't make tandoori chicken in a microwave,' replied the chef airily. Then he seemed to notice, for the first time, the bird clutched in Chopra's arms. 'Why are you carrying a vulture?'

'Her wing is broken. I'm going to keep her here till it heals.'

Lucknowwallah plucked the cheroot from his mouth and stared at him. 'Is that so?'

'I have to keep her somewhere,' said Chopra desperately.

'This, my friend, is a restaurant. One does not keep a carrion-eating scavenger near a kitchen.'

With some effort Chopra stopped himself from noting that his mother-in-law was already employed front-of-house.

'This is *my* restaurant,' he mumbled.

'Well then,' said Lucknowwallah acidly, 'perhaps *you* would like to take charge of this evening's service?'

Chopra gave up. 'Very well,' he said. 'I will find somewhere else.'

He walked through the kitchen, where the sous chefs Rosie Pinto and Ramesh Goel were busily prepping the evening service, and into his office.

Here he found Rangwalla waiting for him.

Chopra set the vulture gently down on to the tiled floor, where she immediately attempted to gouge a chunk out of Rangwalla's leg.

His assistant detective leapt up from his chair, back-pedalling smartly to the room's corner, as the bird waddled after him, her one good wing flapping furiously in the confined space. 'Get this damned thing off me!' he spluttered, ending with a strangled cry as the bird lunged for him again.

Chopra grabbed the creature and shoved her under his desk, where she huddled into herself. 'It's probably your aftershave,' he muttered.

Rangwalla gave his boss an acerbic look.

The former policeman had served as Chopra's deputy for twenty years at the local Sahar station, and had always suspected that Chopra was a little too straightforward for his own good. Rangwalla believed that sidling up to a problem was often the best way to catch it unawares. He came from an upbringing where, usually, the only thing that stood between success and failure was a swift kick to the nether regions. After Chopra had left the force, Rangwalla had found himself in the crosshairs of ACP Suresh Rao. Infuriated at Chopra's final act of rebellion – pursuing a case that Rao had declared off-limits – but unable to do anything to the man himself, Rao had taken out his frustration on his second-in-command, securing Rangwalla's dismissal from the force on trumped-up misconduct charges.

As if to underline the stark difference in the two men's moral compasses, it was Chopra who had subsequently come to his former sub-inspector's rescue, offering him a role at the detective agency.

Rangwalla, a slight, bearded man with a dark, volcanic complexion, invariably dressed in a black kurta and blue jeans, had always possessed the uncanny ability to blend into the streets; it was a skill that Chopra had yet to master, and for this reason alone his old deputy had proven to be a valuable addition to the agency.

They sat to discuss the day's events. It was a ritual they had established when Rangwalla joined the agency; in this way Chopra could keep abreast of the cases he had delegated.

'There is someone I wish you to meet,' said Rangwalla, glancing nervously under the desk. He had pulled his chair well back, in case the vulture attempted a surprise attack. 'He's waiting outside.'

'A new case?'

'Potentially.'

Chopra hesitated. 'I have just taken on something important. It may tie us both up for the foreseeable future.'

He quickly outlined the Zorabian investigation, and his early inroads into the matter.

'Those Parsees are crazy,' said Rangwalla. 'It's all that drinking and inbreeding. Is there anything you need me to do?'

'Not yet,' said Chopra. 'I am still working my way through the original investigation.'

'In that case, will you meet this man?'

'Is he an acquaintance of yours?'

'Yes. He lives in my building.'

'What is the case?'

'It's better if he explains it himself.'

Chopra frowned. It was not like Rangwalla to be so cryptic. His suspicions were always raised when his deputy avoided giving straight answers.

'Very well.'

Rangwalla left the room, returning briskly with a bald, elderly gentleman in tow. The man – who must have been in his sixties – wore wire-frame spectacles, a wispy white moustache, and was dressed in a plain shirt, trousers and sandals. A row of pens poked out in regimental fashion from the front pocket of his shirt. Rangwalla introduced him as Prem Kohli.

Chopra bade him take a seat, which he did. 'How can we help?' he asked.

Kohli blinked, as if composing himself for a difficult task. There was a quality of sadness about the man that Chopra recognised. It was the distinctive air of tragedy.

'Two years ago, my daughter was killed. She died when the building she was working in collapsed. Many others died with her. The official investigation ruled that it was an accident – a gas cylinder had exploded, causing a fire, which, in turn, led to the collapse. I do not believe this. I wish you to investigate. I wish to know the truth.'

'What makes you think the investigation is at fault?'

'It does not feel right,' said the man. He patted his chest. 'Here. It does not feel right here.'

Chopra leaned back in his chair. 'Please explain.'

'I am a structural engineer by background,' said Kohli. 'The building where my daughter died is located in Marol. It was scheduled for demolition by the BMC. The owner of the property, a man named Hasan Gafoor, is an old friend. He gave my daughter a job at my request. She was studying textile design at Bombay University and wished to gain some practical experience.

'Gafoor asked me to look over the property after the BMC engineers filed their demolition order. I did so. My conclusion was that there was nothing fundamentally wrong with the building, certainly not enough for it to be condemned. Gafoor threatened to challenge the BMC ruling. A short while later the building collapsed. Everything became moot, after that. The shock of losing my only child sent me into illness; it took a long time for me to recover.'

'Is that why you have waited two years?'

'That and the trial. I wanted to see if justice would be done, if the truth would come out. I am convinced that it did not.'

Chopra knew that he was in a difficult position. Dealing with a parent's emotions was something that had always to be handled with care. Besides, he had already taken on one investigation that challenged the official version of events – did he really wish to take on another? The BMC – the Brihanmumbai Municipal Corporation – was a powerful outfit. As the body responsible for the civic infrastructure and administration of Mumbai, it had a budget larger than most states in the country. Such wealth, combined with the power BMC officials wielded, meant that the organisation was routinely accused of corruption and malpractice. Yet that same Byzantine structure made any investigation into its inner workings an endeavour fraught with difficulty.

Kohli reached into the pocket of his trousers, then set down a thick bundle of five-hundred rupee notes. 'I am willing to spend every rupee I have. I must know why my daughter had to die. If necessary, I will mortgage my home.'

Chopra glanced at Rangwalla. He knew now why his deputy had brought the matter to him. Saying no to this man would have been beyond him.

'Put your money away,' he said eventually. 'We will look into the matter. But I can make no promises. If it appears that the original investigation was sound then we will proceed no further.'

'And if it does not?'

'Then we will do whatever we can to uncover the truth,' said Chopra.

'That is all I ask for,' said Kohli.

AN ENGLISHMAN'S OFFICE
IS HIS CASTLE

Cyrus Zorabian maintained an office not far from his home. At precisely 10 a.m. the following morning Chopra left Ganesha in the van and was shown into a newly reno-vated tower block on Lal Bandar Road by William Buckley, the deceased industrialist's PA.

Buckley had agreed – at Perizaad Zorabian's request – to assist Chopra in poking around Cyrus's office; but he did not seem particularly happy about it. 'This was Mr Zorabian's most private place,' he said, as he unlocked the door. 'It has been left untouched since the police investigation.'

Chopra shouldered his way past the PA, shaking himself out of a halo of maudlin thoughts from the previous evening . . .

As he had suspected, his wife had been less than thrilled to discover that he had returned home with a vulture in tow. Poppy was a woman of vast emotional latitude – less than a year earlier she had given Ganesha sanctuary for a night during a monsoon deluge that had almost drowned the little elephant – but this was one vertebrate too far. She had vowed not to speak to Chopra until the carrion-eating menace was removed from her home. Her mother, the widow Poornima Devi, had been little better. 'Who do you think you are? The vulture whisperer?' she had sneered. 'That scavenger will probably peck out my heart while I am asleep.'

'What heart?' Chopra had muttered, under his breath.

He forced himself back to the matter at hand.

He stood now in Cyrus Zorabian's office, a lavishly appointed space that would not have looked out of place in a Merchant Ivory production. The theme was clearly Edwardian gentleman's study: the walls were lined with oak bookcases, walnut wainscoting and embossed wall-paper. Beneath Chopra's feet was a thick, emerald-green Oriental rug flecked with gold coins. The furniture, including the expansive desk, was baroque; the wing chairs uphol-stered in chintz. The only thing missing was a draconian fireplace.

Chopra inhaled a sense of the man from this space. 'He was an Anglophile,' he concluded.

'The Zorabian family worked closely with the British during their time in India,' said Buckley. 'The respect was mutual.'

Chopra examined the bookshelves.

The bulk of the reading material was non-fiction, ency-clopedias and the like, as well as entire shelves dedicated to yellowing copies of *National Geographic*. There was a

shelf dedicated to classical poets, both Persian and English
– Firdausi, Rumi, Byron, Keats – but Chopra got the feeling
these had been ordered wholesale for the purposes of flesh-
ing out the canvas.

'Was he a big reader?'

Buckley hesitated. 'Mr Zorabian regretted not having as
much time for reading as he would have liked.'

In other words, thought Chopra, this was all largely for
effect. What did that say about the man whose murder he
was attempting to solve?

'What exactly was Cyrus's role in the family business?'

'He was the CEO,' said Buckley simply.

'How long has he been at the helm?'

'He took over when his father died. And then he handed
the business over to his son a few years ago, but when *he*
left, Mr Zorabian stepped in again.'

'Why did his son leave?'

Buckley blinked rapidly behind his spectacles, as if he had
let slip something better left unsaid. 'Mr Zorabian and Darius
had a difference of opinion regarding the direction they wished
the business to go in. In the end, it was deemed prudent by all
parties that Darius should branch out on his own.'

'So Cyrus kicked his son out,' mused Chopra. This was
something he could not recall reading in the newspapers.

'It was a mutual decision,' countered Buckley stiffly.

'I wonder if Darius would agree?'

'Perhaps you can ask him when you speak to him?' replied
the Englishman testily.

Chopra gave a brisk smile. 'You don't approve of Perizaad
hiring me, do you?'

'It is not my place to question Miss Zorabian's decision,' said the PA, his eyes drilling straight ahead.

'Tell me, Buckley, why are you still here?'

'What do you mean?'

'I mean, it has been three months since Cyrus's death. You were his PA. He is no longer around. So why are you?'

A flush stole over Buckley's parched cheeks. 'The winding up of Mr Zorabian's affairs has been a complex process. I have been helping with the arrangements.'

'Is Perizaad the new CEO?'

'Yes.'

'Are you her PA?'

Buckley pushed his spectacles up his nose. 'She has her own personal assistant.'

Chopra allowed the awkward silence to stretch, until Buckley could stand it no longer. 'It is my hope that I will be retained. If not, I shall move on. There are plenty of opportunities for a man of my experience.'

'How did you end up working for Cyrus?'

'How does anyone end up anywhere?' replied Buckley cryptically. 'I grew up in England, but travelled extensively for many years, working all over the world before arriving in India. I found employment with a British expat living in Mumbai. Eventually he decided to return to the UK. He recommended me to Mr Zorabian before he left. The rest is history.'

'Did you like him?'

'Like him?' echoed Buckley.

'Cyrus. Did you like him?'

'We had an excellent working relationship,' said Buckley. 'I was by his side for nine years. He was a great man. A great man.'

So great, you had to say it twice, thought Chopra.

He was beginning to get a measure of the Englishman, and what he sensed made him uneasy. There was something about Buckley that didn't quite ring true. He wondered if Perizaad Zorabian had sensed it too, and that was why she had not offered him a new role.

He made a mental note to take a closer look at the man's background.

Chopra next took out a photocopy of the sheet found in Cyrus Zorabian's wallet, with its enigmatic jumble of letters: INDUKNAAUIKBAHNXDDLA.

'Have you any idea what this means?'

'The police already asked me this. No, I have no idea.'

'Does it seem curious to you that the first five letters are IND and UK?'

'Curious? Why?'

'One might read them as "India" and the "United Kingdom".'

'If that is indeed what they stand for, then, yes, it is curious. But what of it?'

'You are from the UK. Cyrus was from India.'

'I do not see your point.'

Chopra continued to lock eyes with the man, then put the paper away. He wasn't sure what his point was. The line of text would have to remain an enigma for now. He struck out in another direction. 'The police gave me a movements timeline for Cyrus on the day of his death. That morning

72

he visited a woman named Geeta Lokhani. Lokhani has been in the news recently. She is one of only a handful of very senior women in the BMC – Mumbai's municipal council. But she is leaving to enter politics. She plans to run for member of the state Legislative Assembly. By all accounts she is a shoo-in for her local seat when the elections take place later this year. Why was Cyrus meeting with her?'

'He met with many politicians. He was a man of influence, constantly being courted for his patronage. There was nothing unusual in that.'

'Was this the reason the chief minister disliked him? Lokhani is running for the key opposition party.'

'I don't know,' said Buckley. 'He never discussed that with me. But it was no secret that he and the CM didn't see eye to eye.'

'I would like to speak with Lokhani. Today, if possible. Can you arrange it?'

'I will try,' said Buckley, somewhat sullenly, Chopra felt.

He turned his attention to his immediate environment. 'I need to go through Cyrus's desk.'

'The police have already searched the office.'

'I suspect their search would have been cursory, at best,' said Chopra. '*If* Perizaad's assertion is correct that they had been all but ordered to bungle the investigation.'

Over the course of the next hour he went through the desk, and then the rest of the office, meticulously looking into every nook and cranny, pulling out books from the various shelves and checking behind them, exploring any potential hiding places. Buckley stood in silence, watching him with a cold look in his blue eyes, as if he fully expected Chopra to make off with the family silver.

It was as he was leafing through one of the poetry books – a copy of Omar Khayyam's *Rubaiyat* which had caught his eye because of its worn spine – that a folded paper fell out.

He scooped it up from the floor.

It was a clipping from a popular Mumbai newspaper. The story was about a burned car wreck in which two unidentifiable human bodies had been discovered. The article was dated four months earlier.

He held up the clipping. 'Do you know anything about this?'

Buckley scanned the article. 'No,' he said eventually.

'Why would Cyrus have kept this article?'

'How do you know Mr Zorabian put it there?'

'Most of the books here have never been touched. But this one is the most well-thumbed of the lot. You say he wasn't much of a reader, but I think he liked it.'

Buckley said nothing.

Chopra scanned the clipping again. There was little he could glean from the scant details provided. He noted, however, that the car had been found in an out-of-the-way corner of Marol, the neighbouring cantonment to his former police station in Sahar, the biggest in the region. That gave him a thread, at least, because it meant that any investigation might well have landed up at his old station.

He continued to stare at the article. There was something about the deaths, the horror of burned flesh, that sent a shiver through him, a premonition, perhaps, that this seemingly insignificant and possibly unrelated crime – if, indeed, it was a crime – would somehow haunt him.

Why had Cyrus held on to this? What did it mean to him? Because there was no doubt that it meant *something*. If there was one thing Chopra had learned over the course of his career it was that seemingly inconsequential details often helped shed light on what made a man tick. So often, that was the difference between solving a case or not.

He folded the clipping into his pocket, then put the book back. 'Is there anything else you would like to tell me? About Cyrus's affairs? Anything that might be tied to his murder?'

'No,' said Buckley.

Chopra bit his tongue. The Englishman's clipped responses were infuriating. 'Very well. I will wait for your call regarding the meeting with Lokhani. Thank you for your time.'

When he was once again inside his van, Chopra called Perizaad Zorabian. 'How much do you know about William Buckley's past?'

'He was my father's man. Why do you ask?'

'I get the feeling he wishes you hadn't employed me.'

She gave a tell-tale sigh, one of tiredness, stress. 'William believes the matter should have ended with the police investigation. He feels there is little to be gained by pursuing things further. That, in some ways, I am refusing to allow my father to find peace. Perhaps he is right.'

'We shall see,' muttered Chopra.

Rangwalla wavered in the street, lunchtime crowds passing by him in a din of chatter and industry. Before him was the Sahar police station where he had spent two decades of his working life, until he had been unceremoniously ejected from the ranks of the Brihanmumbai police. Even though he knew it was ACP Rao who had engineered his dismissal, he could not help the bitterness he still felt towards his old employers.

And yet without his khaki uniform, he felt strangely naked, and, more importantly, vulnerable. For the first time, perhaps, he understood how daunting it was for the ordinary Indian citizen to enter such dens of law enforcement, given the dubious reputation of the service.

He walked across terracotta tiles towards the saloon-style doors of the station. As he reached them, a jeep screeched into the courtyard behind him. He turned to see two policemen, one he did not recognise, the other the man he had come to see, spilling from the vehicle, dragging behind them a ragged-looking individual wailing at the top of his lungs: 'But it wasn't my fault! They didn't have any cash – what was I supposed to do?'

Rangwalla winced as the larger of the two cops thrashed the man across the back of his legs with a wooden truncheon. 'Tell it to the judge,' he said, bundling him through the doors.

His colleague's eyes widened in recognition. 'Rangwalla Sir!' He snapped to attention and shot off a quick salute.

'How are you, Surat?' said Rangwalla.

Constable Surat – now Sub-Inspector Surat – had once been Rangwalla's understudy at the station. Young, over-weight and irredeemably idealistic, Surat had seemed to Rangwalla to encapsulate everything that was wrong with the modern generation. He had taken the recruit under his wing, attempting to educate him in the ways of the world, but, for some strange reason, his cynical view on matters had simply washed off the junior policeman's back.

'How is Inspector Chopra Sir?' asked Surat. He had always hero-worshipped the man, Rangwalla now remembered.

'He needs your help. That's why I am here.'

Surat practically vibrated with enthusiasm.

'About two years ago there was a fire at the Gafoor Fashions Textile Factory over in Marol. The building collapsed, killing a number of the employees working inside. A police complaint was registered against the build-ing's owner – here at the Sahar station. The investigation ruled it an accident, caused by negligence, but the father of one of the victims believes there was more to it. I need to talk to the officer who carried out the investigation.'

'I remember the case.' Surat nodded. 'It was handled by a colleague sent here from another station – he was an expert in that sort of thing, apparently. But he has since been transferred to Kolkata.'

Rangwalla swore under his breath.

Kolkata was on the far side of the country.

'However, a copy of the case file is still lodged with us. Would you like to see it?'

Rangwalla hesitated. Surat had always been an expert on stating the obvious. But he did not wish to place the young man in a moral quandary. He knew that the woman who now ran the station was not the type to look kindly upon outsiders rooting around in official police records. Malini Sheriwal – known in the force as Shoot'em Up Sheriwal – had once served on Mumbai's notorious Encounter Squad, taking down gangsters at will, usually in a hail of bullets. Rangwalla had no desire to become the focus of her ire.

'It is OK,' said Surat, sensing his indecision. 'The case is officially closed, so no one will mind if you take a look. In fact, I will show you the site, if you like. It will give us a chance to catch up.'

The boy has become a man, thought Rangwalla, a lump stealing into his throat.

Surat vanished into the station, returning swiftly with the file. As he hopped into the jeep, Rangwalla couldn't help but ask him about the miscreant he had dragged in earlier.

Surat grinned. 'He is surely the most stupid criminal I have come across. Yesterday he attempted to rob an electronics store, only to discover that they carried almost no cash. You know, ever since the government recalled all five-hundred and one-thousand rupee notes.'

Rangwalla understood. The government's recent demonetisation push had been an attempt to clamp down on money laundering, counterfeiting and 'black money' – money that had escaped the taxman's attentions or had otherwise been obtained through corrupt means. One of the unintended consequences had been the effect on small businesses, many of which ran almost entirely on cash.

'And so our thief asked them to write him a cheque,' said Surat. 'In his own name.'

For an instant Rangwalla was speechless, and then he burst into a wild bray of laughter as Surat edged the jeep out into the road.

A STAR IN THE MAKING

For all his intransigence, Buckley was as efficient as his word.

Soon after leaving Cyrus Zorabian's office, Chopra received a call to inform him that Geeta Lokhani was willing to meet him. He was asked to make his way to Opera House where she had agreed to talk to him between engagements.

The drive across the city took less than an hour.

The Opera House region was named after Mumbai's century-old and recently renovated Royal Opera House, the venue for Chopra's meeting with Lokhani. The area was also known for its glut of jewellery stores. The last time Chopra had spent any length of time in the congested enclave was shortly after he had first arrived in the city, one of his earliest postings, patrolling a beat in the area.

He parked the van behind the grand old building, then walked into the lobby with Ganesha in tow.

The Royal Opera House had a storied history.

Completed in 1916, it had been inaugurated by no less a patron than King George V. The three-tiered building featured an auditorium, gilded ceilings painted with murals of luminaries such as Shakespeare and Newton, stained-glass windows and an ornate foyer combining both European and Indian detailing. For years it had hosted both opera and live performances by Indian artists, before being turned into a movie hall when cinema came of age in the city. Following Independence, the grand old venue had stuttered along until falling into disuse in the nineties.

Now, restored as part of Mumbai's much vaunted cultural renaissance, it was proving a magnet for the city's jet set.

He found Lokhani in the auditorium, being filmed by a camera crew with the sweeping tiers of maroon-cushioned seats serving as a backdrop. As he looked on, a curious Ganesha drifted behind him on to the stage, clambering up a short access ramp. He was intrigued by the towering cut-out scenery, left over from a prior performance, and featuring a host of characters from Indian mythology.

'Cut! Cut! Cut! What the hell is that elephant doing in my shot?'

A short man with the boiled-down body of an ascetic and wearing an obscene toupee bounded towards the stage. The toupee jounced around on his skull with a life of its own.

Ganesha froze.

His trunk dangled between his front legs, and his tail swished nervously as the man berated him. Before Chopra could give the overbearing oaf a piece of his mind, Geeta Lokhani rose from her seat. 'Oh, leave him alone, Raghu.'

The man subsided instantly, retreating back to his post behind the main camera rig while continuing to stab hostile glances in Ganesha's direction.

'Chopra, I presume,' said Lokhani, extending a bangled hand towards him.

Chopra nodded, suddenly on the back foot.

Geeta Lokhani, a small, dusky and attractive woman, exuded a sense of supreme confidence, her voice as refined as her appearance. Floating along in an immaculate maroon and gold sari, clutching an iPad in her hand, she gestured Chopra to a make-up room where they might talk. 'Treat my guest with care,' she warned the glowering cameraman, nodding at Ganesha.

Once inside the anteroom, she sat down before a mirrored dresser. 'I must apologise. We are filming a promotional video for the opera house, and the director is somewhat highly strung about the whole thing.'

'We?' said Chopra.

'As head of the BMC's Planning Committee for many years, I was heavily involved in the opera house's renovation. The city authorities felt it would be judicious for me to speak in a short advert promoting the venue's new programme.' Her expression became serious. 'Buckley said that you wished to talk to me about Cyrus Zorabian?'

Chopra quickly explained that he had been employed by Cyrus's daughter to re-examine the investigation into her father's death. 'Cyrus met with you on the day that he was murdered. I would like to know why.'

'It is a simple matter,' said Lokhani. 'The Parsees have always been known for their philanthropy, particularly in Mumbai. Cyrus merely wished to follow in this tradition. He was lending his support to an important BMC initiative.'

'What sort of initiative?'

Lokhani seemed to consider whether or not to provide further details.

'It would not take long to visit the BMC and find the details I need,' said Chopra mildly. 'You could save me the time and effort.'

Her lips stretched into a smile. 'I'm sorry. I am still in the habit of being tight-lipped about BMC ventures. So many projects begin with great fanfare before falling foul of red tape and political interests that in latter years I have tried to keep public exposure to a minimum. The last major initiative I helmed – the one that Cyrus was also involved with – was a slum resettlement project on the outskirts of the city, in Vashi. Fifty acres of reclaimed land that we have proposed to build twenty apartment towers on, comprising over two thousand new units. These units will be used to rehouse slum dwellers from Mumbai's southern districts, infinitely improving their lives. We called the project New Haven.'

Chopra had heard of a number of such projects.

Coming from a rural village, with its wide-open expanses, the pressure on housing in Mumbai was something that had always astonished him. Each year thousands continued to pour into the 'city of dreams', more often than not ending up on the city's streets. This never-ending influx – which some equated to lemmings blindly charging over a cliff – created an upward surge in land values which only exacerbated the problem. The result was some of the most expensive property on earth sitting side by side with some of the world's most deprived slums.

Recently, the issue had become a political hot potato.

Social organisations and prominent activists, incensed by the endless self-aggrandising of the government lauding the country's sustained economic boom, scathingly enquired as to when this fabled wealth might actually reach the poorest echelons of society. The old policy of simply bulldozing the slums, sending the cops to round up their former denizens, and then dumping them beyond the municipal borders, was no longer considered a viable stratagem for the succour of the disenfranchised. And so slum demolition had been replaced by slum redevelopment, slum rehousing, and – Chopra's favourite – slum rehabilitation, which always put him in mind of an alcoholic being nursed back to sobriety.

He knew that Vashi was out in Navi Mumbai – or New Mumbai – a deliberately planned township that was and was not part of the city, depending on who you spoke to. Certainly, the residents of Vashi were conflicted on the matter, some wishing to preserve their independence from the city-monster on their doorstep, others keen to bask in the dubious glamour of being known as Mumbaikers.

'That is all very admirable,' he said. 'But what has it to do with Cyrus?'

Lokhani smiled grimly. 'A development of this type is an exceptionally expensive endeavour. It cannot be funded by the state government alone. Few people understand the true cost of rehousing slum residents. Did you know, for instance, that, as per the tenets of the Slum Rehabilitation Scheme, slum dwellers cannot be "materially disadvantaged" by such a move? What this means, in short, is that they cannot be asked to pay the sort of purchase prices and rents that a build of this type would usually attract and which would repay the cost of construction. Frankly, a project like this is only viable when subsidised by private donors and patrons from the world of commerce. That is where Cyrus came in.

'As the head of one of the wealthiest Parsee clubs in the city he had vast influence with those who might contribute financing. With a few phone calls he could have opened doors for us that we cannot hope to open ourselves.' Lokhani's smile was tinged with sadness. 'Losing Cyrus has been a major blow to the New Haven project. He was a generous man who gave of his time freely. I believe he felt this would be his legacy, a cause worth fighting for.'

Chopra considered this.

Clearly, there was more to Cyrus Zorabian than he had at first thought. He knew of wealthy men – and innumerable politicians – who pretended to a philanthropy that rarely made it past soundbites for the media. But Cyrus seemed genuinely committed to those at the poorest end of Mumbai's social spectrum.

'How did he seem to you that day?' he asked. 'The day he died, I mean. Did he behave strangely in any way? Was anything troubling him?'

'Not at all. He was his usual self. Gregarious. Bombastic. Flirty.'

'Flirty?'

Lokhani smiled. 'It was harmless, though I dare say in his younger days he must have been quite the charmer. He had a certain aura about him; larger than life. I always thought of Cyrus as a roaring fire. The sort of man you could warm your heart by.'

'You were fond of him.'

'Yes. In a way, I was.'

Chopra hesitated. 'Forgive me for asking . . . but was his visit more than just business?'

Lokhani looked momentarily puzzled, then caught his meaning. Her cheeks coloured. 'He was twice my age,' she said, an unmistakable admonishment in her tone. 'But, to answer your question, no. There was nothing between us.'

'You are married?'

'No. Should I be?' She did not wait for an answer. 'It's funny how often men look at me and think that everything I have achieved could not have been possible without the guiding hand of a man.'

Chopra had thought no such thing, but decided not to labour the point. He struck out in a different direction. 'Is it true you are entering politics?'

'Yes. In actual fact, my last day at the BMC was two weeks ago. But I had already agreed to help with this video, which is why I am here today.'

'Why did you leave?'

Lokhani sighed. 'I worked for the BMC for years, Chopra. I have seen the desperation of those who have little or nothing in our city. I tried to help in whatever way I could, but the truth is that my hands were always tied – largely by the machinations of politicians who control how Mumbai's executive branches operate. I believe that in order for me to do the most good I must aspire to such a position.'

'It is a noble sentiment.'

'Some call it foolhardy. To leave the safety of my role at the BMC and wade into the polluted waters of politics. Nevertheless . . .' Lokhani rose gracefully from her seat. 'Forgive me, but I am pressed for time.'

She led Chopra back into the auditorium where he was astonished to discover the director Raghu poised below the stage, hands forming a sort of viewfinder through which he was examining Ganesha with a critical eye.

On the stage, Ganesha, hunkered before a fifteen-foot-high cut-out of his namesake, the elephant-headed god Ganesh, blinked in the overhead arc lights as the director framed his shot.

Chopra sighed.

The little elephant was notoriously fond of having his photograph taken. He knew, by now, that elephants possessed a range of human-like emotions; had he known that vanity was one of them he might have put his foot down when the young calf's tendencies first exhibited themselves.

'Ganesha,' he said sternly, 'it's time to go.'

'One more shot,' pleaded the director, who had clearly changed his tune. 'He's a natural.'

Chopra swung his gaze on to the stage where Ganesha was looking at him expectantly. His irritation drained away. 'Very well. Just one more shot.'

The building site was little more than a concrete super-structure, all but suffocated by trellises of bamboo scaffolding. Labourers scampered along the scaffolding in the manner of daredevil trapeze artists or flying lemurs. Some carried hods loaded with bricks, lengths of copper piping, or tools. Rangwalla's heart leapt into his mouth as one emaciated worker in a string vest and checked dhoti, swinging a bucket in one hand, appeared to stumble. For a brief steepling second, he teetered on the brink of plummeting to his doom, but then righted himself before shimmying through an open doorway. A jaunty whistle echoed down to those watching below.

And that, thought Rangwalla, was Mumbai in a nutshell.

He had heard Chopra once say that the city was a magnificent high-wire act. At any moment in time, it lurched from one potential catastrophe to another, somehow defying its own destruction. No wonder it bred madmen!

He glanced at the developer's signboard: NEW WORLD DEVELOPMENTS. FIFTY LUXURY APARTMENTS FULL OF LUXURIOUSNESS. BUY NOW! ONLY 50 LAKHS EACH!

Only fifty lakhs, thought Rangwalla sourly. Five million rupees. These were not homes for the ordinary Mumbaiker. These were homes for those who had already broken out from the swamp of poverty that defined the 'ordinary' Mumbaiker.

'They're moving along at a furious pace,' commented Surat, beside him. 'A year ago, this site was a great big hole in the ground, filling up with monsoon water.'

'The building that was here before this, it was a textile factory, right?'

'Yes. A very old building; three storeys, if I remember. Belonged to the same family for decades. The most recent owner was a Hasan Gafoor.'

'My understanding is that he ended up in prison. Following the collapse, I mean.'

'Correct. Although it was ultimately ruled that the fire that led to the collapse had been an accident, Gafoor *was* held responsible for not maintaining the building to the required BMC regulations.'

'Yes. We were told that the building had been declared unsafe by the BMC, but Gafoor had done nothing about it.'

'I suppose like most landlords he did not care about such things,' said Surat grimly. 'In the end, the BMC issued a demolition order against the property. Gafoor was accused of bribing BMC officials to stay the order, though that was never proved. Nevertheless, he was convicted of "culpable homicide not amounting to murder". You will have to go to Central Prison if you wish to talk to him.'

Rangwalla looked back up at the half-finished edifice.

From the ashes of misfortune, opportunity was rising. Soon new lives would inhabit this place; new stories would be written. Thus it had always been in this city of dreams.

But what about those who had been disinherited, those who had lost their lives? Perhaps their spirits would remain, doomed to haunt this tower of stone until they obtained deliverance.

And now it had fallen upon Rangwalla to help them find that release.

In spite of the day's early heat, the former sub-inspector shivered.

THE BEST OF RIVALS

Chopra's next port of call was Boman Jeejibhoy, the man who, according to Zubin Engineer, secretary of the Vulture Club, had quarrelled with Cyrus some time before his death. There was nothing in the police investigation about Jeejibhoy. Chopra knew from Engineer that this was because the Parsees at the club had not wished to air their dirty laundry in public. Their natural insularity had compelled them to discretion. He suspected that not a single one of them had even entertained the notion that Jeejibhoy might have had anything to do with Cyrus's murder. In a collective failure of imagination, they could not conceive of anything that might bring shame upon their clan.

Engineer had arranged for him to meet with Jeejibhoy at his business offices, a forty-minute drive from Opera House, west to east across the city, to the Haji Bunder port district.

Upon arrival Chopra parked his van in the forecourt of the gleaming office complex, and let Ganesha out of the back.

He looked up at the façade of the building before him, a broad expanse of tinted glass panels and pristine white columns, topped by a row of pennants fluttering from the flat roof. A grand signboard above the arched doorway read: PERSEPOLIS BOATS & MARINE CONSTRUCTION. It was from here, Chopra had learned, that Boman Jeejibhoy ran one of the biggest boat-building operations in the country.

Inside the lobby, Chopra spoke to a receptionist, who led them smartly out to the rear of the building, to a private dock where a number of sleek yachts were berthed. The receptionist skipped up a ramp on to a fifty-metre-long, triple-masted sailing yacht inscribed with the name *Xerxes' Dream*. The boat reminded Chopra of an old clipper, one or two of which could still be seen sedately gliding around the coast of Mumbai on occasion.

They found Boman Jeejibhoy on the foredeck, bellowing up at a technician fiddling with the foremast rigging. The man seemed relieved to be high above the irate industrialist, and even more relieved when the receptionist redirected Jeejibhoy's attention to his visitors.

For some reason, Chopra had imagined Jeejibhoy as a thin, dry, old specimen. Instead he found himself confronted by a bullish man with the physique of a wrestler, hands like hams, sweating profusely in an ash-grey safari suit. Jeejibhoy had blunt features and a thick head of grey curls. His pale face seemed incapable of mirth. To Chopra, he had the look of someone who would gladly kick a fallen opponent in the stomach as he lay on the ground.

He started to introduce himself, but Jeejibhoy inter-rupted him. 'I know who you are. Engineer explained every-thing. Though he didn't say anything about an elephant scuffing up the deck of my new yacht.' He glared from beneath heavy brows at Ganesha, who was trotting around the foredeck examining his intriguing new environment.

'I simply wish to ask a few questions,' said Chopra.

'And I simply wish to pick you up and hurl you into the sea,' growled Jeejibhoy. 'It is a good thing we cannot all just do as we wish.'

Chopra wasn't sure if the man was joking or not. 'You were lifelong friends with Cyrus,' he said hurriedly. 'Yet you quarrelled, and then cut off all contact with him. What did you quarrel about?'

'And if I were to tell you that it is no business of yours?'

'I would ask again,' said Chopra. 'And keep asking until I got an answer.'

His reply seemed to surprise Jeejibhoy. 'Well,' he said eventually, 'at least you have a backbone. I can't remember the last time anyone spoke to me like that. Not even my own reflection would dare.'

'Perhaps Cyrus did. Is that why you fell out?'

'Hah! That man – the man was an ingrate. Fifty years we were friends. *Fifty years!* And then he betrays me.' Jeejibhoy seemed to be talking to himself. His eyes had clouded over; he was lost in the past.

'Exactly *how* did he betray you?'

Jeejibhoy did not seem to hear. 'You know, when we were young we used to sail together. We won the Seabird class at the National Championships back in 1977. But he was never a true sailor. Couldn't tell the difference between a bowline and a cleat hitch to save his life. It was me who did all the heavy lifting. He just wanted the glory.' He shook himself back to the present. 'It was a business deal gone bad. That's why we fell out.'

But the offhand manner in which he said this gave Chopra pause. 'What sort of business deal?'

'Does it matter?'

'Perhaps.'

'We had agreed to partner in a new venture, one that had been years in the making. A family business. I put up my half of the deal. At the last second, Cyrus reneged on his half. The agreement fell through, causing me . . . a great loss.'

'Surely it could not have mattered that much. Given your wealth, I mean.'

'I made a great *personal* loss,' said Jeejibhoy. 'We shook hands on the deal. My word is my bond. And so, I thought, was Cyrus's. I was wrong.'

'Do you know why he pulled out?'

Jeejibhoy ground his jaw. 'It does not matter why. The only thing that matters is his betrayal.'

'He hurt you deeply. You felt a great anger towards him.'

'Do you think I am a fool? I know why you are here, what you are trying to insinuate. The fact is that if I had wanted Cyrus dead I would not have waited all that time. And I would not have attacked him from behind. I would have throttled him in front of those doddering old vultures at the club.' His meaty fists clenched repeatedly by his side as if he was, even now, imagining them around the deceased man's throat.

'What were you doing that evening? The night Cyrus died?'

'I was at home.'

'Alone?'

'Yes. My wife passed away years ago. My daughter was out for the evening. The servants had gone home.'

'Can anyone verify that you were there? For the whole night?'

'No. Because I was not. I went out for a drive.' Jeejibhoy's expression dared Chopra to make something of this.

'Did you have a driver with you?'

'No.'

'Where did you go?'

'Nowhere in particular. I just drove around. I like to do that sometimes. Is there a law against that?'

Chopra hesitated. 'Can you think of anyone who would have wanted to harm Cyrus?'

'Yes,' said Jeejibhoy emphatically. 'Me. Unfortunately, someone else did what I should have done.'

A loud cry caused them to turn.

Ganesha, who had been fiddling with the rope coiled beneath the foremast, scurried across the deck in alarm, just as the technician fell from the mast, his feet caught up in the rigging. Like a bungee jumper, the rope pulled him up short just before he ploughed into the deck, snapping his body taut with such force that all those watching could not help but wince. The man wailed again, before finally coming to rest, hanging upside down, his legs tangled in the rigging rope.

'That – that elephant is a menace!' he sobbed.

Ganesha looked crestfallen. His ears flapped in distress, and he trotted forward to pat the man reassuringly with his trunk.

The technician wriggled like a fish caught in a net. 'Keep him away from me!'

'Come on, Ganesha,' said Chopra. 'It is time for us to leave.'

He led the forlorn calf off the boat, Jeejibhoy's penetrating stare following him all the way.

Ten minutes later Chopra eased the van to a halt, this time at a nearby restaurant. His stomach had informed him that it was time for lunch. He had stopped at a vegetarian eatery named the Pakora Palace, located opposite the Mumbai Plant & Herbaceous Fauna Quarantine Station.

He thought it a strange place to site a vegetarian restaurant.

Then again, nothing could be taken for granted in the food business. His own restaurant had become something of a haven for police officers, and, as a consequence, a tourist curiosity. He would often wander into the evening service to find locals taking selfies with the cops eating there. On more than one occasion he had even discovered well-known street criminals coming along to meet their police 'friends' – much to the embarrassment of said officers.

He sat now on the restaurant's rear porch, which faced out into the silty port waters, crowded near the concrete sea wall by a vast mat of mangroves. A warm breeze blew in off the water, ruffling his moustache.

He ordered a vegetarian thali, a steel dish containing a range of vegetarian curries, lentils, potatoes and rice. Ganesha waited impatiently as his own order of a heaped tray of raw vegetables arrived. As the little elephant began happily shovelling carrots and turnips into his mouth with his trunk, Chopra took out his notebook and reflected on what he had learned so far.

There was little to go on.

As Kelkar had stated, Cyrus Zorabian did not appear to have an array of enemies, or skeletons in his closet that might hint at an alternative motive for his murder. By all accounts he was a well-liked man, a man who sought to do good for his fellow citizens. He had fallen out with Boman Jeejibhoy over a business matter – beyond that there was nothing to link the man to Cyrus's killing.

The fact was that there were few inconsistencies in the original police investigation into Cyrus's death. As much as it galled him to admit, it was increasingly looking as if Rao and Kelkar's verdict fitted the available facts – at least as much as any other theory.

Then again, it was too soon to draw a line under his own efforts. There *were* certain matters that remained unresolved. They bothered him, like ants crawling up his leg on a hot summer's day. The newspaper clipping he had discovered in Cyrus's office, the key in his wallet, the sheet with the strange line of text . . .

He pulled out the copy Kelkar had given him and re-examined it:

INDUKNAAUIKBAHNXDDLA

He knew that Kelkar and Rao had wasted little time on this puzzle. In all probability, it had nothing whatsoever to do with Cyrus's death. But there must be a reason Cyrus had kept the paper on him; it was the sort of insignificant detail that bothered him. He stared at the letters, mentally rearranging them. Perhaps it was an anagram.

INDIA AND UK BALD . . . his effort petered out.

BAN IND AND UK . . .

LAND IS A BANK . . .

After ten minutes of futile endeavour, he gave up. If it was an anagram, it was a convoluted one. Perhaps, instead, it was a code or cipher?

Chopra knew, from his love of Sherlock Holmes, that the master detective had been adept at decoding ciphers. In *The Adventure of the Dancing Men* he had cracked a cipher made up of stick figures using a method called letter frequency analysis. In *The Adventure of the 'Gloria Scott'* he deduced that every third word in a terrifying letter was the key to the puzzle. In *The Valley of Fear* he worked out that a book cipher was being utilised by a spy within Moriarty's organisation.

The more he thought about it, the more he felt he might be on the right track. He decided to follow through on this line of thought.

He took out his phone and began searching the Internet for websites about cracking ciphers. He quickly discovered that there were a great many such codes.

He spent thirty minutes trying various types of cipher on the enigmatic line of text before finally alighting on one that appeared to show promise. It was something called a Rail Fence Cipher. The cipher scrambled up text by splitting it across a number of rows – called rails. Chopra read the instructions on how to decode it, and then began to apply them systematically to the line of text before him.

First, he counted how many letters were in the text – twenty. Next the website asked him to work out how many rows – or rails – the cipher was using. He had no clue, but he guessed that Cyrus would have kept it relatively simple. He started with two rails. The next step was to calculate the width of the puzzle, which would tell him how many 'units' – i.e. letters and blank spaces – were in each rail. In order to do this, he had first to calculate the 'cycle', i.e. how the letters were arranged up and down the rails. Each cycle of letters ran from the top row, down through each subsequent row, and then up again, but stopping before reaching the top row again. The website provided an equation to allow him to calculate the cycle:

$$\text{Cycle} = (\text{No. of rails} \times 2) - 2$$

This meant that, if he assumed Cyrus had indeed used two rails, the cycle would be $(2 \times 2) - 2 = 2$. Next he had to calculate the width of each rail by dividing the total number of letters in the cipher by the cycle. This gave $20/2 = 10$. Chopra separated the line of text into two lines of ten:

INDUKNAAUI

KBAHNXDDLA

Then, using the cycle of 2 letters, going up and down the two rails, he tried to decipher the puzzle.

I-K-N-B-D-A-U-H-K-N-N-X-A-D-A-U-L-I-A

Chopra stared at the letters . . . But it was no good. The line was still nonsense. He had got it wrong. Either he was using the wrong cipher, or Cyrus had not used two rails as his base.

Undeterred, he decided to try a three-rail permutation.

Perhaps he had underestimated the old Parsee.

He began again with the equation to calculate the cycle, coming up with: $(3 \times 2) - 2 = 4$. Then he calculated the width of each rail. This gave $20/4 = 5$. However, according to the instructions on the website, when there were more than two rails, the top and bottom rails always had half as many units per cycle as any middle rows. This meant that in a three-rail cipher – one containing 20 letters in total – the top and bottom rows would have 5 letters, and the middle one would have 10.

Quickly, he divided up the text in this way to give:

INDUK

NAAUIKBAHN

XDDLA

Now, going up and down the rows, he came up with:

INXANADUDIDKUBLAKHAN

He stared at the text. At first glance it still seemed like a nonsensical string. And yet . . . Something was itching the back of his brain. There was something familiar here.

And then he had it.

With a growing excitement, he wrote out the line again – this time inserting spaces.

IN XANADU DID KUBLA KHAN

He stared at his notebook.

It was always this way, the moment of discovery, of revelation. It was not a question of savouring such a moment, for hubris was not one of Chopra's traits. It was more an instant taken to acknowledge that his own efforts had aligned with the stars, and in that alignment a light had winked on that might guide him a step closer to the truth.

He reached into his pocket and took out the book of poetry found on Cyrus's body, and within which the code sheet had been lodged.

Flicking through the book, he quickly fell upon Coleridge's famous poem: *Kubla Khan*. His eyes scanned the text, searching for another clue, for he was certain that the enigmatic code had been meant to guide whoever read it to this very poem.

> In Xanadu did Kubla Khan
> A stately pleasure-dome decree:

Where <u>Alph</u>, the sacred river, ran
Through caverns measureless to man
Down to a sunless sea.

Alph. It was the only word in the whole poem that had been underlined. Twice. Why? What was important about that word? He thought about why Cyrus would go to these lengths. Clearly, the whole exercise had been designed to protect something. And wealthy men like Cyrus usually had something of great value to protect.

His thoughts circled around in his mind . . . and then there it was.

The security locker.

Kelkar had said that a security key had been discovered on Cyrus. The initial investigation had failed to find out which bank the locker belonged to. Which meant that Cyrus had taken pains not to use one of the major banks. But there *was* a bank, an international bank that had recently arrived in the city, following in the footsteps of operations such as HSBC, Credit Suisse, Deutsche Bank and Bank of America.

The Alpha Bank, one of Greece's largest private banking outfits.

Chopra recalled their advertising campaign. One of the products they had aggressively marketed was bank lockers. Such lockers were popular in India, where the wealthy often had undeclared cash and other items of value to stash away from the prying eyes of the tax authorities.

He picked up his phone and googled 'Alpha Bank Mumbai'. The bank had only one branch in the city.

Back in Bandra, close to the Vulture Club.

In a bid to stand out from the entrenched players in the market, the Alpha Bank had set out to impress. Spread over three marbled storeys, the bank's Bandra branch reminded Chopra of the sort of vast jewellery emporiums that had recently become commonplace in the city, rather than a hub of financial services.

Walking up to a row of pristine glass doors, Ganesha trailing behind him, he saw that a snake charmer had set up shop on the pavement out front. The snake charmer, a dark man in a ragged dhoti and particoloured turban, had attracted quite a crowd. He had also attracted the attentions of the bank's security guards, two beery specimens in smart black uniforms, wielding truncheons as thick and shiny as aubergines. The pair kept attempting to hustle the snake charmer away from the bank. But each time they stepped towards him, the charmer would give a quick blast on his flute and one of his pet cobras would slither towards the hapless duo, causing them to fall over one another as they beat a hasty retreat.

Inside the bank, Chopra found Perizaad Zorabian waiting for him.

'You said on the phone that you had discovered something important?' she said, rising to meet him.

'I have discovered something,' said Chopra. 'Whether it is important remains to be seen.'

He had asked Cyrus's daughter to meet him at the bank, and to pick up the locker key from Inspector Kelkar at the CBI offices, but not to tell him about what they had found. Not yet, at any rate.

There was a second reason he wished her to be here. He suspected that even armed with the key the bank might be reluctant to allow him access to Cyrus Zorabian's locker. The man had been murdered, after all, and Chopra could not be sure of the exact protocols that now applied.

He quickly explained his discovery to Perizaad. 'Why would your father go to such lengths? I mean, surely he wouldn't forget which bank he had a security locker with?'

Perizaad's brow furrowed. 'I'm not sure. The truth is that his memory *had* begun to fail him of late. I suspected early onset Alzheimer's – dementia runs in our family, I'm afraid. As usual my father refused to even admit the possibility. He hated the idea of showing weakness, particularly mental weakness. Parsees of my father's generation are very sensitive about such labels, accused as we often are of "eccentricity". In these last couple of years he had become increasingly paranoid about forgetting the smallest things. My birthday, for instance. He'd write it down all over the place, just so he wouldn't forget that he was organising a surprise party for me.' She smiled sadly. 'As for the code . . . my father loved puzzles. Always had done, ever since we were children. This' – she pointed at the code sheet – 'this has his signature all over it.'

He saw that she was struggling to hold back tears. For all his faults, Cyrus was a man who had inspired devotion. Chopra saw now the great love that powered Perizaad's quest for the truth, her refusal to accept the police's interpretation of her father's final moments on earth. He wondered if that love had been returned by Cyrus. If so it might better explain why he had gone to such trouble to hide the locker, creating a code that few would have been able to crack. Perhaps it hadn't been just Cyrus worrying about a failing memory – perhaps it had been more to ensure that should anything happen to him then his daughter might eventually follow his trail of breadcrumbs and find her way here.

What *exactly* was waiting for them in that locker?

They met with the bank's manager, a man named Mendonca. Having grasped the situation, he led them down into the bank's locker vault, though he requested that Ganesha remain in the lobby. If the elephant's presence inside his bank surprised him, he did not show it. After all, there was no telling how much the elephant's guardian was worth. If Mendonca had learned one thing in the banking business it was never to judge an elephant by its cover.

Inside the vault – a long, narrow room lit by strip lights and housing floor-to-ceiling banks of gleaming brushed-steel lockers – the manager led them swiftly to Cyrus Zorabian's box.

Perizaad Zorabian rummaged in her handbag, then gave Mendonca the key.

He gave a small smile. 'And the code?'

'What code?'

'I am afraid that a key is not enough to open our lockers.' He gestured at the keypad prominent on the front of the locker, containing both the numbers 0 to 9, and the alphabet. 'Each client is also required to input a code.'

Perizaad looked at Chopra in confusion. He hesitated only for a moment, then turned to the keypad, and typed in:

IN_XANADU_DID_KUBLA_KHAN

The keypad beeped, then the words 'WELCOME BACK, MR ZORABIAN' flashed on the display screen, followed by: 'PLEASE USE YOUR KEY TO OPEN THIS LOCKER WITHIN THE NEXT TWENTY SECONDS. FAILURE TO DO SO WILL ACTIVATE ANTI-TAMPERING PROTOCOLS.'

A countdown began on the screen: 20 . . . 19 . . . 18 . . . 17 . . . 16 . . .

Chopra nodded at Mendonca, who stepped smartly forward, and, inserting the key, opened the locker. He peered inside, then reached in and removed a large steel box.

They followed the bank manager to a viewing room where he set the box down on a marble-topped table, then excused himself to allow them privacy.

Chopra waited as Perizaad opened the box, reached inside, and set its contents on the table.

The box contained three sets of items.

First, there was a sheaf of architectural blueprints. As Chopra examined them, he realised that they were for the new property development that Geeta Lokhani had told him about, called New Haven, the project that Cyrus had become heavily involved with, a slum resettlement scheme out in the suburb of Vashi. The blueprints were stamped with the words 'Original – Confidential'. In a legend was the name of the holding company that owned the plot, and the site developer. The holding company was Karma Holdings Private Limited; the developer Kaveri Constructions.

The second item was a linen bag full of bundles of cash. Each bundle contained a hundred two-thousand rupee notes. Quickly, he counted the bundles – there were fifty in all.

Ten million rupees.

Though not an astronomical sum for a man like Cyrus, nevertheless it was a substantial amount. He wondered, briefly, if it was money that Cyrus had intended to donate to the cause of the resettlement complex.

But that made no sense. Why keep it here, in a secret locker? And why in cash? Particularly given the current government crackdown on 'black money'?

The third item in the box was a set of letters, half a dozen in all, bundled together with a rubber band. Each letter was inside a pristine white envelope with Cyrus's office address neatly typed on the front, together with a postage stamp. The letters themselves were all the same. They contained single sentences typed in a large font. The sentences were all different; similar in only one aspect – they all appeared to be in Latin.

He held out a couple to Perizaad. 'What do you make of these?'

She read out the text: '*Boni pastoris est tondere pecus non deglubere*,' and '*Faber est suae quisque infortunii*.' Her expression crunched into a frown. 'It looks like Latin.'

'Why would someone be sending your father cryptic messages in Latin?'

'I don't know. My father studied Latin in school. So did I, as a matter of fact, but it never took.'

'With your permission, I will get them translated.'

Perizaad nodded. She stepped forward, and ran a hand over the cash. 'More confusing to me than the letters is this.'

Chopra raised an eyebrow. 'It can hardly be surprising to you that your father held cash in his locker.'

'You don't understand,' said Perizaad. She licked her lips, then plunged on. 'At the time of his death my father was bankrupt.'

PRISON IS NO PLACE FOR THE PIOUS

Unlike most policemen of his acquaintance Abbas Rangwalla had never been comfortable around prisons. He derived neither a specious pleasure nor a malicious glee from observing those in the system being made to pay for their crimes. He sometimes wondered if Chopra's antipathy towards the Indian judicial apparatus had rubbed off on him during the long years of their association. Corrupt law enforcement officers, a court system that barely functioned, a prison service that might have doubled as most people's imaginings of hell. It was little wonder that the general public had such a low opinion of those appointed to protect their interests.

And there was also, lurking at the back of his mind, the sneaking suspicion that, but for the grace of God, he might well have found himself an inmate of the same prison that he had now come to visit.

Rangwalla had grown up in the tough environs of Bhendi Bazaar, running wild on the streets until his exasperated father had taken him by the ear and thrust him into the police service.

Five years later, he had been posted to the Sahar station, where he had discovered that the man in charge was something of an anomaly. Incorruptible, unwaveringly committed to his own sense of justice, and implacably resolute of purpose, Chopra had defied Rangwalla's expectations. His previous commanders had been, at best, lazy and ill-disciplined; at worst, no better than the crooks they were employed to thwart. Having spent two decades at the station, there were moments when without Chopra to keep him on the straight path he might well have drifted into that nebulous grey waste of the soul that had claimed so many promising policemen in India.

The door to the interview room opened and a prison guard led Hasan Gafoor into the room, depositing the handcuffed man into a chair bolted to the floor. He hitched his pants over his protruding belly, then left with a grunt. 'Thirty minutes.'

Gafoor was a small man with an avuncular face, a thin grey beard, and a round head partly covered by an Islamic skull cap. His eyes were deep-set, and, surprisingly to Rangwalla, serene.

'Who are you?' he asked.

Rangwalla explained his mission. 'Your friend Kohli believes that there was more to the collapse of your building than the official investigation revealed. He has asked us to investigate.'

Gafoor's hands were constantly in motion, clutching and unclutching a prayer book. Rangwalla recognised the volume of Hadiths – sayings of the Prophet Mohammed; he was himself a Muslim, though he left it to others to say whether he was a devout one. It had always amused him how readily men behind bars rediscovered their faith. It seemed that a stint in a dank cell, serviced by rats, cockroaches and other even lower forms of life in the shape of their fellow prisoners, was enough to drive anyone back to God.

'What good will it do?' said Gafoor. 'Digging up the past will not bring his daughter back. Nor any of the others who died that day.'

'No,' agreed Rangwalla. 'But perhaps it will bring him peace. Are you a father? Perhaps you can understand.'

'I *was* a father,' said Gafoor. 'After my arrest my wife took my son and moved back to Lucknow to live with her parents. Now . . . now I am just a man living from one day to the next.'

'Do you think you will find absolution in that prayer book?'

'What makes you think I am looking for absolution?' He held Rangwalla's gaze, then said, 'I did not kill those people. My father left me that building and the business that came with it. I made no money from it. I begged, borrowed, did whatever I had to, to keep it afloat. Not for myself, but for those who earned a living from the employment I provided. So that their children did not go hungry at night; so that they did not have to sleep in the streets. They were my true family. The worst thing was not that I was convicted and sent here. The worst thing was that I was accused of killing my family.'

'You were accused of ignoring BMC warnings. You were accused of trying to bribe BMC officials.'

'Lies!' snarled Gafoor, his face animated for the first time. '*They* destroyed my building. They caused that fire. They caused the collapse.'

'They? Are you saying the BMC was responsible?' Rangwalla could not keep the scepticism from his tone.

'Not the BMC. The goons who tried to buy my site. They first came to me four years ago. They wished to build luxury apartments, they told me. Promised to make me rich. I asked them only one question: what happens to the people who work for me, the people I am responsible for? Of course, they had no answer.'

'Who were they?'

'I don't know. They claimed they were only agents, representing a large property company. But they did not wish to reveal the identity of the interested party until they had firm agreement from me that I would sell.'

'Agreement that you never gave.'

'No,' said Gafoor. 'In the end, they bribed officials at the BMC to declare my building structurally unsafe, and then, when that did not work, to issue a demolition order. They thought that would force my hand. When I still refused, they collapsed the building.'

'How?'

'The fire. The investigation ruled that it was caused by a gas cylinder explosion; I kept one in the pantry so that my workers could make meals for themselves. But I was standing outside the building when the explosion happened. I saw the fireball – it did not come from the pantry. It came from the building's main support columns.'

'You're saying that someone deliberately caused that explosion?'

'It would not have taken much. The building was old – but not so old that it would have collapsed without outside intervention.'

Rangwalla was momentarily silent. Could Gafoor be right? Or was he listening to a deluded fool, or, worse, a consummate liar? His gaze rested on the man before him. Even in his filthy prison uniform Gafoor exuded a sense of dignity. Whatever anger may have possessed the former textile manufacturer it appeared to have burned itself out. Now he seemed simply a man who had come to terms with the hand fate had dealt him.

'Your plot is being developed by a company called New World Developments. Do you think they were behind this?'

'I do not know,' said Gafoor. 'All I know is that that day, when the building fell, I could not save my people. When the dust settled, I tried digging, with a shovel, with my bare hands. I could hear a scream, coming from deep inside. Someone was still alive in there. The authorities arrived, but could not get to whoever was down there. Eventually, the screaming stopped. There was nothing I could do. Now I hear that scream every night, in my dreams.' He gave Rangwalla a look of infinite sadness. 'Only God forgives, my friend. And only He understands why. I wish you well, but whatever truth you uncover will not change the past. It is God's will.'

A FOOL AND HIS MONEY

'I have had to do a lot of growing up in the past three years,' said Perizaad Zorabian, her eyes fixed on the pile of cash on the table. 'Ever since my father lost his mind.'

Chopra waited. In the silence of the locker vault, buried deep beneath Mumbai's streets, the only sound was the soft hum of the air-recycling unit. It was clear that Perizaad was dredging through difficult memories; whatever it was she was seeking to tell him would soon become clear.

'Three years ago. That was when he disinherited my brother and threw him out of our home, and out of the family business, to the ruin of us all. The Zorabian fortune was built on traditional industries. But India has changed. These industries are not as important as once they were – and only those organisations that have adapted, or those that have become the most efficient, have survived. We did neither.

'My father sent my brother abroad, to study business management at Harvard. When he returned, he

immediately took stock of all the Zorabian enterprises –
and concluded that if we did not make immediate changes
we would be bankrupt within the space of a few years. He
wanted us to shut down all our big, non-profitable businesses and venture into modern fields such as telecommu-
nications and software. My father disagreed. He saw
himself as something of a patron to all those employed in
his old businesses. He was horrified at the thought of
moving into industries he did not understand. I am afraid
that he was a little set in his ways.'

'He would not be alone in that,' said Chopra.
'Nevertheless, it seems a harsh reason to disinherit his only
son.'

Perizaad gave a sad smile. 'That was not the reason he
disinherited him.'

Chopra waited once more, but this time Perizaad did not
expand. Instead, she said, 'That is my brother's tale to tell,
not mine. Besides, it has nothing to do with my father's
death.'

'You must allow me to be the judge of that. When I took
the case, I promised you that I would be thorough. I must
speak with your brother.'

Perizaad hesitated, then nodded. 'I will ask Buckley to
give him a call.' She sat down, picked up one of the bundles
of cash, eyed it morosely. 'After my brother left, the business continued its ruinous decline. My father, incensed to
be told that he had husbanded our ancestral wealth into the
ground, tried to shore up the existing businesses, throwing
good money after bad, and then, as the futility of his efforts
began to dawn on him, he finally took my brother's advice

and began investing ludicrous sums in new businesses. The problem was that he did not actually take my brother's advice. In fact, he decided that he did not need anyone's advice.

'He invested badly. All manner of ridiculous ventures, things he read about in the papers, things someone at the racetrack told him about, things he saw on the Internet. An Uber-style business for handcart delivery-wallahs. A social media dating site for pampered pets. Do you know he even ploughed millions into a tech firm that intended to build novelty robots to serve as bridge partners for the wealthy? He made these investments via new companies he set up – just to try to disguise his involvement.' She shook her head. 'Of course, I only found out all this after he died. My father said nothing about it all – only his chief accountant knew, and he was sworn to secrecy. I suspected things were bad, but I had not realised that he had all but squandered what had once been one of the largest private fortunes in the country.'

'I do not remember seeing any of this in the news.'

'That is because my father – and then I – did everything within our power to keep it from the media. We are a privately owned company, which has made it that much easier. There are no shareholders to report to, no public accounts to be published. I have been quietly working to try to stop the rot, to salvage what is left.'

Chopra realised once again how superficial Rao's investigation had been, to have failed to uncover the fact of Cyrus Zorabian's true financial situation. 'You should have told me about this,' he said, allowing his irritation to show.

'I did not think it was relevant,' she said. 'More importantly, I did not want to risk word of our precarious financial situation leaking out. It would hinder my attempts to turn the business around. It's hard to obtain credit when lenders already believe you are finished.'

'It is my job to exercise discretion,' said Chopra sternly. 'The state of your father's business affairs means there were potentially many with a financial motive for wishing him ill. Had the police known this they might have followed up, though it would not have been feasible for them, or me, to track down and interview every such individual. I have to wonder,' he added gravely, 'do you really wish your father's murder to be solved or not?'

'Of course,' she said, colouring.

'Then I must ask you to stop keeping information from me.' He relented. 'Given the state of your father's commercial ventures, why did you not ask your brother for help?'

'I did,' she said ruefully. 'But he refused. I'm afraid we had a falling out.'

'Is that why Buckley has to call him to make an appointment, and not you?'

She looked pained. 'He won't take my calls. He feels that I sided with my father when he threw him out. He is right, of course. Back then I thought my father could do no wrong. It has been a painful experience to find out that the man I held up as a giant had feet of clay.'

Chopra did not tell her that this was a rite of passage for many children, the discovery that their parents were only human, with all the fallibilities of ordinary mortals.

'Did your father leave a will?'

Perizaad nodded. 'He changed it just before he died. Left it all to me, much good that it did me.'

Another reason for Darius and his sister to fall out, thought Chopra. Had Darius known about the will? If so, it might have been the catalyst for a confrontation with his father . . .

He picked up the blueprint of New Haven, the Vashi slum redevelopment. 'I'd like to hold on to this as well. There must be a reason Cyrus kept this under lock and key.'

Perizaad nodded. 'Yes. Of course.'

'There was something else.'

He took out the newspaper clipping he had discovered inside Cyrus's office about the burned car, and the bodies found inside it. 'Does this mean anything to you?'

Perizaad examined the article. 'No.'

'Why would your father have kept this? I found it hidden inside a book in his office.'

'I honestly have no idea.'

'Very well.' Chopra returned the article to his pocket. 'One last thing: William Buckley. I wish to know more about his background.'

Perizaad frowned. 'Buckley was my father's man.'

'Yet you did not take him on as your own PA when you took the reins.'

She hesitated. 'No. I needed a clean break from the past. But that does not mean I think less of him. Frankly, without his help it would have been difficult for me to make any headway with my father's affairs following his death.'

'Nevertheless, I am certain that he has not been completely truthful with me. And given that he was one of the people closest to your father . . .'

'William Buckley served my father loyally for almost a decade,' said Perizaad. 'There is nothing for you to find there.'

'When he joined your organisation, were background checks carried out on him?'

'I assume so.'

'Such records would be with your Personnel office?'

'Yes. I suppose so.'

'May I have access to them?'

She hesitated, then shrugged. 'If you feel it necessary. But frankly, you are wasting your time. If there is anything you wish to know about William Buckley, you should ask him directly. My father always believed him to be a scrupulously honest man.'

Back in the van, Chopra called Homi. 'Darius Zorabian,' he said. 'Can you tell me why he was disinherited by his father?'

Homi asked him to hold. He heard sounds of banging and shouting, then, 'The official version was that Darius was branching out on his own. The prodigal son flexing his Harvard-educated business muscles while his father sat back and gave him room to breathe.'

'But that wasn't the truth, was it?'

'Of course not. Nothing was ever publicly confirmed, but we're a small community. Gossip travels fast. And there's nothing we Parsees like better than a family scandal.'

'Scandal? What scandal?'

'It was to do with Darius's wife,' said Homi.

Chopra listened. By the time he ended the call, he had decided that it was high time he confronted the victim's son.

THE PRODIGAL SON

He drove to the industrial district of Kala Qila – Black Fort – a relatively sparsely built-up area on the marshy banks of the Mahim Creek just twenty minutes from the Alpha Bank, and a short drive across the Sion-Bandra Link Road bridge. It was in this sprawling estate of small- to mid-sized industrial units, nestled around the western edge of the Maharashtra Nature Park, that Sun4Life Incorporated was located.

He parked the van opposite the local bus depot, where a gang of bus drivers were playing cards in the street as they ate a late lunch from steel tiffins. As Ganesha drifted by, they paused their game and watched with interest. The little elephant, drawn by the smells wafting from the open lunch boxes, stopped to investigate, hoping, perhaps, for a light afternoon snack.

'Pick a card for me, little one,' said one of the drivers, grinning broadly as he puffed on a hand-rolled cigarette. He tapped the deck splayed before him. Ganesha reached out and gave the deck a quick poke with his trunk. The driver swept up the card, took a quick look, then set down his hand triumphantly. He pulled the pot of cash towards him and turned to Chopra. 'This elephant is lucky. Why don't you leave him with us?'

Chopra gave a rueful smile. 'I would rather he did not become a gambler. He has enough vices already.'

Good-natured laughter followed them along the dusty track as they walked to the Sun4Life unit, a large shed-like space with crumbling brick walls and a tin roof. It was a far cry from the wealth and pomp Chopra usually associated with Parsee-run enterprises.

The temperature inside the tin shed was even higher than outside, a miasma of dead air and indolent heat.

Chopra's shirt stuck to his back. Sweat poured freely from his forehead, drenching his moustache. He wondered how anyone could work in this sauna-like environment.

Then again, millions of Indians did precisely that, in microbusinesses and low-rent factories up and down the land. There was a reason they were called sweatshops.

A large man in a pair of shabby shorts and a torn T-shirt was poking around inside the guts of a piece of compli-cated-looking machinery. 'Ho, there,' said Chopra by way of greeting. 'I am looking for Darius Zorabian.'

The man straightened.

He was tall, with a dark crew cut and an impressively dynastical nose. It was the nose that gave him away. 'You must be Chopra,' said Darius.

His eyes flickered to Ganesha who was already eyeing the machinery with interest. The elephant calf was insatiably curious.

'Is he with you?'

'Yes.'

'Handsome beast.'

'Don't tell him that.'

Darius raised an eyebrow but forbore from further comment.

'Thank you for agreeing to see me,' said Chopra.

'Do not thank me yet,' said Darius. 'I only agreed to speak with you out of curiosity.'

Chopra's eyes drifted around the space. A number of labourers – men and women – were engaged at various workstations employing simple tools on bits of machinery.

'Solar micro panels,' said Darius, noticing his expression. 'It is an assembly line.'

'Solar panels?' echoed Chopra. It was not what he had expected to hear.

Perhaps Darius caught the note of scepticism in his tone. He launched into a passionate explanation of his enterprise. 'Did you know that a quarter of India's population lives outside the power grid? Our politicians crow about "India Shining", but in most rural homes even the lights don't shine half of the time. Despite the government's promises to "electrify the nation" there is not enough profit for the power companies – and not enough votes for local politicos – to bring electricity to the remoter villages. That is where entrepreneurs like myself come in. The low-cost panels we create can be installed very cheaply. They generate very low amounts of energy – but enough to provide lighting for a single-roomed home, or power for a fridge, for a mobile phone, for an irrigation pump. Slowly but surely, we are transforming the lives of thousands of people.'

Chopra felt that this impassioned speech was one Darius had given many times.

'It cannot have been easy,' he said. 'To leave your family business and strike out on your own.'

'The fact you're here means that you already know that I did not *leave* my family business,' said Darius stiffly. 'I was kicked out. Disinherited. I am sure my sister told you.'

'She did,' said Chopra. 'She was very distressed by what happened.'

'Not so distressed that she stood by me.'

'I believe that is something she deeply regrets. She told me that you and your father disagreed on how to run the business.'

'Run? The only running my father did was running our business into the ground.'

'Your father was a stubborn man.'

'He was more than that. He was the worst type of fool. One who doesn't know that he is a fool. Allowing him to continue to direct our business was like handing a toddler a loaded gun.'

'The pair of you quarrelled over it?'

Darius smouldered, but did not reply.

'And yet,' continued Chopra, 'that is not why he disinherited you.'

'Perizaad told you?'

'No. I discovered it for myself. It was your marriage that caused the rift.'

Darius's eyes gleamed with anger. 'My father threw me out because I married against *his* wishes. Because I married outside the Parsee community. When I was at Harvard I fell in love. With an American, a Christian. I asked her to marry me. When my father found out he gave me an ultimatum. Leave her or leave my home. I chose her.'

It was Chopra's turn to pause. He knew that the subject of marriage in the Parsee community was a delicate one. Indeed, in the country as a whole, marriage outside one's caste, community, tribe, or religion was generally the cause of much angst; the phenomenon of honour killings was more prevalent than most liked to believe or admit. But in Parsee society the interdiction was both deeply entrenched and paradoxical – for they were among the most highly educated and enlightened of communities.

He noticed that Ganesha had picked up the screwdriver with his trunk and was poking it inside the solar panel that Darius had been working on. He frowned at his young ward, who deftly turned his bottom to him, so that he could carry on his investigation without censure.

'Did you speak to your father after leaving the family home?'

Darius's gaze shifted away. 'No.'

Chopra sensed that this might not be the whole truth. 'I am no longer a policeman,' he said gently. 'I am merely trying to discover what really happened to him.'

'What happened to him was stupidity,' spat Darius, suddenly furious. 'He was a stubborn, foolish, old man. He refused to listen. Who was he to tell me who I should or should not marry? As for the business . . . A blind man could have told him he was heading for ruin. He has single-handedly squandered my birthright.'

'Your sister is doing her best to salvage things.'

'My sister. Hah! By rights that should have been me.'

'She wishes you were by her side.'

'She told you that? It's funny, I don't recall her inviting me back.'

'She feels your anger has clouded your judgement. That it is preventing you from behaving reasonably. Perhaps she is right.'

Darius's eyes narrowed. 'You don't know the first thing about me.'

'I was a policeman for thirty years. I have seen the very best and worst of human nature. You say your father was blind, unreasoning. Perhaps there is more of him in you than you suppose.' He paused before continuing. 'Can you tell me where you were on the night of his death?'

'I wondered when you would get around to that. You need not excite yourself. The police asked me the same question. I was at home, with my wife.'

Chopra had read this in the police report, but he had wanted to hear it again from Darius. On the face of it, the man had an ironclad alibi for his father's death. But how much was an alibi from a spouse really worth? It was another example of ACP Rao's shoddy attention to detail. 'I'd like to speak with her,' he said.

'Why?'

'Routine questions.'

'I don't think so,' growled Darius. 'My wife is not well. Stay away from her.'

Chopra did not pursue the matter. The man was in a truculent mood. He would have to find another way to talk to Mrs Darius Zorabian. 'Can you think of anyone else who may have wished your father harm?'

Darius blinked. In that moment, as he stood, alone and defiant, a man cut adrift from the fraternity of his people, Chopra's words seemed to strike something deep inside him. A gong of regret that tolled within the hollows of his heart. His shoulders slumped. 'My father was an infuriating man. He stopped listening to those around him, those who cared about him. Yet he could be charming and charismatic when he wanted to be. He could inspire insane devotion or incandescent hatred.'

'Do you know of anyone who hated him enough to kill him?'

Darius shrugged. 'The last time I saw hatred like that . . . Did Buckley or my sister mention Anosh Ginwala?'

'The head corpse-bearer at the Towers of Silence?'

'You've met him?'

'I spoke with him yesterday.'

'I visited Doongerwadi a week before my father was killed. I may have married a non-Parsee, but my faith is still important to me. I encountered Ginwala. He had been drinking. He recognised me and started talking about my father. Apparently he had turned down a series of demands by the corpse-bearers: a long-overdue pay rise, a request for better housing, better living conditions. He had led them on for years, and then, finally, told Ginwala it was never going to happen. That if he ever mentioned it again he would be fired, his family thrown out of Doongerwadi. In that instant, I saw murder in Ginwala's eyes.' Darius paused. 'They say that, given enough time, history will denounce anyone. Well, my father *deserves* to be pulled down from his pedestal. He was a tyrant, Chopra. Oh, he cultivated the image expected of him – the Parsee with a heart of gold – but it was just a front. He ran our business like a fiefdom. He ruled over Doongerwadi in the same way. He did exactly as he wished, and no one had the power or guts to stop him.'

A QUESTION OF JURISDICTION

On the way back to the restaurant, Chopra first stopped at the offices of the Zorabian organisation. He made his way to the Personnel department, where, citing Perizaad's permission, he obtained background documents on William Buckley, including photocopies of his passport and a letter of reference from his last employer, a Mr Peter Brewer.

Brewer's praise had been effusive, and, on the face of it, genuine.

Chopra tucked the paperwork away, then headed for the door and home.

Half an hour later he detoured towards the Sahar police station.

Evening was fast approaching, but he wished to meet with the station-in-charge. It had been a day of small revelations, and slow, steady progress. Yet the day had also revealed new threads that he could not help but pull at, in the hope that they might unravel some greater truth. It was in pursuit of one of these minor threads that he entered the station and made his way to the office of Inspector Malini Sheriwal.

Outside the door to the office – *his* old office, he couldn't help but think with a squirt of nostalgia – he found Constable Qureshi facing the wall with a terracotta plant pot over his head. The sight was so incongruous that it caused him to halt in his onward progress. 'Qureshi? Is that you?'

Constable Qureshi, a stick-thin, knobbly-kneed fifty-five-year-old, had spent a lifetime on the force without managing to graduate out of his blue constable's shorts. His supreme incompetence had made him something of a legend, and meant that he enjoyed the dubious distinction of being one of the most transferred officers in the service. As the grandson of a once prominent political family, it had been deemed by those in charge that Qureshi could never be fired. He was, instead, passed from station to station, as welcome as a bout of gonorrhoea. He had only just arrived at the Sahar station when Chopra was forced into retirement, but in that short space of time had driven his commanding officer to distraction.

'Yes, sir,' came Qureshi's muffled voice.

'What the devil are you doing, man?'

'Inspector Sheriwal's orders, sir.'

'Orders? She *ordered* you to stand here with a pot on your head?'

'Yes, sir.'

Chopra's expression was mystified. 'Why?'

'I am being TAUGHT A LESSON, sir,' intoned Qureshi. 'Inspector Sheriwal believes that STRONG DRINK IS A

MOCKER and that I must be made to see the ERROR OF MY WAYS.'

Chopra was speechless.

He had heard rumours that Qureshi had something of a drink problem when he had agreed to take the man on, but he did not think that this was the remedy. From what he knew of addiction, standing by the wall with a pot on one's head was not the answer. 'You are dismissed, Qureshi.'

Qureshi somehow contrived to look uncertain, even though the pot was obscuring his face.

'Inspector Sheriwal will be displeased, sir.'

'Go. Now!'

Qureshi scurried away, hands holding on to the sides of the pot.

Chopra knocked on the door to the office, then entered.

Malini Sheriwal was a tall, broad-shouldered woman who wore her khaki well. A head of glossy black hair was pulled back from a not unhandsome face, the most promi-nent features of which were a strong, Roman nose and widely spaced brown eyes.

Sheriwal, he knew, was a woman of firm opinions, and even firmer action.

Betrayed by her first and only husband, she had shot the man in the foot, before divorcing him.

As a member of Mumbai's notorious Encounter Squad, she had brought terror to the city's underworld, notching up numerous kills with her infamous ivory-handled revolver. So cavalier had her shooting spree become that eventually the city's authorities had been forced to disband the squad, and send the ace sharpshooter off to lie low.

After her adrenalin-fuelled days on the Encounter Squad, the mundanities of running a small suburban station had proved to be Sheriwal's worst nightmare; her frustration inevitably found a lightning rod in the less competent officers under her command.

She looked up from her desk as Chopra came in, blinking in momentary confusion, before recognition bloomed.

'I am sorry to interrupt your work,' said Chopra. 'But I wonder if you have a few minutes? I require your help.'

Sheriwal put down her pen. 'It seems that helping you is becoming a full-time job for me.'

Chopra coloured. He realised that he had never properly thanked the policewoman for helping him out of a recent jam. In actual fact, it was Poppy that Sheriwal had helped, aiding her in locating Chopra when he had gone missing, courtesy of ACP Rao's machinations. But for Sheriwal's intervention, Chopra might well still be incarcerated in one of the worst prisons in the penal system.

'Your assistance was appreciated. As one officer to another, I offer you my heartfelt thanks.'

This seemed to please her. She waved at the chair on the far side of her desk. 'What can I do for you?'

Chopra took the proffered seat, then reached into his pocket, and took out the press clipping he had found in Cyrus's office. 'What can you tell me about this case? I believe the burned vehicle was found in your jurisdiction.'

Sheriwal scanned the article. 'I remember the investigation. Mainly because we were unable to make much headway.' She abruptly bellowed: 'Qureshi! Get in here!'

When there was no response, she opened her mouth again, but was cut off by Chopra. 'I am afraid Qureshi is gone,' he said. 'I told him to go.'

Anger flared in Sheriwal's eyes. 'You countermanded my orders?'

'Qureshi is a good man. A bad cop, but a good man.'

Sheriwal was silent a moment. 'He has managed to elevate incompetence to an art form.'

Chopra chuckled. 'Policing is certainly not his strong suit.' He waited as Sheriwal picked up her phone and called outside. A constable arrived at the double, somewhat breathless from his sprint, and handed her a file. He salaamed crisply, then backpedalled from the room just as smartly.

Sheriwal held the file out to Chopra. 'Be my guest.'

Chopra flicked through the paperwork.

The burned-out vehicle had been found in a deserted industrial complex scheduled for demolition; no one had seen it being driven into the complex, or being torched. The make and model had been determined as a Maruti Baleno, one of the most common cars in the city. The number plates had been removed, as had the VIN number, making an identification of the vehicle's registered owner difficult. When the owner had finally been tracked down – through a lengthy process of elimination – it turned out that the car had been stolen months earlier. As for the bodies – they remained unidentified.

He pulled out a series of photographs, taken in situ, showing the blackened cadavers, both in their seats within the burned car, and laid out on stretchers by the authorities.

The images were gruesome, the bodies twisted by the reflex contraction of muscles during the process of burning.

The faces, in particular, were hellish, props from a horror movie.

Sheriwal's eyes lingered on his face. 'I suppose it's some consolation that they were both already dead prior to being burned,' she said. 'Shot in the back of the head. We matched the bullets to 9mm Mungers, made in Bihar. A weapon of choice for Mumbai's underworld.'

'It says here the autopsy identified the corpses as a male and a female.'

'Correct. We were also able to determine their approximate ages. For the female: twenty-one to twenty-three; for the male: twenty-seven to twenty-nine. No identifiers were left with the bodies – they had been stripped naked.'

'Someone went to a lot of trouble to ensure their identities would remain hidden.'

'Yes,' agreed Sheriwal. 'Our working theory at the time was that they were young lovers running away from families that disagreed with their relationship. Perhaps one, or both, of the families hired thugs to take care of the problem. It would not be the first time in this fine country of ours.'

It was a sound hypothesis, thought Chopra. 'I assume you checked against the missing persons lists?'

'Of course,' said Sheriwal, a trace of annoyance entering her tone. 'But if the families *had* been involved they would not have reported them missing. And if they were not involved . . . Well, the number of missing persons in this city at any one time is beyond reckoning. There was simply not enough information for us to narrow down the list of potentials to a practical number, not with the manpower at my disposal. And, frankly, who in this city cares about two unclaimed bodies? As a former policeman, you should know the golden rule: don't do anything until someone raises a stink.'

Chopra understood what she meant. Due to the lack of resources, policing in Mumbai was often a matter of triage, of doing the best you could with what little you had.

But sometimes a crime would grab hold of your throat and refuse to let go.

This was one such crime.

Perhaps Sheriwal sensed his thoughts. She leaned back and fixed him with a thoughtful look. 'What is this *really* about?'

Chopra considered saying nothing. Then again, *he* was the one asking for help. Trust cut both ways.

He quickly explained his investigation into Cyrus Zorabian's death.

'So this is what you do now? Run around second-guessing real police work?'

He bristled. 'I do what the police should have done in the first place.'

'Who made you judge and jury of our competence?'

Chopra glowered. 'Either you can help me or not. The choice is yours.'

She continued to stare at him, then muttered, 'You can take the cop out of his khaki, but you cannot take the khaki out of the cop.' She raised a placatory hand. 'I didn't say I would not help.' She tapped the article where it lay on her desk. 'Why would Zorabian have kept this? Do you think he knew these two?'

'I don't know. I am learning more about the man by the hour. I get the feeling that I have only scratched the surface.'

'Then I guess we are back to square one.'

'There may be something we can do. To identify these bodies, I mean. But I will have to speak with a colleague first.' He scraped back his chair. 'I will keep you informed. Thank you for your cooperation.'

AN OLD FRIEND COMES IN HANDY

Back at the restaurant Chopra left Ganesha in his compound, then waited in his office for Rangwalla to arrive. When his associate detective finally showed up, wiping the dirt and sweat from his throat with a dirty handkerchief, he seemed less than satisfied with his lot in life.

'What is the matter?' asked Chopra.

'I was thrown out of a rickshaw,' said Rangwalla, smacking dust out of his jeans.

'What did you do?'

Rangwalla scowled. 'Why is it that whenever something like this happens you automatically assume *I* was the one at fault?'

Chopra waited.

Rangwalla slumped into the seat before him. 'The rickshaw driver had a picture of his father on the dashboard. I merely commented that he was a striking-looking man.'

'He took offence at that?'

Rangwalla had the decency to look away. 'Apparently, it was not a picture of his father. It was his wife.'

They ordered fresh lime juices. Irfan brought them in, whistling a jaunty Bollywood tune as he entered.

'Did you finish your homework?' he asked as Irfan set down his glass.

Irfan puffed out his cheeks. 'Yes.'

Chopra raised an eyebrow.

'Weell . . . I've finished *most* of it,' said Irfan.

Chopra smiled. Irfan had grown up on the streets and as a consequence had received little in the way of formal schooling. Poppy had tried to rectify the matter by hiring a tutor to visit him at the restaurant, in between his shifts. Initially reluctant, Irfan had, in time, taken to the new regime. He still refused to move into their apartment, however, preferring to stay at the restaurant where he could be close to Ganesha.

In a way, Chopra was glad.

The boy had a streak of independence, a rebelliousness that he hoped he would never lose. Poppy's intentions were well-meaning, but she didn't quite realise that Irfan's upbringing had left him with a mind all of his own.

'What case are you investigating now?' Irfan asked.

'A very complicated one.'

'Uncle Rangwalla said you were working with Parsees?'

Uncle Rangwalla. Chopra tried to picture his deputy in an avuncular light, and failed.

'It's true that my latest case involves the Parsee community.'

'Is it true that they are all crazy and that they secretly eat their dead when no one is looking?'

'Where did you hear that?' said Chopra.

Irfan's eyes swivelled towards Uncle Rangwalla, who looked as if he'd swallowed a small bird and was now choking on it.

'That is untrue as well as being unkind,' said Chopra eventually. 'We should never make fun of others just because they are different.'

'But Uncle Rangwalla is always telling jokes about the Parsees.'

Chopra glared at his assistant detective who blushed under his beard.

He stood up and ruffled Irfan's hair. 'Go on. Off you go.'

Irfan paused at the door. 'You're very busy these days, aren't you?'

Chopra understood the question behind the question. 'I'm sorry. I *have* been very busy. But I promise, once I make some headway on this case, I will find time to take you out. Perhaps a day trip to Elephanta Island? We'll take Ganesha as well. He will enjoy that.'

'That boy's as eager as a Gurkha with two grenades,' said Rangwalla, after Irfan had left.

Quickly, Chopra brought him up to speed with the investigation into Cyrus Zorabian's death.

'You seem to have waded into a swamp,' commented his deputy. 'Do you really think there was more to his death than a random attack?'

'It's too early to say. But there are matters here that I believe the initial investigation either did not uncover, or could not be bothered to follow through.'

'Does it surprise you? With Rao in charge?'

'I suppose not. Anyway, how did *you* get on?'

It was Rangwalla's turn to describe his prison meeting with Hasan Gafoor.

'Do you believe him?' asked Chopra, when he had finished.

Rangwalla looked uncomfortable. 'He seemed genuine. Perhaps he's the one true innocent in this city. The mythical virgin in a whorehouse.'

Chopra winced. His deputy had always had a colourful grasp of language. 'What will you do next?'

Rangwalla shrugged. 'What do you think I should do?'

'I think you should use your initiative. You are no longer my junior officer, Rangwalla.'

Rangwalla gave him a sour look. He hated the idea of using his initiative. In his experience using one's initiative usually got people like him into trouble.

'You're enjoying this, aren't you?' he muttered.

Chopra suppressed a smile. He had always suspected that his former sub-inspector had a keen mind, though one that worked in a different manner to his own. Men like Rangwalla hated the limelight; yet, so often, when the dung hit the fan, they rose magnificently to the occasion.

Rangwalla squirmed in his seat for a few moments longer, before a flash of insight jolted him upright. 'I need to find out who it was that tried to strong-arm Gafoor into selling his plot.'

Chopra nodded approvingly. 'And how exactly will you do that?'

Rangwalla hesitated. His mind had gone alarmingly blank, as if the effort of deduction had drained him of further inspiration.

Chopra relented. 'Do you remember ACP Ajit Shinde?'

'The one with the wooden leg? Married whatshisname's sister, the girl with the squint and the donkey? Used to drag it around with her everywhere she went. She was a bit soft in the head, by all accounts. Then again, Shinde was no catch himself.'

'No,' said Chopra stonily. 'That was Constable Shankar. Shinde always used to say that in situations such as this, the best thing to do is to follow the money. If I were you I would find out *precisely* who benefited from Gafoor's misfortune.'

When he entered his apartment Chopra's first task was to check on his impromptu houseguest. He stepped into his office, expecting to find the vulture lodged on the perch she had found for herself on his bookshelf.

But there was no sign of the bird.

'Poppy,' he said, stepping back out into the living room, 'where is the vulture?'

Poppy, who was sitting at the table filling out a compli-cated-looking form, did not look up. He guessed that she was still upset about the matter. 'I think my mother took him,' she finally ground out.

Chopra paled. 'Your mother?'

'Yes.'

'Why?'

'I don't know.'

'You didn't ask?'

'I was busy,' said Poppy, signing her form with a flourish.

'Where did she take her?'

'Her?' Poppy looked up.

'Yes. The bird is a she.'

Her brow furrowed. 'It's strange. I've never thought of a vulture as a *she*. I suppose there have to be female ones otherwise they'd die out. Possibly due to lack of common sense.' Chopra smiled, but Poppy did not smile back. 'I think she said she was taking *her* up to the terrace.'

When Chopra reached the building's roof he discovered his mother-in-law, Poornima Devi, sitting with Mrs Subramanium in a pair of bamboo chairs, the pair of them bent deep in conspiracy. Before them lay a steel tray upon which were stretched out a trio of dead rats, the vulture hunkered in front of the tray.

As Chopra looked on, the bird grasped one of the rats with a talon, then tore off its head with her beak.

'What are you doing?' he gaped.

'What does it look like we're doing?' replied Poornima, pulling at her white sari as a gobbet of half-masticated rodent fell from the bird's mouth to land beside her sandalled foot. 'We are training the bird to eat rats.'

'Why?'

'So that it can help clean up this building. We are infested with them at present; all coming over from that new slum. Belligerent ones, too. The other day one of the little devils was sitting on my dresser, bold as brass.'

'I must say, Chopra,' chimed in Mrs Subramanium, 'we haven't always seen eye to eye, but this is a most excellent idea of yours.'

'Mine?' said Chopra weakly.

'Well, you brought the bird home, didn't you?' said Poornima.

'That *bird* is part of an ongoing investigation,' protested Chopra.

'That doesn't mean it cannot earn its keep while it is staying with us.'

'But you're feeding her dead rats!'

'It is a vulture,' pointed out his mother-in-law acidly. 'What were you intending to feed it? Lentil soup? Samosas?'

Chopra realised that for once, contrary to all that was holy, his mother-in-law had a point. He looked down at the vulture; the arch scavenger had gobbled down the first rat and was tearing enthusiastically into the second.

'There really is no need to get your bowels in an uproar,' continued Poornima, squinting at him out of her one working eye. 'Bahadur will bring it back down again when we are done.'

Feeling somewhat light-headed Chopra returned to the flat where he found Poppy humming around the kitchen; she had completed her form and was beginning preparations for dinner.

He noticed the form was still on the table.

He picked it up and scrutinised it.

It was an application to join the Poo2Loo campaign's 'Volunteer Leaders' programme. The form began with a formal petition, which each applicant was required to sign:

Hon'ble President of India,

I call on you as Head of State to ensure that India rises to the challenge of ending open defecation. As a citizen of India, I am proud of our country's rich and varied culture; we have a beautiful land. However, over 620 million people do not use a toilet and nearly as many accept this practice. The result is an unacceptable level of filth in our environment. This is why I have chosen to take a stand. Together we can change India.

Poppy's complicated signature was inscribed beneath the text together with two carefully drawn hearts and the official mascot of the movement – an animated turd named Mr Poo.

Chopra, shaking his head, put down the form, then took out his notebook.

As Poppy made dinner, chattering animatedly about her upcoming activities on behalf of the campaign, he went through his notes from the day. He counted his blessings that she appeared to have temporarily forgotten about Vulturegate.

The investigation had thrown up more questions than it had answered. He felt the ripple of familiar currents moving around him; the swirl of things both seen and unseen. The cash found in Cyrus's locker, the Latin letters, the feud with Boman Jeejibhoy, the press article about the dead boy and girl. Again he sensed that there was more to Cyrus Zorabian than had met the eye.

But was that not often the way?

How often during his career had he dug behind the public mask only to discover an altogether different reality underneath?

He had learned to rely on his instincts. Those same instincts now nagged him to pick up his phone and dial a number he had not employed for some time.

'Superintendent Bomberton, please,' he said, when the phone was answered.

'That's *Mr* Superintendent to you,' said Maxwell Bomberton on the other end of the line.

Chopra smiled. 'If they keep promoting you at this rate you'll soon be commissioner.'

Bomberton gave a growl of laughter. 'How are things over in the cesspool of dreams, Chopra?'

'Don't let the Mumbai tourist board hear you call it that.'

They shared a chuckle.

A few months earlier Max Bomberton, a senior detective in the UK's Metropolitan Police, had assisted Chopra in the recovery of the famed Koh-i-Noor diamond. The priceless jewel had been brought to Mumbai as part of a special exhibition of the British Crown Jewels, only to be promptly stolen in a daring heist. With Bomberton's help Chopra had managed to track down and recover the diamond, earning the gratitude of both British and Indian governments. Bomberton's star had been on the rise ever since.

'I need your help with something,' said Chopra.

'What can I do for you, old friend?'

'I have been hired to look into the murder of a wealthy industrialist. His personal assistant is an Englishman. He grew up in a place called Yeovil. I need some background.'

'Is he a suspect?'

'I don't know. But something about him is not sitting right with me. I suppose I am simply being thorough.'

'Why change the habit of a lifetime, eh?' said Bomberton. 'Do you have some details for me, or shall I just read your mind?'

Chopra took out the photocopy of William Buckley's passport provided to him by the Zorabian company's HR office, photographed the relevant pages using his mobile, then texted them to Bomberton. He also sent over details of Buckley's previous employer in Mumbai – Peter Brewer – the Englishman who had eventually returned to the UK.

'It would be useful if you could also locate *this* gentleman,' said Chopra. 'He may provide valuable insight into Buckley's past.'

'Anything else I can do for Your Highness? Back rub? Breakfast in bed?' Bomberton's sarcasm dripped down the phone.

'No. This will be enough,' said Chopra, who was tone-deaf to irony.

'Grim-looking bugger,' remarked Bomberton, meaning Buckley. 'I'll get someone on it asap. Right. Must dash. Got a meeting with the chief super. He's not in a good mood. Hairdryer at the ready, if you catch my drift.'

Chopra frowned. 'Your commanding officer styles your hair for you?'

'I mean he's a shouter,' snapped Bomberton. 'Last week he gave my deputy such a blast the man's glass eye fell out.'

HOMI HAS AN IDEA

'Have you ever seen a four-month-old corpse? It is not a pleasant sight.'

It was the following morning and Chopra was splayed in a plastic seat inside the badly air-conditioned office of Homi Contractor, deep within the bowels of Sahar Hospital.

He had arrived at the facility half an hour earlier, his first stop of the day, and had spent the better part of that time trying to convince his old friend to help in the identification of the two burned bodies. He still had no idea if they had anything to do with Cyrus Zorabian's death, but his instincts were once again making a nuisance of themselves.

And besides, there was an unspoken obligation here.

Call it fate, karma, or simple bad luck, but the burden of unravelling these two brutal and unsolved deaths had fallen to him. The sight of those blackened corpses would haunt his nightmares for years to come; it was not within him to walk away from their unspoken plea.

'I am in need of some expert advice,' he had said when he had entered the cramped office to find Homi writing up an autopsy report.

'Really?' Homi had replied without looking up. 'When *I* need expert advice I usually consult myself.'

Chopra smiled. Modesty had never been one of Homi's strong suits.

Quickly, he had launched into an explanation of the circuitous path that had brought him to his friend's doorstep.

Homi had considered the problem; he was less than enthusiastic. 'I remember those two – we did the autopsies right here. Shot in the head, then burned to a crisp. Someone had used an accelerant on them. Wanted to make sure there was no chance of an ID. It worked, too.'

'There has to be something we can do.'

'Ah,' said Homi, staring curiously at his friend. 'It's one of *those* cases, is it?'

'What do you mean?'

'I've seen all this before, you know,' replied the pathologist evenly. 'When something gets under your skin. It's like watching a man with a terminal case of haemorrhoids. You simply cannot stop yourself from scratching.'

Chopra coloured. 'We owe it to them.'

'If we all started thinking like you, the whole system would collapse in a week. Our resources are limited. And there is only one of me. If I could clone myself, I most certainly would. My gift to the world. But alas that is not possible.'

'If it is a question of funds . . .? That can be arranged. Within reason.'

Homi's ears perked up. 'Is that so?'

'The Zorabian organisation is not without means.' Chopra did not bother to mention that Cyrus's company had fallen on hard times.

Homi's eyes glittered. 'Well, there is *something* we might try. A procedure I saw at a medical conference in Helsinki last month. I've been itching to give it a go, but have never been able to convince our budgetary taskmasters at the hospital. It's expensive – I'd have to liaise with a couple of overseas experts. There's also some rather costly software I'd need to buy . . . But, yes, I think it could be done.' He seemed to be talking to himself, his rubbery features suddenly animated. He leaned forward over the cluttered desk, his autopsy report temporarily forgotten. 'Have you ever heard of forensic facial reconstruction?'

'I have come across it. On TV documentaries. Do you think such a procedure can provide us with a likeness of their faces?'

'As good as makes no difference,' said Homi confidently. 'We would have to dig them up. It won't be a pretty sight. Bodies that long underground.'

'Out of interest: how is it that they were not cremated?'

'It's the law, I'm afraid. Without a positive ID we could not ascertain their religion. So into the ground they went. Can you imagine the fuss if we'd cremated them, and then it turned out they were Muslims? Or, even worse, Parsees? I'd never hear the end of it.'

Chopra could well believe it.

It had always struck him as faintly ridiculous the rituals that human beings had invented to make the cold hard reality of death more palatable. Ceremony, prayer, meretricious outpourings of grief, convoluted burial practices. The simple fact was that once a man passed into the next life – or wherever the soul went after death – there was nothing but an empty carcass left behind. Anything you did to it or for it was moot, an exercise in pointlessness.

'How soon can we get this done?'

Homi had stood up and was pacing his office. 'We need a court order to exhume the remains. I know a couple of friendly judges, so that shouldn't take long. Then we need approval from the city's Public Health Department. They're a real pain to work with. But you leave that to me. The head man owes me a favour. I am pretty sure I can get him to fast-track the application.'

'Application?'

'Digging up the dead is a dicey business, old friend. You wouldn't believe the paperwork involved. But I will take care of all that for you. With a fair wind we'll have those cadavers breathing fresh air by this evening.' Homi clapped his palms together. 'This will be a first in Mumbai. I shall document the whole process. There'll be at least half a dozen papers in it. Maybe even a TV documentary. "Homi Contractor – the face of Indian forensic facial reconstruction." Get it? The face of?' He grinned wolfishly.

Chopra could see that his friend was intoxicated with the possibilities. He hoped that he did not forget the reason behind the endeavour.

'Two young people were brutally murdered,' he said, in mild admonishment.

'Well, *you* didn't murder them, did you?' replied Homi. 'Neither did I. We cannot change what happened.' He scooped up a polished skull that he kept on his bookshelf, a souvenir from his college days. Turning to face Chopra, he worked the skull's jawbone up and down in a parody of speech. 'Alas, poor Chopra! I knew him, Horatio. A fellow of infinite jest, of most excellent fancy.'

Chopra did not smile. He got up, gave Homi his sternest look, then turned for the door.

The skull's jawbone rattled again: 'My name is Gladiator.'

Chopra grasped the handle. 'Keep me informed,' he muttered, as he swept from the room.

'*I* am your father, Luke!'

A LATIN DETOUR

Chopra arrived at the St Xavier Catholic School for Boys in the plush suburb of Juhu as it was approaching midday. The temperature had already risen into the upper thirties, with little breeze to leaven the baking atmosphere. As he and Ganesha entered the extensive grounds he saw that the grassy fields were already turning brown from the heatwave.

The school, over a century old now, had begun life as an orphanage, the legacy of Portuguese missionaries who had been zealously active once upon a time, eradicating poverty, doling out Christian charity, and converting the heathen. A hundred years on and St Xavier was routinely ranked as one of the finest educational establishments in the city.

It was also the place of employment of one Poppy Chopra, the first and, to date, only woman to serve on the school's staff roster.

Chopra remembered the fuss when his wife had discovered this peculiar omission; the fact that in a hundred years the school had not seen fit to utilise the talents of a single member of the gentler – and, in his wife's opinion, wiser – sex had incensed her. A campaign of aggressive petitioning had followed, almost driving a number of the school's ageing trustees into early graves, the end result of which had been the appointment of Poppy as St Xavier's first drama and dance tutor.

Chopra had suspected that, having made her point, Poppy would quickly tire of the role. She had never worked before, contenting herself with pursuing a never-ending catalogue of social causes over the years of their marriage.

But she had surprised him.

The job seemed to suit her perfectly. By all accounts, she was a big hit.

'Hello!'

Chopra turned.

Talk of the devil.

There was Poppy now, striding purposefully over the grass towards him in a bright yellow sari, her dark hair pulled into its usual bun.

Chopra always felt his good fortune most acutely in the presence of his wife. They had married young – Poppy was only in her early forties, and he himself, though in his late forties, did not feel a day over thirty – passing a quarter of a century together, a union that had seen its share of ups and downs. Nevertheless, he believed – no, he *knew* – that both their lives would have been poorer without the other. They had grown up in the same village together, out in the Maharashtrian interior; their fathers had been the best of friends – so in some sense perhaps destiny had played its part.

Yet it had remained for them to live out the partnership they had committed to, and in that living, define each other. That they had done so successfully, in spite of the vicissitudes of fate – most notably in their childlessness – was a testament to the decision they had made all those years ago.

Ganesha bounded over to her, wrapping his trunk around her waist as she leaned down and hugged him.

Chopra's gaze, however, was drawn to the man jogging behind her, struggling to keep up, clad head-to-foot in a strangely unsettling costume. He looked for all the world like a giant mound of chocolate ice cream, or a brown Michelin Man from the tyre adverts on television. There was something queasily familiar about the whole thing . . .

'Who is this?' he asked.

Poppy turned to the man, who was bent double, hands on knees, gasping for breath. 'This is Mr Poo. The mascot of the Poo2Loo campaign. I have invited him to deliver a talk to the boys today.'

Chopra felt once more the surreal disembodiment that stole over him whenever he encountered the Poo2Loo campaign. It still seemed fantastical to him that a country touting itself as a global superpower was struggling to control the profligate bowels of its populace.

'But that is – that is *preposterous*,' was all he could find to say.

The mascot straightened. He lifted a hatch from the 'face', revealing wide eyes and a sad little moustache. 'Oh, you think my life is easy, do you? Parading around in this outfit?' He lit a cigarette. 'You think I dreamed of being a giant turd when I was growing up? I trained at the Prithvi

Theatre. I have performed Shakespeare. The *Ghatkopar Express* called my Macbeth a "most acceptable" performance.'

Still shaking his head, Chopra followed his wife into the school. He had asked Poppy to arrange a meeting with the school's principal.

'I must warn you, he is not in a good mood,' she remarked as they arrived at the frosted-glass door of Brother Augustus Lobo's office.

'Has he *ever* been in a good mood?' muttered Chopra.

'I must leave you to it,' said his wife. 'I will see you afterwards for lunch.'

'Take this,' said Mr Poo, handing Chopra a leaflet. The slogan read: *Defecation need not be desecration.* He watched the six-foot-tall turd waddle after his wife, before vanishing around a corner.

Taking a deep breath, he knocked on the principal's door.

'Come!' bellowed a voice from within.

Chopra entered to find Principal Augustus Lobo hunched over his desk, fountain pen in hand.

The principal of St Xavier was in his early nineties, but, with his thick grey hair, looked like a man in his sixties. Lobo, a strict disciplinarian, was a man who believed in the 'stick and bigger stick' approach to tutelage; he had been meting out such salutary lessons at the school for more than half a century, passing on his own sense of moral righteousness to cadres of bright (and not-so-bright) young men who had gone on to shape Indian society. Politicians, businessmen, film stars – many famous backsides had felt the ire of Augustus Lobo's cane during their formative years.

'Ah, Chopra,' said Lobo, glancing up. 'Short back and sides today, man.'

Chopra blinked in confusion. 'I – ah – I am here about the Latin letters.'

Lobo's expression crunched into a glare. 'What does a barber need with Latin?'

'I am not a barber. Sir.' Chopra wondered why he instantly felt reduced to his ten-year-old self in the presence of the old man. 'I am Poppy's husband. Here about a case.'

A light came on in Lobo's eyes. 'Ah! The detective with the elephant. You helped us with that dreadful statue business.'

A sense of relief washed through Chopra. The agency had recently assisted the school in recovering a missing bust of one of its founders, thereby averting both a scandal and Lobo's incipient hernia.

Chopra pulled out the sheaf of letters discovered in Cyrus Zorabian's bank locker. 'Poppy tells me that you are fluent in Latin. These were recovered as part of an ongoing investigation. I would be most grateful if you could translate them.'

Lobo took the letters, adjusted the pince-nez spectacles balanced on his nose, then furrowed his great, winged eyebrows. 'Hah! Typed!' he muttered. 'Where have the days of penmanship gone, eh? In the old days, you could tell where you stood with a man just by examining his handwriting.'

Grumbling under his breath, Lobo worked swiftly. In his neat hand, he wrote each translation on to a single sheet alongside the original Latin.

Chopra waited for the ink to dry, then picked up the sheet, and began to read:

Salus populi suprema lex esto.
The welfare of the people is the highest law.

Radix malorum est cupiditas.
Greed is the root of all evil.

Bonum commune communitatis.
Common good of the community.

Sit sine labe decus.
Let honour stainless be.

Boni pastoris est tondere pecus non deglubere.
It is a good shepherd's role to shear his flock,
not to flay them.

Faber est suae quisque infortunii.
Every man is the artisan of his own misfortune.

'What do they mean?' he murmured to himself.

Believing that the question had been directed at him, Lobo responded: 'They are fairly well-known exhortations to moral behaviour. From the likes of Tiberius and Cicero. It would seem that whoever sent these was urging your victim to reconsider his actions. Possibly the man was in some position of responsibility and had failed in discharging that duty. The world is rife with immorality, Chopra.' Lobo rose from his desk. 'At any rate, I have Brother Machado's lecture to deliver. Bloody fool managed to stop a javelin with his foot out on the sports field. Not paying attention, too busy fiddling with his mobile telephonic device. Hah! Divine providence, if you ask me.'

Back out on the grounds, Chopra found a whitewashed bench where he waited for Poppy.

He watched Ganesha playing soccer with a group of boys out for their physical exercise class. The little elephant was surprisingly nimble with a ball at his feet. His presence delighted the youngsters, and the sound of their laughter drifted over the tinder-dry grass.

Lobo's translations circled each other inside Chopra's head like a flock of honking geese.

Who had sent those letters? Why?

Clearly, Cyrus had taken them seriously enough to secrete them inside his bank locker. Yet they were hardly threatening. There was no overt malice, merely a rather condescending sense of moral righteousness. Was it possible that the Parsee industrialist was being blackmailed? If so, what for?

This line of thought opened up complicated new avenues of investigation, and Chopra spent the next thirty minutes scratching in his notebook.

When Poppy arrived, she plopped on the bench beside him, startling him.

'We shall eat together,' she announced, rattling her tiffin at him.

Chopra checked his watch. He could spare the time.

As the beguiling aromas of home-made chicken kolhapuri and saffron rice wafted around them, his thoughts lingered on the letters.

If the possibility of blackmail was set to one side – for Chopra really had no reason to suppose this – then what else might these letters mean? What was it Lobo had said? That the phrases indicated a man who had failed to discharge his duty. Cyrus Zorabian had ground his ancestral business into the dirt. How many lives had been affected by the decisions he had made, by his pig-headedness, his refusal to listen? Could it be that someone had written these letters to wake Zorabian up to the effect of his actions? Any number of employees would have been justified in sending these missives – those who had their ear to the ground and had put two and two together, at any rate – including his disinherited son.

But why in Latin?

Chopra could only guess.

Perhaps, by writing to Zorabian in this way, the sender had hoped both to attract the Parsee magnate's attention – Perizaad had stated he had studied Latin – while also disguising his or her own identity. Which hinted that the sender might be known to Cyrus. But who . . .?

'Have you taken your pills?'

Chopra shook himself out of his mental divagations. He smiled at his wife. 'I was just about to.'

Poppy poured him a glass of water so that he could gulp down the angina pills that were the bane of his existence.

'How did it go with Lobo?' she asked.

'Very well. I have inched a little closer to the mountain. What about your talk? How did the kids take to, er, your friend?'

'Boys will be boys,' said Poppy, arching a rueful eyebrow. 'I am afraid they were quite merciless. In the end, he tore off his suit, shouted "I quit", and ran off. He was arrested in the street. He was not in the habit of wearing anything beneath his costume, you see. Because of the heat. It has not been a good day for Mr Poo.'

Chopra stared at his wife. Something moved in his gut. He tried to ignore it, but soon he found his shoulders shaking. And then he could control it no longer. The laugh erupted from inside him, a great, convulsive roar of glee. His wife looked on in astonishment, as tears of mirth squeezed out from the corners of his eyes. It was so rare to see her husband this way.

Chopra was, and always had been, the soberest of men.

'Mr Poo!' he gasped. 'Only in India! No one would believe it in the west.'

'It is a noble endeavour,' she said sternly, suddenly suspicious that he was laughing at *her*.

'I am sure it is, Poppy,' he replied, calming himself. 'And you are a noble woman.' His phone rang, and he answered it, glad of the distraction.

It was the vet Lala. 'So, the blood test came back on your vulture. Most curious. She had significant quantities of diclofenac in her system.'

'Diclofenac?' Chopra mentally riffled through his notes. 'The chemical that almost wiped out the vultures a decade ago?'

'The very same.'

'Did you not tell me that it had been banned?'

'I did, and it has.'

Chopra's mind ticked over silently. 'What does this mean?'

'I took the liberty of checking with some colleagues. Diclofenac is definitely *not* being administered to livestock any more. There are still old stocks of it lying around, but no farmer would be foolish enough to use it – the government has been very harsh on transgressors. This leaves us with two possibilities. Either your vulture accidentally stumbled across some diclofenac and ingested it – though heaven only knows why she would do that; no vulture would touch it in its raw state – or . . . or someone intentionally fed it to her. Inside a carcass. A dead rodent. A small monkey. That sort of thing.'

'Why would anyone do that?'

'Don't you read the papers? Plenty of people – non-Parsees, I mean – want Doongerwadi shut down. Those Parsees have made some powerful enemies with their body disposal routine. I suppose the logic would be: kill off the vultures and you kill off Doongerwadi. Then again, it might be someone closer to home. Someone who had access to the place, someone disillusioned with the whole damned business. A disgruntled employee, perhaps.'

Chopra suddenly had a vision of Anosh Ginwala, the head corpse-bearer at Doongerwadi, a man who had professed exactly the sort of sentiments Lala was describing. Cyrus had publicly stood up for the old values, sacking two priests for deviating from the millennia-old tradition of leaving it to the vultures and instead cremating bodies. It wasn't beyond the bounds of possibility that Ginwala had played a hand in that incident. Or perhaps, bitter at Cyrus's refusal to meet his demands for better pay and conditions, Ginwala had simply decided to sabotage Doongerwadi's operation.

'This is most helpful,' he said. 'Perhaps you can do something else for me? I wish to know the names of all those holding diclofenac in the Mumbai Metropolitan Region.'

'Let me guess, you intend to ask if they have sold any of it to someone connected to your client's death?' Lala scoffed. 'And you think they will happily incriminate themselves by telling you?'

'You would be surprised what people will say when put on the spot. Besides, I doubt that it would have been illegal for them to sell the diclofenac on.'

'I have a better idea. Why don't you let *me* follow up for you? At least I know what I am talking about when it comes to this chemical.'

Chopra was surprised by the offer. 'You wish to help?'

'I've always wondered what it might be like. Playing detective. Kicking down doors, slapping suspects around. Eating enormous meals at the taxpayers' expense.'

Chopra frowned. 'If you are to help you must take this seriously. A man has been murdered.'

'It was just a joke,' said Lala. 'I will be the very definition of sober when I question these people. Besides, it doesn't sit well with me that someone has been out there trying to kill off these endangered birds. At least we now know how you managed to run that vulture over. The quantity of diclofenac your bird ingested was not enough to kill her, but more than enough to give her the mother of all hangovers. As bad a driver as you may be, Chopra, even you couldn't hit a healthy vulture. They have a sixth sense for predators. They're used to eating with one eye open.'

Rangwalla had had few occasions to visit the BMC head-quarters in south Mumbai. As the seat of urban govern-ance for the Mumbai metropolitan region, the municipal HQ had long discouraged the average citizen from casual visitation. A man had truly to be in desperate need to enter the Byzantine administrative swamp that resided within the century-old neo-Gothic edifice.

As he weaved his way across the crowded square from the CST train station, blasted from all directions by a frenzy of rabid horns – this was, after all, one of the most congested junctions in the city – he craned his neck upwards to take in the building's magnificent façade.

With its cusped windows, dominating arches and lion-headed gargoyles, the place gave off a distinctly colonial air: the British had built it as a definitive marker of author-ity; now it had become simply another facet of the city's architectural heritage, a proud symbol of India's commit-ment to self-rule.

The area around the building had once been called Gallows Tank. It was here that criminals convicted by the Portuguese founders of the city had been publicly hanged, left to swing in the street, covered in cow dung and egg shells, as an example to others.

Inside the main doors, Rangwalla was confronted by a sweeping stone staircase rising out of a softly lit central hall. As he made his way up to the Citizen Facilitation Centre he couldn't help but notice how the much vaunted renovation had transformed the place since the last time he had set foot here, over a decade earlier. Gone were the rickety old benches, clunky steel cupboards and creaky ceiling fans. In their stead were plush couches, air-conditioning and chandeliers. Lovingly restored Minton tiles, stained-glass windows and buffed Burma teak roof arches added to the newfound grandeur of the place.

At the citizen's centre, he found his onward progress halted by a queue. He took a ticket and sat down to wait.

It was an hour later that he was finally able to present his request to the pleasant-looking woman behind the counter. As he explained what he was after, the woman looked him up and down, and then down and up, as if he had demanded from her an answer to the very meaning of life. Finally, she asked him to wait, then scuttled off to fetch someone who might be able to make something of his unusual query.

Another hour passed, and then, just as Rangwalla was drifting off to sleep on the comfortable couch on which he had ensconced himself, a short, grey-haired man sporting bottle-bottom glasses and dressed in the national uniform of the Indian bureaucratic flunky – untucked white shirt and dark trousers – tapped him on the shoulder. 'Please come with me.'

Rangwalla followed the fellow to an office.

Once they were both seated, the man fixed him with a wobbly look through his glasses. 'My name is K.D. Soman. I am a senior administrator here at the BMC. You have requested information about a matter that we have marked as closed. Can you tell me what this is about?'

Rangwalla hesitated, wondering how much it was prudent for him to reveal. After all, if Hasan Gafoor was correct, BMC officials may well have been involved in the sordid attempt to strong-arm the textile factory owner.

Eventually, he decided that he would have to take a leap of faith. Without Soman's help, he was at a dead-end.

Quickly, he explained the situation that had brought him to the bureaucrat's desk.

The man picked up a pen and absentmindedly tapped on a small bronze of the god Krishna. His expression had compacted into one of concern. 'This is most irregular,' he said. 'We have a complaints division to investigate precisely this sort of matter.'

'You know as well as I do that that could take months,' said Rangwalla. He did not bother to add that there were documented cases of complaints made against the city's civic authority that had taken so long to resolve that the complainant had, literally, died of old age. Instead, he nodded at the picture on Soman's desk of a young man who, from the facial resemblance, he presumed was his son. 'I see that you are a father. The man who hired me lost a daughter in that building. Can you imagine if such a thing happened to you?'

'That is unfair,' said Soman. His eyes involuntarily went to the photograph, a face that only a father could love. He sighed. 'Do you know what it takes to run a city like Mumbai? It is akin to spinning a million plates in the air at the same time. If you upset the balance, everything could come crashing down.' He sighed again. 'But neither can we function if there is grit in the engine of governance. Let me see what I can find.'

GINWALA TAKES A STAND

On his second visit to Doongerwadi in the space of three days Chopra was let in, this time through the main, western gate, by Ramin Bulsara. Anosh Ginwala's deputy in the community of corpse-bearers was a plump man with sloppy white whiskers that seemed to have washed up on his face like debris on the tide.

Bulsara led Chopra to a rundown collection of brick houses – little more than hovels – a hundred yards from the gate, hidden from inconvenient eyes by a screen of fig trees. In the dusty courtyard between the homes, Chopra found a gang of red-hatted corpse-bearers sitting on frayed char-poys, chatting, smoking and watching a soap opera on a small TV set. Children ran around them, and women called occasionally from inside one of the shabby homes.

Chopra paused. An idea had occurred to him.

He hovered by the men, Ganesha eliciting curious glances, then sat down beside them and began to gently probe them for information. He discovered that they were only too happy to talk. Like Ginwala they had a bellyful of complaints about their circumstances. He gradually steered the topic around to the night of Cyrus's death. The men became more animated, each attempting to outdo the other in their supposed revelations about the affair. Chopra casually asked them about Ginwala discovering the corpse, his hatred of Cyrus. This set off another round of animated gossip. Even Bulsara became vocal. Chopra got the impression that there was little love lost between the deputy and his senior.

By the time he moved on, he had a wealth of new information. His next task would be to sort out the truth from the hyperbole.

He was led by Bulsara along a dirt path to another rundown dwelling set apart from the main group. Bulsara waved at the squat little home. 'He is in there,' he muttered. 'Don't ask me to go in with you. He is not in a good mood.'

He scuttled off the way he had come.

Chopra knocked on the open doorway, then ducked inside.

Here he discovered a red-eyed Ginwala chopping up a chicken with a cleaver, hacking at the denuded bird with repeated blows.

There was something hypnotic about the act, and for a moment Chopra simply watched.

Finally, Ginwala sensed his presence. He froze momentarily in shock, the cleaver raised above his shoulder, then lowered it, and fixed him with a sour look.

Behind Chopra, Ganesha poked his head in the doorway, decided that the two-roomed dwelling was too small and grim for his liking, and shuffled back out into the dirt path.

'The last time we spoke you were less than truthful with me,' began Chopra.

Ginwala's sullen expression did not change.

By way of reply he fished a packet of cigarettes from his pocket and lit one. A halo of acrid smoke mushroomed around his head.

'You harboured a grudge against Cyrus Zorabian. He had treated you badly, you and your fellow corpse-bearers. Refusing your demands for a pay rise, for better working conditions. He was a poor employer, and you had had enough.'

Ginwala continued to stare at him.

'I spoke to the others. They told me that your wife left you just over three months ago, soon after Cyrus last refused your demands. Just before he died, in fact. She had had enough. By your own admission her life as a corpse-bearer's wife was a difficult one. Now it was also financially untenable. She took your son with her. Your friends say you blamed him for your misfortune. Hours later, he was murdered.'

Ginwala's expression had frozen.

'Where were you that night?'

Still Ginwala said nothing. Smoke continued to rise from the cigarette burning between his fingers, making slow swirls about his writhing jaw.

Chopra waited, allowing the silence to spin itself out. Usually this well-worn tactic would be enough, but Ginwala was a man of unusual restraint. He decided to try a different tack.

'And now I discover that someone has poisoned one of the vultures here. Your colleagues tell me that this is not an isolated incident. There's been a spate of dead vultures recently.'

Finally, Ginwala blinked. 'Are you accusing *me*?'

'Are you denying it?'

'Have you lost your mind? Why would I harm the vultures? They are holy animals. Besides, without them our work becomes infinitely more unpleasant than it already is.'

'Perhaps that was the point. You knew that Cyrus was facing increasing opposition from those wishing to shut down Doongerwadi. Without the vultures, the situation would have dramatically worsened. It would have placed pressure on him to improve your circumstances. After all, with no vultures, he would need to rely ever more on you and your men to dispose of the bodies.'

Ginwala ground out the cigarette on his chopping board. 'You can bark all you wish, Chopra. But I do not answer to you. Cyrus Zorabian was an arrogant, cruel man. He had all the wealth in the world, yet his heart was empty of the smallest charitable impulse. We were nothing to him; our lives were nothing to him. They say that every man earns his own fate. Cyrus more than earned his.'

Chopra mentally contrasted Ginwala's depiction of Cyrus with the impression Geeta Lokhani had painted of a man hell-bent on philanthropic works. 'Where were you that night?' he repeated.

Ginwala stared at him. 'I was sick. In bed, all night. I could barely move.'

'Did you call a doctor?'

Ginwala laughed. 'You think we can afford doctors, even if they were willing to come out here?'

'Who can testify to your illness?'

'No one has to. It is the truth.' He shifted on his feet. 'You are a dog chasing shadows, Chopra. And I have nothing more to say to you. Get out of my home.'

Chopra realised that he was not going to get any further with the obstinate corpse-bearer. He had no direct proof that Ginwala had poisoned the vultures at Doongerwadi, and even less evidence of his hand in Cyrus's murder. Yet there was little doubt that Anosh Ginwala had had the means, the motive and, quite possibly, the opportunity.

He walked back to the other huts, found Bulsara. 'Ginwala says he was ill on the night Cyrus died. Can anyone verify that?'

Bulsara frowned. 'I don't know about ill, but he was definitely in his hut that night. I went there in the evening, then again later, around eleven. I wanted to plan out the next day's corpse cleansing – a number of bodies had come in late that day. He was in his bed both times, dead to the world. So, yes, he could have been ill. Or, more likely, flattened by booze. He doesn't like anyone to know that, of course. Our patrons wouldn't be impressed if they discovered the head khandia was a drunk.'

Chopra sensed Bulsara's naked ambition. Nevertheless, his testimony meant that Ginwala could not have murdered Cyrus. Cyrus had been killed almost a mile away on the far side of Doongerwadi. Bulsara's account placed Ginwala in his hut during the time of the murder, dead to the world, drunk or ill. Either way, it was highly unlikely that he could have risen from his charpoy and stumbled through the forest to commit murder.

His phone rang in his trouser pocket. He fished it out, then stepped away from Bulsara.

'The thing about a good steak, Chopra, is that it needs to be eaten at exactly the right time. Eat it too soon and it's not rested enough. Leave it too long and it becomes cold cuts.'

'Please tell me that you did not call me simply to advise me on the qualities of a good steak.'

'Just wanted you to be aware of the sacrifices I make for you,' said Max Bomberton. 'Here I am, sitting down to dinner in a lovely little restaurant just off Parliament Square, the sort of steak you'd sell your grandmother for, and guess who should call?'

'I cannot guess,' said Chopra. 'Nor do I wish to.'

'All right then, let me tell you. Detective Superintendent Todd Wilson. Of the Avon and Somerset Police. The Avon and Somerset Police, in case you didn't know – and I am pretty sure you didn't – is where Yeovil is located. Do you know what DS Wilson had to tell me?'

'No,' said Chopra. 'I do not. If I did I would be a mind reader. Which I am not.'

'Someone's in a foul mood,' observed Bomberton. 'I had phoned up Wilson and put him on the task of digging up what he could about your man Buckley. He was only too glad to help. It's not every day a cop in his shoes gets tapped up by a big cheese from the Met Police.'

'By "big cheese" are you perhaps referring to yourself?'

'Who else would I be referring to?'

'I have never understood this expression. Big cheese. Why "cheese"? There is nothing inherently prestigious about being a bigger cheese than another cheese. I was under the impression that the quality of a cheese is entirely dependent upon its taste.'

Bomberton was momentarily speechless. He had forgotten about Chopra's literal bent. 'I'm surprised you don't know,' he muttered. 'It actually comes from India. The word "cheez" means "thing" in Urdu. Big cheez literally meant "big thing" during the Raj. Over time it became "big cheese".' Chopra heard his old friend bellowing at a waiter. 'Anyway, you're ruining my story. Let me tell you what Wilson found out. It appears that this Buckley was born in Yeovil and grew up there. Only he wasn't born Buckley. He was born as one Adam Beresford. We identified him from his birth date and his photo.'

'Why did he change his name?' asked Chopra.

'I was getting to that,' said Bomberton irritably. 'It seems that young Beresford was a troubled young man. Lost his parents when he was eight. Grew up in a foster home. In and out of young offenders' institutions. Shoplifting, petty thuggery. Eventually graduated to the big top. Car-jacking, burglary, fraud. He served a five-year stretch in his twenties for violent assault – the fact that he had a record made it easier to find him. And then he vanished.'

'Vanished?' echoed Chopra.

'Pfft. Into thin air. Blew his parole, never came back. I guess he decided to relocate. Probably also when he changed his name. Fresh start and all that. I'd like to believe he wanted to turn over a new leaf, didn't need his old life trailing after him . . . but I don't.'

'You are assuming he simply fled to continue a life of crime elsewhere. But if he had indeed wished to start again, unencumbered by his past, then why abscond? Why not complete his parole?'

'Who knows? Maybe he couldn't be bothered to wait. Or, like I said, maybe he wanted the fresh start, but not a new life. Probably been up to no good ever since he left the UK.'

'How did he end up in India?'

'I have no idea. He left England twenty years ago. He's had plenty of time to get around.'

'Did you get in touch with his previous employer? Peter Brewer?'

'Yes. And what a surly old bastard he turned out to be. I had to practically threaten the information out of him. He told me Buckley had been a model employee. Said he'd just walked into his office one day, following an ad he'd put out, and asked for the job. Brewer couldn't believe his luck. He was working on a big Indian contract, but didn't really like it out there. Couldn't get a grip on the native way of thinking – can't imagine why. Then along comes Buckley. A fellow Englishman, speaks the lingo, a dab hand at the admin. An absolute godsend.'

'Buckley speaks Hindi?'

'Better than speaks it. Reads it, writes it. By all accounts, the man was the perfect PA. No wonder your Zorabian chap kept him on the payroll all those years.'

'Did Brewer say where Buckley came from? Prior to working for him?'

'He did, but not until he'd given me an ear-bashing. He'd kept all his old paperwork from his India years, just in case of any tax issues. Dug up Buckley's original job application. There're a few previous employers on there. I'll scan it over to you.'

'Thank you, my friend. You have been most helpful.'

Rangwalla checked his watch. He'd passed an hour in the BMC office of K.D. Soman, waiting for the man to return with information about the municipal authority's involvement in the Gafoor case. His stomach gave an ominous rumble. He clamped down on his incipient hunger just as Soman returned with a stack of manila folders and computer printouts.

He sat down, then, licking his thumb and forefinger, began flicking through the paperwork. 'In the year that Gafoor's building collapsed, the BMC listed more than six hundred premises as unsafe. We categorise such buildings according to how badly their structural integrity has been compromised – which also reflects how much of a danger they represent to their occupants – labelling them C1, C2, or C3, with C1 being the most dilapidated, and deemed beyond repair.' He handed a sheaf of papers to Rangwalla. 'Here is the first structural audit report submitted for Gafoor's building – this was just over three years ago. As you can see it was graded as a C2. Ten months later, a second structural survey upgraded it to C1.'

'Gafoor claims that no such surveys took place. He remembers BMC officials coming to the building, but they were not there long enough to carry out an official inspection.'

'That is not what this report says. It was signed off by our technical committee.'

'We both know that signatures have a habit of appearing on official documents even when they have no right to be there.'

Soman bucked his head, as if offended at the suggestion. But his anger dissipated as quickly as it had arrived. He sighed. 'Of course, you are correct. The BMC wields incredible power. And power corrupts. Despite our best efforts, there are still unscrupulous individuals in our civic administration. They work hand in glove with surveyors, structural engineers, property developers and even the police, to turn a blind eye. After all, how often does a building collapse? How often is someone convicted, even if it does? When the odds are stacked in your favour, there will always be those willing to roll the dice.'

'Well, this building *did* collapse, and Gafoor *was* convicted.'

'Yet you are convinced of his innocence.'

Rangwalla hesitated. It was one of those questions that demanded an examination of one's own convictions. He realised that he trusted Prem Kohli's belief in Gafoor's innocence. What's more, to his own surprise, he understood that his own conscience had delivered its verdict after visiting the man in prison. 'I am,' he said.

Soman dug back into the papers before him. 'Following his conviction, the plot that the building was on was possessed by the BMC, by order of our technical committee.'

'How is that even legal?'

'I assure you it is very much legal, though it is not something that happens often. In the case of this particular property, it was possessed under the law of "eminent domain". This allows the state or federal government to forcibly acquire private land when the public good is considered pre-eminent. It was this same doctrine that was used during land reform following Independence, when land was taken from the old nawabs, princes and feudal landlords to redistribute as shareholdings to the rural classes.'

'But Gafoor's plot is being used to build private apartments,' said Rangwalla, his brow furrowing in confusion. 'Surely that cannot be classified as a public service.'

'You are correct. But if you look here' – he held out a further set of papers – 'you will see that the plot was possessed with the stated intention of building a government-funded cancer hospice. However, a short while later, following a new land-use survey, it was deemed that the location was unsuitable for such a facility, and so the usage categorisation reverted back to "private development". That was when it was sold off at auction.'

Rangwalla sat back and considered the chain of events that had overtaken Hasan Gafoor.

First, he had been approached by unnamed parties to sell his property. When he refused, BMC inspectors had visited, purportedly to survey his building, subsequently declaring it unsafe – at least on paper. When he continued to refuse to sell, the BMC had reclassified his building as so dilapidated that it would have to be condemned. Even this did not convince Gafoor to cave in. Shortly afterwards, a fire – caused by a suspicious gas cylinder explosion – had brought the building down, killing over a dozen people. Gafoor, who had been there that day and witnessed the explosion, believed that the official explanation was a lie. Nevertheless, he had been arrested, tried for negligence, and sentenced to a lengthy jail term. In the meantime, the plot on which his building had once stood had been possessed by the city's municipal council, on the grounds that it would be used for the 'public good'.

But this too had proven to be a lie of convenience.

Once the BMC had legal possession of the land, a reversal had quietly been put into effect, and the plot once again made available for private development. It had subsequently been sold off at auction.

What had Chopra said? Follow the money.

'May I have a copy of these documents?'

Soman hesitated. His eyes wobbled behind his glasses, two fish swimming manically around a bowl. 'Legally, there is nothing here that can be challenged. There is a full and proper paper trail; everything has been carefully documented.'

'But we both know that something stinks,' responded Rangwalla. 'You seem like an honest man. You could have chosen not to help me. But you did. My guess is that you have seen too much of this sort of thing. You can live with corruption for only so long before it begins to seep into your soul. A friend of mine says there comes a point in every man's life where he must decide his own legacy. What will yours be, Soman?'

K.D. Soman seemed to consider Rangwalla's words. It was obvious that his sentiments had struck a chord with the municipal bureaucrat.

Finally, he spoke: ' "It is the duty of all leaders of men, whatever their persuasion or party, to safeguard the dignity of India. That dignity cannot be saved if misgovernment and corruption flourish. Misgovernment and corruption always go hand in hand." Do you know who said that?'

Rangwalla shook his head.

'It was Gandhi. He wrote those words in 1947, just after Partition. He knew, even then, that in this new country of ours there would be those who placed themselves first, their nation second, their fellow countrymen last.' He waved at the paperwork before him. 'Take it. Take it all. If you can use it to root out those who do not deserve to serve this great city, then I am content.'

'Thank you,' said Rangwalla. 'And your words, Gandhi's words? I know a man who would appreciate them dearly.'

'We are custodians, Rangwalla, mere custodians. The only real legacy we can pass on to our children is our integrity. They are the ones we must face one day, when they come of age. What will I say to my son then? What will you say to yours?' He gestured at the edifice around him. 'I am not the only honest man here. I am not the only one who cares.'

'I do not doubt it,' said Rangwalla.

The crows had gathered in force. They were lined up on the crumbling roof of St Angelo's Church in Marol, and weighed down the branches of a banyan tree on the edge of the plot. There was a sense of predatory anticipation to them that reminded Chopra of the vultures he had seen in the Towers of Silence. A gaggle of curious langurs had joined the fray, fighting for space on the tree's lower branches. An elderly, white-cassocked priest watched the audience of crows and monkeys with trepidation.

'It's a nice night for digging up bodies,' remarked Homi Contractor beside him.

Chopra's response was to scowl. Ever since Homi had called with the news that he had successfully negotiated the paperwork needed for the exhumations, the pathologist had been insufferable, exhibiting what was, to Chopra's mind, an unseemly exhilaration at the prospect of disturbing the rest of the two unidentified corpses.

Homi clapped him on the shoulder. 'Cheer up! At least we're not digging up anyone you know.' He took out a tub of menthol ointment, smeared some under his nose, then held it out to his colleague. 'They're going to smell a little on the ripe side.'

Chopra ignored him and looked back at the graveyard.

The church maintained a section for unidentified burials, the final resting place for a small number of the two thousand-plus unclaimed corpses that turned up in Mumbai each year, on railway lines, in open sewers, in burned-out illegal dwellings, beneath concrete flyovers, on the edges of slums. The vast majority of those corpses ended up at one of the city's designated crematoriums, as per official state policy. A few – where it was deemed judicious by the pathologist or the police services investigating the death – were consigned to unnamed burials, ostensibly in the interests of justice.

More often than not, that justice failed to materialise.

Chopra knew that the expiry date on such inhumations was usually a decade, at which point the corpses would be dug up, incinerated and their resting places turned over to the next nameless occupant.

Two sweating gravediggers, in shorts and vests, were busily excavating twin graves, marked by simple headstones, labelled, respectively, 'Unknown Male' and 'Unknown Female', with the date of death neatly engraved below.

A crowd had gathered, as was usual in Mumbai whenever the possibility of unexpected public entertainment reared its head. Housewives, street vendors, bicycle delivery boys, homeless children, retired pensioners, pedestrians and passing rickshaw drivers, leaning out of their vehicles as traffic backed up behind them. In other countries, Chopra had learned, exhumations took place at night to avoid creating a spectacle. In Mumbai it made no difference – night or day, the crowds were the same. Helpful commentary accompanied the efforts of the two gravediggers.

'Put your back into it!'

'Swing from the hips, lad, not the shoulder.'

'They've got this all back to front. They're supposed to be putting them into the ground, not taking them out.'

A guffaw accompanied this last observation.

One of the gravediggers paused to smear a sweaty forearm over his brow. Dust tickled his nostrils and he sneezed mightily into the half-dug grave, causing the Department of Health officer standing beside Homi Contractor to shudder.

'I've sent plenty of men to their graves,' remarked Inspector Malini Sheriwal by Chopra's shoulder. 'This is the first time I've had the pleasure of welcoming someone back.'

Chopra did not appreciate the gallows humour.

At the far edge of the plot Constable Qureshi was enjoying a quiet roll-up, blowing smoke away from the direction of his senior officer and into the vicinity of Sub-Inspector Surat who was looking distinctly green around the gills.

'Never a good thing disturbing the dead,' mused Qureshi. 'You never know how they're going to take it.'

Surat said nothing.

He was, by nature, a credulous man, the result of a strict religious upbringing. The notion of disconsolate spirits floating about the graveyard, possibly holding a grudge against those who had disturbed their rest, was not one he considered conducive to his immediate wellbeing.

As the evening wore on, and darkness descended, Ganesha, sticking close to his guardian, became increasingly agitated. Long before the humans gathered beside him could detect the odour of decomposed remains, Ganesha's trunk had begun to twitch – elephants possess one of the keenest senses of smell in the animal kingdom. When the gravediggers finally hauled the two cheap wooden caskets to the surface, and crowbarred open the lids, the little elephant's ears flapped in alarm, and he turned tail and fled for the relative safety of the van.

One of the gravediggers lost his grip on the casket he was manhandling, and it hit the ground, split, and disgorged its grisly contents. Because the other end of the casket was still being held up by the second gravedigger, the cadaver sat up straight and faced its audience with a macabre parody of a smile.

A gasp of shock rose from the audience.

'Now that's not something you see every day,' murmured Qureshi.

Beside him, Sub-Inspector Surat turned away to disgorge his own grisly contents on to the road.

The putrid odour of decaying flesh floated about the plot, curdled by the heat, gradually dampening the chatter. The sense that Chopra had felt, of lives ended too soon, an affront to the natural order of the cosmos, seemed to envelop all those present. The public health officer stepped forward, fitted a mask over his face, then moved in to carry out his inspection, ticking boxes on a clipboard.

When he had finished, he ripped off the sheet, handed it to Homi, and fled.

The corpses were zipped into cadaver bags, then loaded into an ambulance.

Homi turned to the crowd. 'Show's over, folks. You have been a wonderful audience. Do come again.' He looked at Chopra. 'If you want to see what happens next, meet me at the hospital tomorrow morning at ten.'

Back at the restaurant, Chopra found himself dwelling on the bodies. He had decided to eat a late meal in the court-yard. Poppy and Irfan had joined him; Ganesha had trotted over to poke at Irfan under the table. Chopra had spent some time kicking a ball around with the pair of them, an activity his young ward was usually keen on. It seemed to have helped bring Ganesha out of himself, at any rate. Now, as he observed them, the chirp of crickets floating on the warm night breeze, the closeness of his family seemed a thing never to be taken for granted. Life was fleeting, and full of unexpected turns. The two bodies they had exhumed, presumably, also had families, loved ones. Where were they now? Waiting for news, perhaps resigned to the worst.

'Whatever it is, it can wait till tomorrow. This chilli lamb won't.'

He looked up at Poppy, who was watching him with concern. Once again, he felt a sense of pride. It was his good fortune indeed to find a life partner who shared his own ideals, and was willing to fight for them, in small and big ways. 'I was just thinking about the bodies.'

'I know,' said Poppy. 'But now is not the time.'

'Is there a good time to think of lives lost needlessly?'

She realised he was speaking to himself, and did not answer.

He reflected once again on the inequalities that plagued this great city. On one side Poppy was fighting to bring basic rights to the poorest members of society; on the other, he was struggling to unravel the murder of a privileged man who had probably taken advantage of those same people. A man who may have been involved in the death of two unknown victims. And, perhaps, *that*, more than anything, powered his desire to uncover their identities and their fate. In some way the resolution of one investigation might balance out his participation in the other. There was no rulebook to his chosen profession. Justice was a concept you couldn't measure or hold in your hands. But you knew it by its absence, and you knew it when you had scaled the mountain and saw the world for what it was.

BRINGING BACK THE DEAD

At precisely ten the next morning Chopra and Inspector Malini Sheriwal entered the autopsy suite at the Sahar Hospital.

The corpses had been divested of their cadaver bags and laid out on the room's two steel autopsy tables. Homi had pulled on scrubs and was fiddling with his recording equipment.

Chopra and Sheriwal watched him from an anteroom adjoining the suite, peering in through a Plexiglas viewing window as he prepared to get down to work. Homi's voice filtered nasally through a speaker located beside the window.

Homi had been joined in the suite by an Australian forensic anthropologist, a white man by the name of Decker Coin.

Coin was the first Australian Chopra had met in the flesh, though he had seen plenty onscreen, and a few hurling themselves around the Wankhede Stadium when the

Australian cricket team toured India. Coin did not fit the mould of the average Aussie that Chopra had discovered lodged unwittingly inside his head. There was no mop of bleach-blond hair, no rugged chin, no flinty eyes squinting into the horizon. Coin was a small man with an abnormally large and preternaturally bald head. This bowling ball of a pate reminded Chopra of volcanic protrusions; it was a fiery red in colour as if the superheated mind within had literally boiled the hair from Coin's skull. He wore yellow-framed glasses, a red polka-dot bow tie and braces, as if he had just come from the stock exchange. The only thing Australian about Coin was his strong Tasmanian accent, and the 'CUDDLY KOALA? THINK AGAIN' badge pinned to his shirt. Chopra peered closer. Under the badge's bold header, in smaller script, were the words: *Koalas are nasty, aggressive and spread chlamydia.*

The anthropologist had flown in from New Delhi that morning.

Homi, in his search for expert advice, had alighted on Coin's profile, and then, to his delight, discovered that he was already in India for a research meeting at the Jawaharlal Nehru University.

The pair chatted for a while, before Homi signalled to his assistant, Rohit, who had been roped into manning the video camera, and was slumped behind it in his bottle-green scrubs like the eternal bridesmaid.

Homi swivelled to face the camera, coughed ostentatiously, and began: 'My name is Dr Homi Contractor, Chair of the College of Cardiac Physicians and Surgeons of Mumbai. I am joined at the Sahar Hospital in Mumbai by

Dr Decker Coin, Head of the Forensic Anthropology Research Group at Griffith University in Australia. Dr Coin is a recognised expert in the identification of human remains and has worked extensively with the Australian Defence Force to identify recovered servicemen. Dr Coin will assist me as I attempt to use a technique known as forensic facial reconstruction in order to aid in the identification of these two cadavers' – he waved at the autopsy tables – 'Unnamed Male 1 and Unnamed Female 1. This will be the first time such a technique has been employed in India. The bodies have been interred for a period of less than ninety days, but, due to the ambient environment, and the poor construction of the burial caskets – both of which appear to have been breached by micro-organisms – we find them in a relatively advanced state of decomposition. The victims died from close-range gunshot wounds to the head, and their bodies were subsequently immolated using a high-temperature accelerant. No identifying artefacts were discovered on the cadavers, or at the scene. At the request of the Brihanmumbai police service the bodies have been exhumed in order to apply this technique to their identification. I will now ask Dr Coin to explain the process.'

Coin's voice sailed forth authoritatively. 'Forensic facial reconstruction is the process of recreating the face of an individual from their skeletal remains through an amalgamation of forensic science, anthropology, anatomical sciences and artistry. The process is somewhat controversial because it does not uphold the usual standards of legal admissibility for expert witness testimony. The subjectivity involved in the method means that reconstructions of the same set of remains by different forensic experts vary. Nevertheless, the technique has gained significant traction in the past few years as the methodological underpinnings of the process continue to be advanced.'

'What language is he speaking?' muttered Sheriwal. 'These academic types love the sound of their own voices. I wonder if a well-placed bullet in the foot would speed him along.'

Chopra gave her a sideways look.

'It was a joke,' she said, with a fleshless grin.

Coin continued with his explanation. 'In this instance the sex, age and race of the individuals have already been ascertained through traditional forensic anthropological techniques, permitting us to utilise the three-dimensional clay reconstruction method popularised by Taylor and Angel.' He turned to the bodies and pointed at the two gooey skulls. 'As we can see, both these cadavers display extensive remnants of soft tissue. This allows us to estimate tissue thickness when reconstructing the facial features. Our first step will be to take a complete set of digital images of the facial skeleton.'

Coin excavated an expensive-looking camera from his bag, and connected it to a laptop. He fiddled with the computer, then took the camera and began moving around the two corpses, requesting Homi to manipulate the skulls so that he could photograph them from all angles. The software on the laptop converted the images into a complete 3D rendering of the skulls. 'The next step is to clean the skulls, and examine them,' continued the Australian.

Homi bent to the gruesome task of detaching the two skulls from their cadavers.

Then, together, using jet scalpels, bone brushes and a chemical bath, they removed the remaining putrefied skin and soft tissue from the twin craniums, revealing the clean white bone beneath.

Homi pointed each skull at the camera. 'Note the extensive damage caused by the gunshot wounds. In both instances the victims were shot at close range in the back of the head. In the case of Unnamed Male 1, the bullet entered through the occipital bone, and exited through the right eye socket. In the case of Unnamed Female 1, the bullet entered through the parietal bone and exited through the frontal bone.'

Chopra shivered.

He understood that Homi was a professional, and had carried out more autopsies than Chopra could imagine, yet the dispassionate manner with which he catalogued the death of these two individuals bothered him. Somehow, he felt the occasion deserved more, a sense of empathy that was missing from the cold scientific analysis.

Next Coin carried out a detailed naked-eye examination of the skulls, explaining that he was looking for bony pathologies, unusual landmarks, and wear of the occlusal surfaces. Any one of these features would have an effect on the shape and contours of the individual's face. He then took another complete set of 3D photographs of the naked skulls.

The next step was to prep the skulls for a plaster cast.

With Coin showing Homi the way, the two men repaired the damage to the skulls caused by the bullets, using sealing wax and modelling clay. Coin removed a jar from his bag, from which he took out two sets of prosthetic eyes. These he set, with great care, into the eye sockets of the skulls.

'Not bad,' he remarked. He turned to Homi. 'Now for the cast.'

The next hour was spent in the creation of the casts, first creating a mould of each, and then a cast from the moulds. Chopra sensed Sheriwal's growing impatience. The woman kept checking her watch, and stepped out a couple of times to make calls on her phone.

'You do not have to be here,' he said.

She gave him a cold look. 'This is *my* case.'

When the casts were done, Coin turned to the camera once more. 'Now we must wait for the casts to set. We will then use them to model the facial features of the specimens.'

Homi patted his colleague on the back, grinned at the camera, then stepped out of the autopsy suite. 'Why don't you two come back later this afternoon, around five, say? I have invited a forensic artist from Germany to help with the reconstruction. Her flight will be landing in a few hours. We should have something for you by the end of the day.' He was about to duck back into the suite, but stopped by the door. 'By the way, something just floated up in my memory. This whole Zorabian thing. Did you know that they tried to get rid of him last year?'

'Get rid of him?' said Chopra. 'What do you mean?'

'The Vulture Club. There was a vote of no confidence carried out by the club's managing committee. Apparently they were trying to oust Cyrus. They didn't succeed, but I thought it was worth you knowing. Caused a big stink in Parsee circles. We had a good laugh over at the Cyclists Club, I can tell you.'

Aside from being one of the city's top medical practitioners, Homi was also on the board of the city's other big Parsee association, the Cyclists Club. There was little love lost between the two outfits, stemming back to a perceived slight when, decades earlier, the Vulture Club members, attending a dinner at the Cyclists, had cast aspersions upon the dhansak recipe served by their rivals. The Dhansak Cold War, as it became known, had rumbled on for longer than anyone cared to remember, with no end in sight.

'Are you sure?' said Chopra. 'No one at the club mentioned this when I paid them a visit.'

Homi gave him a withering look. 'I am a pathologist. I am always sure. You can't be a little bit dead, Chopra.'

As they stepped back out into the street, Sheriwal, checking her watch, turned to the former policeman. 'I usually take lunch at this time.'

'As it happens I was headed to my restaurant,' said Chopra. 'It is nearby. Why not join me? We can carry on discussing the case.'

At the restaurant, the lunchtime service was in full flow.

Chopra scouted around for a table, but then realised that he and Sheriwal were attracting a great deal of attention. A number of junior policemen slid off their chairs and slunk out from the restaurant leaving their meals half-eaten.

Chopra suspected that their initiative in policing the restaurant – no doubt to ensure that it was not stolen in a world-first whole-eatery theft – would probably not be appreciated by their commanding officer.

He led Sheriwal into his office, then rang for the chef.

Lucknowwallah turned up red-faced from the service. 'Ah, Chopra. What brings you back at lunchtime?'

'This is a colleague. Inspector Malini Sheriwal. We are working together on a case.'

'Nothing like a duet!' said the chef, who seemed to be in unnaturally high spirits. Either that, thought Chopra, or the man was unnaturally high *on* spirits. He knew the chef had a weakness for good whisky.

'We would like to order some lunch. Could you also make sure that Ganesha is fed?'

'Your dish is my command,' said Lucknowwallah, with a wink.

In short order, menus were presented and food ordered. Chopra was intrigued to discover that Sheriwal was a vegetarian. The fact shouldn't have surprised him. India had more vegetarians than the rest of the world put together. But there was something about Sheriwal's aggressive reputation that made him feel that the woman ought to be a carnivore.

Once the waiter had left, Chopra asked, 'How are things at the station?'

Sheriwal shrugged. 'I don't know how you did it for so long. No offence, but it is hardly the most exciting posting in the service.'

'We are there to resolve problems, to uphold the rule of law,' bristled Chopra. 'Excitement was never a factor.'

Sheriwal snorted. 'Spoken like a true idealist.'

'What about you?' said Chopra. 'Do you really think that charging around as "Shoot'em Up Sheriwal" made a difference?'

'I always disliked that name.' The policewoman scowled. 'I did what I did because it had to be done. The underworld had become a cancer in our city. It was the only way to treat the problem.'

'What about due process?'

Sheriwal shrugged. 'There are some who transgress so far beyond the limits that they do not deserve due process.'

'What gives *you* the right to decide?'

Another awkward silence hovered between them. Chopra searched for a less fractious topic. He had never been good at small talk. In such situations Poppy always asked after family. Yes. That was what was needed here: a subtle conversational gambit. 'You are divorced, aren't you?'

Sheriwal glared at him. Finally, she spoke. 'Yes. My husband was a scoundrel.'

'Relationships can be complicated,' stuttered Chopra, reaching for the nearest available cliché.

'I have found that when you have a gun in your hand they can quickly become very uncomplicated.'

Another silence. 'Do you have children?'

'I have a daughter. But she lives with my ex-husband. In Pune. I rarely see her.' Sheriwal picked up a marble figurine of an elephant trapped inside a trelliswork Taj Mahal, spun it around with her long fingers. 'What about you? Do you and, ah, Poppy, wasn't it, have children?'

'No. We were unable to.'

'That is unfortunate. And now you have an elephant.'

Chopra wondered if the woman was making fun of him. It was hard to tell. Malini Sheriwal was possibly the only person he had ever met with less of an ear for social niceties than himself.

'The elephant was bequeathed to me. I am his guardian. I do not take such a responsibility lightly.' He realised that he sounded pompous, but Sheriwal's condescending manner had riled him.

'Ah, yes. Myself, I have always thought a little responsibility can go a long way. Like pickle. Besides, if you begin to take things too personally it dulls your objectivity.'

'I have always thought the opposite,' said Chopra, feeling his cheeks flush. 'For me, each and every case is a personal matter. It is the only way we can be sure to see things through.'

'Is that why you care so much? About those two bodies?'

'If *we* don't care, who will?' It was as good an answer as he could give.

The door opened and Rangwalla walked in.

He skidded to a halt at the sight of both of his former commanding officers, staring in horrified fascination as if doubting the evidence of his own eyes. His hand twitched involuntarily as if it were contemplating saluting Sheriwal without necessarily first engaging in a discussion with his brain. A sheen of sweat broke out on his forehead as he remembered his recent hijacking of Sub-Inspector Surat's time for the purposes of his own investigation.

'Rangwalla,' began Sheriwal, 'you appear to have seen a ghost.'

Rangwalla winched his lips into a skeletal grin. 'Ah ha. Ha ha. How are you, madam?'

'What are you doing here?' asked Chopra.

The junior man turned to his boss. 'I, ah, I had a few loose ends to tie up on current investigations. Plus I obtained a mountain of paperwork from the BMC yesterday regarding the Gafoor case. I was going to go through it with a fine-tooth comb. Following the money, as you suggested. I didn't realise you had, ah, company.'

Chopra gave him a stern look. 'Sheriwal and I are attempting to identify the two burned bodies linked to the Zorabian case.'

Rangwalla's gaze dropped to the plates of food on the desk. 'Yes,' he said pointedly. 'I can see that.'

Chopra had had enough.

He reached into his pocket and took out a printout, holding it out to his deputy. 'This is a list of former employers of William Buckley, Cyrus Zorabian's PA. Buckley was once Adam Beresford – he changed his name following a prison sentence. I need you to call everyone on that list and see what else you can find out about him. Did his employers know about his criminal background? Did any incidents occur while he was employed: theft, fraud, violence, that sort of thing?'

'You think Buckley may have killed Zorabian? What was his motive?'

'I have no idea if Buckley's past is even linked to Cyrus's death. Perhaps it is exactly as it appears: Buckley wished to turn over a new leaf, so he changed his name, eradicated his past, and fled abroad.'

Rangwalla smirked. 'An emu cannot go backwards, sir.'

Chopra frowned. 'What are you talking about? What emu?'

Rangwalla's face fell. 'It is an expression I heard on the television. The emu is a flightless bird. It cannot walk backwards. What I meant was that a leopard does not change its spots.'

'Then why the hell didn't you just say so?'

Rangwalla took the paper, then practically ran from the room.

'He is a strange one,' said Sheriwal.

'But curiously effective, in his own way.'

Sheriwal rose to her feet, checking her watch again. 'I have some work back in the office.'

Chopra pushed back his chair. 'Yes. I too have some urgent business to attend to.'

'We will meet again this afternoon.'

A VOTE OF NO CONFIDENCE

There was a commotion on the busy thoroughfare outside the Vulture Club.

A youngish, dishevelled-looking man was standing on a soapbox, vehemently denouncing the government. A band of supporters were gathered before him, throwing fists into the air, banging steel drums, and generally raising a ruckus. A trio of policemen looked on somnolently, leaning against their police jeep, but made no move to interrupt proceedings.

Chopra paused for a moment to listen to the man speak. He knew that this was another of the ongoing series of protests currently convulsing the country.

Ever since India had become a republic, the country had sought to address the disadvantage suffered by the poorest elements of society by enshrining within its constitution a series of affirmative action measures for so-called 'backwards' castes and tribes. These measures 'reserved' access to seats in the various legislatures, to government jobs and to enrolment in higher educational institutions for those so categorised, in this way redressing the historic oppression, inequality and discrimination faced by such communities.

Recently, however, the debate had shifted.

With India aspiring to the status of a true meritocracy, many argued that it was time to do away with this antiquated 'reservation system', and that only talent should determine opportunities. To this end the government was considering a bill to de-list some of the 'backwards castes' qualifying for the reservation system, a development that had ignited protests around the country, such as the one Chopra was presently confronted with.

Only in India, he thought, would people fight to be labelled backwards.

He found Zubin Engineer, the club secretary, in the Vulture Club's grand hall, supervising a cleaning effort that appeared to consist of a solitary gentleman even older than Zubin pushing an enormous, industrial-strength floor polishing machine around at the general speed of continental drift. Ganesha, trotting behind Chopra, was instantly beguiled by the thunderous piece of equipment, and padded forward to investigate. The ancient cleaner leaned on the handle watching him with interest.

'You were not completely honest with me,' said Chopra, raising his voice above the din of the monstrous contraption.

Engineer blinked from behind his spectacles. 'What do you mean?'

'A year ago, the club tried to remove Cyrus from his role as chairman.'

Engineer seemed to deflate. 'Not the club,' he finally said. 'Boman.'

He led Chopra to his office, leaving Ganesha behind in the grand hall.

Once the door was closed, he hobbled to the sideboard, poured himself a whisky, then sank into a padded armchair. 'It was shortly after they had that fight in the lobby. Boman came to me and told me that he wanted the committee to declare Cyrus unfit for the post of chairman, and to elect him instead.'

'Why did he want Cyrus replaced?'

'He would not say. I suppose it was all to do with what-ever had caused them to fall out in the first place.'

'What did you say to the request?'

'What *could* I say? There has always been a Zorabian as chairman here. He was the face of the club. Besides, there was no reason to oust him.'

'What did Boman do when you refused?'

'He called an emergency meeting of the managing committee, then raised a vote of no confidence in Cyrus.'

'He could do that?'

'As a member of the committee, yes. As long as he found someone to second the motion.'

'Which I assume he did.'

'Boman has his own coterie within the club,' affirmed Engineer. 'Family friends, and those who do business with him.' He sipped his whisky. 'Not that it did him any good. The vote went Cyrus's way, by a large margin. Boman thundered out of here in a rage, vowing to get even.'

'And you did not feel that the authorities should be informed of this?'

'Boman is a hothead, but he is no killer. Besides, as I told you before, we prefer not to air our dirty laundry in public.'

Chopra absorbed this. 'Who is the club's current chairman?'

'I thought you knew,' said Engineer. 'Perizaad, though technically I suppose she is a chair*woman*, the first we have ever had. When her father passed, I asked her – on behalf of the committee – to take on the role. She accepted.'

Chopra considered this fact, wondering why Perizaad had not mentioned it. But then, why would she? It was hardly pertinent to her father's death. He tacked in another direction. 'What do you think of William Buckley?'

Engineer's brow puckered. 'Cyrus's PA? He is a very competent man. Very organised.'

'Did you know that he is a convicted criminal? Did Cyrus know?'

Engineer's eyes wobbled behind his spectacles. 'Surely not!'

'It was a long time ago.'

'If Cyrus knew, he never mentioned it.' Engineer leaned forward. 'You think Buckley could have wished Cyrus harm? Why? Cyrus always spoke highly of him.'

'I don't know.' Chopra took out the Latin letters, with the sheet of translations, and showed them to Engineer. 'Cyrus received these before his death. Did he mention them to you?'

Engineer examined the letters and the translations, then shook his head. 'No. What do they mean?'

'I'm not sure.'

Chopra now took out the architectural plans he had found inside Cyrus's bank locker. He spread them before the club secretary. 'Cyrus was involved in raising finance for this development in Vashi. Did he discuss it with you?'

'No. But Cyrus was involved in so many things. As I told you, he was the head of our philanthropy programme.'

'What if this wasn't about philanthropy?'

'What do you mean?'

Chopra hesitated. The notion that he wished to express had been slowly forming. The discovery of the architectural plans, and the cash, coupled with the fact of Cyrus's dire financial circumstances, had led him to speculate on a possible motive for the Parsee mogul's murder.

'What if Cyrus was not involved purely as a benefactor? What if he was using his position at the club to generate funds for the development in order to line his own pockets?'

Engineer looked aghast. The glass of whisky almost fell from his grasp. 'I do not believe it. Such a thing would go against everything the Zorabian name stands for.'

'Desperate times lead men to desperate acts,' said Chopra. 'Perizaad tells me that her father's business was ailing. He was facing bankruptcy. Perhaps he did what he thought he had to.'

Engineer shook his head. 'Cyrus, an embezzler? No. I cannot believe it.'

A few days ago, Chopra would not have believed it either. But now, he found himself increasingly plagued with doubt. He was a man ruled by his conscience. Each case he took on was weighed on the scales of that conscience. He found himself striving to solve the murder of a man who, with each passing hour, was slipping in his estimation. His thoughts drifted to the two burned bodies. If there was anything that set him apart in his own mind, it was that many in this venal city would take money to help the likes of a Zorabian, but few would exert themselves for two nameless corpses.

'It might explain the letters,' he said, returning to the moment. 'Perhaps someone found out, and was trying to obliquely warn him, encourage him to desist. Or, alternatively, it might have been someone setting the scene for a blackmail attempt.'

'Latin is common in the Parsee community,' said Engineer. 'We tend to go to the same schools, and nearly all have Latin on their curriculum. It could have been anyone.'

Chopra got to his feet. 'It's just a theory for now. There may be nothing to it.'

'What will you do next?'

'I think it would make sense for me to talk to Boman Jeejibhoy again, don't you?'

Returning to the grand hall, Chopra found Ganesha pushing the vacuum cleaner around by ducking his head and shoving it along from behind. The veteran cleaner was sitting on a chair, enjoying a cup of tea as the little elephant moved in happy circles around the room.

Chopra paused before the waxwork statue of Rustom Zorabian. He recalled the portrait of Cyrus that he had seen in the Samundra Mahal. In the right light, the two could have been twins. Rustom, with his throne-like seat, his princely clothes and mace, looked every bit as regal as Cyrus had in the portrait.

But the problem with kings was that, sooner or later, they always overreached themselves.

Which is why so few ever died in their beds.

Rangwalla poked his head around the door. The office was empty. He sagged with relief.

The thought of coming face to face with Malini Sheriwal again had been giving him palpitations. He understood, of course, that the woman no longer held any authority over him. The only problem was that Sheriwal was as unpredictable and volatile as a keg of dynamite. During the short time he had served under her at the Sahar station he had learned that the only way to avoid the woman's wrath was to stay well out of her way.

He wondered again why Chopra had brought her into his investigation. There was nothing wrong with police officers – former or otherwise – helping each other out, of course, but the least Chopra could have done was to have given him fair warning. Walking in on the woman earlier that day had almost led to an unscheduled emptying of the Rangwalla bowels.

At least they were both gone now.

Which was just as well, because he needed the office. It was the only quiet space he could find to work on the files he had obtained from the BMC. His own cramped apartment was besieged by his children, at home from school with a stomach bug.

He hauled the box of files on to the desk, then gradually placed them into neat piles, ordered by year.

He sat down, opened a large ruled notebook that he had taken from his son's schoolbag, squinted at the end of the blunt pencil he had fished from his pocket, and made a very deliberate note of the date. He studied the date, then under-lined it.

Twice.

For a brief, terrifying instant, his mind was filled with a paralysing blankness. This sort of thing was not his forte; he had always felt most comfortable discharging his duties as an officer of the law out on the streets, poking vagrants in the ribs with his nightstick, cajoling his network of street informants for gossip, occasionally sticking the boot into some wife-beating hoodlum in need of a salutary lesson. Wading through a paper trail was the sort of advanced policing that left him feeling woefully out of his depth. He understood, well enough, that this was an essential part of the process. Hadn't Chopra drilled that into him over the long years of their association? But during his time at the station there had always been someone even lower on the totem pole for him to delegate such onerous tasks to.

Dung, as they said, always rolled downhill.

Sighing, he lifted the uppermost file from the stack before him and untied the string holding it together. Inside, he found the first of the purported notices issued by the BMC to Hasan Gafoor with regard to their unfavourable assess-ment of the state of his premises.

Rangwalla's dark eyes moved along the inked paragraphs, his lips slowly forming the words.

A clock ticked unnoticed on the wall as he lost track of time, becoming engrossed in his investigation, occasionally stopping to make a belaboured scribble in his notebook.

BOMAN JEEJIBHOY
REVEALS THE TRUTH

Chopra found Boman Jeejibhoy at his boatyard.

The industrialist was in his office, a large, wood-panelled space cluttered with balsa wood models of boats of various designs. The walls were lined with framed accolades from the boatbuilding industry, and photographs of Boman with grinning celebrities inaugurating a medley of yachts and other marine-going vessels.

As Chopra entered the office, the industrialist looked up from the half-finished model of a catamaran on his desk. He unhitched the jeweller's loupe from his eye.

'What are you doing here?' he growled.

Chopra did not waste time with pleasantries. They would be wasted on a man like Boman. 'Why did you ask for a vote of no confidence in Cyrus Zorabian at the Vulture Club?'

Boman's chin sank into his chest. 'We had a difference of opinion.'

'What do you mean?'

'I thought he was a scoundrel. He did not.'

Chopra moved closer. 'It is time to tell me the truth. Sooner or later I will discover it, even if I have to speak to every Parsee in the city.'

'The truth,' spat Boman. 'What will you do with the truth? You are an outsider. You would not understand.'

'Try me.'

Boman's hard eyes glinted in the sunlight filtering in from the room's blinds. Finally, he came to a decision. 'Very well. Do you remember the last time we spoke I told you that Cyrus betrayed me?'

'You said that he had agreed to partner with you on a business venture, and then reneged.'

'What I actually said was that it was a *family* venture, and that after I put up my half of the deal, he did not fulfil his side of the bargain.'

Chopra waited. He sensed that Boman Jeejibhoy was actually looking forward to finally speaking his mind. His heartbeat quickened. Could it be a confession . . .?

'You know of course that Cyrus has a son. Darius. Well, I have a daughter of the same age. Dinaz. She is my only child, the most precious thing in the world to me. Many years ago, when Darius and Dinaz were still children, Cyrus and I agreed that they would be married. We shook hands on it. As the children grew, we encouraged their friendship. My daughter fell in love with Darius. I assumed the reverse was also true.

'Just before Darius was due to begin his year at Harvard, I spoke with Cyrus. And he spoke with his son. Cyrus

208

assured me that as soon as Darius returned, he would announce an engagement between the two. My daughter was overjoyed by the news. She was always a trusting soul.' Boman paused, his face aglow with the awful light of the past. 'When Darius came back, I held Cyrus to his word. But something had changed. My "friend" began to avoid me, to make excuses. Darius refused to see my daughter. When he finally did, I discovered what I had already begun to suspect. He no longer wished to marry her. He had found someone else. My daughter had been discarded.' The old Parsee lashed out with a huge fist, obliterating the model boat on his desk. Wooden chips exploded in all directions. 'He ruined her! Since that day, she has become a shadow of herself. My beautiful, happy, healthy child has become a recluse, wasting away in our home like a pale wraith.'

'Surely you cannot blame Cyrus for his son's decision? For that matter, how can you blame a young man for falling in love? No one can predict the vagaries of the human heart.'

'This isn't about Darius falling in love!' bayed Boman. 'This is about what is *right*. The Parsees have always kept our bloodlines pure through intermarriage. The match between Darius and Dinaz was perfect. For them, and for our dwindling community.'

'Some might argue that marrying outside the community would be a step in the right direction for the Parsees.'

'Such people do not understand us,' Boman ground out. 'Our traditions, our history. We do not tell others in this country of a million factions how they should live. We do not expect to be preached to.'

Chopra knew that this was a sore topic, and one that he had no real wish to wade into. He decided to head in another direction. He took out the clutch of Latin letters and handed them to Boman. 'Did you send these to Cyrus? Was this your way of getting him to understand that by not forcing his son into marrying your daughter he was, in some sense, letting the Parsee community down?'

Boman scanned the letters, then set them down on his desk. 'I have never seen these before. They are nothing to do with me.'

'But you read Latin?'

'So do thousands in this city. What does that prove?'

Chopra hesitated. 'Are you sure there is nothing more you wish to tell me? About the night Cyrus died? By your own admission, you have no alibi for the time that he was murdered.'

Boman rose to his feet. Anger curled from his bullish features like smoke. 'You think you can come here and sling accusations at me? Have you any idea of what I have endured because of Cyrus and his son? My daughter's life has been destroyed by the Zorabians! She will never be the same.'

'You may be surprised. People are resilient.'

Boman's eyes narrowed. 'You know nothing. Now, get out.'

Back in his van, Chopra took out his phone and dialled Darius Zorabian. It was time for another talk with him. He was surprised when a woman's voice answered.

'Who is this?' he asked.

'This is Lucy, Darius's wife. He forgot his phone this morning. Can I pass on a message?'

Chopra considered the offer. An unexpected opportunity had presented itself. 'My name is Chopra,' he said. 'I need to speak with Darius. But, perhaps, I might speak with you first, if that's OK?'

'Chopra? Are you the man investigating Cyrus's death?'

'Yes. Darius told you about me?'

'He did.' A hollow silence floated down the line. 'I – ah – yes. Why don't you come to our home?'

'When would suit you?'

'Perhaps it would be better to speak immediately. There are some questions I have for you too.'

NOT EVERY FAIRY TALE
HAS A HAPPY ENDING

Darius Zorabian's home was not quite what Chopra had expected. A shabby, twelve-storey tower in a rundown part of the mid-town Dadar district, the building, with its flaking grey walls, caged balconies, cheap advertising hoardings and thickets of snaking electrical and phone cables, looked severely ill, as if it had contracted some sort of debilitating architectural disease.

Chopra was unsurprised to discover that the solitary lift was out of order.

Indeed the 'out of order' sign itself was out of order; it was hanging loose from one side and had been spat upon repeatedly with betel-nut fluid, and possibly worse.

Chopra trudged up the stairs, passing a gang of sari-clad women on the fourth floor, each clutching a seemingly identical child to her hip. The women, chattering animatedly before his arrival, clammed shut the moment he trudged into view, then eyed him beadily until he vanished up the stairwell before resuming their heated discussion.

The Zorabians' apartment was on the tenth floor, high enough to avoid many of the smells that had assaulted Chopra on his climb. He knocked on the door, then stood back, his thoughts momentarily alighting on Ganesha, who he had left in the compound below. The elephant's spirits were much improved. Perhaps Lala had been right. Ganesha was an emotional creature and, like everyone else, entitled to good days and bad days.

After all, humans did not have a monopoly on feeling blue.

The door swung back and Chopra found himself face to face with a statuesque red-haired white woman, with green eyes and a smattering of freckles across the bridge of her nose. She wore a pair of slacks and a T-shirt imprinted with the words MINNESOTA OR BUST. The baggy garment could not hide the fact that she was heavily pregnant.

'I'm Lucy Mulvaney,' she said.

Chopra followed her into the cramped apartment. It was even smaller on the inside than he had supposed, and a great deal messier.

As if sensing his thoughts, Lucy waved apologetically at the chaos. 'Sorry about the mess. I haven't had a chance to clean up. We had to let the maid go, and . . . I just get very tired. With the pregnancy, you know?'

Chopra didn't know, but nodded sympathetically. 'When is your baby due?'

'A couple of months. I was hoping to be in a better apartment by then, but that hasn't quite worked out.'

He sensed a note of bitterness. He guessed that life in India hadn't quite turned out the way Lucy Mulvaney had anticipated. For Darius too, such reduced circumstances must have been chafing, fuelling his sense of outrage, and stoking his anger towards his father.

She gestured for him to sit on the worn two-seater sofa in the middle of the room, taking a firm-backed wooden seat opposite him. He fell into the sofa . . . and kept falling. The springs creaked exhaustedly, a death rattle that left him with his bottom scraping the floor, even as his knees swung upwards towards his ears. He felt like a praying mantis, and wondered just how he was going to get up again.

'Sorry,' apologised Lucy. 'It came with the flat. Darius said we'd replace it as soon as we could afford to, but . . .'

Chopra decided to plunge straight in. 'I understand that you and Darius met at university?'

'Yes. We were at Harvard together. I was there on a scholarship. I don't come from money like Darius. My folks are farmers; they've pretty much lived hand to mouth for as long as I can remember. One bad harvest and they'd lose everything. I suppose they hoped I'd take over one day, but I could never see myself doing that. I was always ambitious. I wanted to see the world. I guess I got my wish, much good that it did me.'

'You and Darius were on the same course?'

'No. He's a few years older than me. He was on a one-year executive MBA programme; I was an economics undergraduate, there for the long haul. I met him when an Indian friend of mine invited me to a Republic Day celebration that the Harvard Indian Society was holding. He was there dressed up as Gandhi – you know, all wrapped in a white robe with a bald wig on. And then he got on stage and started doing this ridiculous breakdance routine. I thought it was hilarious. We started chatting and hit it off. A year later, when he was finishing up his studies, he asked me to marry him. I was only twenty-two, but he was dashing, funny, exotic. You could say he swept me off my feet. I still had a year to go on my degree – and so I told him I needed time. He was a gentleman about it. Said that he would wait for me. He was as good as his word. After the year was up, he invited me to India so that he could introduce me to his family. I couldn't think of a place further from the life I'd known – and so I said yes.'

'And when you came to India did you meet his father? Cyrus?'

The smile died in her eyes. 'Only the once. Darius took me to Samundra Mahal. It was a big mistake. Darius hadn't told him about us. When he sprang it on him – the fact that we were going to be married – Cyrus went ballistic. Darius asked me to step out of the room, but I could hear them shouting through the door. When he came out again, he was as white as a sheet, practically dragged me out of his home. We stayed at a friend's house for two weeks before he found this place. His father had cut him off completely, you see. No allowance, no financial support of any kind. He gave his son an ultimatum. Ditch me, and marry the girl *he'd* chosen for him, or face being disinherited.'

'You knew that Darius was heir to the Zorabian fortune?'

'What you mean is, did I marry Darius for his money?' She waved her hands around the room. 'If I did, it hasn't exactly worked out for me, has it? Look, I'm no gold-digger, but I'd be lying if I said that Darius's wealth wasn't part of the attraction. I've always had a practical head on my shoulders. I promised myself a long time ago I wouldn't marry the first village idiot to flex his biceps at me.'

'Why did you go through with the wedding? I mean, you knew that Cyrus was going to disinherit his son if he married you.'

'I thought it was just bluster. I thought the old man would calm down once he saw that we were serious about building a life together. I guess I didn't realise just how stubborn they both were.'

'Did you know that Cyrus had all but run the Zorabian empire into the ground before his death?'

Her eyes widened. 'No. I didn't know that.'

'Darius didn't tell you?'

'He doesn't tell me much. I think he's a little disappointed that I haven't exactly taken to our reduced circumstances. Hah! I have a degree from Harvard. By rights, I should be scaling the ladder at one of the world's top companies. Instead, I'm stuck. And on top of it all, I'm about to have a child.'

'The child is an issue between you?'

Lucy rubbed her belly. 'It wasn't exactly part of the plan. I thought we were being careful; clearly not careful enough. Before you ask, yes, I thought about getting rid of it. But Darius wouldn't hear of it. Our baby became another pawn in his battle with his father. The Parsees, as you probably know, are hyper-sensitive about their low birth rate. They're always pushing each other to have kids. I saw this cartoon, once, on the wall of my gynaecologist's office. A couple of grumpy pandas in a cage. One says to the other, "So much pressure on us to breed – what do they take us for, Parsees?" ' Her lips cracked into a mirthless smile. 'I have half a mind to take the kid back to the States when it's born. But the thought of running back to my parents with my tail between my legs, back to the farm I swore I'd have nothing to do with . . .'

Chopra gave the woman a sympathetic look. 'Where is Darius? I need to talk to him.'

'He's gone to Pune for the day. To try to nail down a big contract for his solar panels. He's obsessed with those things, convinced he's going to strike it rich. He's borrowed heavily, put everything he has – *we* have – into it. If things don't turn a corner soon, we'll be out on the street. What kind of a life will that be for our child?'

Chopra sensed, finally, the deep despair sloshing around behind Lucy Mulvaney's façade of brittle cynicism. The woman was drowning; life had hit her hard, the vicissitudes of fate a rude awakening she had been wholly unprepared for.

He pushed his sympathy to one side. He had a job to do, and difficult questions to ask.

'Lucy, did Darius ever threaten his father?'

Her eyes flashed. 'What do you mean?'

'I am working on the theory that the person who murdered Cyrus was known to him, that it wasn't a random crime.'

'Surely you don't suspect Darius? I mean, I know he was angry with his father, but—'

'Just how angry was he?'

'Furious. But that doesn't make him a killer. If rage was all you needed *I'd* be on the Most Wanted list by now.'

Chopra considered this, then asked, 'Does Darius read Latin?'

'Latin? Yes. He studied it in school. He went to the same school as his father; it was a point of pride for them, the Zorabians, I mean. But what has that got to do with anything?'

Chopra dug out the letters and showed them to her, with the sheet of translations. 'Cyrus was sent these before his death.'

Lucy's brow furrowed. 'You think Darius sent these?'

'I do not know.'

She shook her head slowly. 'No. This isn't Darius's style. He's a bull in a china shop, a regular chip off the old block. When he wants to make a point, he goes charging in, all guns blazing. This is too cryptic for him.'

Chopra took the letters back. 'This is a difficult question, but on the night that Cyrus died, where was Darius? He claims that he was at home with you. At least, that's what he told the police.'

A look of surprise flashed over Mulvaney's features. 'I – ah – well, yes, of course he was.'

'Lucy,' said Chopra gently, 'I need the truth. It is important.'

'He's my *husband*. The father of my child.'

'If Darius had anything to do with his father's death – and I am not saying that he did – surely you would wish to know?'

Lucy bit her lip, her expression troubled. She rubbed her belly, unconsciously. Tears welled in her eyes.

'It's a boy,' she said. 'You know, I suggested to Darius that we name him after his father. I thought it might be a gesture, help get them talking again. Darius tore my head off. Even the idea of it sent him spinning into a rage.' Her face cracked. 'The way he looked at me. I – I never thought I'd see so much hate, such anger in him. He was such a funny, good-natured guy when we first met. Now I hardly recognise him.'

Chopra leaned forward. 'Lucy, listen to me very carefully. Providing someone with a false alibi is a criminal offence. My instincts tell me that you have not been entirely truthful. I will make you a promise. If you tell me the truth, it will remain between us, unless and until I find other evidence that Darius may have been involved in his father's death.'

Mulvaney shuddered, and then, to his shock, collapsed in on herself, burying her head in her hands. He sat back, watching as her body heaved with sobs. A dam had burst, and he sensed that Lucy Mulvaney had finally reached a crossroads.

Eventually, she brought herself under control, and looked at him, her face scarlet with tears. 'You promise me that this will stay between us?'

'You have my word. Anything you tell me will be used only to see justice done. I am not Darius's enemy.'

She wiped a sleeve across her face. 'All I can tell you is that he *was* with me that evening, at the beginning, at least. Then I fell asleep – I was tired; I'd had a prenatal appointment earlier in the day – but he stayed up to watch TV. It was the sound of the TV that woke me a few hours later. Darius wasn't in the living room, though the TV was still on. I didn't think anything of it. He often goes out for a walk late in the evening. He's never been a good sleeper. I went back to bed, and the next morning he was right there beside me.'

'What time did the TV wake you?'

She shrugged. 'Around half nine.'

Chopra pushed himself to his feet. 'Thank you. I know this hasn't been easy.'

'Look, whatever else my husband is, he's no killer.'

'I pray that you are right,' said Chopra. 'For the sake of your unborn child.'

On the way back down to his van, Chopra reflected that Darius Zorabian had now leapt to the top of his list of suspects. Disinherited, desperate, angry and with no alibi. The man was a walking time bomb; had that bomb exploded on the night of his father's death?

DEAD MEN *CAN* TELL TALES

Chopra arrived back at the autopsy suite at the Sahar Hospital at five. He found Homi in his office deep in conversation with Dr Coin and the German forensic artist he had invited to help with the reconstruction, a large woman with square-framed glasses, close-cropped hair and an austere expression that Chopra found a trifle condescending. His impression was reinforced when the woman stood to introduce herself. 'My name is Klara Bekker,' she said, in a clipped, heavily accented tone. 'I am one of the world's foremost experts in this field.'

'That is good to know,' said Chopra, glancing at Homi. Clearly, the woman had as much use for modesty as his friend.

'The gang's all here,' said Homi, clapping his hands briskly. 'Let's get this show on the road.'

They made their way to the autopsy suite, ploughing through the crowded hospital corridors.

Back outside the suite, Chopra saw, through the viewing window, that the bodies had been returned to cold storage;

the two white plaster casts stood on their pedestals, ghost-like in the room's dimmed lighting.

'Ah, the patients are ready,' said Bekker, with a grim smile. She pulled on latex gloves, snapped the edges. 'And Gott said: let there be light!'

Homi hurried to the socket panel, and wrenched the switch, so that the room was bathed in its usual bright white light.

'Yes, yes, come to me, *meine Lieblinge*.' Bekker advanced on the casts, a dreamy look overtaking her blunt features. 'I shall raise you from the dead as Jesus once raised Lazarus!'

'Is that woman sane?'

Chopra turned to find Sheriwal at his shoulder.

'I am not entirely sure.'

They watched as Bekker hefted a boxy chrome make-up suitcase on to a bench, snapped open the latches, examined the array of tools within, and selected a dusting brush. She turned to the casts, ran a critical eye over them, and said, 'You have done an adequate job, gentlemen. Now stand back and permit me to do my work.'

Homi and Dr Coin exchanged glances. *Adequate* job? But neither man had the courage to challenge the German woman's assessment.

Silently, they drifted to the rear of the autopsy suite.

Bekker began by placing coloured plastic markers at twenty-one sites around each cast. These corresponded to landmark areas inferred from the reference data, providing a contour map of facial thickness based on the race, age and sex of each cast. Next, she removed a tub of modelling clays, selected the correct shade, then began to work it on to the first cast.

Over the course of the next hour she layered on to each cast the facial muscles – the temporalis, masseter, buccinators and occipito-frontals – and, finally, the soft tissues of the neck. She then reconstructed the lips and nose. 'For the lips, one usually takes the interpupillary distance as a good approximation,' she said to her rapt audience and for the benefit of the video-camera – once again manned by Rohit, who was gazing at Bekker with a love-struck expression. 'It is the nose that is the problem.'

They watched as she took a steel ruler from her bag, and bent to measure the width of the nasal aperture, and the nasal spine. 'We can estimate the length of the nose by using a calculation of three times the length of the nasal spine multiplied by the tissue depth estimate at this point. It is a remarkably effective method.' She wheeled on Homi, causing him to flinch involuntarily. 'Your nose, for instance, is unusually big. But I am certain that if your skull came before me I would be able to estimate its length to within the nearest few millimetres.'

Homi passed a self-conscious hand over his bulbous nose. He noticed that Rohit had turned the camera towards him, and was smirking from behind it. He scowled at his assistant, who hurriedly swung the instrument back on to the forensic sculptor.

'Getting the pitch of the nose right is a different matter,' continued Bekker. 'It is down to experience and instinct.' She bent to the task, aggressively moulding clay in her hand, then applying it to the cast.

'This is pointless,' muttered Sheriwal. 'This woman is making it up as she goes along.'

'Let us see what she comes up with,' said Chopra. 'This technique has worked in a number of high-profile cases abroad. Perhaps it will work for us too. At this point, we have nothing to lose.'

Sheriwal subsided with a grumble. She glanced at her watch. 'I shall be back,' she said, and slipped out of the anteroom.

Once the nose had been completed to Bekker's satisfaction she began to build up the outer layers of the face, using her thumb to work the modelling clay, creating the contours of the cheekbones, jawline and chin.

Gradually, the facial thickness markers that she had put in place at the outset vanished below the clay.

Bekker stood back to examine her handiwork.

She seemed to consider the blank face before her, then stepped forward and began to use her fingers and a plastic forensic spatula to work the clay, adding superficial detail to the face: wrinkles, facial lines and micro-contours. The countenance took on a more human aspect, became something more than just a lifeless doll.

As Chopra looked on, the ghost of a shiver eased up his spine. There was something inherently discomforting about watching the dead revivified in this way. Rationally, he knew that what Bekker was doing was little more than a best-guess reconstruction of what-had-once-been. But a deeper, primordial part of his brain imbued the act with a significance that spoke to the basic humanity that was part and parcel of a life, and that was shed at the moment of death. If there was such a thing as a soul, it seemed to him that Bekker's act of recreation had somehow breathed that nebulous vapour back into these wax-like visages.

Another hour passed as the German woman completed the second face.

Then she returned to her bag and extracted two black-haired wigs. She looked at Homi. 'Based on what you have told me, I felt these would be most suitable.'

She adjusted the wigs on to the casts. The female wig was traditionally Indian in style, hair parted in the middle of the head, and gathered into a long ponytail. The male hairstyle was simpler, short on all sides with a neatly combed parting on the right.

'Of course, you can photograph the casts and use modelling software to apply different hairstyles to them.'

Bekker stepped back, her demeanour suggesting the word: 'Voilà!'

Homi and Coin looked at each other and then moved tentatively forward, like two errant schoolboys approaching the headmistress. 'Fabulous!' ventured Homi. 'You have done a remarkable job.'

'Yes,' said Bekker matter-of-factly. 'I am very pleased with the outcome.'

'Of course, one must be careful to note that there is always a degree of subjectivity involved in such reconstructions,' said Coin.

The temperature in the room fell several degrees.

Bekker turned slowly and incinerated the Australian with an icy look. 'Thank you for your input, Herr Coin,' she said. 'However, it is the experience and skill of the forensic artist that ultimately determines how closely the end result might match the deceased person. I believe that with the data made available to me, no one could have done a better job.'

'No, no, of course not,' said Coin hurriedly, backtracking at Olympic speed. 'I merely meant that our detectives should view these models as a starting point. In the eventuality that they have no immediate success in identifying the deceased parties.'

Bekker subsided with a final glare.

Chopra took out his phone, then said, through the speaker, 'I'd like to photograph the casts.'

Homi and Coin both looked at Bekker. 'Yes,' she said imperiously. 'You may.'

As Chopra emerged from the autopsy suite, he found Inspector Malini Sheriwal bearing down on him, swinging a thick folder by her side.

'Just in time,' said Chopra. He held up his phone. 'This is what our two victims *may* look like.'

'Assuming this entire charade has any validity whatsoever,' responded Sheriwal. She hefted her folder. 'I have brought along all the missing persons photographs that we accumulated during the initial investigation. We narrowed it down to one hundred and twenty-seven potentials. Too many to make any headway. Perhaps we can use these reconstructions to narrow that number down further.'

Chopra waved a hand along the corridor. 'We can use Homi's office. I am sure he will not mind.'

Over the course of the next hour they sat in Homi Contractor's cramped and badly ventilated basement dungeon, and went through the folder, comparing each of the pictures with the photos of the newly reconstructed faces. Of the male victim they found no sign. 'In all likelihood, he was never reported as a missing person,' remarked Sheriwal. 'Many people vanish in this city every day without anyone even realising that they have gone.'

Chopra knew that this was the unfortunate reality of life in a place as obscenely overcrowded as Mumbai, a city that attracted migrants, drifters and desperadoes from all over the subcontinent. Many came to the metropolis having left their families behind in villages dotted around the interior, promising to send money orders once they found work. Often they were never heard from again.

They had better success with the female victim.

Halfway through his stack of photos, Chopra was struck by a bolt of lightning.

The woman in the photograph was young – twenty-six according to the accompanying missing person's profile – pretty, with a dusky complexion, twinkling eyes and full lips. Many aspects of her features did not quite match the reconstruction by Bekker – the flare of her nostrils, the thickness of her lips, the arch of her eyebrows. The girl wore her hair short, shoulder-length, a modern hairstyle at odds with the ponytail that Bekker had chosen for the cast.

Yet the similarities could not be dismissed as mere coincidence. He knew, instinctively, that they had found the person they were looking for.

He held out the photograph to Sheriwal. The police-woman examined it, then compressed her lips. 'Possibly.'

'It is her,' said Chopra.

'What you mean is, you *want* it to be her.'

'I *know* it is her.'

Sheriwal gave him a sceptical look. She glanced down at the profile. 'Arushi Kadam. Her mother filed a missing person's report four months ago.'

Chopra looked uneasily at the photograph.

Arushi Kadam had been captured smiling breezily at the camera, a pair of sunglasses parked in her short hair, her eyes crinkled in self-aware amusement. She seemed every inch the image of modern Mumbai youth, a head full of dreams, her life shimmering before her.

Sheriwal was right. There *was* a chance that he had it wrong, that his instincts had betrayed him. The similarity between this girl and the reconstruction was noticeable but by no means definitive. Perhaps his own unconscious bias was at work here, his overwhelming desire to find a connection so that he might progress his parallel investigation into Cyrus Zorabian's death.

He vacillated, considering how the girl's parents would react if he told them that their daughter had been murdered, her body burned beyond recognition.

'What would *you* do?' he finally asked.

Sheriwal shrugged. 'If this is truly Arushi Kadam, her parents have a right to know that she is deceased. It is not our responsibility to consider how they will come to terms with their grief.'

A MOTHER'S GRIEF

Arushi Kadam's home was located in an area called the Postal Colony, a tortuous forty-five-minute drive from the Sahar Hospital. Evening traffic congested the winding thoroughfare that led there. Tempers had clearly frayed at the end of another busy day in the city of dreams, and Chopra was forced to smear his horn at numerous attempts to overtake the Tata van by those around him. Ganesha joined him enthusiastically, tooting with his trunk each time he banged the wheel.

They left the van on a patch of dry wasteland pock-marked with ancient boreholes and littered with left-over concrete pipes from abandoned building projects. The pipes now served as home for a number of street families, and various wild animals.

Kadam's apartment tower, optimistically named Grace Oasis, was rundown, in dire need of repair. Chopra pegged it as a refuge for lower-income families, clinging tenuously to their foothold on Mumbai's social cliff-face; one wrong move – a missed rental payment, a loss of employment – and they would plunge into the seething chaos of the slums below. The state of the building brought him momentarily back to Cyrus Zorabian's involvement in the Vashi slum redevelopment project, and his own suspicions that Cyrus's intentions in the matter had not been entirely philanthropic.

He had always suspected that true altruism, the kind that entailed a genuine cost to the individual and yet offered no reward in return, was rare. Cyrus Zorabian, renowned for his philanthropy, had been facing bankruptcy. The more Chopra discovered about the man, the more he was convinced that the Parsee industrialist may have been willing to get his hands dirty in order to save his business.

The door to Arushi Kadam's apartment was flung open by a late-middle-aged woman in a white blouse and checked slacks. Her hair was cut short, like Arushi's; her facial similarity to the victim told Chopra that they had found Arushi's mother.

The woman stared at Sheriwal's uniform, then at their sombre expressions, and her face collapsed. 'I knew that you would come one day. I prayed that it would be with good news, but in my heart I knew that was no longer possible.'

She led them inside the small, neat flat, ushered them on to a sofa. She asked them to wait, then went into the bathroom. They heard her weeping gently behind the door.

Chopra glanced at Sheriwal. The policewoman sat rigidly beside him, lips grimly pursed. It was impossible to know what she was thinking.

His eyes wandered around the room. Polished marble floor. A porcelain pot on the sideboard, Japanese in design. An African death mask on the wall. A stylised black and white print of a classic Bollywood movie from the fifties.

A modern home, with modern sensibilities.

When the woman returned, she dropped into the wing chair before them, her demeanour once again businesslike. 'My name is Mona. As you may have gathered, I am Arushi's mother.'

Chopra quickly explained how Arushi's remains had been identified, also clarifying his role in the investigation. He hesitated before describing the gruesome nature of Arushi's death, but realised that the woman had a right to the truth. Mona Kadam's jaw tightened as she absorbed her daughter's final moments, but otherwise she did not react. He took out the photo of the reconstruction and showed it to her. She examined it with hollow eyes, then nodded. 'Yes. That's Arushi. It cannot be anyone else.'

Chopra was willing to take the woman's word for it, but privately decided that a final confirmation might be in order later.

'Is Arushi's father here?' Sheriwal asked.

Mona shook her head. 'He passed away seven years ago. A heart attack. I have never remarried.'

'Do you have any other children?'

'No. It is just Arushi and me.'

'Can you tell us about her?' asked Chopra.

Mona grimaced. 'She was intelligent, and strong-willed. I suppose she got that from me. I always urged her to be independent, especially after her father passed. She studied hard, got a degree from Bombay University in business administration. She wanted a career, wanted to achieve something with her life.'

'I take it that she was the outgoing type?'

Mona frowned, as if perhaps Chopra had impugned her daughter's character. 'She was a lively, pretty girl. She had a circle of friends, and she enjoyed going out with them. She loved Bollywood movies; she loved music. And she loved social causes.'

'This is a delicate question, but did Arushi have a boyfriend?'

'Why is it a delicate question?' barked Mona. 'Are you one of those who still think women in India must conform to some outdated notion of virginal purity, while men get to run around with whomsoever they please?'

'Not at all—' Chopra protested.

'Let me tell you, *Mr* Chopra,' interrupted the suddenly irate woman, 'I always encouraged my daughter to break through barriers that men like you seek to put in her way.'

'But I assure you—' Chopra spluttered.

'*My* daughter,' continued Mona, mowing him down beneath the bulldozer of maternal indignation, 'was an attractive, proud Indian woman. If she chose to have a boyfriend, then more power to her.'

Chopra waited, in case there was more to come. He glanced at Sheriwal who, he couldn't help but notice, was struggling to suppress a smirk. Finally, he risked opening his mouth again. 'I apologise if I have caused offence. The reason I ask is because Arushi's body was found with a male victim, of similar age. We were hoping you could help us identify him. They were both murdered in the same way. To be frank, it has all the hallmarks of an honour killing.'

Mona sat back in her chair, momentarily overcome by fresh grief. 'There *was* a boy. I don't know his name, but Arushi was quite taken with him for a while. I only found out because a neighbour saw her on a motorbike with him. I asked Arushi about him, but she wouldn't tell me any details.'

'I thought you encouraged your daughter to be *modern?*' said Sheriwal.

Mona glared at her. 'Just because she was modern it doesn't mean she wished to share everything with her mother.' She sniffed. 'All I know is that Arushi was obsessed with her career. If she was in a relationship then it was not serious, and certainly not the most important thing in her life.'

Chopra realised that there was little to be gained by pursuing the matter, and so he changed tack. 'Can you tell us where Arushi worked?'

Mona's response was immediate. 'A property company. A firm called Karma Holdings.'

Chopra froze, the name tolling in his mind. He had seen it somewhere before, recently. He flicked open his note-book . . . And there it was.

Karma Holdings.

The same company that had prepared blueprints for New Haven, the Vashi slum redevelopment project that Cyrus Zorabian had been involved with.

Like most good investigators, Chopra did not believe in coincidences. Here was an unambiguous link between

Cyrus and the two deaths the industrialist had, for reasons that were not yet clear, taken a keen interest in.

He stood up. 'We will do whatever we can to find your daughter's killer.'

Mona did not bother to see them out. Her eyes were hollow, locked on to her own memories. 'But that will not bring her back, will it?'

On the short drive back to the station Chopra told Sheriwal he planned to visit the offices of Karma Holdings the following day, the address of which he had obtained from Mona Kadam.

Sheriwal frowned. 'I am tied up for the next three days. I have been tasked with running some training classes at the academy in Nasik on the mechanics of encounter shootings. First, they stick me in the back of beyond for shooting criminals, and now they want me to teach the next generation how to do it properly.'

'At least you will be able to get back to doing the only thing you seem to enjoy,' muttered Chopra.

Sheriwal stiffened. 'What does that mean?'

'Nothing,' he said hurriedly.

Sheriwal glared at him. 'If I allow you to carry on with your investigation, I expect to be kept up to speed with everything that you discover.'

'If *you* allow *me*?' Chopra almost swerved into the rickshaw puttering along to his right.

'This is a murder case,' said Sheriwal coldly. 'Now that one of the bodies has been identified, it falls within my jurisdiction to continue the investigation.'

'You would not have identified the body at all without my intervention.'

'That may be so, but it does not change the fact that this is a police matter. And you are no longer a policeman.'

Chopra ground his jaw. He slammed the horn at a passing and entirely blameless motorcyclist. 'I have been hired by the Zorabian family to—'

'Yes, yes. So you have already said.'

A heated silence fell between them.

Ganesha looked from Sheriwal to Chopra and back again. His ears flapped earnestly.

Finally, Sheriwal coughed. 'However, as I am due to be otherwise engaged, I think that perhaps, in this instance, and in the cause of furthering the investigation in the speediest possible manner, it would behove *my* team to work with *your* team.'

A muscle worked on Chopra's forehead. 'That would seem to be the most expedient way of moving forward,' he finally managed.

No further words were exchanged for the remainder of the drive.

Having dropped the prickly policewoman back to her office, Chopra headed for the restaurant. Here he discovered Rangwalla apparently slumped unconscious over his desk, folders, printouts, and the remains of a lamb biriyani spread messily around his prone form.

Chopra had to jab him three times in the ribs before his deputy finally stirred to life.

Rangwalla looked up blearily. 'Wah?'

'This is not a hotel,' said Chopra sternly.

Rangwalla's brain returned from whatever distant planet it had been orbiting. A look of panic swarmed over his dark features, and he sprang to his feet, a windmill of flailing arms and legs, sending sheets of paper and the biriyani dish cartwheeling into the air. A well-gnawed chicken bone struck Chopra in the face, then slid down his shirt and into his front pocket.

He glared stonily at Rangwalla, then, very deliberately, removed the offending article, and set it down on the desk.

'I presume you have accomplished something more than simply eating biriyani?'

Rangwalla, now ramrod straight, gave a rictus grin. 'I thought this would be the best place to go through the BMC paperwork.'

Chopra waved away his annoyance. 'Sit. Tell me what you have found.'

Rangwalla gingerly lowered himself back into his seat.

He excavated his notebook from under the mound of paperwork, then laid it out before Chopra. The senior man could make nothing of the untidy, looping handwriting, which reminded him of a phalanx of dead spiders squashed between the pages of a book.

'I have boiled it down to a few key documents,' explained Rangwalla. 'First are the two BMC structural surveys of Gafoor's building that he claims never took place. These were initiated after he was approached by agents of an unnamed company wishing to buy his site. Gafoor refused and the next thing he knew the BMC had declared his building unsound. When he continued to refuse his would-be buyers, the BMC issued a demolition order.

'Instead of capitulating, Gafoor threatened to take the BMC to court. Conveniently, the building collapsed not long after, supposedly due to a gas cylinder explosion. At least, that was the cause cited in a BMC report of the disaster, though Gafoor is adamant it couldn't have happened that way.

'Following the collapse Gafoor was arrested, tried for negligence, and sentenced to a lengthy prison term. In the meantime, the BMC issued a repossession order for the site – based on another report that stated that the site would be used for "the public good". Once the repossession was complete, however, the BMC reversed the ruling with a new land use classification order, reverting the property back to private use. This then allowed the BMC to put up the site for auction; where it was purchased by a private company. But the intriguing thing is this: all these documents – the structural surveys, the demolition order, the collapse report, the repossession order, the land use re-categorisations and the auction sale order – were countersigned by the same individual.' Rangwalla paused, allowing the tension to build. 'One Geeta Lokhani. Head of the BMC's Planning Committee.'

He sat back, clearly pleased with his efforts.

For the second time in the space of an hour Chopra felt the ground shift beneath him.

The fates, it seemed, were playing games with him.

For here, now, was a second connection to the Cyrus Zorabian investigation, one he could not possibly have foreseen. Cyrus had visited Geeta Lokhani before his death; he was involved in helping her with the Vashi slum redevelopment project. Yet Rangwalla had uncovered if not evidence, then at the very least tangible cause for concern as to Lokhani's integrity as a senior BMC official. If Gafoor's suppositions were correct, then he had been railroaded off his property by the machinations of the BMC, all in the interests of selling the plot to a private buyer. No doubt a vast sum would have changed hands, and further fortunes would be made when the new apartment development on the site was complete. With so much money sloshing around, it was inevitable that many stakeholders would be wetting their beaks, including those at the BMC.

Chopra was forced to reassess his own first impressions of Lokhani.

He had to admit to himself that he *had* been impressed by the woman – intelligent, successful, attractive. A deep disappointment wound through him, like a crocodile wading through the murk at the bottom of a river. In Lokhani he had sensed a kindred spirit, someone committed to redressing the inequalities built into the fabric of the city in which they both lived. He felt . . . betrayed. Why hide from it?

'What was the name of the company that bought the site?'

'The company currently building apartments on the site is called New World Developments,' said Rangwalla. 'But then I remembered what you said about following the money and who really benefits. And so I said to myself, Rangwalla, dig deeper.'

Chopra reserved comment. It was never a good sign when his deputy began to talk to himself. He braced himself to be underwhelmed.

'I asked Soman, the BMC official, to help me locate the deeds of purchase. It turns out that the plot was actually bought by a property company by the name of Karma Holdings.'

Shock rippled through Chopra.

Karma Holdings.

Yet again he was confronted by the same interconnecting thread, snaking itself around his investigation. What was that old saying? Once, an accident; twice, a coincidence, and three times . . . a conspiracy.

'You recognise the name?' said Rangwalla, peering at him.

Quickly Chopra filled in his deputy, outlining the link between Karma Holdings and Cyrus Zorabian, and also the fact that Arushi Kadam had worked for the company.

'It looks like we're working the same case,' said Rangwalla.

Together they went over the tangle of connections; but the pieces would not fit.

Finally, Chopra gave in to the realisation that there was little headway they could make at present. They were grasping in the dark; they needed more information about Karma Holdings.

He asked Rangwalla if he had had any luck with his investigations into William Buckley's past.

'I spoke to a number of his former employers. None of them were aware that he had a criminal past. By all accounts he was a model employee.'

'What sort of work did he do?'

'All sorts. The last couple of roles were PA and general admin. Before that he worked as a tutor.'

'Tutor? What did he teach?'

Rangwalla leafed through his notebook. 'Ah. Here it is . . . He taught Latin.'

As Chopra pulled the van into his compound, he was astounded to find himself confronted by a giant turd. 'Mr Poo?' he said, his voice a disbelieving rasp.

Mr Poo saluted, then lifted the hatch to unveil a mousy set of all too familiar features. 'It is me, sir. Bahadur.'

Chopra goggled at the building's security guard. 'What are you doing in that get-up?'

'Poppy Madam requested me to put on this costume. I am to tell everyone who enters the compound to please use the lavatory when vacating their bowels and not the street.' Bahadur pulled back his narrow shoulders. 'It is for the good of India.'

When Chopra reached his flat, he found his wife shuffling mounds of campaign leaflets around the dining table, each one stamped with the UNICEF logo.

Irritation flared through him, and then just as quickly vanished, to be replaced by a sudden upwelling of pride. He contrasted the likes of Cyrus Zorabian, a man who had purported to help the disadvantaged yet had only sought to help himself, and his wife, who toiled selflessly for the greater good. Nevertheless . . . 'You are deliberately provoking Mrs Subramanium,' he said mildly.

'Charity begins at home,' countered Poppy. 'Besides, Bahadur needs the extra income, and *we* are in need of a new mascot.'

'But there's a giant turd greeting everyone who enters the building!'

'Exactly. It is a talking point. That is how the message will be spread far and wide.'

Chopra recognised the futility of argument.

He put a hand on Poppy's shoulder, drew her into him, and said, 'You are an amazing woman.'

Her face brightened with warmth and surprise.

He went off to check on the vulture, discovering to his own surprise that she was looking distinctly perky, shuffling villainously back and forth on the shelf she had made her own within his office. He poked his head out of the door. 'Did you feed her?'

'Yes,' said Poppy, without looking up. 'Mother brought a bucket of raw entrails from the restaurant. She has actually been less trouble than I had imagined – the vulture, not my mother. It's really no different to looking after a parrot.'

Except that parrots don't usually peck out their owners' livers after they die, thought Chopra.

An hour later, having showered, changed and wolfed a hurried dinner, Chopra closeted himself in his office, took out his notebook, and began to jot down his thoughts on a clean sheet of paper.

The case was in danger of tying itself into knots.

What had begun as a straightforward investigation into the death of Cyrus Zorabian had now splintered into multiple criss-crossing lines of enquiry.

Quickly, he clarified the situation as he now saw it:

CZ killed in Doongerwadi, body dumped in a Tower of Silence.

CZ on verge of bankruptcy.

CZ involved in raising funds for new Vashi slum redevelopment project. Project being managed by Karma Holdings; BMC permissions handled by Geeta Lokhani. Was CZ using the project to embezzle funds to shore up his failing business? Did Lokhani know?

Suspects

CZ estranged from son. Darius Zorabian married against CZ wishes. Darius angry with CZ for disinheriting him. Darius has no alibi.

CZ and Boman Jeejibhoy fell out over Darius spurning Boman's daughter. Boman, enraged, threatens CZ. Boman has no alibi.

CZ angers Anosh Ginwala, head corpse-bearer at Doongerwadi. Ginwala loses family, blames CZ. Ginwala has motive, means, but not opportunity.

CZ PA William Buckley is a former criminal, convicted of violent assault. Did he have grudge against CZ? If so, why?

Parallel investigations

CZ received Latin letters before his death, accusing him of ??? What exactly? Bankrupting his business? Being a bad Parsee? (Note: Boman, Buckley and Darius all know Latin.)

CZ kept news article about two burned bodies. One body identified as Arushi Kadam – worked for Karma Holdings. Who was the other victim? Why were they killed? Why did CZ care?

Hasan Gafoor's building burns down in Marol. Multiple victims. Arson suspected. Was Gafoor being strongarmed out of his land? Were the BMC involved? Site eventually sold to Karma Holdings. Geeta Lokhani signed off all BMC paperwork. What is Lokhani's link to Karma Holdings?

Chopra sat back and stared at his notes.

Behind him he heard the vulture's talons scraping along the shelf.

There was little doubt that Cyrus Zorabian, far from being the picture-perfect Parsee with a heart of gold, was instead a man who had harboured dark secrets, a man with a penchant for making bad decisions. The net result was that there were now a number of suspects with motives valid enough to have driven them to murder. Running through and around this was his potential involvement with former BMC official and prospective politician Geeta Lokhani in a major property development scam, possibly in collusion with the property company Karma Holdings.

Chopra tapped his pen on the desk, his thoughts swirling.

Karma Holdings.

Like a bad penny the name kept cropping up everywhere he turned.

He glanced around at his vulture companion. 'Three times is a conspiracy,' he muttered.

The bird hunched her shoulders and gave him a beady glare.

Chopra's instincts rarely needed a second invitation. In essence, his next course of action had been dictated to him.

There was little doubt that Karma Holdings would be his next port of call.

But before that there was one other thread that he needed to chase down.

Cyrus Zorabian's less than straightforward personal assistant William Buckley.

SHEDDING AN IDENTITY

Unusually for Chopra, he overslept the following morning.

The previous day, with its circuitous loops around the city, had taken more out of him than he had realised.

By the time he lurched blearily from his bedroom Poppy and his mother-in-law had both left for the day, Poornima for the restaurant, Poppy for the St Xavier School for Boys. Harried by the nebulous feeling of guilt that always overcame him on such occasions, he quickly showered, shaved, dressed, checked the oven for the breakfast he hoped Poppy had left for him, found, somewhat to his disappointment, that there was none, gulped down a bowl of cereal instead, then checked on the vulture.

The bird raised her head from between her shoulders, and gave a low, guttural hiss.

'Good morning to you too.'

Satisfied that the creature was as comfortable as he could make her, he left the apartment.

Thirty minutes later he had picked up Ganesha from the restaurant and was on his way to meet Buckley.

Buckley had agreed to see him at a coffee shop just yards from Cyrus Zorabian's office.

The coffee shop, one of hundreds that had mushroomed around the city in the past few years, was unique in that it had a distinctly English feel to it. Indeed, the sign above the doors said *Ye Olde English Coffee Shoppe*. Chopra suspected that the name's not-so-subtle humour would be lost on most of his compatriots.

Inside, he spotted Buckley hunched at a table in the corner. He was prevented from making a beeline for him by Ganesha tugging on his arm. The elephant pulled him to the counter, where the display of cakes, pastries and various other delicacies had caught his eye. His trunk twitched at the warm gust of delicious aromas.

The young barista behind the counter – who looked about as English as Chopra's moustache – stared at them. 'Um, is that an elephant, sir?'

Chopra refrained from asking what the young man thought it might be if *not* an elephant.

'It is just that pets are not allowed on the premises. For hygiene reasons.'

'That is good news,' said Chopra sternly. 'Because he is not a pet.'

He ordered a coffee and a tray of confectionaries for his ward.

The barista picked up a pen. 'What is your name, sir?'

Chopra frowned. 'Why do you need to know my name?'

'It is so that I can write it on this coffee cup.'

'Why do you need to write my name on my cup?'

'Um. So that we can easily identify your order.'

Chopra looked around at the almost empty shop. 'I am standing in front of you. Simply make my coffee and hand it to me.'

The barista gave a desperate grin. 'But it is store policy, sir.'

Chopra stared at the man. Once again, the inscrutable mores of the modern world left him bewildered. 'Very well. My name is Palaghat Kolungode Vishwanatha Narayanaswamy Singanalluru Puttaswamayya Mutthuraju. I am from the south,' he added. 'Make sure you spell it correctly.'

As Chopra set his coffee down, Buckley looked up from the English newspaper that he had been immersed in: the *Guardian*. The pale Brit was dressed immaculately in a crisp blue shirt and tie and his usual peppery crew cut. His eyes fell momentarily to Ganesha.

The little elephant was practically dancing on his toes as he waited for the barista to set down his tray of delicacies on the floor.

Moments later, his face was smeared with cream as he inexpertly shovelled a mille-feuille into his mouth with his trunk.

Buckley was drinking tea from a porcelain cup. His ornate watch, which Chopra had noticed when he first met the man, lay face down beside the cup.

Something about the watch tugged at Chopra, a speck of grit blown into the corner of his eye. But he had no time to waste on trivialities.

He looked back up, and faced the PA squarely.

'This place has been a haven for years,' said Buckley, apropos of nothing. 'A small slice of home.'

Chopra said, 'Did Cyrus know that you have a criminal record? That your real name is not William Buckley but Adam Beresford?'

Buckley froze.

A car hooted outside the shop. A man shouted loudly. A herd of goats bleated past.

Buckley pulled off his spectacles, wiped them very deliberately with a handkerchief. 'I haven't heard that name in a long time.'

'You went to great lengths to conceal your past. You skipped parole; you fled the UK; you invented a fraudulent new identity.'

Buckley's eyes flashed. 'When I changed my name, I *shed* my past, Chopra. I left behind the life fate had set out for me.'

'Changing your name was not necessary to accomplish that.'

'How would *you* know? For someone like me, trying to make a new life without changing my identity would have been like leaping out of a sinking boat with an iron ball around my ankle.'

'I have known many criminals who aspire to change. Rarely do they find a way out from the labyrinth of their own natures.'

'How very Zen of you. But you know nothing about me. Adam Beresford died the day I left prison. I made a choice, and I never looked back.'

'Why not complete your parole? Do it the right way?'

Buckley stirred his coffee, then set down the spoon. 'I had no choice. If you've seen my record you know that I was convicted of violent assault. The man I assaulted was a senior member of the criminal outfit I worked for. We got into it because I refused to do a job for him, a burglary. I had decided, you see, that I had had enough. I wanted out of the life. But, of course, it's easier to step into quicksand than to pull yourself out. I was too good at what I did. He wouldn't let me go. We fought, I defended myself, and my reward was to spend the next five years in a six by ten cell.' Bitterness laced the Englishman's words. 'He tried to have me killed in prison, three times. I have the scars to prove it. When I got out on parole, I knew that it would be only a matter of time before he finished the job. And so I fled. Got myself a new passport, a new identity – I still had useful contacts willing to help me. I landed in South America, and I've never looked back.' He picked up his watch and snapped it on to his wrist.

The action set gears moving at the back of Chopra's brain. What was it about the watch that was bothering him . . . ?

'Anyway, what has any of this to do with Mr Zorabian's death?'

'In one of your earlier roles – before you came to India – you taught Latin.'

Buckley's face registered surprise. 'What of it? I've had a lot of jobs. I've taught a number of languages.'

'Where did you learn Latin?'

'In prison. There was a course. Most of my fellow inmates were learning woodcraft, or how to fix engines. I wanted to do something that kept me away from them. It just so happened that I turned out to have a knack for languages. It was one of the reasons Mr Zorabian hired me.'

Chopra fished out the Latin letters, smoothed them on to the table. 'Did you send these to Cyrus?'

Buckley examined the letters. 'Where did you find these?'

'Inside a bank locker that he maintained. I believe he was being sent these in the months before his death.'

'You think his killer was communicating with him?'

'Possibly. The tone appears to be one of general disapproval.'

Buckley took a second look at the letters. 'I did not send these,' he said finally.

'Are you certain?'

'Why don't you put your cards on the table, Chopra? Are you suggesting that I had something to do with Cyrus's death?'

'Did you?'

'I had no reason to kill the man. He was my boss. I considered him a mentor, and a friend.'

'But did he think of you in the same way? What if he had discovered your criminal past? And that you had kept it a secret from him? A man like Cyrus might consider that a betrayal. Perhaps he decided to dismiss you. Perhaps you reacted badly to being confronted with the fact of your duplicity.'

'And perhaps you were a fantasist in an earlier life,' Buckley responded heatedly. 'Even if Cyrus *had* found out, he would have discussed it with me. In the past nine years, I have given him no cause to mistrust me.'

'Since our first meeting I have discovered that Cyrus was a more volatile character than I had been led to believe.' Chopra shifted in his seat. 'You were Cyrus's PA. Why didn't you know about the state of his finances?'

'As I told you before, he kept financial matters between himself and his chief accountant. We were close, but, in many things, he was a secretive man.'

Chopra considered Buckley's words. The Englishman seemed earnest. But he was also a convicted felon, a man who had breached his parole, a man who had lived under a false identity for years. 'Where were you on the night Cyrus died?'

Buckley replied a little too quickly. 'I was at home.'

'Alone?'

'Yes. I live alone.'

'You do not have a, ah, partner?'

'No. I mean, I've dated on and off, but at present I'm single.' Buckley grimaced. 'I'm afraid I can't furnish you with a convenient alibi, Chopra. But then I don't need one. I had nothing to do with Cyrus's murder. Why would I want to kill him, for God's sake?'

That was the question to which Chopra had no real answer. What motive would Buckley have had? Even if Cyrus had discovered his criminal past surely that wouldn't have been cause enough to commit murder.

Buckley straightened his shoulders. 'What happens now? Will you turn me in?'

'Turn you in?'

'I skipped parole. Technically, I'm on the run. There's probably still an arrest warrant out for me, buried in some dusty police file somewhere.'

Chopra hesitated. Had he still been a police officer, he would have felt compelled to arrest Buckley, and hand him over to the proper authorities. Yet set against this was the fact that the Englishman had worked hard to carve out a new life. Twenty years was a long time to be on the run without slipping up. Perhaps he really was exactly what he claimed to be: a reformed criminal.

He stood up. 'I advise you not to leave the city.'

'I have no plans to go anywhere,' said Buckley. Something flickered through his eyes. 'I have a request. Don't tell Perizaad about my past. I don't think she would take kindly to the idea that a former convict had been by her father's side for almost a decade.'

'I make no promises,' replied Chopra. 'I suspect there is more here than you are telling me. But I do not have the authority to arrest you, and I do not want to hand you over to Rao at the CBI. His methods of extracting information are not to my liking.' He looked down at Ganesha, who had polished off his plate of pastries. The elephant's cream-smeared face looked as if he had inexpertly attempted to apply a clown's make-up. 'Did anyone tell you that you are becoming a glutton?' he muttered as he led his young ward back out into the street.

Ganesha happily stuck the end of his trunk into his mouth and sucked up the last of the cream.

A MEETING WITH KARMA HOLDINGS

The plaque in the lobby listed a dozen companies ranged over the nine floors of the gleaming new tower in Juhu.

Karma Holdings Private Limited had its offices on the eighth floor.

As Chopra made his way up in the lift, he considered the forthcoming encounter.

The initial police investigation into Cyrus Zorabian's murder had concluded that his killing had been a crime of opportunity, a random encounter. But Chopra's own efforts had revealed multiple motives that might be tied to a possible crime of passion. Darius Zorabian, Boman Jeejibhoy, Anosh Ginwala, all had reason enough to wish Cyrus dead. And then there was William Buckley. Though his instincts were telling him that the Englishman was not the man he was looking for, he was not yet willing to erase him from his list of suspects.

His instincts had been wrong before.

Any one of these men might have murdered Cyrus

Zorabian. All had grudges and a personal dislike for the victim.

But he was increasingly beginning to suspect that perhaps something more calculated lay behind the Parsee industrialist's murder.

Cyrus's ham-handed attempts to shore up his failing business by wading into the murky waters of fraud – under the guise of philanthropy – might well have led to his undoing. Chopra knew that he would have to confront Geeta Lokhani at some point. Yet he also knew that as a senior BMC official she would have signed hundreds, if not thousands, of documents. Could she really know, or be held accountable for, the machinations – nefarious or otherwise – behind each one? The fact that Cyrus had gone to meet her on the day of his death had taken on a darker significance, but Chopra had no direct evidence that Lokhani and Cyrus had colluded to embezzle funds meant for the Vashi slum redevelopment project.

It was only instinct that told him something was awry; it would take further effort to unravel the truth.

And the first stepping stone on the road to that truth was Karma Holdings, the thread that connected Cyrus Zorabian and Geeta Lokhani. He paused for a moment. Karma Holdings might be the agency behind multiple as yet unexplained deaths. If that were true then he would be stepping into their crosshairs. What exactly was he trying to achieve by walking through the front door like this?

The answer hovered before him.

He needed confirmation. He needed to know that something was rotten here. In order to flush out whoever was behind this, he had no choice but to reveal his own hand.

It was worth the risk.

At the reception counter, he flashed his identity card, introduced himself as 'Inspector' Chopra, and asked to see the person in charge. The ID card listed Chopra as a 'Special Advisor to the Mumbai Police' and was signed by the commissioner – a deal he had struck following his work on an earlier case. Though he was no longer on the force, it was a tactic he often employed, subtly bending the truth to his advantage.

The young girl behind the counter reacted with alarm, then swiftly vanished behind the scenes. Ten minutes later Chopra was led into a large office, where he was greeted by a man introducing himself as the company's managing director, a John Reddy.

Reddy was a tall, dark and handsome man, with a head of thick Bollywood hair, Brylcreemed into a suitably fashionable mop. He wore gold-rimmed spectacles, and a snazzy waistcoat-and-tie ensemble that clung pleasantly to the contours of his beefy frame. When he grinned, a mouthful of perfect teeth blazed Chopra with a pearly white light, as if he had stepped inside the gates of heaven. He reminded the former policeman of a gameshow host, or a salesman at a luxury car showroom.

Reddy's handshake was firm, his palms moist. A gust of cologne stung Chopra's throat; he gasped his way into a chair.

Reddy eased himself into his own executive chair, joined his palms together in a pose of pastoral contemplation, and gazed expectantly across the expanse of his marble-topped desk. 'How can I help you, Inspector?'

Chopra took out a photograph of Arushi Kadam that he had obtained from the missing person report her mother had filed, and set it down on the desk. Reddy's eyes fell to the photo. His hulking frame stiffened; a muscle twitched at the corner of his mouth.

'Do you know this woman?'

Reddy licked his lips. Chopra could almost hear the gears grinding inside the man's head.

'Yes. Of course. Her name is Arushi. She used to work here.'

'Used to?'

'Well, she left a few months ago.'

'Why did she leave?'

Again, Reddy seemed to consider his response. Chopra sensed he was trying to gauge just how much his visitor knew; which implied he was also trying to judge just how much truth he could get away with. 'I don't know. She simply vanished.'

'Vanished?'

'Yes. Just didn't come in to work one day.'

'Did you contact her parents?'

'Why would I do that?'

'To find out why your employee had stopped coming to

work, perhaps?' Chopra allowed a trace of sarcasm to enter his tone.

Reddy shrugged. 'Frankly speaking, Arushi was not the best of workers. And it is not my habit to chase those who do not wish to be here. There are plenty of talented young-sters in need of work in Mumbai. After three days, I simply told the HR office to look for a replacement. I am sure they must have spoken with Arushi's mother.'

'What did she do here?'

'She was an administrator. Filing. Paperwork. Records. That sort of thing.'

Chopra took out another photograph, this time of Arushi's burned and blackened corpse.

'Arushi did not vanish. She was murdered. Shot in the head, and then burned.'

Reddy's elbows slipped from the desk. He stared, slack-jawed, at the gruesome photograph. 'That – that is terri-ble,' he finally managed.

Chopra continued to examine his face. Was the man's reaction genuine?

'Can you think of anyone who wished her harm?'

Reddy was still transfixed by the picture.

'Mr Reddy?' Chopra prompted.

'No. No,' mumbled the man. 'Why would anyone want to do *this* to Arushi?'

Chopra held his gaze. 'She was very attractive. Could she have been the object of infatuation? Someone in your company?'

'No. She had a boyfriend.' Reddy bit his tongue. The words had slipped out, and he seemed to instantly regret them. Chopra realised that the man was sweating, in spite of the impressively powerful air-conditioner thundering away at the back of the office.

'A boyfriend?'

'Ah. Yes.' It was too late to backtrack. 'He also worked for us. In fact, they met here.'

'What was his name?'

'Vijay Narlikar.'

'I would like to speak with him.'

'I am afraid that is not possible. You see, he vanished at the same time as Arushi. We thought they had run away together.'

'Why would they run away?'

'I believe Arushi's mother disapproved of the match.'

'She told you this?'

Reddy winced. 'No. I mean, it was just office gossip. You know how it is.'

'No,' said Chopra. 'I do not know how it is. I have always discouraged gossip.' He continued to stare Reddy down, certain the man was being less than truthful. 'Do you have an address for Vijay? I would like to speak with his family.'

'Vijay was an orphan,' said Reddy hurriedly. 'A real loner. He only came to Mumbai recently. He really didn't know anyone.' His shirt had begun to stick to his back. He pulled at it, then stood up, and examined his watch ostentatiously. 'I have another meeting . . .'

Chopra remained rooted to his seat. 'What exactly does Karma Holdings do?'

'We are a property company. We buy and sell property.' Reddy's voice steadied as he found himself on firmer ground.

'Do you also work on property development?'

'On occasion. Yes.'

Chopra took out the architectural plans for the Vashi development that he had obtained from Cyrus Zorabian's bank locker and set them on the desk. He tapped the organisation names inked in the title legend. 'Karma Holdings.'

Reddy sank back into his seat like a deflated tyre. 'We are involved in many developments. What of it?'

'This is New Haven, a major BMC-led initiative. It is being championed by a woman named Geeta Lokhani. Do you know her?'

Reddy hesitated. Once again Chopra got the feeling he was gauging just how much he could safely reveal. 'Yes. Of course. We work extensively with the BMC's Planning Committee. She is the head – though I believe she recently resigned. So, naturally, we are acquainted. But what has this to do with Arushi?'

'I will get to that. In the meantime, perhaps you can tell me about another development that Karma Holdings appears to be involved with, a site in Marol that was once owned by a man named Hasan Gafoor. The building on the site – a textile factory – collapsed in a fire, and the land was subsequently possessed by the BMC who sold it on at auction. To Karma Holdings. It is now being developed into apartments.'

A fresh lather of sweat gushed from Reddy's pores. 'These are private commercial matters,' he stuttered.

'It is all in the public record.' Chopra leaned forward. 'The interesting thing is, Geeta Lokhani was heavily involved in that transaction too. Some might say she was instrumental in ensuring Karma Holdings acquired the plot.'

'As I said, she was the head of the BMC's Planning Committee. We liaised with her office regularly.'

'The owner – Gafoor – believes he was strongarmed out of the site.'

Reddy pushed his spectacles up his nose. 'We cannot be held accountable for what some crazy old fool *believes*.'

'What about Cyrus Zorabian?'

Reddy's chin sank into his neck. 'Who?' he squeaked. He was clearly unused to being interrogated in this way.

'Cyrus Zorabian,' repeated Chopra. 'He was a Parsee industrialist, murdered some three months ago. He was heavily involved in raising finance for the Vashi slum redevelopment project you are involved with. He also appeared to have had a keen interest in the deaths of Arushi Kadam and Vijay Narlikar.'

Reddy shook his head, slowly. 'The name does not ring a bell. No. I don't think I have ever met the man.'

'Strange,' said Chopra, 'because when I showed a picture of Cyrus to the lobby receptionists they clearly remember him coming here to visit Karma Holdings on numerous occasions, right up to the time of his death. He was a larger-than-life character – an easy man to remember. His name is in the visitors' ledger. Right alongside yours.'

Reddy winced again.

An uncomfortable silence passed as Chopra allowed the man to squirm in his seat.

Finally, he spoke. 'Oh, yes. Cyrus *Zorabian*. Completely slipped my mind. I deal with so many people, it's sometimes hard to keep track of them all. Yes. He came here a few times. To find out more about the Vashi project. So that he could better promote it to his wealthy friends.'

'Did he meet Arushi Kadam while he was here? Or Vijay Narlikar?'

'No. Why would he?' But Reddy's flushed cheeks told Chopra a different story.

Chopra set down another photograph on the desk, this time of Vijay's blackened corpse. 'Arushi was found with another body. Based on what you have told me I suspect that it was Vijay Narlikar. They were murdered together. Shortly afterwards Cyrus Zorabian was also murdered. I have no doubt that their paths crossed in this office. What passed between them that led to the deaths of Arushi and Vijay?'

'I don't know what you mean.'

'What if I told you that Cyrus had kept a newspaper article about the two burned bodies discovered in Marol? This was well before we identified them as Arushi and Vijay. How would he have known that it was them? What did he know about their deaths?'

'I have no idea,' said Reddy. 'You seem to have arrived at a convoluted conspiracy theory involving Cyrus, Arushi and our company. But you could not be more wrong. We are a legitimate firm. We do not involve ourselves in the private lives of our employees, our clients, or those who work with us.' He rapped his desk with his knuckles as if drawing a line under the matter. 'And now, I think you should leave.'

'You realise that this is now a police matter?' said Chopra. 'You can expect the authorities to crawl through your records. If there is something to find, we will find it.'

Reddy said nothing; merely gave a nervous grimace. Chopra saw that sweat had seeped from under his arms to create dark patches around his ribs.

Chopra got to his feet. 'This is just the beginning, Mr Reddy.'

He turned and left the office.

As the door closed behind him, he did not see Reddy slip a phone from his pocket and begin to dial with trembling fingers.

Chopra's next port of call was the workshop of Darius Zorabian.

Darius's wife had arranged for Chopra to meet her husband for a second time; he had returned from his business trip to Pune and had, reluctantly, agreed to talk to the private detective at his place of business.

When Chopra arrived, he found the victim's son in a foul mood.

Darius was ensconced in a tin shed that served as his office, loudly berating his foreman, a wilting man in a raggedy, torn uniform, who kept wiping his forehead with a dirty rag as if this might somehow deflect the storm of invective coming his way. Chopra knocked briskly on the corrugated metal door – which hung halfway off its hinges

– and entered. Darius gave the foreman a final venomous glare, then ordered him back to work.

The man fled, flashing Chopra a look of grateful relief.

Darius stood, a looming presence in the claustrophobically small and hot room. There was no air-conditioner here, Chopra saw, not even a table fan. 'I have a busy day, Chopra. What is it you wish to talk about? Lucy was very vague. She said you had come to the flat with some follow-up questions.'

'How did your trip to Pune go?'

Darius's perpetual expression of boiling constipation seemed to deepen. 'It went badly. Those blinkered idiots turned down the order.'

'That is unfortunate.'

Darius shrugged. 'I will find other buyers. I do not give up easily.'

'I do not doubt it.' Chopra straightened. 'I took the opportunity to speak to your wife when I visited your home. She told me that on the night that your father died you were not there, at least not for the whole time, as you had originally stated. Your alibi no longer holds.'

Darius blinked. The air seemed to go out of him. 'Impossible,' he wheezed. 'Lucy would never have said that.'

'She is an honest woman. She is worried. Life in India has not worked out the way she had hoped.'

These words struck Darius with the force of a physical blow. His knees buckled, and he fell back into his tatty seat. For a moment there was silence, broken only by the sounds of industry drifting in from the shop floor. Darius's gaze was distant.

'We've spoken about it, of course,' he said. 'But I never realised just how deeply she felt. Or perhaps I never wished to realise. I have disappointed her. She is the only woman I have ever truly loved.'

'And Boman Jeejibhoy's daughter? Did you love her?'

Darius looked up sharply. 'You know about Dinaz?'

Chopra nodded. 'I spoke with Boman.'

'That man is insane. Yes, there was a time when I thought I might love Dinaz. But we were children then. Once I went to America, I saw just how big the world was. And Lucy was so different. Dinaz is a lovely girl, but she has no ambition, no *fire*. She is content to follow her father's instructions, to tread the same weary path as our much venerated Parsee ancestors. I cannot live like that. I *will not* live like that. And so I made my choice. I chose Lucy.'

'Boman claims your decision has destroyed his daughter's life.'

'And for that I am truly sorry. I would not hurt Dinaz for all the world. But some things cannot be helped. What cannot be cured must be endured.'

'Your father was furious. You caused a rift between him and one of his oldest friends. Your decision also cost him a great deal of standing within the community – after all, he was Cyrus Zorabian, guardian of Parsee traditional values. And here was his own son flouting one of the most cherished customs. His response was to disinherit you. Your anger towards him must have been overwhelming.'

'What are you suggesting?'

'Where did you go when you left your apartment on the night that he died?'

Slowly, Darius got back to his feet. 'You are not a police-man. You are a private investigator hired by my sister. You are lucky I do not throw you through the wall.'

'You can try,' said Chopra. He held the younger man's burning gaze until Darius looked away. 'Did you phone your father that evening, after you left your home, asking him to meet you in Doongerwadi?'

'Whatever I did that evening is none of your business.' Darius bunched his shoulders. 'Most of us experience Oedipal rages at some point or another. It does not mean we act on them. Now, I must ask you to leave. I will answer no more questions.'

WHAT LIES BENEATH THE SHELL

The meeting with Darius Zorabian once again put Chopra into a quandary, reminding him that in spite of the wider conspiracy theories now working their way into his investigation, there was still the distinct possibility that Cyrus had simply been killed in a moment of rage. Perhaps no longer by a random killer, but by someone known to him. The man clearly had no problem in inspiring hatred. And Darius's refusal to clarify exactly where he had been during that critical period on the night his father had died was telling.

Chopra's destination was the Western Region office of the Ministry of Corporate Affairs, located on Marine Drive, in the southern half of the city. Here he hoped to be able to dig into the background of Karma Holdings. John Reddy's suspicious manner had ignited his curiosity; he was certain there was more to Cyrus Zorabian's visits to the company's office than the managing director had told him. He knew that, in due course, he would have to apprise

Inspector Malini Sheriwal of his suspicions – the deaths of Arushi Kadam and Vijay Narlikar were, after all, active police investigations. It was imperative that he learn as much as he could before that eventuality, for there was no guarantee how accommodating Sheriwal would be once she had the scent of blood in her nostrils.

The woman seemed to blow hot and cold.

The thought caused him to smile thinly.

Reddy may have found the interview with him to be challenging, but thirty minutes with Sheriwal might convince the man not only to tell the truth, but possibly also confess to the assassination of Mahatma Gandhi back in 1948, years before Reddy had even been born.

But Sheriwal was otherwise occupied at present, and Chopra could not wait for her to bulldoze her way into Karma Holdings for the information he sought.

Fortunately, there was more than one way to milk a cow, as Chopra's late father had often been fond of saying. (Chopra himself had never understood this. As far as he could determine the only way to milk Layla, the cross-eyed and vicious old dairy cow that his father had kept back in their village in Jarul, was to approach her when she was at her most torpid, grab her by the teats, pull as hard as you could, and hope to hell she didn't kick your teeth in.)

Having left Ganesha in the MCA lobby, happily gurgling his trunk in the fountain that had recently been installed there, Chopra made his way up in the elevator to the sixteenth floor.

Here, in a relatively plush reception – by the standards of most government offices – he asked to meet with one Ajay

Rangoon, a bright young MCA employee who had helped him with his recent investigation into the death of an American tycoon at the city's most prominent hotel, the Grand Raj Palace.

When Rangoon arrived, he was sporting a heinous new haircut, with three stripes mowed down one side of his head, the rest dyed blond and pulled over into a curtain that obscured half of his face. The haircut was such an affront to common decency that Chopra was left momentarily speechless.

Rangoon appeared not to notice. 'Mr Chopra!' he beamed enthusiastically. 'How nice to see you again.'

His one visible eye blinked in welcome.

'Ah, yes,' Chopra stuttered, unable to take his own eyes from the offending coiffure. He shook himself back to the task at hand. This was modern India, after all, ground zero for every MTV and pop-culture innovation – good or bad – that swept in from the west. There were probably worse hairstyles loose on the streets of Mumbai, though Chopra hoped never to encounter one. 'I require your assistance.'

'We are here to serve,' said Rangoon pleasantly. 'Please tell me what you require.'

Quickly, Chopra explained.

'But that is very straightforward,' said Rangoon, as if disappointed that Chopra had not set a greater challenge for his prodigious skills. He led his visitor inside, to a bank of computers, fell into a seat, flicked back his curtain of hair, then began to hack away at the keyboard.

In short order, he printed out a sheaf of documents, led Chopra to a meeting room, then explained what he had discovered. 'The company that you are interested in, Karma Holdings, is a shell company. This man John Reddy, the managing director, is one of a number of what we call "nominee" office bearers. The actual "owners" of the company are other companies; quite a few of them, in fact.' He ran his fingers down a list of a dozen corporate names, none of which meant anything to Chopra.

'Can you find out the details of these other companies? I mean, who owns *them*?'

'I can try,' said Rangoon. 'But you have to understand that shell companies by their very nature are secretive. In fact, it is only in the past few years that the government has attempted to crack down on them. They have been used extensively for money laundering, tax avoidance and as fronts for illegal activities. But now, with the demonetisation initiative, the central government has decided enough is enough. It has recently allowed us to share information with the tax office which has made it a lot easier to track such entities. Nevertheless, it will take some time for me to get the details of all these companies. You may wish to wait downstairs.'

Chopra went down to check on Ganesha, then took the elephant with him to a hotel café further along the road, where he ordered a fresh lime juice for himself and a bucket of the same for his ward.

Together, they watched the passing traffic on Marine Drive, one of Mumbai's busiest boulevards, a curving, four-kilometre stretch of palm-lined promenade that meandered around the bay, and was clogged, day and night, with locals and tourists alike.

A donkey cart passed by, hauling a load of bricks. A wiry youth sitting on the bricks whipped at the donkey with a switch. The donkey, head down in the sweltering heat, tongue lolling, nostrils flared grimly, seemed on the verge of collapse. The load it was hauling was far too heavy for its lean and undernourished frame.

Chopra simmered with anger.

At any given moment, this same scene was replayed a million times across the country; the unthinking cruelty, the brutal manner in which men treated the beasts of burden they employed aroused a rage within him that he found difficult to contain.

And then he realised that he did not have to.

He rose from his seat, marched out into the road, and hauled the shocked young thug from his perch. He picked up the switch, flexed it between his hands, then whacked the oaf around his buttocks. The boy leapt a foot off the ground, yelping with pain. 'I suppose you did not enjoy that,' said Chopra. 'What gives you the right to inflict such pain on this dumb animal?'

'Have you gone mad?' yelled the boy. 'I shall call the police!'

Chopra took out his ID card and pushed it against the boy's nose. 'Go ahead. Do you know what the sentence is for animal cruelty?'

The boy looked askance at the crowd that had materialised, as if by magic, around them. This was better than a free ticket to the circus.

'Go on. Give him another whack,' said a dumpy woman. 'Kids these days don't know they're born.'

'If I had a rupee for every time my father gave me the cane, I'd be … a moderately wealthy man,' opined a gummy elder struggling with grocery bags.

'Look at that poor donkey. He's on his last legs.' A tall woman in jeans and sunglasses glared at the boy. 'Shame on you.'

'But it's not my fault,' wailed the object of their collective ire. 'If I don't get this load to the kiln, my boss will fire me. Then who will feed my mother and two sisters?'

'He's got a point,' admitted the first woman.

This, thought Chopra, was the subcontinent's essential dilemma.

It was easy for a man like himself to judge. Fate had been kind to him. He could afford the luxury of a conscience, of high-minded morals. But for those at the bottom of the pile, eking out a living on the mean streets of Mumbai was a daily struggle. The fate of one donkey rarely factored into the equation.

He looked down at Ganesha, who looked back up at him with solemn eyes.

Chopra threw the switch away.

'But how will I make the donkey go without it?' wailed the boy.

'Use an aubergine on a rod,' advised the old man.

'Don't you mean a carrot?' said the woman beside him.

'It has never been empirically proven that a carrot works better than any other vegetable,' said the man, with an air of superiority.

Chopra considered the problem. Then he took out his phone and made a call.

Twenty minutes later a haulage van arrived in a cloud of exhaust fumes that almost finished off the poor donkey. Chopra explained the situation, and paid the bemused driver. In short order, the bricks were transferred to the van, and it sped off to make the delivery.

The boy mounted his cart, and with a last wary look over his shoulder, eased the donkey back into the traffic. By tomorrow, Chopra knew, the poor beast would be once again back in harness. He was fighting the tide.

Yet, as he looked at the happy little elephant beside him, he knew that sometimes even an unwinnable battle was worth fighting. As Gandhi himself had once said: 'The greatness of a nation and its moral progress can be judged by the way its animals are treated.'

'So,' announced Ajay Rangoon, 'this is what I have discovered.'

He handed Chopra another sheaf of printouts. 'These are the details of all the companies that hold stakes in Karma Holdings. Unfortunately, they are also all shell companies. The only individuals listed are nominee office bearers, people who have no actual control over the companies in question. The ultimate aim of this convoluted structure is to safeguard the anonymity of the true owner of Karma Holdings – known as the Beneficial Owner – the person who benefits from this network of organisations.'

'How do I identify this Beneficial Owner?'

'The first step is to go back in time. I have tracked the evolution of this incredibly complex spiderweb of firms back to a handful of shell companies with the oldest incorporation dates. However, there is a problem. These companies have all been red-flagged.'

'Red-flagged?' echoed Chopra.

'Yes. Ever since the government crackdown on shell companies, a system of red-flagging has been in effect. Whenever we come across a corporate entity that may potentially be a front for illegal activity we red-flag it on our system. Such companies are then automatically referred to the Serious Fraud Investigation Office who follow up and decide whether to shut the company down, and, possibly, prosecute those behind it.' He grinned. 'It just so happens that my uncle is a senior investigator there. I suspect that you would like more information about these red-flagged companies?'

'You suspect correctly.'

'I will give him a call. Their offices are not far from here. He will help you. He is a helpful man. He even got me this job here. I wanted to be a rock star, but he thought I should have a real career first.'

The Serious Fraud Investigation Office building was located on Mahatma Gandhi Road in Fort, barely a twenty-minute walk from the MCA offices. Feeling the need to stretch his legs – and those of his ward – Chopra chose to navigate the early evening crowds washing along the esplanade on foot, rather than drive.

The route proved to be a boisterous exhibition of modern life in the city.

They passed a crowded Burger King sandwiched cosily between a Louis Vuitton store and a small art gallery. A minor soap opera star was shooting an advert outside the Burger King, holding an enormous burger to her mouth as camera bulbs flashed and popped. Starving beggars looked on from the sidelines. Clumps of foreign tourists – sporting expressions ranging from stunned to bemused – wandered through the thronged streets, pursued by lepers, street urchins, flute players, eunuchs and hawkers selling everything from samosas to bootleg books to stolen car parts. Skyscrapers towered on either side of the road: the Abu Dhabi National Bank, the Life Insurance Corporation of India. Gridlocked traffic greeted them at Veer Nariman Road under the disapproving gaze of the statue of Sir Edulji Wacha, another of the Parsee grandees who had helped found the Indian National Congress, the party Gandhi would go on to lead.

The SFIO offices were yards from the Cross Maidan Garden. Chopra left Ganesha to have a trot around the neatly manicured space, paying a watchman to keep an eye on him, and then wandered across the road.

Enquiring at the lobby, he was quickly directed up to the third floor and the office of the second Ajay Rangoon he had encountered that day.

Rangoon Senior was a quite different animal to his nephew.

An overweight, sloppy-looking individual, he looked at Chopra from a pair of droopy, deep-set eyes, an air of world-weary cynicism emanating from his every pore. His shirt was untucked, his collar flung open, buttons undone halfway down his chest revealing an off-white vest. He clutched a burger in one hand. Chilli sauce was smeared over his chin and had dripped on to his shirt.

He waved Chopra into a seat, then flopped down into a chimpanzee slouch behind a desk covered in dunes of paper and manila files. 'My nephew explained what you were looking for. My hourly fee is five hundred rupees.'

Chopra raised an eyebrow. 'I thought this was your job.'

Rangoon waved at the paper on his desk. '*That* is my job. You are not the police. You are asking me to expend my time helping you with a private investigation, presumably one for which you are being paid.'

Chopra nodded. 'Your point is well made.'

'Cash, please. In advance.' He bit off a mouthful of burger, and chewed it with bovine passivity.

Chopra reached into his wallet, and passed over three hundred rupees. 'That is all I have. You may bill me for the rest.'

Satisfied, Rangoon leaned back. 'Shell companies are a cancer in our economy – for decades I have watched them choke the machinery of our financial system. Thankfully, we now have the resources to begin tackling them.'

'Why has it taken so long?'

'You're forgetting, Chopra, that many of our esteemed politicos have used them for years, to hide their own ill-gotten gains. They are everywhere. I myself have shut down a thousand of them in the past year alone. I once led a raid on a single building in Dadar where more than two hundred "offices" were registered. Most consisted of a single cupboard-sized room, with a padlock that hadn't been touched in years. These companies exist largely on paper, fronts for their true backers.' He set down a printout in front of Chopra, a complex maze of interconnected boxes. Inside the boxes were the names of various corporations, including those Rangoon Junior had narrowed down as the primary shell companies that owned Karma Holdings. 'These companies control everything. And they in turn are controlled by one man. He is not a director, an employee, or even a listed shareholder – those are all nominee office bearers, just like your man John Reddy. The person you are looking for – the Beneficial Owner – is the man who truly runs this web of shell companies, and thus Karma Holdings. The puppet-master.'

'Who is he?'

'His name is Om Kaabra. Once upon a time he was known as the Black Cobra. Have you heard of him?'

Chopra shook his head.

'Officially he is a businessman, a coconut oil exporter. Unofficially, he graduated from the Mumbai underworld. Low-level street rackets, extortion, that sort of thing. He did a stint in jail for passport fraud. After that, he decided, like many of his contemporaries, to diversify. Began to dabble in the property market. And, by dabble, I mean extort properties from their owners at below market prices, collude with developers to build expensive new premises, and then sell on at a handsome profit. *Unlike* many of his peers, Kaabra has been extraordinarily successful at it. What's more he has managed to keep a low profile. He only came to our attention a few years ago; we have been following his progress with keen interest since, though it has proved impossible to gather enough evidence to prosecute him. No one will testify against him, and he keeps himself far removed from the more unsavoury aspects of the business. And, as you can see, he has become a master at disguising his involvement via these shell outfits.'

'Where is he based?'

'To be frank, we don't know. We think Delhi, but he has properties around the country. We don't have the manpower to track his whereabouts. Besides, Karma Holdings is just *one* of the many front companies he uses. He has different ones in different cities. Kaabra is a smart operator, he knows not to put all his eggs in one basket.'

'Do you know of his links with the BMC? Specifically, a Geeta Lokhani?'

Rangoon shook his head. 'The BMC is an enormous organisation. It is not within our remit to investigate them – that would be a matter for the CBI. But it would not surprise me that officials there are in Kaabra's pay. They are hardly a bastion of integrity, and a man like Kaabra knows how to grease the wheels of corruption.'

'What about a man called Cyrus Zorabian? Parsee industrialist, murdered in the city three months ago. Have you come across him in any of your investigations?'

Rangoon dredged his memory. 'No. The name has not cropped up.'

Chopra scraped back his chair. 'You have been most helpful.'

Rangoon took another enormous bite of his burger. 'Where shall I send the bill?' he said, flashing a craggy smile.

RUN OFF THE ROAD

Darkness had fallen by the time they returned to the van.

As he drove back north, towards home, Chopra's mind whirled with possibilities. Old policeman's reflexes snapped and crackled through him as he considered all that he had recently learned.

Kaabra was not a name he was familiar with, but he knew the type.

During his years on the force Chopra had had numerous run-ins with the Mumbai underworld. For decades, they had practically run the city, until a major crackdown in the late nineties had seen many of them either shot dead – via specialist units such as Malini Sheriwal's so-called Encounter Squad – or dispersed through citywide task-forces. Though their influence had waned, the old dons were far from a spent force. They had regrouped, retrenched and returned to the fray, although now most had the sense to maintain a low profile.

In the ensuing vacuum low-level operators such as

Kaabra had seized the opportunity to carve out their own shadowy empires.

There was little doubt in Chopra's mind that Kaabra was the man behind the murders of Arushi Kadam and Vijay Narlikar. Their killings had all the hallmarks of a gangland slaying. The two youngsters had worked for Kaabra's front company, Karma Holdings, and had clearly done something to attract his ire. Chopra was also certain that Kaabra and the BMC official Geeta Lokhani were working together. Lokhani was no doubt being paid handsomely in order to smooth the path for Karma Holdings to acquire property via underhand means, and then to develop those properties for vast financial gain.

But what was the link that tied them to Cyrus Zorabian?

Cyrus, facing bankruptcy, had clearly got into bed with the wrong people.

Had he sensed an opportunity when Geeta Lokhani first approached him to raise funds for the Vashi slum redevelopment project? Had something subsequently gone awry, causing Kaabra to order Cyrus's death? Cyrus had visited Karma Holdings on a number of occasions – had something happened there that had effectively sealed not only *his* fate, but also the fates of Arushi Kadam and Vijay Narlikar?

Questions, questions, and no answers.

The truth was that Chopra could not yet link Cyrus's killing to Kaabra or Lokhani. The Parsee industrialist's murder might be completely unrelated to his dealings with the pair.

So absorbed was he with these conundrums that he did not notice the dark grey four-by-four with the blacked-out windows following them through the evening traffic.

It was only when he turned off the Western Express Highway to take a short cut through the largely derelict Gold Spot quarter that he noticed the vehicle's lights flashing through his rear window. At that point, he thought little of it. The short cut was well known, though usually avoided by all but the sturdiest vehicles due to the terrible state of the road that wound between the crumbling apartment blocks and industrial units waiting for demolition. The site had been scheduled for gentrification for over three years; the plans were currently mired in red tape, awaiting various official stamps, which in turn awaited pay-outs to a long line of those involved in the approval process.

Chopra idly wondered if Geeta Lokhani had been one of those individuals.

Here and there were the crude fires of those who had chosen to risk sleeping in these hollowed-out concrete shells, any one of which might come down on their heads at a moment's notice.

The van bounced over a pothole, lifting Chopra's bottom from his seat. He cursed and held on to the wheel, as the Tata Venture skidded around a corner.

Behind him, Ganesha trumpeted in alarm.

And then, just as he had regained control, he heard the growl of an engine; bright beams flared into the van. The Tata Venture was struck aggressively from behind; Chopra found himself wrestling with the steering wheel as the van was pushed roughly along the rutted road.

'Hold on!' Chopra shouted.

He swung the wheel, and managed to pull away from the vehicle behind.

But the respite was only momentary.

A gunshot blasted through the night air; the van's rear side window exploded inwards, showering Ganesha with shards of glass. The little elephant's ears shot out like sails on either side of his head.

'Keep your head down, boy!'

Chopra slammed the accelerator, attempting to outpace the four-by-four.

But the van's engine was not powerful enough.

More gunshots zinged into the night, peppering the side of the van.

Chopra ducked low, cursing, face lathered in sweat. He hurled the van around a corner. A rusted sign flashed by: DANGER: THESE BUILDINGS HAVE BEEN SCHEDULED FOR DEMOLITION.

The van bounced over another pothole – and for a terrifying instant all four tyres were off the ground.

Another bullet rang out in the darkness. Chopra felt a sting in his right ear.

He risked a sideways glance.

The chasing vehicle had pulled up alongside. The rear window was rolled down. He saw an automatic poking out; and then the orange bloom of a muzzle flash. He felt one of the van's tyres disintegrate under them. And then the vehicle lurched sharply to one side, the steering wheel all but wrenched from his hands. He cried out in alarm as the Tata Venture swung off the road, barrelled through a chain-link fence, then careened down a slope into the underground parking level of an abandoned apartment tower – little more than a concrete shell – hurtling past a succession of pitted columns, before finally crashing into a pockmarked wall at the rear of the darkened space.

Chopra's head bounced from the steering wheel; Ganesha skidded into the back of his seat, bellowing in alarm.

A moment of blankness, then Chopra shook himself alert.

His head sang, and he could feel blood flowing freely down his forehead and into his eyes.

But he was alive.

He released his seatbelt, wriggled out of the driver's seat, raced to the rear, and looked inside, his heart in his mouth. 'Ganesha!'

The elephant was sprawled on the floor.

Chopra ducked inside, slapped his arms around Ganesha's neck, and heaved. Slowly, the calf stumbled to his feet. 'Come on, boy.'

Together they emerged from the van, then ducked behind a concrete pillar.

He could hear voices echoing in the vast underground space. Concrete dust filled the darkness. He suddenly remembered something. 'Wait here!' he hissed, then raced back to the van.

Steam gushed from under the Tata Venture's bonnet. The windows had been shot out, and the left passenger-side wheel was now a mess of shredded rubber.

Chopra reached in, yanked opened the glove box, and took out his old service revolver.

He scrabbled his way back to Ganesha.

'Where is he?' came a voice. 'I can't see anything in here.'

The beam of a torch speared into the darkness, picking out the van. It swung sideways, and flashed across the pillar that Chopra and Ganesha were crouched behind.

'There!'

A bullet whipped into the stone, scattering chips in all directions.

Chopra ducked back.

Beside him, Ganesha flapped his ears in terror.

Chopra wiped the blood from his eyes, and hefted his revolver. It was the trusty Anmol that he had used for many years before they had been replaced with the newer automatics. When he had retired, he had forgotten to return the gun as protocol dictated.

He was not a man who believed in prayer, but at that moment he wished fervently that any gods who were in the vicinity might deign to look his way.

He flung himself around the pillar, and fired at their assailants.

He heard a loud cry, and then: 'He has a gun! Where did he get a gun from?'

'I'm hit! I'm hit!'

More bullets rang out. The torch fell; there was a tinkle of glass, and then it fizzled out.

'I can't see a thing!'

Chopra fired in the direction of the voice.

'He's firing at us! *He's firing at us!*'

'Will you shut up, you idiot! I'm bleeding here!'

Chopra fired again; another yelp of alarm tore through the darkness.

'I've had enough! This building could come down any second!'

Chopra heard the men scrambling away.

He waited until he heard the rumble of the four-by-four driving off. And then he fell bonelessly against the pillar, closing his eyes as relief washed through him.

He was still alive! They were both still alive.

He limped to his feet. As the adrenalin began to fade, the pain of his bruised and battered body was making itself felt.

'Come on, Gan—' he began, and the ground fell away beneath his feet.

FLOATING IN DARKNESS

When he opened his eyes, he thought for a moment that he was back in the village in which he had grown to adulthood, down by the banks of the river where he would often go as a boy to spy on the village maidens from the branches of a peepal tree.

Clear spring water gurgling over rocks.

He realised he was in darkness.

The last thing he remembered was the floor collapsing under him, falling into a void.

He was in an underground room, waist deep in water.

The gurgling sound he heard was from a burst pipe, pouring water into the narrow space. Something bumped his hip, whipping him around in alarm – but it was only a plastic bottle adrift in the frothing water.

He looked around him, his eyes slowly adjusting to the gloom, then waded to the room's door. He grasped the rusted handle, and pulled.

It came away in his hand.

Cursing, he tried to insert his fingers around the frame, but it was impossible. With the water pushing against the door, there was no way to open it from the inside.

He would have to find another way out.

He waded back into the centre of the room, and took stock of his surroundings. Pipes lined one wall, with bracket shelving bolted to a metal siding on the wall opposite. He was in some sort of maintenance room.

There were no windows, he realised, with a numbing shock. A bloom of panic flowered around his heart.

The water had now risen to his chest.

A wooden pallet caught him a glancing blow. Something slithered by his elbow, and he thrashed out in fright.

And then it came to him . . . *How was it that he was able to see anything at all in this darkness?*

He looked up.

He had fallen through the ceiling – a gaping hole in the corner permitted a trickle of light to seep into the tiny room. Chopra splashed his way over so that he was directly below the hole. He attempted to leap up and grasp the edge. It was too high. He looked at the wall before him. Perhaps he could scrabble up?

But the wall was smooth, slick with water; there was nothing for him to use as a handhold to scale the concrete surface.

The panic became a raging fire. His heart thumped in his ears. How ironic it would be, he thought, if he died of a heart attack before he drowned. He imagined Homi carrying out the post-mortem, what his old friend might have to say about that. And Poppy . . . He shuddered. It did not bear thinking about.

He would never hear the end of it, even in the afterlife.

Think!

There had to be a way out of this.

Perhaps he could climb on top of something?

He surged through the swirling water, grabbed the floating pallet, and wrestled it back to the corner. He tried to clamber on top of it, but it bobbed out from under him.

It was impossible.

The water had risen to his neck.

And now the thought that he had attempted to suppress came roaring to the front of his mind.

I cannot swim.

The water was now above his chin. He closed his eyes.

So this is how it ends.

An ignoble finish to a career devoted to doing the right thing. But then, no one had ever promised him that doing the right thing would guarantee a happy ending. That simply wasn't the way life worked.

He heard a soft bugle above him.

His eyes snapped open, and he peered upwards. Outlined above was Ganesha's head, his trunk curling down into the cavity. The elephant vacillated nervously on the lip of the hole.

'Step back, boy!' warned Chopra.

Ganesha looked at him forlornly, trumpeting his distress.

'There is nothing you can do.'

Still the elephant did not move. 'Go on! Get out of here! Before the whole place comes down on you.' His teeth chattered in the dark. He hadn't noticed how cold the water was. His body felt numb; a dreamy feeling was beginning to rotate upwards from the core of his body. This wasn't such a bad way to die, he thought. He'd lived a good life, hadn't he? He'd fought the good fight; he'd made a difference.

And through it all, the good times and the bad, he had kept his integrity.

No one could take that from him.

He looked up again, saw that Ganesha had vanished.

'Good boy,' he mumbled, as the water rose above his mouth, and he was forced to lift himself on tiptoe.

In the car park above, Ganesha raced to the rear of the crashed Tata Venture. The little calf understood that Chopra was in trouble, that he needed help. An idea, a memory of something he had seen, bloomed in his mind . . . Two weeks earlier, Chopra had helped out a stranded woman by towing her broken-down car.

Ganesha reached down below the van's bumper to where a large red tow hook poked out from its embedded storage cavity. He curled his trunk around the hook, then turned and trotted back to the hole in the floor.

Behind him, the towline unspooled with a mechanical humming sound.

Chopra strained on tiptoe, his nostrils now the only part of him clear of the swirling water.

Perhaps it would be easier to just let go. What was the point of struggling for a few extra seconds of life? What did it mean in the grand scheme of things?

But then again, perhaps that was precisely why it *did* matter.

Every second was precious, and the preservation of life – because of its very rarity – was what gave meaning to the cosmos.

A shape appeared in the haze above him . . . Ganesha!

No! He didn't want the elephant to see him die . . . and what exactly was he *doing*?

Chopra's eyes widened as he watched the elephant grip the towline, and, foot by foot, lower it down into the room.

Impossible! How had he . . .?

But there was no time for that now.

Chopra pushed forward, reaching up with his arms. The hook dangled just out of reach. Just a few more inches . . . He lifted his face above the water, took a deep breath, then bent his knees, submerging his whole body, before pushing back up, and thrashing himself out of the water like an over-weight salmon. His arms flailed for the hook . . . He had it.

The towline reeled out swiftly, causing Ganesha to let go, and stumble backwards. Chopra felt panic grip him again as he fell back into the water. He held his breath, grasped the line with both hands, and pulled, hand over hand, as fast as he could.

Finally, the line had run out to its maximum length, and he had a firm purchase.

He hauled himself out of the water, then clambered up the line, using the wall to brace his feet.

Reaching the lip of the hole, he let go of the rope, grasped the edges of the cavity, and, with a monumental effort, wriggled his body over the edge, his legs kicking out into the empty space below.

Finally, he flopped on to his back, spluttering out the last of the water lodged in his throat.

His chest heaved, and his eyes blinked back tears of relief as Ganesha wavered into view.

The elephant palpated Chopra's bruised and battered face with his trunk, as if to reassure himself that he was still alive.

Chopra attempted to speak, but he was beyond words.

A ringing silence descended on him. And then there was only darkness.

NO PLACE TO BE SICK

It was unfortunate for all concerned that the first thing Chopra saw when he opened his eyes was the face of his assistant investigator Abbas Rangwalla, looming over him in relief.

He cried out in alarm, and raised his hands to ward off the bearded apparition.

Rangwalla fell backwards, almost tripping over his own feet. 'What kind of way is that to greet a friend?' he said sourly.

Chopra blinked rapidly, his mind a terrified blank.

He was lying on a bed in a whitewashed room bathed in bright light. His memory appeared to have deserted him; he ransacked his panicked brain. Where was he? What had *happened*?

And then it flooded back: the chase, the crash, the shootout, the escape from the flooded room.

And then . . . a wash of fatigue as the adrenalin drained away, and darkness fluttering down on to him.

He struggled to a seated position in his hospital bed. The movement sent splinters of lightning forking around his skull, and a gasp of pain escaped him.

'Take it easy,' said Rangwalla. 'You've been through a lot.'

'What happened?' asked Chopra, clutching at his head.

'I don't know. An ambulance picked you up in the Gold Spot district. You were passed out in some derelict building. One of the doctors here knows Homi and had heard of you. Homi called *me*.'

'How did the ambulance find me?'

'Some homeless guy who lives there called it in. He says Ganesha led him to you.' A smile split Rangwalla's beard. 'That is one smart elephant.'

'Where is he now?'

'Back in his compound, safe and sound. Do you want to tell me what happened?'

Quickly, Chopra brought his deputy up to speed on all that had transpired since they had last spoken.

'You think this Kaabra tried to have you killed?' Rangwalla said when he had finished.

Chopra evaluated the question, the possible chain of events since he had visited John Reddy at Karma Holdings. 'Yes,' he said finally. The certainty of it coiled around his guts.

'If he's the power behind Karma Holdings,' continued Rangwalla, 'I suppose it means he is, directly or indirectly, also the one behind what happened to Hasan Gafoor's factory.'

Chopra nodded again. 'It fits with his modus operandi. Bully landlords into signing their properties over to

Karma at below market rates, then redevelop them for profit.'

'And if they put up a fight, resort to any means possible to acquire the land. Up to and including collapsing a building on to thirteen innocent people.'

'That's not all of it,' said Chopra. 'The boy and girl who were shot and burned in Marol? It turns out they worked for Karma Holdings.'

Rangwalla grimaced. 'This is bad.'

The door to the room swung open, and Homi Contractor breezed in. 'Ah. Bollywood's ugliest action hero is awake. What would you like to do for an encore, old friend? Lie down in front of a train?'

'How soon can I get out of here?' asked Chopra. He was in no mood for Homi's caustic sense of humour.

'Get out of here, he says!' Homi threw up his hands. 'When they brought you in here you were stretched out like a corpse. You have suffered concussion, a hairline fracture of the clavicle, multiple bruises and lacerations. And, for the icing on the cake, what looks like a bullet wound. Luckily for you, it just clipped your ear.'

Chopra raised a hand to his right ear, and the plaster that now encased it. Suddenly, he was back in the condemned building, the smell of cordite in his nostrils, adrenalin flying wild in his blood.

'I don't suppose I have to say it – and it wouldn't do any good if I did – but you are lucky to be alive.'

Weariness washed through him. He leaned back into the glut of pillows behind his head, and momentarily closed his eyes. Perhaps Homi was right. He had survived a brush with death; his body, his mind, his very heart had been bruised and battered. He needed to rest, if only to regain the strength to continue his pursuit.

He heard the door swing open and opened his eyes again.

Poppy advanced into the room, then stopped short as she saw her husband stretched out on the bed. A shudder trembled through her. She glanced at Homi who shrugged as if to indicate that Chopra's condition was none of his doing, then, sensing her mood, nodded reassuringly at her.

She stepped forward and lowered herself gingerly down on to the edge of the bed. 'How do you keep getting yourself into these situations?'

'I *would* blame fate,' mumbled Chopra, 'but I don't want to get him into trouble.'

Poppy frowned. 'This is all a joke to you, isn't it? But you are not the one who has to take the call telling you that your husband has just been wheeled into hospital suffering from God knows what.'

'No,' agreed Chopra. 'But then, I don't have a husband.'

Poppy looked at him, temporarily speechless. Behind her, a snicker escaped Homi before he could clamp a hand over his mouth.

Poppy straightened, then smoothed down the front of her sari with ominous deliberation. 'I am surrounded by children,' she said, her voice tight with anger.

'There's really nothing to worry about,' Homi chimed in. 'A few bumps and bruises. We'll keep him here for a night to observe him. Couple of days and he'll be right as rain.'

Poppy wheeled on him. 'Is that so? Well, in that case, why don't *you* look after him, Mr Right-as-Rain? Perhaps he can live with *you* for a while, and then *you* can chase around after him, make sure he takes his tablets, and try to keep him from having another heart attack?'

Without a further word, or a backwards glance, she stormed from the room.

'Was it something I said?' muttered Homi.

'Did you just get thrown out of your house?' said Rangwalla in wonder. 'I thought that sort of thing only happened to me.'

Chopra swung his legs out of bed. His bare feet trembled on the cold floor; a waft of air snaked up his breezy hospital gown.

'There's no point going after her until she's calmed down,' said Homi.

'I am not going after her,' said Chopra. 'I am going to the bathroom. It is a lot safer in there, I think.'

When he returned, Homi had gone.

Rangwalla, however, was still waiting for him. 'A hospital is no place to be sick. As my father used to say: they're just waiting rooms to the grave.'

'Thank you for your positive sentiments,' muttered Chopra.

'Is there anything you need me to do?' Rangwalla asked. 'Given that you are temporarily out of action.'

'I am not *out of action*,' said Chopra irritably. 'My brain is still functioning.'

'Fine. In that case, did you get the number plate of the goons who chased you?'

Chopra shook his head. A thought occurred to him. 'My van. There was paperwork inside it. From the Serious Fraud Investigation Office.'

Rangwalla beamed at him. He reached down into a bag set beside him on the floor. 'Do not worry. I have it all here.'

Chopra was surprised. 'You went into a condemned building to recover evidence? That was courageous of you.'

Rangwalla had the decency to look embarrassed. 'Well, I didn't exactly go into the building myself. I paid a couple of locals. I thought I would help them out. Giving back to society and all that.'

'You thought you would help them out by sending them into a condemned building that might collapse at any moment?' Chopra's tone could have stripped the paint from the walls.

'Well, *they* didn't seem to mind. Cost me fifty rupees, too. I suppose I can claim it back as expenses?' His tone was hopeful.

Chopra took the grubby-looking sheaf of papers from Rangwalla. He glanced through them, considering his next course of action.

His investigations had clearly stirred up a hornet's nest. His visit to the offices of Karma Holdings – and his enquiries into the deaths of Arushi Kadam and Vijay Narlikar – had, in all probability, led to Om Kaabra issuing the order to have him attacked.

But what now?

Would they continue to come after him?

Had they just intended to warn him off or did they plan to stop him for good?

The response seemed disproportionate. After all, the evidence Chopra had collected was largely circumstantial. Enough to weave a convincing narrative, but not enough to build a case in court.

And there was also the question that continued to pulse at the very heart of the puzzle: *how exactly did this all tie in with the murder of Cyrus Zorabian?*

He looked at the papers in his lap, at the names of the shell companies that lay behind Karma Holdings.

'Your contact at the BMC,' he said. 'The one who helped you. What was his name?'

'Soman? What about him?'

'Do you trust him?'

Rangwalla's dark brow corrugated into a series of worried grooves. 'You think *he* put Kaabra on to you?' He shook his head. 'No. He wouldn't have bothered helping me if he was on Kaabra's payroll. Besides, he seemed like an honest man. And I have met so few of them in my life that they are easy to spot.'

Chopra gave this due consideration.

'In that case there is something I would like you to do.'

It was an hour later, a few minutes before midnight, when the door was flung open and Assistant Commissioner of Police Suresh Rao marched into the hospital room, closely followed by Inspector Avinash Kelkar.

Chopra was halfway to his bed, limping back from the toilet.

He froze as Rao ran his eyes over him. 'The exposed bottom suits you,' he said dryly.

Chopra flushed with that singular sense of humiliation that one feels only when embarrassed before a mortal enemy. 'What are you doing here?' he ground out, turning to face the ACP.

'I heard that you had been in an accident. I came to reassure myself that you had been gravely hurt. Alas, that does not appear to be the case.'

Chopra scowled. 'Who told you that I was here?'

'That is irrelevant. What is not, however, is the fact that you have not filed a single report with Kelkar.'

'Report? You seem to keep forgetting: I do not *report* to Kelkar. Or to you.'

'And *you* seem to be forgetting that the murder of Cyrus Zorabian is still, officially, a police investigation. You may think that your client has influence with the commissioner, but sooner or later you will trip over your own feet and cause a stink. We will see just how willing he is to tolerate you running roughshod over the force then.'

'I doubt it,' retorted Chopra. 'He has tolerated *you* doing exactly that for thirty years.'

Rao's face swelled with rage. 'Always the joker. We will see who is laughing at the end of your so-called investigation. What exactly have you discovered so far? Nothing, I will wager.' He stepped forward. 'Two days. I will give you two days, and then I will personally speak with the commissioner. He is a political animal. He will not permit a private investigator to embarrass the service.' He spun on his heels, and would have made an impressive exit from the room had he not barrelled straight into Kelkar, the pair of them tumbling to the floor in a flail of arms and legs.

Rao extricated himself from his deputy, and leapt to his feet, his jowls quivering with fury. 'How many times do I have to tell you not to stand behind me! Again and again, and still you do it!'

Kelkar wilted before the onslaught.

Rao's face expanded and contracted like a bullfrog. He jammed his peaked cap on his head, and stalked from the room.

Kelkar gave Chopra a painful grimace. 'He's not as bad as he seems.'

'I hate to disillusion you,' said Chopra. 'I worked with him for years. He is *exactly* as he seems.'

'He does have a point. This was supposed to be a *co-operative* endeavour.'

'It will be a cold day in hell before Rao and I cooperate on anything.'

Kelkar sighed. 'I am just trying to do my job.'

Chopra examined the younger man with a critical eye. Perhaps he was being unfair. It was hardly Kelkar's fault that fate had conspired to saddle him with Rao as a commanding officer. 'Very well. I will tell you what I have discovered. On one condition. That you do not pass on the information to Rao. Not yet, at any rate. I do not trust him, and nothing you say will convince me otherwise.'

Kelkar hesitated, then took off his peaked cap, ran a weary hand through his hair, and collapsed into a seat. 'Very well.'

Over the course of the following thirty minutes Chopra brought the policeman up to speed on all that he had discovered since their first meeting.

When he had finished Kelkar looked deflated.

'You have made a great deal of progress,' he said in a wilting voice.

Chopra suspected the man was feeling, acutely, the short-comings of his own initial efforts. 'Don't doubt yourself. Your investigation was as sound as it could have been with Rao on your case. One thing I have discovered since becoming a private investigator is that people are far more willing to talk to a man in a shirt than an officer in khaki.'

Kelkar heaved himself up and out of his seat. 'So, your conjecture is that Cyrus had got into bed with the wrong elements, and this led to his murder?'

'Yes.'

'And now these same forces are intent on shutting down your enquiry? To the point of attempting to kill you?'

Chopra nodded.

Kelkar drew back his shoulders. 'How can I help?'

Chopra considered the offer.

It was well-intentioned, and he hadn't the heart to turn the man down. 'Perhaps you could ask around. What does the Brihanmumbai police service know about Om Kaabra? If he is on the radar of the Serious Fraud Investigation Office, then his activities may be known to others. Any information would be useful.'

'I will do my best.' He walked to the door, then stopped. 'I have been on the force twenty years. In all that time I have never suffered so much as a scratch, never fired my weapon in anger . . . What does it feel like? To be in a life-and-death situation, knowing you might not make it to the morning?'

Chopra stared at him. 'Perhaps the next time I walk into a hail of bullets I will invite you along.'

Kelkar appeared not to notice the sarcasm. His eyes shone. 'Really?'

Chopra gave him a withering look before turning back to his bed.

THE WORM IN THE APPLE

Poppy returned just before lunch the next day, accompanied by Irfan.

She found her husband dozing in his bed, papers strewn over his quilt. She gently banged the steel tiffin she had brought along on his bedside trolley, snapping him awake. His haggard features brightened into a smile. 'I am glad you came back.'

'I brought you some food,' she said. 'God knows what they're feeding you in here.' She turned away and began fiddling with the tiffin.

Moments later the room was filled with the redolent smell of potato and cauliflower curry. Chopra felt his mouth gush with saliva. When was the last time he had really eaten?

Having laid out the meal, Poppy straightened. 'I apologise for shouting yesterday. I suppose by now I should be accustomed to you getting into this sort of situation.'

'Are you still angry with me?'

'It's not anger,' said Poppy. 'It's concern. You cannot understand how hard it is, knowing that you are out there treating life as if it is some sort of "plucking the chicken" game.'

Chopra turned this around in his mind. Ah. 'You mean "playing chicken".'

'What does it matter if it's plucking or playing?' said Poppy. 'The chicken always ends up dead.'

'You are being unfair. I did not ask for this. I was merely following through with my investigation. I had no idea where it would lead.'

Poppy unleashed a deep sigh. 'I know,' she wailed. 'It's just – it's just . . . Why is it always *you*?'

Chopra paused before replying. 'Because I care,' he said simply.

Her face cracked into the ghost of a smile. 'So do I. About *you*.'

She sat down, set his tray on the bed, and watched him eat.

Irfan, deeming it now safe to approach, came up and gave Chopra a hug. 'I made you this,' he said. He handed him a card. The front showed a crude drawing of what looked like a hillock with legs, and a stick figure with a moustache slightly bigger than its head. 'It is you and Ganesha.'

'It is wonderful,' said Chopra.

Irfan beamed.

'My mother sent you laxatives,' said Poppy.

'Poppy, I ran my van into a building. I do not have constipation.' He munched on a pickle. 'How is Ganesha?'

'He is grounded. A day or two indoors will be good for him.'

Chopra could not argue with that. The little elephant had gone above and beyond the call of duty, and was lucky to have come away from the episode unscathed. It always bothered him that his activities sometimes placed his ward in harm's way. Yet he would rather have the little elephant by his side than not. Chopra did not believe in luck. But if there was such a thing then Ganesha was, certifiably, two hundred kilos of good fortune.

He changed the topic. 'How goes it with your, ah, initiative?'

'The Poo2Loo campaign?'

'Yes.'

'We have had a minor setback.'

'Oh? What happened?' Chopra smiled. 'Did Mr Poo run off again?'

'No,' said Poppy gravely. 'Mr Poo accidentally set fire to himself.'

Chopra nearly choked on his chapatti.

'As you know, Bahadur was our new campaign mascot. He tried to smoke a cigarette without taking off his suit and somehow set fire to it. He is unharmed, thank God.'

Chopra tried to imagine a giant turd running down the street aflame. His imagination failed him.

Rangwalla arrived just as Poppy was washing out the tiffin in the sink.

He marched across the room, and set down a leather satchel on Chopra's bedside table with a triumphant flour-ish. 'Soman was more than helpful. In there you will find copies of all documents pertaining to properties purchased by Karma Holdings and its nested shell companies in the past decade which involved BMC permissions or approvals. Many of them were, in fact, repossessions by the BMC – buildings that had been condemned and seized – and later sold on at auction to Karma Holdings. There are over seventy of them inside Mumbai's municipal limits.' He paused. 'You were right. In almost every single case, Geeta Lokhani signed off on the seizure and the subsequent sale to Karma. There is additional paperwork attached to some of the cases. It appears that a number of the owners of these properties attempted to initiate court action against the BMC's orders. They either quickly changed their minds, or else mysteriously vanished. In at least two cases, they were killed in freak accidents.'

Chopra considered this wealth of new information.

His instincts may have led to the discovery, but Rangwalla's industry in putting flesh around the bones of his conjecture impressed him greatly. 'Well done, Rangwalla,' he said. 'This is superb investigative work. You have outdone yourself.'

His former deputy preened, basking in the rare moment of glory.

'Did you bring the map?'

'Also in the folder.'

Chopra spread the map of Mumbai on the bed.

Rangwalla rummaged in his bag and held out a red felt-tipped pen. 'You might need this.'

Chopra smiled. 'Your initiative is improving in leaps and bounds.'

'Shall I read out the addresses?'

'That would be helpful.'

One by one Rangwalla dipped into the satchel and removed the documents he had obtained. He riffled through the pages and read out the address of each property purchased by Karma Holdings and its associated companies, as Chopra made a corresponding mark on the map, together with a date of purchase. They quickly became engrossed in their work, and barely noticed when Poppy and Irfan made their farewells and left.

As much as she wished to stay, she had another busy day ahead on the Poo2Loo campaign.

She paused at the door, looking back at her husband, his injuries seemingly forgotten. If she was honest with herself this was how she had always pictured him, engrossed in the work that gave meaning to his existence. Would she truly wish him to be any other way?

A sad smile flickered over her lips, and then she slipped out quietly, unwilling to disturb them.

Ten minutes later a nurse shuffled in, wheeling an ECG monitor. She bumped into Rangwalla, took one look at his face, and shrank back in fright. 'My God, you are much worse than they told me!'

'I am not the patient,' said Rangwalla stonily.

The nurse donned a pair of spectacles hanging from a chain around her neck and peered closely at him. 'Are you sure? You could give a corpse a fright.'

Chopra concentrated on the map.

A pattern had begun to emerge.

At first the properties that Karma Holdings had bought up were scattered at sites around the city, but then, over the past three years, those sites became concentrated around one particular region. As he continued to mark the map, a suspicion began to form, gradually hardening into certainty. He began to understand exactly what Om Kaabra had been up to, and the audacity of it took his breath away.

He felt his hands closing around the truth.

And with this insight came the blinding realisation that perhaps, just perhaps, he had finally uncovered the true motive behind Cyrus Zorabian's death.

VOTE FOR GEETA LOKHANI!

The campaign offices of Geeta Lokhani, prospective member of the Legislative Assembly, were located on the ground floor of a well-heeled building in the wealthy suburb of Juhu. On one side was a designer fashion boutique, on the other a trendy patisserie.

The doctor in charge of Chopra had been unhappy about discharging him, in spite of reassurances that he was feeling fine. It had taken the intervention of Homi Contractor to engineer his escape. Homi had pulled the junior man aside and informed him, briskly, that Chopra was well known for his Lazarus-like powers of recovery.

'Poppy will kill me if she finds out,' he had said to his friend on the way out.

'Join the club,' Chopra had muttered in reply.

He glanced back at the police jeep that had brought him this far.

Behind the fly-splattered windscreen Inspector Kelkar waited nervously.

Two hours earlier Kelkar had arrived at the hospital with a manila file in hand. In the file was the information on Om Kaabra that Chopra had requested, cobbled together from a variety of police sources.

Chopra had swiftly gone through the material.

Kaabra had been born in a slum in Marol, near the Marol Pipeline. He had grown up in the Marol area and knew it well. His father had sold shaved ice drinks from a handcart, but had died during a stampede at the Elphinstone railway station that claimed thirty-eight lives. Kaabra's mother had died in his teenage years of lung disease. She had worked for years on unregulated building sites. The boy had grown up wild, drifting into begging, then later into petty criminality. He had joined a gang of teenage pickpockets. His work had not gone unnoticed. Recruited into a larger operation, he made his mark in the underworld with thievery, violence, extortion. Over the next three decades he had enjoyed a number of stays at the government's pleasure, for offences ranging from fraud to blackmail.

And then he had dropped off the radar.

This was the period when, according to Ajay Rangoon at the Serious Fraud Investigation Office, Kaabra had been building his property empire. He had been smart enough – smarter than many of his contemporaries, at any rate – to steer clear of those activities that might have seen him reincarcerated: guns, drugs, racketeering. He had also been smart enough to spread his new wealth around. It was now in many people's interests to keep Om Kaabra out of the spotlight and out of jail.

Yet the man had a ruthless streak.

His hand was suspected in the deaths of dozens of individuals around the country, mainly those who did not fall into line with the expansion of his property business. Direct evidence against him was in short supply. Witnesses refused to cooperate or had a bad habit of vanishing.

But perhaps Chopra had found a way to change that.

Having gone through the folder he had asked Kelkar to get the commissioner on the line.

Half an hour later, Chopra had the reassurances he needed.

Now, standing outside Lokhani's office, he turned once more to Kelkar, nodded, then walked towards the building.

He entered the office – a large, open-plan space lit by swathes of light falling in from tall sash windows – to find a scrum of mainly young people furiously spinning about the room. There was a manic energy to the place, a sense of sleeves being rolled up in pursuit of a cause. A shadow clouded his features as he realised that he would soon bring all this crashing down; he would dash the aspirations not only of Geeta Lokhani, but of all those who had pinned their hopes to her ascendancy.

And then he thought once more of Arushi Kadam's burned and blackened corpse and steel returned to his resolve.

A trumpet sounded by his ear, almost concussing him.

As he reeled from the blast, the eager young thug who had delivered it lunged forward and slapped a round sticker on to his shirt. Chopra looked down. The badge said: 'Vote for Geeta Lokhani!' Below this, in smaller font: *A woman who knows how to get things done in a city that needs things to be done.*

As a motto, it was somewhat of a mouthful, Chopra thought.

'How many hours can you spare today, sir?'

'What?' Chopra stared at him. 'Hours for what?'

'For distributing leaflets, of course!' The cadet gave a maniacally cheerful grin. If he had been a bottle of Coca-Cola, Chopra thought, the top of his head would have fizzed off, such was his unholy zeal for the job.

'How about none?' he growled. He ripped off the badge, then headed for the glass-walled office at the rear of the room, where he could see Geeta Lokhani speaking on the phone.

He charged in and was immediately confronted by a short, grim-looking woman in a pair of baggy trousers and a *Vote for Geeta Lokhani* T-shirt. 'Geeta is busy,' she snapped, hands on hips. 'And you cannot just barge in here. Next time make an appointment.'

'There will not be a next time,' said Chopra sternly. He took out his ID card. 'I must speak with you,' he said, facing Lokhani.

'Now look here—' interjected her PA, but Lokhani waved the woman away.

She put down the phone, and stared up at him, her features suddenly drawn. The PA looked between them, then stomped out, banging the door behind her.

Chopra set down the folder that Rangwalla had given him. 'In there are BMC documents approving the seizure and subsequent sale of numerous properties in Mumbai to

Karma Holdings and its associated companies. Nearly all are signed by you. Karma Holdings is run by a criminal by the name of Om Kaabra – but I suspect you already know that. Kaabra's modus operandi is to extort the owners of these buildings into selling to him at below market rates. If they do not, they are threatened, assaulted, even killed. Thirteen people died in a building collapse in Marol that I am certain Kaabra was behind. More recently two employees of Karma Holdings were murdered – Arushi Kadam and Vijay Narlikar – on his orders. Before his death Cyrus Zorabian visited Karma Holdings numerous times. I believe that his murder is tied up with Kaabra's property dealings. And I believe that you are also involved.'

The muscles of Lokhani's jaw twitched. She seemed stunned, yet not altogether surprised.

'You knew I would come for you, didn't you?' said Chopra. 'From that first moment at the opera house, when I came in asking about Cyrus?'

She blinked. 'You seemed the tenacious type.'

'And today? Now? Did your friend Kaabra warn you that I was on the trail?'

'He is not my friend!' She said this with such vehemence that he was momentarily taken aback.

'You have helped him build an empire, an empire built on the ashes of many hopes and dreams.'

'You are mistaken. I was merely an employee of the BMC.' She tilted her chin in defiance. 'Whatever you may *think* I have done, you cannot prove it.'

Chopra pointed at the folder. 'These records are now with the Central Bureau of Investigation. The commissioner of police and the chief minister have been informed. They have unleashed their dogs. The paper trail will be followed. Interviews will be conducted with those whose properties were taken. There is no hiding from what you have done. It will all come out. All this' – Chopra waved at the office – 'is over. A CBI officer is waiting outside to take you into custody. The best you can hope for now is to avoid imprisonment by cooperating with the authorities. Help bring Kaabra in.'

Lokhani seemed to collapse in on herself. A dark silence pulsed in the office. 'It was never meant to be like this. All I wanted to do was help this broken city. When I was a girl, my father once said to me: "Whoever owns the land, owns the wealth of Mumbai." Such power in the hands of a privileged few!' Her eyes danced with anger. 'Seven years ago, Kaabra came to me with a proposition. He told me that if I used my position at the BMC to help him gain a particular parcel of land, he would ensure it was developed into housing for the poor. I was younger then, naïve. I thought that, with a flourish of my pen, I could set right the legacy of inequality that our feudal system bequeathed us. So what if I had to bend the rules? The only people being hurt were wealthy elitists who had made that wealth off the backs of the disenfranchised.' She looked at him finally, her face full of regret. 'But it never worked out that way.'

'It never does,' murmured Chopra.

'Kaabra betrayed me. Once he had the land, he sold it to a mall developer. Instead of homes for the poor, he gave the city another shopping centre. I tried to fight back, but his

314

goons paid me a visit. I was threatened. I told them to get out; they broke my arm. And then he blackmailed me. If I made a fuss, he would expose my collusion. I would lose the post I had worked years to attain. I would be cast out, back to a life of nothing.'

'And so you continued to help him.'

'I had no choice. I was in so deep, there was no way out. I tried to rationalise it to myself. I told myself that these new developments created jobs for the poor, that one day Kaabra would see the light. But I was wrong.'

'Kaabra built those places on the backs of other people's misery. Extortion, blackmail, even murder.'

She was silent. There was nothing to say.

'Your only chance is to strike a deal. I have the commissioner's reassurance that if you help convict Kaabra, you will go free. You will never work for the BMC again, and you will never run for office. But if you don't take this deal I am sure there are others in the BMC or at Karma Holdings who will.'

Chopra opened the folder to show her the map of Mumbai upon which he had marked the properties that Karma Holdings had recently acquired. He pointed at the concentration of purchases made in the past three years. They made a neat ring around Doongerwadi, home to the Parsee Towers of Silence.

'There is only one reason that Kaabra would acquire these properties. It is because he anticipates their value rising dramatically. And *that* will only happen if something monumental is due to change in the immediate landscape.' Chopra paused to allow his words to sink in. 'At first I thought Cyrus Zorabian was embezzling funds from the Vashi slum redevelopment project under the guise of philanthropy. But I was wrong. My guess is that he had agreed to *sell* Doongerwadi to Om Kaabra, via Karma Holdings. That was how he intended to save his failing business empire.

'But he knew he could never accomplish that without the BMC's help. Doongerwadi is holy ground. If it is taken from the Parsees then something else must be given in return. That was where you came in. The Vashi slum redevelopment site – New Haven. The BMC, in other words *you*, secretly agreed to approve a "change of use" proposal for the Vashi development from a slum rehousing scheme to a new site for the Towers of Silence, out on the edge of the city. By doing so, Cyrus could sell Doongerwadi, and still have something to placate the Parsee community that he had betrayed. The storm would be terrible, but he was confident he could ride it out. Besides, what choice did he have? Doongerwadi is a prime property. Kaabra stands to make a fortune by developing it. No doubt he agreed to pay Cyrus handsomely for the site. I have already discovered what appears to be an initial fee – ten million in cash – in a bank locker Cyrus kept from his family.

'Of course, where there are winners there are always losers. And the losers in all this are the slum dwellers that *you* had promised a new home. Their old homes will be demolished; but there will be no Eden waiting for them in Vashi. They will be homeless, at the mercy of your "broken city".'

Lokhani did not reply. The mask had shattered; silent tears leaked from her eyes.

Chopra leaned over the desk again, and opened the folder to a photograph of Arushi Kadam and Vijay Narlikar's burned corpses. 'Tell me why they were killed.'

Lokhani stared sightlessly at the wall behind him. A poster of Gandhi looked back down at her.

'Arushi's mother will never know peace until she knows why her daughter died.'

Finally, she blinked. 'Arushi and Cyrus met at the offices of Karma Holdings. He seduced her. Turned her head with talk of his wealth, hinted that he was on the lookout for a second wife. It began as harmless flirting, a lecherous older man and an impressionable younger woman. Yet somehow Arushi fell for his charms, such as they were.

'She worked in the records section of Karma Holdings. I don't know exactly how it happened, but somehow she found out that the Vashi redevelopment was just a front, and that Cyrus was going to sell Doongerwadi to Kaabra. Or perhaps Cyrus told her himself. Bedroom whispers. The vanity of an old man.

'Of course, none of this would have mattered, except that Arushi already had a boyfriend. Vijay.

'Vijay found out about the affair – and about Cyrus's plans for Doongerwadi. He became enraged, bitter. He confronted Arushi in the office, threatened to expose Cyrus, as a way of getting back at her. He was overheard by the wrong person. He was just lashing out; he didn't understand that he was signing his own death warrant.'

'Kaabra had them both killed.'

Her head jerked into a nod. 'He couldn't risk word of the Doongerwadi sale getting out before the formalities had been completed. He knew there would be a public backlash from the Parsee community; they are powerful and politically connected. Given a chance they would have buried the sale in red tape, perhaps for years.'

'They were murdered in cold blood, then burned.' Chopra's voice was cold with fury. 'Part of that responsibility rests on *your* shoulders.'

'Don't you think I know that?' Her eyes were pinpricks into oblivion.

'What about Cyrus?' said Chopra. 'Why was *he* killed? Did he get cold feet? Try to back out of the deal? Or did he just get greedy?'

'Kaabra had nothing to do with Cyrus's murder.'

'You expect me to believe that?'

'You said it yourself. Kaabra *needed* Cyrus. Cyrus's death has ruined his plan. The power to sell Doongerwadi rests with the Zorabian family. Now his daughter, Perizaad, has that power. But she will never sell to him.'

'He has approached her?'

'Not yet. Cyrus's death has thrown everything into confusion. Kaabra knows that Perizaad is unwilling to let her father's murder go. He cannot approach her until the matter is settled. And Darius – he is out of the fold, disinherited.'

'If Kaabra did not kill Cyrus, then who did?'

'I do not know. That is the truth.'

As Lokhani folded into the back of Kelkar's jeep, Chopra pulled the man aside. 'Have you arrested John Reddy at Karma Holdings?'

'He is being taken to CBI headquarters as we speak.'

'You must play them off against each other; offer them protection from Kaabra. They will give you everything you need to bring him to justice.'

Kelkar smiled. 'I have done this before, you know.'

Chopra nodded. 'Forgive me. I sometimes forget that I no longer wear a uniform.'

'There is nothing to forgive. This will be the making of me. Frankly, I am amazed you are handing me Kaabra on a platter.'

'There is nothing more I can do. I do not have the authority or the resources to bring him in. My only concern is Rao. How will *he* react to this?'

'I went behind his back to the commissioner. When he finds out he will blow his top. But by then it won't matter.'

Chopra spent a few dreamy seconds picturing the moment ACP Rao would discover that he had been made a fool of. It was the sort of memory he wished he could press into a scrapbook, and then take out again when he was old and wizened, lodged by a winter fire with a glass of sherry in his hand, just so that he could gloat.

He stuck out a hand. 'I wish you the best of luck.'

Kelkar shook his hand. 'The day you retired was the force's loss. Sir.'

Chopra sat in the coffee shop next door to the campaign offices, ordered a fresh lime juice, and contemplated his next move.

The facts of the case had worked their way into his mind like smoke; he was infused by them, choking on them, yet could not gain clarity. He was sure that Lokhani believed what she had told him, namely that Om Kaabra had played no part in the murder of Cyrus Zorabian. But that did not necessarily make it so. There was still a chance that Kaabra had had the Parsee industrialist killed.

But why?

Why kill him if he needed Cyrus's cooperation? Unless . . . Cyrus had done something to incur his wrath.

Had he reneged on the deal to sell Doongerwadi? That would explain much, including why the murder itself had the markings of a crime of passion. Perhaps Kaabra had sent one of his underlings to talk sense into Cyrus, and when the prickly Parsee had refused it had ended in disaster. A moment of madness. Might this also be why Cyrus had kept hold of the article about the burned bodies of Arushi Kadam and Vijay Narlikar? A reminder to himself of what Kaabra was capable of? Or perhaps he had kept the cutting out of a sense of guilt, guilt that had later fuelled a change of heart in his dealings with the gangster? It was impossible to know for sure, though what he had learned of Cyrus Zorabian did not inspire any confidence that the man had suddenly grown a conscience.

Which left him back exactly where he had started.

He took out his notebook.

VASEEM KHAN

Over the course of the next hour he carefully went over everything he had learned. There was something here that he had missed, there had to be . . .

His concentration was broken by the ringing of his phone. It was the vet Lala. 'I couldn't get that vulture of yours out of my head.'

'At least she's only in your *head*,' muttered Chopra.

'Yes. I'd heard you'd lodged her in your house.' His mirth was apparent down the line.

'I'm glad my discomfort amuses you.'

'I should have warned you. They are *very* territorial. At any rate, you asked me to follow up for you—'

'You volunteered to follow up.'

'Semantics!' said Lala. 'Do you want to hear what I have to say or not? I have a buffalo in need of a colonic waiting for me.'

'Go ahead,' growled Chopra.

'I decided to start by having a poke around Doongerwadi myself. I gave your client Perizaad a call to help arrange entry. I hope you don't mind.' Lala did not wait to hear if Chopra minded or not. 'I spoke to a few of the corpse-bearers – fascinating people! Apparently, there's been a spate of these poisonings in the past months.'

'I already know this,' said Chopra.

'I am sure you do, being an all-powerful detective,' said Lala breezily. 'But I don't suppose you managed to find out where the bodies of some of the others had been buried? And I don't suppose you then dug up those decomposed remains and had them tested for toxins?'

Chopra hesitated. 'No. I did not.'

'Ah. Well, not quite omnipotent then,' said Lala. 'At any rate, I now have the results back. I can confirm that all the vultures were poisoned. By the same toxin.'

'I had already assumed the same.'

'Well, yes, Mr Know-it-all, but did *you* trace all known supplies of diclofenac in the Mumbai Greater Metropolitan Region? Did *you* then contact the holders of those supplies, and threaten to send inspectors from the national Pesticide and Animal Medicines Regulatory Agency to their premises if they did not reveal any recent clandestine sales of their stock?'

'No,' said Chopra. 'That is what you agreed to do.'

'That's right,' said Lala triumphantly. 'And a bloody good job I did too. There were only four individuals who had access to the quantity of diclofenac needed to kill off the number of vultures my estimates show have perished in the past year at Doongerwadi. I visited each one. It turns out that one of them sold roughly such a quantity to a man calling himself Firdous Chichgar. Tall, bullish, pale-skinned older gentleman with a head of curly grey hair. Wearing a fine linen suit and cravat. Sound like anyone we know?' Before Chopra could answer, Lala went on. 'When I showed him a photograph of Cyrus Zorabian, he confirmed that it was the same man.'

Chopra was stunned.

Cyrus Zorabian had poisoned the vultures at Doongerwadi. But why?

The answer, in light of recent revelations, was obvious.

Cyrus had secretly planned to sell Doongerwadi to Om Kaabra, and move the Towers of Silence to the new site at

Vashi, the plot ostensibly set aside for a slum redevelopment project. He knew the backlash that would follow from his own community would be terrible, and so he had prepared the ground. By killing off the vultures at Doongerwadi his intention had been to bring to a head the long-running argument that it was now unsound for bodies to be left in the towers to decompose with little assistance from scavengers to dispose of them. This was probably also why Cyrus had sacked the priests who had attempted to introduce cremation to Doongerwadi. He could not afford to have the site being used in this alternative way, facilitating a possible route to its continued viability.

Clearly, Cyrus had planned everything, down to the last detail.

For a moment, Chopra marvelled at the man's resolve.

Poisoning the vultures would have meant repeated visits to Doongerwadi, having injected the diclofenac into the bodies of rodents or other small animals that vultures would be tempted to eat, and then scattering them strategically around the forested site. And all of this without being found out. At least it explained his recent penchant for wandering about Doongerwadi late at night.

It had not been for the purposes of solitude, after all.

The ingenuity of the murdered Parsee was almost worthy of admiration. Almost . . .

He thanked Lala, ended the call, then went back to his notes.

He turned back to the page upon which he had listed all the suspects:

CZ estranged from son. Darius Zorabian married against CZ wishes. Darius angry with CZ for disinheriting him. Darius has no alibi.

CZ and Boman Jeejibhoy fell out over Darius spurning Boman's daughter. Boman enraged, threatens CZ. Boman has no alibi.

CZ angers Anosh Ginwala, head corpse-bearer at Doongerwadi. Ginwala loses family, blames CZ. Ginwala has motive, means, but not opportunity.

CZ PA William Buckley is a former criminal, convicted of violent assault. Did he have grudge against CZ? If so, why?

He considered each suspect in turn, turning over in his mind everything he had learned.

Nothing sprang out from the morass of detail.

Time ticked away.

He checked his watch, then tapped at it with a fingernail. The damned thing was stuck again. The only reason he held on to it was in memory of his late father, who had given it to him on the day of his wedding. He took off the watch, held it beside his ear, then set it down on the table, beside his cup.

The sight triggered an unexpected memory, and he was gripped by the strange sensation that he had seen this before . . .

Buckley.

When he had met Buckley at the coffee shop, the PA's watch had also been set down on the table, beside his coffee cup. It had been flat on its face, the straps stretched out like the arms of a penitent. And on the back of the casing, inscribed in Roman script, had been words.

At the time, something had bothered him about the watch. He now knew it was the inscription. The words hung before him, outlined in fire. And in those words: revelation.

A MAN OF PRINCIPLE

The Samundra Mahal was as he remembered it, white-washed and breezy against the blue dome of the sky. This time he was let in by a creaking houseboy who led him down the ancestral fairway to the same drawing room in which he had met Perizaad Zorabian for the first time.

Buckley was standing by the window, silhouetted by the falling light. A glass of what looked like whisky was clutched in his left hand; his right foot tapped lightly against the mosaic floor, revealing his inner agitation. From her seat behind the desk, Perizaad Zorabian watched him with an expression of concern.

When Chopra entered they turned as one to watch him make his way to the centre of the room.

'What is this about?' snapped Buckley.

'It is about a watch,' said Chopra calmly.

For an instant, the Englishman's brow clouded with confusion, and then his eyes widened.

Chopra pointed at Buckley's wrist. 'May I?'

He saw the conflict in the PA's smooth-shaven features. He shot a glance at Perizaad, who had risen behind her desk, her hands bunched into fists.

They exchanged a look, and then Perizaad nodded.

Buckley took off the watch and handed it to Chopra.

'I saw the inscription on the back when we met in the coffee shop. But at the time it simply did not register.'

He held the watch to his face, and read the inscription aloud. '*For a man of principle, PZ.*'

Turning to Perizaad, he said, 'You gave him this watch. And so I had to ask myself: why would you do that? Why would you give such a watch, such an inscription, to a man you did not even wish to give a job?'

Perizaad's shoulders straightened. 'You clearly know the answer, so why ask the question?'

'How long have you been . . . together?'

'We are not together. Not really. Being together, truly together, would mean that we could be open about our relationship.'

'What stopped you?'

'You know the answer to that too.'

Chopra nodded. 'Cyrus. He would never have approved of a match between his daughter and his PA. A white man, a non-Parsee, an *employee*.' He faced Buckley. 'When last we met you said to me: "I had no reason to kill the man." We can both agree that that premise no longer holds. Perhaps Cyrus found out about your affair. Perhaps he wished to confront you. You called him that evening, asked him to meet you at Doongerwadi. You knew he liked to go there. You knew he had his own key to the gate. Perhaps your intention was to reason with him, far from prying eyes, listening ears. He let you in, led you into the forest. You talked. The talk flared into an argument. Things got out of hand. Or maybe you planned it that way from the very beginning.'

Buckley was shaking his head. 'You could not be more wrong. Cyrus never knew about Perizaad and me. We were careful to keep it a secret. We knew that we would have to tell him one day, but we weren't ready, not yet. At least, I was not.' He glanced at Perizaad, a curious sense of shame softening his hard features. 'I had nothing to do with his death, Chopra. Do you really think I would murder the father of the woman I love, the woman I hope to spend my life with?'

'I have seen men kill each other for a million reasons,' said Chopra phlegmatically.

'No!'

They both turned.

Perizaad's face was suffused with anger. She moved out from behind the desk, walked to Buckley, and stood by his side. 'You have no idea what you're talking about. William could not have killed my father.'

'Yet you chose to keep your affair a secret from me.' Again, Chopra allowed his annoyance to show. 'You have continually hampered my investigation by not presenting me with all the facts.'

'I didn't tell you about William because I knew you'd jump to the wrong conclusion. You knew my father was a traditionalist. You'd suspect he confronted William about me – exactly the scenario you have just painted.'

'I wonder,' said Chopra, 'if you are in full possession of the facts. Did you know, for instance, that William Buckley was once Adam Beresford, a convicted criminal who served time in a British prison for violent assault?'

She gave a sharp intake of breath, her body stiffening. Beside her Buckley had gone the colour of milk.

'You're lying,' hissed Perizaad.

Chopra said nothing. There was no need.

She turned to Buckley, her eyes frantically searching his face. What she saw told her all she needed to know. 'How could you keep something like that from me?'

Buckley could not meet her gaze. 'Because I did not want to lose your respect. Because you are the most capable, remarkable, intelligent, exhilarating woman I have ever met. Because I was in love with you. And because I was afraid.'

'What about honesty? What about truth?'

Buckley hung his head. 'I wish I could go back and do things differently. I was a coward. Adam Beresford is who I once was. I haven't been that man for many years. There is nothing else I can say.'

She stared at him. And then she reached out and put a hand to his cheek. 'If you had trusted me, I would have trusted you.'

He looked into her eyes. 'I never expected this. To find someone I adored at this stage of my life. I was afraid of losing you.' He breathed deeply. 'But I had nothing to do with your father's death. Whatever happens next, *that* you must believe.'

She grasped his hands, squeezed. 'I know.'

She turned to Chopra. 'I told you before that William could not have killed my father. I meant that as the literal truth. On the night my father was murdered, he was with me. We knew my father would be tied up at the club that evening, so we spent the time together at William's place.'

Chopra's eyes moved over her face. He sensed the truth in her words.

He turned to Buckley. 'Why didn't you just tell me this when we spoke?'

'You know why.'

'I am investigating a murder. Discretion may be chivalrous but it was your duty to tell me the truth.'

Buckley said nothing.

'Is there anything else you haven't told me?' asked Chopra. 'Either of you?'

'No,' said Perizaad.

Buckley shook his head. 'Over the last few years Cyrus has been increasingly secretive. As his PA you probably think I knew everything he was doing or involved in. Nothing could be further from the truth.'

'So what now?' asked Perizaad.

Chopra sighed. 'I am not sure. I was certain I was on to something, but it appears to be another dead-end.'

Back outside, Chopra paused beneath a palm tree looming over the road.

A car raced by in a rush of warm wind.

He had felt so close. Close enough to reach out and touch the answer.

He couldn't shake the feeling that he had all the pieces of the puzzle. He simply had to put them together in the right way.

The truth was that the suspects in most murders were circumscribed by a narrow circle made by the victim's life; the people he knew or had contact with. That limited set of suspects could further be whittled down by the age-old policing stalwarts of motive, means, opportunity. Completely random murders were almost unheard of. People didn't just wander out of their homes, pick up a weapon, and bash in the skull of a stranger.

He took out his notebook.

It was all here, everything he needed.

He ticked off the suspects one by one.

William Buckley. In light of the meeting he had just had he felt confident in eliminating the Englishman from his list of suspects.

Which left Jeejibhoy, Ginwala and Darius Zorabian.

A certainty had slowly formed in him that Cyrus's killer was someone close to him. Someone who could write to him in Latin, obliquely threatening him. Which meant that as much as Ginwala hated the man, he was probably not the killer. Besides, Ginwala had been seen in his hut, dead to the world, around the time of the murder.

Jeejibhoy and Darius, then.

Two men chained together by a broken promise. A promise made by Cyrus to his old friend to unite their two houses. Both men furious at Cyrus, for different reasons.

The thought that had been lurking just below the surface of his mind snapped into clarity.

The killer had summoned Cyrus to Doongerwadi on the night of his death. Cyrus's phone records showed that the call that had drawn him out from the Vulture Club had been made from an untraceable phone. But that was not the point. The point was that the killer had to have known that Cyrus *would* come to Doongerwadi. Would the old Parsee really have done that for Boman Jeejibhoy, a man who had already threatened him publicly? Who had tried to oust him from the club?

No. Chopra could not see that.

Which left Darius.

Surely Cyrus would have been willing to drop everything and meet his estranged son. All Darius would have had to do was to feed his father a story about how he wished to return to the fold. How he would divorce his American wife, and submit himself to Cyrus's edicts. But, once he had Cyrus in the isolation of Doongerwadi, had Darius instead attempted to make his father listen to reason? Chopra pictured a desperate Darius pleading to be re-instated, begging Cyrus to consider his unborn grandson. And Cyrus refusing to be moved. A heart as cold as stone. And the argument spiralling into something worse, the darkness of the woods transforming Darius's pleas into a murderous rage.

Yes, it could have happened like that.

But there was something else, itching away at the back of Chopra's mind.

Why Doongerwadi?

Yes, it was secluded, but it was also holy ground. It *meant* something to the killer. Chopra was suddenly sure of this, the thought flaming brightly like a fire given oxygen.

Cyrus Zorabian had been lured to Doongerwadi because the killer had discovered his plans to sell the place. Indeed, it was now clear to him that this was what the Latin letters sent to Cyrus had alluded to.

He felt the thought slide into place like a brick cemented carefully into position in a great wall. The wall felt solid, unbreachable.

On the heels of this thought came another: the killer had to have had a set of keys to Doongerwadi. Or they had known that Cyrus had his own set.

He felt the truth edging closer.

And then he had it.

A KILLER REVEALED

The late afternoon sun lit up the stone vultures standing guard atop the gates to the Ahura Mazda Parsee Sports and Social Gymkhana. As Chopra approached it seemed to him that their bald heads were aflame.

He stopped at the guard booth, flashed his ID, and spoke to the security guard.

'Who is in charge of security at the club?'

'That would be Anwar Sahib,' replied the man.

'Where can I find him?'

'He is not here, sir. I will have to call him.'

'Please do so.'

Fifteen minutes later a Tata Sumo four-by-four arrived. Mohammed Anwar, head of security for the Vulture Club, a small, neatly pressed man in a dark blue safari suit, got out. 'What's this all about?' he asked.

'I need to ask you some questions. About the night Cyrus Zorabian was killed.'

Anwar considered this, then nodded. 'Go ahead.'

'Who let him out that evening?'

Anwar looked at the guard. 'If I recall, you were on duty that night, weren't you, Mahajan?'

'Yes, sir.'

'Did he say anything to you?' said Chopra.

'Yes. He swore at me to open the gates.'

Chopra raised an eyebrow. 'Was that usual?'

The guard shrugged. 'You never could tell with Mr Zorabian. Sometimes, he'd laugh and joke with you – he knew a lot of dirty jokes – and at other times he looked like he wanted to rope you to the back of his jeep and race through the streets. He had a filthy temper.' A thought seemed to occur to him, and he glanced fearfully at Anwar. 'I hope I'm not speaking out of turn. I need this job.'

'The man is dead,' said Chopra. 'Anything you tell me stays between us. That night, would you say he was agitated?'

'He flew out of here like a tiger with its tail on fire, if that's what you mean.'

'After he left, did anyone follow him from the club?'

'No, sir.'

'Is there another way out?'

'There's a fire exit at the rear,' supplied Anwar.

'Show me.'

He allowed the puzzled head of security to lead him along a narrow, gated alley running by the side of the main building. They emerged into a manicured rear garden, bisected by tiled walkways and dotted with fountains and canopied garden tables. Anwar led him to a bolted door in the club's fifteen-foot-high outer wall.

They stepped out into a deserted alleyway, lined by trees, and backing on to the rear façades of a succession of old buildings. To his left the alley petered to a dead-end. To the right, it travelled a hundred yards before hitting a gate that, he presumed, let out on to the main road.

'Is that gate locked?'

'Yes.'

'Who has the keys to it?'

'There are a couple of sets here. Technically the alley belongs to the club. But we don't really use it for anything.'

A rat ran across the narrow road, vanishing into a drain on the far side.

Chopra turned back to look at the wall of the Vulture Club.

Mounted on the wall, directly above the door, was a video camera.

'Is that camera active?'

'Yes.'

'I'd like to see the recording for the evening that Cyrus was killed.'

'That is not possible. Recordings are on a seven-day cycle, after which they are erased.'

Chopra cursed silently. He looked around the alley, his eyes roving over the confined space. His gaze swept upwards, to the building directly opposite the doorway. A succession of narrow windows looked down on the alley.

'What is that building?'

'That? It belongs to a software company. InterWeb Solutions.'

'Do you know anyone there?'

'I know the head of security. We've shared a cigarette or two.'

'I need to speak to him.'

'Her,' said Anwar. 'Speak to *her*.'

Ten minutes later they were in the air-conditioned office of Shruti Deshmukh. The small, intense woman listened to Chopra's explanation, then rose from her seat. 'Come with me.'

She led them up to the second floor, then out on to an open-plan space criss-crossed by rows of corrals. Inside the corrals, men and women – mostly young – tapped away on computer screens. A buzz of background conversation rose above the sound of keyboards being hacked at with violent abandon. There was an informal atmosphere to the place at odds with the workplace environment that Chopra associated with the India of his youth.

But then, wasn't that the point?

This was no longer the India he had once known.

Deshmukh led them to a corral on the far side of the room. The cubicle abutted a window that looked down on the alley outside the Vulture Club.

A middle-aged man sat in the cubicle, pushing a mouse around. On the screen was a detailed rendering of a tiger.

He looked up as the trio descended on him. For a moment, a look of instinctive guilt flickered over his face, and then he stood to face them.

'This is Yeshwant Dalvi,' said Deshmukh. 'He works a late shift, and seems to be here all the time. Perhaps he may have seen something.'

Chopra introduced himself, then said, 'I am investigating the murder of Cyrus Zorabian. He was the chairman of the Vulture Club. Do you recall the incident?'

'Of course,' said Dalvi. 'It was a big deal around here. The club is our neighbour, after all.'

'On the night that he died, were you here in the office?'

Dalvi nodded slowly. 'It was three months ago, but yes, I was.'

'How can you be sure?'

'Because the next day, when news of his death hit the papers, I remember talking to a colleague about it. The evening he died had been the deadline for a major graphics project I had been working on. I'd been in the office till well past midnight – liaising with our client in the States.'

Chopra was impressed with the man's even tone. 'In that case, perhaps you could answer a question for me. On that evening, did you see anything unusual in the alley below? Any activity at all?'

Dalvi considered this, then said, 'No, I'm afraid not.'

Chopra felt the disappointment as a physical reaction. He racked his brain for another question, but there was no point.

'Thank you,' he said.

As he turned, Dalvi spoke again. 'Actually, now that I think about it, there *was* something. Not exactly *activity* . . .'

Chopra turned back.

'A car was parked in the alley. I've never seen a car in there before – other than the occasional municipal work van – so I remember it clearly. It was there when I arrived for work around 2 p.m. Later, I noticed it had gone.'

'When was that?'

'Around ten. The funny thing is, when I looked back again around midnight it was there again.'

Chopra suppressed the bolt of excitement that flew through him.

'Can you describe the car to me?'

'Actually, I can. It was a red Tata Nexon. One of the new Tata models. I remember because I'm planning on buying one myself.'

Chopra turned to Anwar. 'Does anyone at the club own a red Tata Nexon?'

Anwar nodded slowly, a frown on his face. 'Yes,' he said. 'There is one person.'

And he told Chopra the name.

Chopra made his way up to the club's dining room.

Here he discovered the club's veterans Forhad and Dinshaw huddled over a green-felted poker table playing cards.

'I need to ask you some questions about the night Cyrus went missing.'

'You already did that,' said Forhad. 'Or have you forgotten? I thought we were the ones supposed to be senile.'

Dinshaw snickered.

'Cyrus attended the lecture given by Zubin Engineer,' said Chopra, ignoring the remark.

'Is that a question?'

'No. Cyrus attended but left early. The question is, did *you* stay for the whole lecture?'

'It's not like we had a choice,' said Forhad. 'Engineer gets prissy if we don't muck in.'

'It lasted the whole two hours?'

'Unfortunately,' said Dinshaw.

'How would you know?' said Forhad. 'You slept through most of it.'

'And when it was done?' asked Chopra.

'When it was done Engineer turned the lights back on, took a bow, answered a few questions, and finally led us to supper. My stomach was about to mutiny by then, I can tell you.'

Chopra rose. 'Thank you.'

'That's it?' asked Forhad suspiciously.

'That's it.'

'What are you up to, Chopra?'

'Just trying to piece together a timeline for the evening.'

'Give my regards to that elephant of yours!' said Dinshaw as the private detective left, Anwar close on his heels.

Chopra made his way to the lecture hall. Rows of seats had been laid out, theatre-style, facing the stage. Daylight flooded in from a succession of bay windows.

'Close the curtains,' he said to Anwar.

Anwar did as he was bid, plunging the room into darkness.

Chopra nodded. With the lights out, it was impossible to see a thing. The only light would come from the screen.

He stumbled his way to the panel, and switched on the lights.

Then he walked over to the AV console, a complicated-looking deck of equipment that controlled the screen, USB ports and speakers.

'Is there someone who knows how all this operates?' he asked.

'That would be young Bilimoria. He is our resident IT genius.'

'Where can I find him?'

'You would have to call him. He usually only comes to the club when we need him.'

'Do you have his phone number?'

Anwar hesitated. 'Is this still part of your enquiry into Mr Zorabian's death?'

'Yes.'

'Very well. We have a register of contact details for all members. Bilimoria is a member by virtue of his father. I can dig up his number.'

Chopra waited as Anwar disappeared, then returned ten minutes later with the details scribbled on a chit.

He dialled the number. Once it connected, he quickly introduced himself and explained what he was looking for.

Bilimoria was only too glad to help.

By the end of the conversation Chopra had the information he needed.

Finally, the killer was in his crosshairs.

He closed his eyes and tried to piece together how the murder might have transpired. He could almost visualise everything that had happened, how Cyrus's murderer had planned the killing down to the last detail, how he had executed that plan.

But there was one gap in his reasoning, he realised.

The murder weapon.

Where would his suspected killer have obtained it? How would he have disposed of it? This killer was surely not a person used to the fine art of murder.

His mind spun around in wild loops of conjecture. What was it the pathologist had suggested? That the murder weapon was heavy and blunt, possibly something with a rounded tip.

A rounded tip.

What sort of weapon had a rounded profile?

A baseball bat.

A club.

No.

Neither of those felt right. Not for the killer he had in mind.

What else?

He closed his eyes again, willing the thought writhing around in his subconscious mind to break the surface and flap its way into the light.

A rounded tip. A club. Or a—

He had it.

His eyes snapped open, and he looked over at Anwar who had been watching him patiently.

'Come with me,' said Chopra.

Minutes later, he stood in the lobby before the display housing the waxwork of the club's founder, Rustom Zorabian. So lifelike was the sculpture that he almost expected the plough-nosed old goat to rise up from his seat to confront him.

'Open this case.'

Anwar frowned. 'I cannot do that.'

'Why not?'

'I do not have permission.'

'Whose permission do you need?'

'Well, usually only Mr—'

He stopped as Chopra raised a hand. 'I am giving you permission. By order of the commissioner of police of Mumbai. Do you understand?'

Anwar looked displeased, but nodded.

He trotted off and soon returned with a set of master keys.

Under Chopra's scrutiny he unlocked the glass case and swung back the doors.

Chopra plucked a handkerchief from his pocket, then leaned in, and took the ceremonial mace from the old Parsee's unresisting hand.

He examined the mace minutely, until finally he grimaced in triumph.

There, lodged just beneath the heavy circular dome, encrusted into the splice, were three tell-tale drops of dried blood.

THE MEANING OF DUTY

He found the club secretary Zubin Engineer in his office, painstakingly composing a letter on his computer. Chopra moved over the tiled floor, then set down the mace on Engineer's desk. The man's eyes wobbled behind his spectacles; he exhaled slowly, then fell back against his seat, his frail body suddenly limp.

'When did you find out about Cyrus's plan to sell Doongerwadi?'

Engineer said nothing, merely blinked slowly.

'The notion shocked you to the core,' continued Chopra, 'shook loose something wild and uncontrollable. You knew that you could not sit by and let this happen – not you, secretary of the Vulture Club, custodian of the community's great heritage. What I don't understand is why didn't you confront him? Why send him the anonymous letters?'

Engineer finally seemed to revive. His eyes fell to the mace. A sense of resignation slumped his shoulders; his

345

features softened into melancholy. 'Because I am powerless here,' he said softly. 'Club secretary may sound like an important position, but the truth is that Cyrus has always treated me as little more than a glorified receptionist. Had I confronted him directly, he would have dismissed me. And where would I go then? This place is everything to me. My wife passed years ago. I have no children. The club is my only reason for getting up each morning.'

'And what of your responsibility to your community?'

Engineer snapped his head up. 'Who are you to talk to me of responsibility? I have spent my life trying to uphold our traditions. When I found out about Cyrus's plan I was horrified. He had left his jacket here at the club one evening. As I picked it up the blueprints fell out for his planned new site for the Towers of Silence out in Vashi, together with a land transfer document prepared by him regarding the sale. Once I finished reading it, I put it back inside his jacket, my hands trembling. That was the moment all this began.

'I racked my brain for a way to get Cyrus to change his mind. I thought of going to the other committee members, but that would have been futile. Cyrus is king here, the rest of us mere courtiers. I even considered going public – but then I realised that if I did I would give ammunition to those who have been clamouring for years for Doongerwadi to be moved to another site. After all, if the head of the Zorabian family, the ancestral owner of Doongerwadi, was willing to sell up, then what chance would the rest of us have to save the site? Somehow, I had to dissuade Cyrus without alerting the world.'

'That was when you hit upon the idea of sending him the letters.'

Engineer nodded. 'It was the only thing I could think of.'

'But why in Latin? And why keep them vague? Why not explicitly tell him to stop the development?'

'I dared not risk being too direct. I did not wish to raise any suspicion in him that I was behind them. He has been reading correspondence from me for forty years. Had I been explicit, in English, he would have instantly recognised my writing style. At least, that is what I feared. Perhaps that fear was unjustified. Perhaps if I *had* confronted him none of this would have happened.'

'At some point you realised that your letters were ineffective. That they would not dissuade him.'

'Yes. I overheard him on the phone one day, at the club. He received the call while he was with me and, in typical Cyrus fashion, commandeered my office. I pretended to leave, but hung around outside with the door cracked open. He was talking to someone – I don't know who – about how they would soon break ground on the New Haven plot. He was reassuring the other party that he would easily manage the storm that would arise after he announced the sale of Doongerwadi, that legally the Parsee community could do nothing to stop him.'

'That was the moment you decided that there was only one way to stop him,' said Chopra.

Engineer nodded sadly. 'He made up my mind for me.'

'Tell me about that evening, the evening of his death. Cyrus came to the club for a meeting of the committee. You had scheduled a lecture afterwards. Cyrus decided to attend the lecture – or perhaps you begged him to stay. You made a point of telling me that you were on stage when he received the call summoning him to Doongerwadi. That gave you the perfect alibi. I had to rack my brain to work out how you might have been in two places at the same time . . .

'The only way you could have accomplished that was if your lecture was a recording. You told me that the hall was dark, and that a slide presentation was showing on the lecture screen. It was due to last two hours – Dinshaw said that there were two hundred slides. Once it began, you bowed out to the wings. You switched on the recording you had previously made so that your voice would continue to pump through the speakers in the darkened hall. You had made sure to inform the audience that you would take no questions until the very end. That way you were assured of not being interrupted.

'Once the recording was playing, you left via the fire exit, out into the lane behind the club, and then through the gate at the end of the lane – you are one of only two people who have a complete set of keys. You had left your car parked in the alleyway – a red Tata Nexon. The vehicle was spotted. It is what led me to you.'

Engineer's reaction to this last fact was merely to compress his mouth.

'It was always a risk parking there,' he said. 'But I had no choice. I could not have left via the club's main entrance. The security guard would have seen me. And I could not have taken a cab to Doongerwadi. The driver might later have become a witness.'

'On the way to Doongerwadi, you phoned Cyrus. You told him to leave the lecture immediately and meet you at the eastern gate. You knew there would be less chance of anyone seeing either of you at that gate, or in that section of Doongerwadi. I don't know precisely how you lured him there, but I suppose you must have threatened to expose him. My guess is that you also disguised your voice.' He paused, but Engineer did not confirm or deny this. 'What happened in Doongerwadi? Did you try to reason with him, a last-ditch effort to force him to see sense? Or was it always your intention to kill him? I suspect the latter.'

Engineer was silent a moment. 'Do you know, Chopra, that within these very walls, some of the greatest minds this country has ever produced plotted the road to Independence? The best jurists of the age, working to understand the complexities of the fight, and the even more knotted realities of post-Partition India. In many ways, Parsees helped define the country you now stand in.' He got up, limped to the sideboard, poured himself a whisky, then sat heavily back down. As he drank, the whisky worked its way into his eyes, softened his careworn features. 'Cyrus was beyond listening. There was no guilt. No recognition that he was betraying not only our community, but the storied history of the Parsees in India. The Cyrus I had known since he had been a boy was gone. He was no longer one of us. His soul had turned to ash.'

'My guess is Cyrus told you that you were finished at the club.'

Engineer stared into his whisky. 'Yes, he tried to threaten me. He even suggested that should I speak up publicly about his plans before he was ready to reveal them he would have me killed.'

349

'And that was when you took out the mace that you had brought with you and struck him on the back of the head.'

'He turned away from me,' said Engineer. 'As if I were nothing. As if my words meant nothing.' Fury drove up through the old man like a fist. 'He *dismissed* me, Chopra.'

'You planned Cyrus's murder with great care. You knew that he would never reconsider, that any attempt to get him to change his plans for Doongerwadi would be futile. That's why you called him there in the first place. A quiet, secluded place where no one would see you kill him. That's why you took the mace along. What better murder weapon than a symbol of the very community he was betraying?'

'I called him there so that he might be reminded of our heritage. Of what it means to be Parsee. We are keepers of the flame, the guardians of our legacy. Till the very end I hoped to sway him. *That's* why I took the mace. Rustom's mace. I wanted him to see it, touch it, be connected to that past.'

'I don't believe you,' said Chopra. 'Had that been the case, you would not have arranged such an elaborate alibi.'

Engineer said nothing.

'But why, having killed him, didn't you just leave the body there? What purpose did it serve to drag him to the tower and dump him inside?'

'You *couldn't* understand.'

'Try me.'

Engineer stared into his whisky. 'First, I thought it would make it look like a random killer had panicked and tried to hide the crime . . . But the real reason? I wanted Cyrus to end up in the same towers he had chosen to abandon. I wanted the vultures to take at least a piece of him before the last rites were administered. I wanted them to desecrate his flesh, just as he sought to desecrate our traditions. For years I had seen him put himself forward as the protector of the old ways. After I discovered his plan to sell Doongerwadi I realised it had all been a pretence, a way for him to convince our community that he had always had our best interests at heart. That way, when he broke the news of the move, he hoped to sway many of us to his argument.'

'You wanted to punish him,' said Chopra. 'Even after death.' It reaffirmed his belief that Engineer had premeditated the murder. 'But there is one problem with that scenario. Cyrus is a big man. You are not strong enough to have moved his body. Which means that someone helped you. But who? Boman? Darius? Both had motive and neither has an alibi for that night.'

Silence.

'Or perhaps it was Anosh Ginwala? He discovered the corpse the next day, and planted the convenient notion with the authorities that a trespassing drug addict may have killed Cyrus. The trouble is, he was ill, confined to his bed, with a reliable witness testifying to that.'

'Ginwala has nothing to do with this,' croaked Engineer. 'Nor Boman or Darius. I acted alone.'

Chopra did not believe the man, but it was clear Engineer would not reveal the identity of his accomplice. A new thought occurred to him. 'It has been three months since Cyrus died. Why haven't you gone public with his plans? After all, he can no longer kick you out of the club.'

'What would that achieve except to throw a noose around my neck? Besides, as I said to you earlier, I do not want to provide ammunition to those who, like Cyrus, wish to see the Towers of Silence moved elsewhere.'

Engineer leaned back, closed his eyes. 'When I was seven my father brought me to the club, and stood me before the waxwork of Rustom Zorabian. "Look at him, Zubin," he told me. "That man enshrines everything that makes us Parsee. Integrity, industry, philanthropy. These are the pillars by which we live, and by which we are known. Take away any one of those and we no longer have the right to call ourselves Parsee." Cyrus stopped being a Parsee the day he decided to sell the Towers of Silence. He betrayed not only himself but all of us. He betrayed the legacy of a thousand years of Parsee endeavour.' The old man rose from his seat. 'I have only one request. That when they come for me, I am permitted to walk out of this club for the final time with my head held high. Not cuffed like a common criminal.'

Chopra hesitated. 'I will do what I can.'

OF VULTURES AND ELEPHANTS

The wedding of William Buckley and Perizaad Zorabian took place on a blistering hot weekend a month after the arrest of Zubin Engineer for the murder of the bride's father. The marriage – attended by close relatives of the Zorabian family – was a relatively simple affair, a ritual Parsee ceremony at the fire temple in Juhu, the bride and groom stiff and self-conscious in traditional dress. The venue for the nuptials had already caused a stir. Tradition decreed that non-Parsees were not permitted entry to the fire temple. But Perizaad, in line with many reformers within the community, had decided that she would not be bound by such old-fashioned attitudes. She had declared an intent to shake up other aspects that she felt had no place in the modern world, and had started as she meant to go on.

With the ceremony complete, the wedding party moved en masse to the Vulture Club where the evening reception – a star-studded affair attended by the city's elite – was scheduled to take place.

It was to this latter event that Chopra and family had been invited. Inside the wedding card, Perizaad Zorabian had scribbled the words: 'You must attend! And please bring your little elephant, too.'

And so now, as he tugged at the starched collar of his shirt, and twitched his shoulders inside his well-worn black suit, looking around at the packed hall with its sea of refined gentry, the bride and groom seated, rictus-grinned, on the distant stage, Chopra found his thoughts drifting.

Cyrus Zorabian was foremost in his mind. There was still so much he could only guess at. The man had proven to be corrupt, avaricious, morally reprehensible. He had caused the deaths of Arushi Kadam and Vijay Narlikar. Had he regretted that? Is that why he had held on to the newspaper clipping? They would never know. And what of Doongerwadi? Had Cyrus's belief in the old ways been nothing more than a pretence? Or had he shed those beliefs in the face of necessity? Once again, he was confronted by the greyness of morality. He searched inside and realised that, in the court of his own opinion – the only one that really mattered – Cyrus *was* guilty. Of causing death and incalculable loss – the slum dwellers whom he had purported to help would never see their promised home in New Haven. That project was now suspended, perhaps irredeemably crippled.

Did all this make Zubin Engineer less guilty?

Chopra thought not. Justifying murder was a slippery slope, one that he could never condone, even if he might, at times, understand.

He dwelt on Engineer.

He was certain the man had had help in planning and executing the murder of Cyrus Zorabian. But neither he nor the authorities had made any headway in discovering who that accomplice might have been. And with Engineer insisting that he had acted alone, the police had eventually taken him at his word. The case was closed. But for Chopra, this was the one loose end that continued to nag at him.

He shook away these sobering thoughts and glanced at his wife.

Poppy was in her element, wrapped in a new sari, a vision of gaiety and good humour. Beside her, Irfan – dressed in his own glossy suit and clip-on tie – was leaning down to pat Ganesha on the head. The elephant, reclining on all fours, had attracted much attention, with guests stopping by every so often to take a picture with him. Though usually a maven for the limelight, Ganesha largely ignored these selfie-seekers. He was preoccupied with the conveyor belt of delicacies making their way to him from the kitchen.

Chopra turned back to Poppy as she heaved her enormous handbag on to the table, and took out a thick stack of leaflets.

The familiar face of Mr Poo grinned up at him.

'Poppy,' he said, 'you cannot distribute these here. We are at a *wedding*.'

Poppy merely smiled at him. 'I cannot think of a better time. Look around you. Eight hundred people in one place with nothing to do but eat six kinds of dhansak. This will give them something to talk about.'

'I do not think they wish to talk about' – he lowered his voice – '*excrement* over dinner.' He cut his eyes to either side in case anyone had overheard him.

'I disagree. This is a community that believes in philan-thropy. They will be delighted to learn more about this important initiative.'

'But – but *they* are not the ones who have a problem with this sort of thing.'

Poppy's face hardened. 'Precisely,' she said. '*They* never have to think about where they should do their business. But for those who have no access to clean facilities, or have never been shown another way, it is a daily struggle to conform with the rules society says they must follow. We call them stupid, but we have no right to call others igno-rant if we are not willing to put in the effort needed to educate them. Those at the bottom are powerless to change their environment. But the people in this room – *they* have the wealth and influence to make that change happen.'

He was about to protest, and then realised that his wife was right. He gave her a rueful smile. 'Well, if you're going to do it, you will need helpers.' He turned to Irfan. 'Why don't you give her a hand? And take Ganesha with you.'

Poppy beamed at him, adjusted her sari, then sashayed away, the leaflets tucked under her arm, Irfan and Ganesha trailing her.

Chopra felt a twinge of sympathy for those she was about to accost. Like skiers before an avalanche, they had no idea what was coming.

He looked around the hall again, spotting Darius Zorabian and his wife Lucy. He knew that Perizaad had made a concerted effort to return her brother to the fold. Her overtures had not been entirely successful – Darius was a proud man. But a beginning had been made, and his presence at the wedding augured well, for the family and for Darius's unborn child.

Chopra was not a sentimental man, but a part of him hoped that the pair – Darius and Lucy – might find their way through their recent troubles. His instincts – based simply on the fact that a man as unyielding as Darius had finally surrendered enough of his own ego to participate in his sister's happiness – told him that this might well be the case.

'Ah, Chopra, the man of the hour.'

He turned to see Forhad and Dinshaw advancing, Forhad wheeling his catheter stand beside him. They collapsed into chairs, caught their breath, then proceeded to fix him with equally belligerent glares.

'I suppose you feel virtuous,' said Forhad. 'Getting old Zubin pinched.'

'He committed murder,' said Chopra sternly.

'That's one way of looking at it,' said Forhad.

'I hadn't realised there was another way.'

'You know what they say,' said Dinshaw. 'One man's murderer is another man's martyr.'

Chopra frowned. 'You don't believe that Engineer's actions deserve censure? What would happen to society if everyone with a grievance decided to settle their issues with violence?'

'Society, schmiety,' poo-pooed Forhad. 'Zubin did what most of the people in this room would gladly have done.

Cyrus sold his soul; he betrayed the legacy of his ancestors. Zubin found out. Instead of creating a public scandal, he did something about it himself. Frankly, I never thought he had it in him, the old goat. He was always such a milksop. Just goes to show.'

'Because of his bravery,' continued Dinshaw, 'we now know what Cyrus was up to, and we can organise a defence. We may not look like much, but we have power, and wealth, and we will kick up such a stink that it will be a hundred years before anyone else tries to kick us out of Doongerwadi.'

Chopra knew that Perizaad had already assured the Parsee community that no such thing would happen during her stewardship of the hallowed site. Yet he marvelled at the divergence between his own thoughts and those of the two ancient Parsees. He had always viewed the world in black and white – each time he was confronted by the ugly grey of reality it caused him to step back and re-examine his convictions.

Engineer's involvement in the murder of Cyrus Zorabian had shocked the club, the greatest scandal in its one-hundred-and-twenty-year history. But the biggest shock had erupted as word spread of Cyrus's plan to sell Doongerwadi. The cloud of rumour had moved outwards, enveloping the BMC, and gradually rippling around the upper echelons of the city's power structure. When the newspapers finally got hold of the story, it ignited a fury of tabloid rhetoric with some hailing Cyrus's alleged plan as 'visionary' and 'long overdue', and others tearing him down as a 'heretic' and 'the ultimate con man'.

The coverage had given wings to the CBI investigation into Om Kaabra.

Kaabra had been arrested at the Indira Gandhi airport in Delhi attempting to flee the country. He was now safely ensconced in an out-of-sight-and-out-of-mind CBI dungeon enjoying the brutal hospitality of various state and federal law enforcement agencies. Inspector Kelkar had obtained full cooperation from John Reddy and Geeta Lokhani, as well as various others willing to testify against Kaabra in desperate bids to save themselves. It was all but certain that the man would spend the rest of his life in prison. Arushi Kadam, Vijay Narlikar and the thirteen dead souls buried beneath Hasan Gafoor's building could finally find peace. As a result, Gafoor himself would soon be released from prison – a matter Rangwalla was pursuing with unusual diligence. In that sense, much good had come from the death of Cyrus Zorabian. And yet . . .

'I am afraid I cannot agree with you. A man has been murdered. That is not something to be taken lightly. Engineer went beyond the bounds of not only the law, but of what is moral. He will pay the price for his actions.'

'I doubt it,' said Forhad.

Chopra stared at him. 'He has confessed.'

'He is a seventy-five-year-old man with a gimpy leg and a tenuous grasp of the world at the best of times.'

'That was not my impression of him at all.'

'Well, then, it's lucky that you are not the one defending him. For the record, the club has appointed Bastavar Screwwalla. Perhaps you have heard of him?'

Chopra's moustache twitched.

Screwwalla.

The most renowned defence lawyer in the country, a man routinely employed by the rich and shameless when they fell into hot water with the authorities. 'Why would Screwwalla—' he began but was cut off by a grinning Dinshaw.

'Screwwalla happens to be the son of a very prominent club member. A true Parsee patriot.'

Of course. Screwwalla was a Parsee.

'Engineer killed a man in cold blood. He will not walk free.' But some of the certainty had slipped from Chopra's voice.

'Nonsense,' said Forhad. 'Engineer is too frail to have killed anyone. Cyrus was hit with old Rustom's mace, right? Well, anyone could have got hold of that. And bashing in the skull of a man as big as Cyrus is no easy matter. Zubin could never have done that – not with his wrist.'

'Wrist? What do you mean?'

'I mean, Chopra, that young Bastavar Screwwalla, defence lawyer extraordinaire, will categorically show that this frail old man, who barely has the strength to lift his cane, could not possibly have wielded that mace. Zubin suffered a car accident years ago which left him with shattered wrists. They have never healed properly.' He gave a smug look. 'This is not as open and shut a case as you may think.' He staggered to his feet, grasped his catheter stand; Dinshaw rose with him. 'You can take consolation from the fact that without your investigation Cyrus's duplicity might never have come to light. I suppose we owe you a debt of thanks.'

He watched them shuffle away, the old Parsee's words still ringing in his ears.

Could it be true? Could Zubin Engineer really escape punishment for his crime?

Chopra had himself lifted the mace that had been used to kill Cyrus Zorabian. It was a heavy instrument, at least seven kilos. He tried to picture Zubin wielding it, with his supposedly weak wrists, repeatedly swinging it above him – for Cyrus was considerably taller than the club's former secretary – and failed.

His mind went back to the autopsy report. What had the pathologist written? The killer had tried to disguise himself, by hitting the victim with blows from both left and right hands. One blow with the right, two with the left.

What if that was an incorrect assumption?

And now Chopra had the image of another man, wielding a different type of weapon, repeatedly hacking down with it . . . using his left hand.

It took him thirty minutes to reach Doongerwadi.

It was a further ten minutes before Ramin Bulsara, Anosh Ginwala's deputy, materialised at the gates. He peered myopically at Chopra. 'What are you doing here?'

Chopra explained his mission. On the way to Doongerwadi he had considered how Ginwala could have been in two places at the same time – confined to his bed, while simultaneously helping Engineer to kill Cyrus Zorabian. Bulsara had said the man had been dead to the world . . . *Dead* to the world . . . Eventually, a grotesque idea had occurred to him, the only plausible way Ginwala could have managed it. 'You told me before that Ginwala was in his hut the night Cyrus died. Did you actually speak with him when you visited him?'

'No.'

'But you called out to him?'

'Yes. He didn't reply.'

'Did you enter his hut?'

'Why would I do that? He gets wild if anyone enters his home without permission.'

'Then how do you know it was him on the charpoy?'

'Well . . . He was wearing his usual clothes.'

'You saw his face?'

'No. He had his back to me. But it was him.'

'You saw a big, dark-haired man on the charpoy, with his back turned to you?'

'Yes.'

Chopra took a deep breath. 'You said that a number of corpses had come in late that day. That's why you went to talk to Ginwala. Tell me, was one of them a big, dark-haired man?'

Bulsara paled as understanding dawned. 'But that is—' He stopped, incredulous.

'Where are the corpses stored?'

'In a refrigerated outhouse, well away from our homes.'

'So Ginwala could have taken a body from there, dressed it in his own clothes, set it up in his bed, then later returned it, and no one would have known?'

Bulsara nodded. 'It is possible, yes.'

Not possible, thought Chopra. Probable. 'Take me to him.'

Bulsara led him past the cluster of huts near the gate, and into the crepuscular gloom of the forest, his lantern flinging waxy shadows before them. When they emerged into a clearing, Chopra held him back. 'I will take it from here.'

Chopra advanced into the pool of light cast by a row of lanterns hanging from the Tower of Silence before him. He saw that the wooden door built into the circular outer wall at the top of the ramp was ajar. Atop the rim of the tower, clustered like gargoyles, were the dark shapes of roosting vultures.

He moved up the ramp and walked into the dakhma.

Standing at the lip of the central well, three tiers down from him, was a large man in a corpse-bearer's uniform peering down into the cavity, a lantern raised aloft, beating back the darkness.

As Chopra's feet scuffed the stone, the man jerked up, then spun around to face him.

Anosh Ginwala's eyes gave away his amazement at the sight of the former policeman standing by the doorway; and then shadows closed around his hard features once more.

'What are you doing here?'

'Zubin Engineer could not have murdered Cyrus Zorabian. At least not on his own.'

Ginwala's eyes narrowed.

He moved forward, labouring up the tiered stone walkway, until he was standing before Chopra. His piercing gaze examined the private detective.

'The CBI already interrogated me. I was sick in bed all night.'

'Your alibi no longer holds. You used a corpse to pretend that you were in your home at the time Cyrus was murdered.'

Ginwala's eyes flared, but he said nothing.

'You did more than help Engineer move the body,' continued Chopra. 'That day when I came to your home, you were using a cleaver to butcher meat. The cleaver was in your left hand. Cyrus's killer hit him with one right-handed blow, and then two blows using his left hand. Our mistake was in thinking those blows came from the same man.'

Ginwala stepped closer. 'Why don't you just say it?' he murmured.

'I think that Zubin Engineer called Cyrus here that night with the intention of killing him. They argued; at some point Cyrus turned his back. That was when Engineer hit him with the mace. Using his right hand. But he could not finish the job. Either because the shock of what he had done paralysed him or because wielding the heavy mace aggravated the old injury to his wrist. I believe he had already planned for you to help him move the body. That is why you set up an alibi for yourself. Engineer knew that you would not refuse him – he knew of your long-running animosity towards Cyrus. Perhaps he even promised to finally help you get the pay rise you wanted, once Cyrus was out of the way.

'He could never have got that body into the dakhma by himself. *You* helped him drag the corpse to the tower. Except that at some point you realised that Cyrus was *not* a corpse. He was still alive. And so you decided to finish what Engineer had started. You took the mace and smashed Cyrus twice more in the back of his skull. *You* killed him.'

In the flickering darkness Ginwala seemed to grow, a malevolent outline that loomed and billowed in the sweltering night. In that instant Chopra sensed something primeval in the man, feral and instinctive. It took all his resolve not to step backwards as the corpse-bearer's gaze burned into him. He was glad that he had his revolver with him. Recovered by Rangwalla's efforts from the condemned building into which he had crashed his van, he could feel its reassuring weight tucked into the back of his trousers.

'Look around you, Chopra. You are standing in a place that is ageless, a place that embodies something greater than the life of one man. These stones, the vultures, the uncountable shades of men, women and children that hover above these towers, they make demands on those of us yet to face the holy fire. I do not expect someone like you to understand.'

'Words cannot change the fact that you killed a man.'

Ginwala grimaced. 'You can prove that?'

'You may have underestimated the abilities of modern science. No killer can interact with his victim without leaving some trace of his presence or taking some trace of the victim away with him. It is known as Locard's Principle. The forensics team will find something. You wielded the mace – perhaps you left traces of DNA upon it? In his haste to return to the club Zubin was unable to clean it thoroughly. I suspect he washed it quickly in one of the club's toilets and then returned it to its cabinet before his talk ended and the others came out again.

'Or perhaps droplets of blood or hair from Cyrus's skull found their way on to your clothes. Did you know that only the deepest wash will remove such evidence? There are a hundred tiny details that you may have overlooked. Once the CBI gets to work on you, they will find something. Sooner or later you will stumble.'

Ginwala's eyes flared. 'Zubin has cleared me!'

'How long before he admits that he did not deliver the fatal blow? He is an old man. Frail. The CBI detective in charge told me today that he was on the verge of cracking, that he wished to amend his initial statement. Perhaps he has finally decided to reveal your involvement. Guilt is weighing heavily on his conscience.'

'You are lying!'

'Can you afford to take that chance?'

Ginwala's face contorted with rage.

He lowered his lantern, and looked down at his sandalled feet. For an instant Chopra thought the fight had gone out of him. And then he erupted with a roar, launching himself at the former policeman, swinging the lantern at his head. Chopra ducked just in time, the lantern bouncing off his shoulder. A thick fist crashed into his midriff, sending a shimmer of pain through him and knocking him off balance so that he fell forward, past Ginwala, and stumbled down the tiers, finally tripping and sprawling on to his stomach with his head dangling over the black well of the central pit. The waft of putrefying human flesh served as a dose of smelling salts; his head jerked back. He scrabbled to his feet in time to see Ginwala lumbering down the tiers towards him.

Heaving a deep breath, Chopra cleared his head, and reached behind him for his revolver.

Which was not there.

Frantically, he patted his trousers, but there was no mistake.

He looked past the bear-like shape of Ginwala and saw the revolver lying on the stonework by the door; in the tussle with the corpse-bearer the weapon had fallen out.

Dammit.

Chopra faced the man before him, and quickly assessed his chances. He was a tall man, broad-shouldered and strong. He had always made it a point to keep himself fit, even after retiring from the force. But Ginwala was bigger, bulkier and hardened like tough leather. And he was powered by a cocktail of hatred, fear and a survival instinct sharpened to the point of a knife.

Ginwala glared at him, the light from his lantern adding a sinister aspect to his craggy features. He reached under his shirt and emerged with a long-bladed knife.

'Sometimes, when a body is diseased, I am forced to cut away the dead portions. It would be sacrilege to allow the vultures to consume tainted flesh.' He raised the knife. 'Men like Cyrus are a cancer. Their greed infects every-thing. They have everything, yet are still willing to take from those who have nothing.'

'It is not too late,' said Chopra, sweat flowing freely down his brow and into his eyes. 'Surrender. Confess, and you may yet get off lightly.'

Ginwala shook his head. 'We both know that is not possible.'

For one instant, a look of infinite regret crossed his worn features, as if perhaps, in another life, under different circumstances, he might have been the man he wished to be. Husband, father, a cherished and respected member of a dwindling community. But the dream was no more tangible than reflections on the surface of a bubble.

He swung his head, as if to clear his mind.

He focused once more on Chopra, his purpose as clear and naked as the heart of a flame.

A growl rumbled in his throat. And then he charged.

Chopra waited, his every instinct urging him to flee . . . *another second . . . just a few more steps . . .*

As Ginwala closed on him, leaping forward with the knife in one hand, the lantern in the other, Chopra spun aside, neatly sidestepping the lunge, and returning with a windmilling slap that caught Ginwala on the back and propelled him towards the gaping mouth of the pit. Off balance, carried forward by his own momentum, there was nothing the corpse-bearer could do to prevent the inevitable.

As he tumbled into darkness, he turned his head towards Chopra, his eyes blinking out a Morse code of shock, surprise, perhaps even grudging admiration.

He vanished over the edge.

Chopra did not wait.

He raced up the tiers, scooped up his revolver, and bounded back to the central well.

Peering into the pit, he saw that Ginwala had landed awkwardly. The corpse-bearer was slumped against the stone wall, his leg twisted at an unnatural angle. The lantern lay on its side, casting a grim yellow light across the horrifying landscape of half-decomposed bodies that had broken Ginwala's fall.

There was a terrible unreality to the sight.

Chopra's stomach did a quick, precise somersault; it took a concerted effort to keep its contents from spewing forth into the black pit.

Ginwala stared up at him, his breathing laboured. A violent, inexpressible hunger lanced from his eyes. 'We are older than you can possibly imagine,' he gasped. 'We will be here long after you are gone. Thus spake Zarathustra.'

Chopra took out his phone, and dialled Inspector Kelkar at the CBI.

Behind him, he heard the rustle and hiss of the vultures that called the Towers of Silence home.

HOMECOMING

'I don't think of her as a vulture any more,' said Poppy.

Chopra glanced at his wife but decided against commenting. It was symptomatic of his wife's character to become attached to a creature that she had, at first, professed to despise.

They had driven to Doongerwadi together.

The Tata van, repaired and with a gleaming new paint job, had ferried them through the midday traffic on their mission of mercy. The vulture – or Mehrunissa, as Poppy had christened her, after an ancient Indian queen – had recovered.

On the way, they had stopped to see the vet Lala, who had rubber-stamped a clean bill of health.

'She's a tough one,' he'd said. 'A real survivor.'

'Anyone who has to spend a month in my home with my mother-in-law had better be,' Chopra had muttered.

Now, as he watched the bird tentatively hop away, he felt a sudden unease.

Doongerwadi may have been rescued from the avaricious designs of Om Kaabra, but the vultures that resided here were precariously placed. They existed in that nebulous haze between survival and extinction; the smallest change in their environment could send them over the edge. They had never been popular. The tiger, the peacock, the elephant – these were the creatures that symbolised India, feted the world over. But for the humble vulture there were only brickbats, curses and an undeserved reputation for malignity. Tigers and elephants between them mauled, trampled and gored to death hundreds of the nation's citizens each year; but vultures provided a valuable service, mopping up carcasses – both animal and human – that would otherwise fester in the swollen heat.

They were unloved because they were unlovely.

Even in the animal kingdom life was a beauty contest.

He watched as the bird gingerly spread her wings and launched herself into a short test flight, skimming low over the ground for a few metres, before skidding down into the dirt. She righted herself, shook out her neck, and clawed at the earth with her talons.

Ganesha trotted behind, a sort of pachyderm Wilbur Wright encouraging vulture Orville to master the power of flight.

The bird appeared to gain a second wind.

She steadied herself, then lunged upwards, thrashing at the air with her wings, sending up a shower of dust that tickled Ganesha's nose, and halted his headlong progress. The vulture rose into the air, then beat her way up to the rim of the Tower of Silence before them.

Moments later, she had inveigled her way back into position among the indignant ranks of her colleagues.

The vultures settled again, staring beady-eyed down at their visitors.

'Are you sure she will be fine?' Poppy said.

'She's a vulture,' said Chopra. 'You heard what Lala said: a real survivor.'

They lingered a moment longer, then turned and headed back to the van.

Behind them, the Tower of Silence, shrouded in myth and mystique, shimmered in the haze of dust and heat, before being swallowed, once more, by the forest.

AUTHOR'S NOTE

For the record: the Take the Poo to the Loo campaign is very real. Widely praised for its innovative approach, this UNICEF-led social media campaign has achieved immense public awareness in India since its launch in March 2014. The initiative, part of the larger Total Sanitation Campaign launched by the Indian government in 1999, emerged from a conference organised by UNICEF India and the Indian Institute of Technology. The Poo2Loo campaign, as it is informally known, has opened up a robust discussion around the previously taboo topic of open defecation.

The petition depicted in this novel is also accurate in its wording, calling upon the President of India to embrace the challenge of ending open defecation.

Finally, as incredible as it may seem to some readers, the official mascot of the movement is indeed an animated human-sized turd by the name of Mr Poo.

Sometimes truth can be stranger than fiction.

ACKNOWLEDGEMENTS

Once again I owe a debt of gratitude to my agent Euan Thorneycroft at A.M. Heath, my editor Ruth Tross at Mullholland, and Kerry Hood at Hodder. Between them, they have cajoled, wheedled, counselled, and, when all else fails, gently bullied me into turning out another half decent novel in the series. For me, this is the best of the lot and no small credit is due to my wonderful team.

I would also like to thank the rest of the gang at Hodder, Maddy Marshall in marketing, Rachel Southey in production, Dom Gribben in audiobooks, Myrto Kalavrezou in publicity, and Ruth's assistant Hannah Bond. Similar thanks go to Euan's assistant Jo Thompson, and the others at A.M. Heath working tirelessly behind the scenes.

Thank you also to Anna Woodbine and Sarah Christie for another wonderful cover, perhaps the best of all – I adore the peckish vulture!

I hope these books continue to be as much fun to read as they are to write.